THAT OTHER ME

A Novel

MAHA GARGASH

HARPER ⬤ PERENNIAL

NEW YORK • LONDON • TORONTO • SYDNEY • NEW DELHI • AUCKLAND

HARPER ⬤ PERENNIAL

THAT OTHER ME. Copyright © 2016 by Maha Gargash. All rights reserved. Printed in the United States of America. No part of this book may be used or reproduced in any manner whatsoever without written permission except in the case of brief quotations embodied in critical articles and reviews. For information address HarperCollins Publishers, 195 Broadway, New York, NY 10007.

HarperCollins books may be purchased for educational, business, or sales promotional use. For information please e-mail the Special Markets Department at SPsales@harpercollins.com.

FIRST EDITION

Designed by Jamie Kerner

Library of Congress Cataloging-in-Publication Data
Gargash, Maha.
  That other me : a novel / Maha Gargash. — First edition.
    pages ; cm
  ISBN 978-0-06-239138-4 (softcover) — ISBN 978-0-06-239139-1 (ebook)
  1. Women—United Arab Emirates—Social conditions—Fiction. 2. Young women—Social life and customs—Fiction. 3. United Arab Emirates—History—20th century—Fiction. 4. Domestic fiction. I. Title.
  PR9570.U543G378 2016
  823'.92—dc23
                                                                        2015011785

ISBN 978-0-06-239138-4

16 17 18 19 20   OV/RRD   10 9 8 7 6 5 4 3 2 1

THAT
OTHER
ME

ALSO BY
MAHA GARGASH

The Sand Fish

THAT
OTHER
ME

ALSO BY
MAHA GARGASH

The Sand Fish

For my Mother
Maryam Ali Gargash
The Diamond of the Family

THAT
OTHER
ME

1

MAJED

Tok, tok, tok, tok, tok.

There are women standing on the other side of my bedroom door, taking turns knocking. There are seven of them, and each is more beautiful than the last. I can tell what they look like—fine-nosed and fair—even though the door is closed. Their accents are flawless, but I know they are not Emiratis.

Tok, tok, tok. I grin at their impatience and wait a moment before inviting them in. "Enter!"

I am young, with not a gray hair on my head. I listen to their light footsteps over the thick carpet. Even though my eyes remain shut, I can see everything. They form a circle around my bed, which sits in the middle of the room. Their gowns float around them, their silhouettes flashing bare when the light hits them from behind.

Yes, there is light, too: hundreds of lines, beaming through tiny holes in the wall. A shaft catches a rising knee; another illuminates a twisting shoulder as an arm twirls. "Come!" I demand, feeling the hairs on my body rise. And when they do, I start grabbing at them.

There! Her hair is soft, and she bends out of the way. *There!* I snatch the air as another one spins away like a wheel. They are so fast, but I don't stop lifting my arms toward the ring of dancing women who loom over me.

Blocking the light, they reach down to caress me. But instead of rapture, I'm filled with horror: they fix their long fingers around my neck. Bold, cold, they squeeze. I am a writhing worm as I struggle to break away, and once I realize it's useless I cry out with a force that shakes the length of me. But there is no sound. I yell again. *"Arree!"* This time it's as shrill as a whistle, and I don't stop until I'm up and on my knees, sweating and shivering on the bed.

I am awake and staring at the face of a child, who holds a bucket in one hand and a rag in the other. My rattled wits are reflected in her tiny eyes. And no wonder! My *wizar*, the checkered cotton wrap I sleep in, has crept up and twisted around my neck. My chest, tummy and all that hangs below are exposed in full view of this girl, who stands frozen in place at the foot of my bed, unable to look away from my sprouting forest of hair. I hurry to hide my nakedness with a pillow, too stunned to ask who she is or what she is doing in my room.

Tok, tok, tok. It's the sound of a hammer breaking cement, and it triggers sharp pain along the length of my forehead. The noise comes from downstairs, not from behind the door, which now opens. My wife, Aisha, rushes in and orders the girl out, admonishing her for having entered the room while I was asleep. "New maid," she says to me. "She doesn't know the ways of the house yet." Her eyes round. "What happened to you?"

I fumble to untangle my wizar, puzzled at the two thick knots. How is that possible? How much did I struggle in my dream? "Can't I wake up peacefully in this house?" I grumble. My throat is parched, and I cough before continuing. "Can't I wake up to silence and privacy?" The curtains are just short of being fully drawn. Only a sliver of white light beams through, but it's enough to drill a hole through my head, just like the bright-green numbers of the electronic calendar on the bedside table—15:01:1995. I search for the aspirin in the drawer.

"I know, I know," says my wife, handing me a bottle of water. "But it's an emergency." She waits for me to swallow the two pills before continuing. "I had to send a driver to Hor Al-Anz to fetch the plumber. He called to tell me that the plumber is away, visiting relatives in Ajman. I tell him, 'Can't you think for yourself?'" She taps her head. "But it seems he can't. So I ordered him to drive out to Ajman."

I slide off the bed and tighten the wizar around my waist. My eyes burn. I want to splash cold water on my face. As I hobble to the bathroom Aisha follows me, continuing her account of the morning's household incident.

"No one expected the pipe to burst. It just did, and the dining room is flooded. I hope the carpets won't be completely ruined. We've spread them outside in the sun to dry. I don't know how long . . ."

My wife utters each detail with relish, as if I care about any of it. I close the bathroom door, but her voice travels through the thick teak wood, crisp and anxious. ". . . Persian carpets. We couldn't hang them, of course: too heavy with all that water. So we spread them over the garden benches, and . . ."

These domestic accounts and complaints are tedious, and fueled by the incompetence of an army of servants. Who killed the purple-flowered bougainvillea by giving it too much water, and the potted gardenias by exposing them to too much sun? Was it our Pakistani gardener or the landscaping company that comes twice a week to maintain the garden? And yesterday's fish, which was fried until the flesh turned rubbery instead of being steamed in the Chinese way, as was instructed. Which of our two cooks was responsible? Was it the Muslim Bengali or the Christian Indian? The cooks, bickering, each pointed his finger at the other. Who can tell with those two? They hold their views on the best way to chop onions or boil rice with the same vehemence as they do their political and religious beliefs.

"The drivers didn't help carry the carpets out. Of course, one of them was getting the plumber. But the other one—well, he conveniently disappeared."

My eyes are red. I lean over the sink and let out a loud belch.

"Once I find him, he'll make an excuse, probably tell me that he went to pray, even though there's still another hour before the muezzin's call for the midday prayer."

She is chattier than usual today. It exhausts me to have to listen to her. The sooner I get ready, the sooner I can leave the house. I turn on the tap. It gurgles and spits air.

" . . . Because we turned the water off."

My tongue feels like a piece of leather. There's the plumber's hammer again, a drill boring through my skull. When will the medicine work? I pull open the bathroom door.

"Of course, lunch won't be affected. There is water in the outside kitchen. But that pipe, that pipe . . ."

"I want to wash my face," I say in a hoarse voice.

Without delay Aisha stops her prattle and hurries to fetch the bottle of water, three-quarters full, from the bedside table. I watch her with a scowl on my face: her willowy build, with only a slight broadening of the hips—a finger's width added, I think, with each of her eight deliveries. I guzzle down enough of the water to relieve my parched throat and, without bothering to lean over the sink, splash the rest over my head.

My wife does not fetch a washcloth as the water slides along the sides of my face and down my torso. Through the gaps of her burka, she narrows her sharp black eyes at the puddle that forms at my feet. I wait, but she says nothing about the mess. She calls the maid, and when no one answers, she tightens her *shayla*, the black head cover, around her head and rushes out of the room.

There's my face in the mirror, swollen and tinged a sickly green, as if I'd been poisoned. It's not the first time. More and more often, this is how it looks the morning after a long night at the Neely—that's the code name for the deep-blue, three-bedroom apartment where I drink (privately, of course) with my friends. Situated a few streets off the main road in Al-Qusais, it has a balcony that overlooks an empty plot of land. Few cars pass there at night because it's in an industrial area, packed with warehouses and printing facilities. This suits us well, but we park our cars out of sight anyway, in the basement garage.

"Finally," I mutter as another new maid enters, carrying two plastic buckets of water. She strains under the weight but, surprisingly, manages to place them in the bathtub without spilling a drop. I bend over, and cry out as soon as I scoop a handful. "Where did you get this water? It's as hot as boiling stew."

She opens her mouth, but no words come out. Aisha rushes in and, with a few well-chosen questions, extracts the necessary information. This second new maid has boiled the water because she was given to understand that everything in this house has to be hygienic. That's why she pulled bottled water from the fridge and poured it into a huge pot. That's why she boiled it before bringing it up.

"Stupid, stupid girl," Aisha admonishes her. She tightens her lips and raises her hand as if to strike, but pulls the maid's ear instead. "Now, run down and get some more bottles from the fridge. Quickly!"

"No can, madam. Fee-neesh." Her singsong voice prompts my wife to pull her other ear.

"I'll make you fee-neesh! Go down. Bring ice. You know ice?"

"Yes, yes, ices." She darts out of the bathroom.

"Now, that first tiny maid comes from some jungle," Aisha says, "but this one who just delivered the buckets is from Manila—at least, that's what is written in her papers." The pain in my head turns sharp and I press my temples to numb it. My wife doesn't seem to notice. She continues her soliloquy. "Being from a big city like that, she should know the basics." She dips her index finger in the water to check the temperature and pulls it out abruptly, cocking her head as if surprised that I was telling the truth. "I'm certain it's those recruitment offices," she continues. "They must forge all the details." I could easily shut her up with one harsh reproach, but the thought fatigues me, and besides, I don't think there's enough saliva in my mouth to speak. So I call up one last bit of patience and herd her out of the bathroom. I'm about to close the door when the ice arrives. The cubes lose shape as soon as the maid empties them into the buckets.

Finally, after Aisha quickly checks whether I need anything more, they leave me alone. I climb into the bathtub and hunker down, pinning my knees to the sides for balance. I scoop water into a plastic jug and pour it over my head several times. The temperature is bearable, and I can hear the birds outside because the plumber has stopped smashing the wall. As I soap my body, I begin to feel better. I am working up a lather when I realize I need to calculate how much water I'll need to wash it off. "A quarter of a bucketful," I predict out loud, and guffaw. Here is one of the richest men in Dubai, crouched on his heels like a coolie, stingy with his water, as he takes his bath out of a bucket.

2

DALAL

The stone flies high into the air. Then there's a deafening crack at the second-story window and muffled squeals from inside the girls' *sakan*, the dormitory of the Emirati college students in Cairo.

I had raised my fist high and thrown blindly. I had not expected my aim to be so perfect. All I wanted was to get Mariam's attention so she would sneak out and meet me. I stand in place, stupefied. A girl—not Mariam—rushes to the window. She is in her nightgown, her head wrapped in a polka-dot head scarf. She would have spotted me had Azza not yanked me out of the glare of the streetlight. We squat down behind a dusty hedge as the window is pushed open.

"*Ehh!* What's going on down there?" That's the voice of the *abla*, one of the matrons responsible for the sakan girls. I try to stay still, but Azza's perfume, a sharp bouquet that is an insult to any flower, shoots up my nostrils. I sneeze, and that gets the matron hollering out into the night again. "I can hear you down there, you mangy hooligans. This is a respectable building with decent people living in it, you hear me? Show me your faces, you cowards." She is a barrel of a woman, blocking my view of the group of girls now huddled tightly around her. "I'm going to call the police. I'm going to call them right now."

I hear a girl suggest that it might be thieves. "Or murderers," a silly one adds. The abla retreats and shoos the girls away. Once she slams shut the broken window we straighten up, and Azza clicks her tongue. "What you go through for your cousin," she says. "What's wrong with just showing up at the door and asking to see her?"

"It's after nine," I reply, brushing the dust off my jeans and silky purple blouse. "You know she can't leave after nine." I gaze at the entrance of the building. I'll have to bribe the doorman. Not willing to part with my money so easily, I'd kept this as a last option. "They're grown women in there," I grumble, "and they treat them like children." Suddenly I'm struck by the importance of this mission. "I will demand that they treat those students—so clever that they are studying law, medicine, engineering—with respect. 'Stop treating them like prisoners!' That's what I'll say. 'Give them the freedom to come and go as they please, to have some fun!'"

"But what if they don't want any of that?" Azza asks. "Maybe they're just here to study and leave with degrees. Don't forget, you're talking about Emirati girls."

"Young women," I correct her. "Seventeen years old, like me. Nineteen, like my cousin Mariam. And older, too."

"But they're Emiratis."

"And what am I?"

"Well . . . yes . . . But your mother is Egyptian, thank God." She raises her arms to the sky. "You've got that Egyptian mischief in you." She starts giggling for no reason. I give her a nasty look, which she ignores. I turn my back to her and start walking away. "Sometimes I think you do things without thinking," she persists as she hurries after me.

"Sometimes you make the stupidest comments. Now will you stop it?" I swing around to face her. There's just a ribbon of moon on this

January night, but I know she can see my glower. She may have brought the car, her father's battered maroon Fiat, but she knows that she is in the company of future promise. Yes, that's how I visualize myself, ever since I found out today that I have a confirmed appointment to meet with the famous composer Sherif Nasr. "Look," I tell her. "All I want is for Mariam to be with me right now, to celebrate my good news."

She points at the doorman. "But what about him?"

"Leave him to me," I say. "Just go and get the car and meet me a few buildings down, at the corner of the street."

"But how will you get past him?"

"Just go, pretty one," I say, even though she's the opposite of pretty, and I march to the entrance of the sakan.

❧

"How did you manage to get me out?" Mariam asks me as soon as we've walked out of the doorman's hearing range. Her eyes are long and slightly hooded; they widen as she searches my face for an explanation.

"He told me to sign and just go, to enjoy the night, not to worry."

"But what about the permission? I didn't get one."

I greet her with a kiss on the cheek and say, "I've made a special arrangement with him."

"What arrangement?" She crinkles up her nose, slightly raising the upper lip of her broad mouth. She is darker than I am, but there's a dazzle to her because of the strange mix of tones in her face. That attractive coppery shine in her complexion is brought out by her bright eyes, which are the color of pale honey, and her auburn hair, which is many shades lighter than her skin.

I blow out air with impatience. Must I explain everything? She should know that I paid him—simple as that. At first the doorman held his fist lightly over his heart in a show of honesty, but then those wily fingers loosened and tapped his chest. It didn't take long for his hand to open, indicating his readiness to bend a rule or two. "I jiggled my breasts and shook my hips at him." I chuckle at the predictability of the gasp that comes out of my dear cousin.

"You think it's just him in there?" she says, fixing her shayla loosely around her head in a way that reveals the full breadth of her glossy bangs. They sit neat and straight, just above her crescent-shaped eyebrows. Like many other Emirati girls studying in Cairo, Mariam does not wear an abaya, a voluminous black robe, but she still dresses conservatively. Her pale-green shirt, decorated with tiny creeping vines, is buttoned at the cuffs. Her ankle-length skirt has the right amount of looseness so as not to cling to her figure. "There's also the night security guard and the abla. If she finds out I'm missing she'll send a letter to the cultural attaché, who will surely call my uncle—*Ammi* Majed will not be happy—and then I could be expelled."

I decide right away that the more books Mariam studies, the slower her mind works. She should know that I gave the doorman enough for him to share. "All taken care of," I say. "Don't worry."

"How can I not?" she says. "You know what it'll mean if I'm found out. No chance for a degree. And then what would I do? My life would be ruined."

"Ruined!" I exaggerate the whine in Mariam's voice. My features freeze into the classic look of desperation that Egyptian actresses put on when faced with the inevitable heartbreak woven so predictably into every drama's script. Tragedies are always hurled at women. I slap my chest and repeat, "Ruined!"

"Stop it," Mariam says, giggling and scolding me while she hugs me. "You are terrible." I relish her scent, the incense on her clothes blending with the clean smell of her skin and that dot behind the ears of *oudh* essence. "So?" she says, pulling back. There's a spark of curiosity in her eyes. To drag her out of the sakan after-hours: of course she knows I have important news to share.

I let out a half hum, half sigh. "Well, nothing. I just thought I would pull you out of your prison for a bit. And when you did not respond to my signal at the window, I had to get you out another way."

"That was you?" Mariam's stunned squeal delights me. So easy to shock, always so proper, that Mariam! She has to be; it's the way she was molded in that household, obligated to follow the stifling rules my father—her uncle—has drawn up to preserve our family's reputation in Dubai's conservative society. I thought she would have loosened up by now, with exposure to Cairo. Always so reserved, so Emirati, so unlike myself: the rebel flame of that same prosperous family, Al-Naseemy. "You know you hit the wrong window, don't you? I'm above, on the third floor."

I reach out for a plush jasmine bush nearby and loosen the blossoms into my palm. After I take a deep breath of their sweet smell, I look back at Mariam's flushed face and declare, "It's happening."

"What is happening?"

"I'm finally going to be a star!" I exclaim.

"What? When?"

She knows how much I've struggled these past ten months to find a composer who would create a winning song for me, but she doesn't know the details. I consider starting from the beginning: all the facilitators and mediators my mother and I kept relying on, all the promises that led to nothing, all the futile appointments. But none of that matters anymore. So I skip it all and fling the jasmine flowers high, bending back my neck so they fall on my upturned face. "Today!" I say, blowing away a bloom that sticks between my lips, "I got an appointment to see Sherif Nasr."

Her lips round to pronounce a soft "Ahh."

"He's famous and distinguished, and when he meets me I know he will recognize my talent straightaway." I grab Mariam's wrists, and together we laugh and hop in a circle.

"You did it! You did it!"

"*We* did it," I correct her. "All those years, you and I, imagining something like this, planning how we could make it happen, plotting our revenge on my father." I let her go and hug my chest. "It won't be long now before I start making my own money, so much money that I won't need anyone anymore. I won't have to rely on my father to take pity on me." A breeze embraces my hot face and fills my nose with the sweet scent of jasmine. I twirl my arms up into the air and let my waist follow. I don't need music; it's already in my head.

Mariam's soft face grows sharp as her grin lifts those cheekbones, which shine like sword blades caught in light. She looks over her shoulder to make sure the street is empty before joining me in my silent dance. I click a rhythm with my tongue and follow it, my belly turning and twisting like a lazy river, the current traveling from my shoulders to my arms and fingers, which twirl like vines, climbing high above my head.

Mariam tries to do the same, and I encourage her with a lift of my eyebrow, thinking all the time how hopeless she looks. I can make out her hip bones jerking back and forth as she struggles to bring some fluidity into her dance. What a waste it is that she can't put to use that slender build and enviable height, made less through her tendency to cave in her shoulders. There is no femininity in her movements. Poor thing, she is as stiff as a wooden doll. Still, it is brave of my sweet cousin to share my mood, my joy.

A honk startles us out of our night dance. As Mariam shies away from the headlights, I tell her, "It's all right. It's for us."

"Who's driving the car?"

"It's just my friend Azza."

She groans, and I can tell she wants it to be just us. "It's just that I haven't seen you," she says, "and there's something I want to talk to you about . . . It's a sensitive . . ."

She's growing moody, while all I'm interested in is celebrating my good news. "Look," I say. "She's not staying. So let's enjoy ourselves, okay? Just don't be difficult."

3

MARIAM

❧

Difficult? What did Dalal mean by that?

She wanted me with her tonight and here I am, fully aware of the consequences of sneaking out of the sakan. I could have refused, but I didn't.

Difficult? Hardly!

All I want is for us to be together, alone, so I can build up the courage to tell her about Adel. Where would I begin? What would she say if I told her about all these months that I have spent observing him from a distance, memorizing his every gesture and expression?

Sometimes he'd smile at me in passing and say, "Good morning." It should have been easy to do the same, but it felt impossible to issue this simple greeting. Always, my courage drained like water down a bathtub. I could almost hear the gurgle and slurp of it as my mouth turned dry. The best I could manage was to frown and walk away quickly, silently cursing whatever it was that made me so self-conscious.

But last week, we spoke for longer—or, I should say, he spoke to me. My cheeks grow hot whenever I think of it. Like me, Adel Al-

Shimouli is an Emirati dentistry student, but he's a year ahead. Naturally, I was surprised when he approached me on campus and asked for help going over some lectures he had missed. I still don't quite know how I agreed so quickly. I'd nodded with the serious face of a disciplinarian to mask my attraction toward him. I regret that I didn't smile. I should have smiled, made it look casual by adding a shrug, perhaps. That would have been best.

Adel had suggested we meet over the weekend at the Emirati Students' Club. I had arrived early to make sure I occupied one of the two private rooms on the first floor of the three-story villa. He was late. Twenty minutes was expected; thirty minutes marked heavy traffic and was forgivable. Forty minutes: well, that's when I began to wonder whether I'd misunderstood the time of our appointment.

As I waited, my fretfulness grew until I chewed the eraser off the end of my pencil. I was giving up my weekend. I was giving up valuable study time. I wanted to move, but I didn't dare walk out of the room. The club was filling up with grim-faced students looking for a quiet space to study. I took a deep breath and put on a serious face, too, staring hard at the notes I'd spread on the desk in front of me and the three textbooks filled with diagrams of teeth, gums, and bridges.

Strangely, by the time he arrived, nearly an hour late, I wasn't illtempered, just relieved that he'd come at all. Wearing a red-checkered shirt pushed into dark-blue jeans, he burst into the room with the freshness of a summer's shower. He kept apologizing, and although I wanted to pretend I was so busy studying that I hadn't noticed the time, I mumbled that it was all right, with a smile that came out exaggerated.

The pink that tinged Adel's eyes and the plump crescents beneath them were proof of the late night he'd had. It made me wonder where he had been, and with whom. All silly, of course, but my mind was flitting about. It was an awkward study session, too formal, too quiet. I kept my eyes diverted from his. There was no trusting them, so easy to read, often revealing too much in their clarity.

"Come on, get in," says Dalal, pulling me back into the present. "We can't wait all night."

I mumble a halfhearted hello to Azza, which she returns through a gum-filled grin. I am about to slide in behind her when I spot a browned apple core on the seat. What a pig! I pull a tissue out of my handbag, pick up the core, and throw it out of the car, then wipe down the dusty seat. Dalal snickers at my fastidious behavior. The sleepy right eye she was born with narrows when she laughs.

I say nothing and sit down, curling my arms tight around my waist. The car groans, and we are off. I stare out at the street as if waiting for something really important to happen, while Dalal and Azza chat away like a couple of parrots about to be rewarded with handfuls of pumpkin seeds. Every now and then, Azza lets out a vulgar laugh that convinces me she's nothing but a girl of lowly upbringing who was never taught good manners. The thought makes me feel superior, and my temper cools as the car turns onto a broad, traffic-choked road.

❦

Azza drops us off at the entrance to the Marriott Hotel in Zamalek. Since the half-term vacation has ended, I was convinced that the Khaleejis would have packed up and flown home by now. But here they are, visitors from Saudi Arabia, Kuwait, Qatar, and the Emirates, filling the hotel's café, an oblong arrangement with a broad walkway that runs from one end of the garden's patio to the other.

Waiters in green aprons flit between the round tables, carrying *shisha* or balancing trays crowded with cups of tea and coffee, and long glasses filled to the brim with ruby-red hibiscus punch or saffron-colored *qamar el-din*, a thick juice made of apricot paste. The light is atmospheric, casting pockets of shadows over the sections of the café bordered by hedges, making them look like little rooms with four to six tables. That's where I want to be, but I follow Dalal. There's a natural sultry swing to her gait that comes with being shaped like that: the perfect symmetry of the crescents of her waist, the dip just above her tailbone that slides out just so, giving the impression of an invisible string holding up her plum-shaped buttocks. What man would not look at her? She struts down the amply lit walkway and I tag along behind her, awkward and too aware of all the eyes following us: a lazy gaze here, a sharp stare a little farther down, furtive glances to take note of what is there and what is not there.

I'd felt a sense of security, but it evaporates as panic builds up in me. What if someone sees me and word gets back to Ammi Majed? He would not approve of my being out at night, and certainly not with Dalal. But I keep my thoughts to myself because there's no point nagging.

I am suspicious of every gaze that lingers too long on us. A middle-aged man, hawkeyed, ambles up and down the walkway. He seems to be a regular, because the waiters keep greeting him by name. He holds a string of emerald-colored worry beads and is doing exactly what I am: scrutinizing faces in the Marriott garden.

I turn my head as we pass two young, smooth-haired Khaleejis sitting on the right. They wear jeans and tight T-shirts, so it's hard to tell which Gulf country they come from. Farther down, three middle-aged men look up at us (at Dalal, really). There is a silent and special recognition—deep, intense, welcoming: that *I-know-you're-a-Khaleeji* look. I toss a sharp glance back at them. No fear of word getting back to my uncle from this lot. Although they wear the same white *kandoras* as Emiratis would wear—loose white ankle-length robes—their head-dresses are bound with ropes too thick to belong to Emiratis. I decide they must be Saudis.

Dalal makes a popping sound with her lips, smooth as rose petals, as she looks around. She has deer eyes, beautiful and empty of complicated thought. Just like her mother's, her skin has the evenness of porcelain, with an attractive luminosity that makes it look as though it shines, even in dim light. "So," she says, fixing her palms to her hips. "Where should we sit?"

I don't give her a chance to choose. She yips as I grip her waist; I maneuver her into one of the more shadowy hedged-in areas and settle to the left of one of the many large marble statues on plinths.

"What's this place?" Dalal objects as soon as I sink into the bamboo chair, hunched low, with my back to the statue. "No one will see us here."

"Yes," I say, looking at the menu so we can order something and get out as soon as possible. "It's better that way. You can afford to be risky, but I can't. You don't have anything to lose, but I do. So, just . . ."

"All right, all right," she says. "Stop getting all paranoid."

"Did you know this is a historical royal palace?" I say, pushing back in my chair, trying to blend into the hedge to my right. "It was built by Khedive Ismail for the Suez Canal inauguration celebrations in 1869." I pretend I don't notice the disgruntled expression on her face and indicate a nearby statue. "And apparently, these are all antiques." I slide the menu toward her so she can read the information printed on it.

Dalal snaps her fingers in front of my nose. "We're here to have fun, and all you can do is give me a history lesson. Look at you, stuck to the bush like that. People will think you're mad. What are you pretending to be, some sort of spy, or a caterpillar?"

I straighten up and giggle. I do look ridiculous. With a vow to loosen up (after all, we are here together to celebrate her breaking into the world of music, her passion), I take a deep breath. The air is filled with the scent of the honey- and apple-flavored tobacco wafting out of the shishas. My gaze drifts over the lavish garden with its high palms and stout bushes, the foliage neatly trimmed and shaped into pyramids and squares, some with strips of tiny lights. I spot a hibiscus (also known as the "Rose of China," because of where it originates) and a cassia tree (fast-growing; from tropical America, yet thriving in Egypt's rich soil).

How is it that I can still remember such details? My father gave me a plant encyclopedia a long time ago, and I treasured it, making sure it stayed next to my bed (where is it now?). What started as a little girl's attempt to please her father turned into genuine interest, a passion even, that for some reason was abandoned with his death.

"So, here we are," says Dalal in a dreamy voice, "having a good time, you know, joking . . ." She flings her head back and rakes her fingers through her curls, a satiny chocolate-brown mass, before turning to survey the walkway. "Flirting . . ." Someone has caught her eye, and I frown to discourage her just as she drags her gaze back to me and says, "All right, say something, quick."

I've seen enough flirting to know where this is leading. She is setting a trap for the boy. She will probably giggle, and he will take it as an invitation. If he approaches us and she decides she's not interested, she can deny having flirted with him because she was doing nothing more than chatting with her friend. I say, "The waiter's here."

She gasps, as if I had just made the funniest comment. Her shoulders quiver as she pretends to stifle a laugh. "Ah, you are too much!"

The games—Dalal is playing her games. "The waiter is behind you," I repeat.

Instead of getting embarrassed (the waiter has been standing behind us, watching), Dalal aims a hard stare at him. He is grinning. "Spied enough?" she says.

He is young, with eyes set close together and a rocket-shaped nose. "Madam? I wasn't . . ."

I give my order quickly. "Pineapple juice."

"I can't bring you that," he says, "but I can bring you a delicious orange juice, as fresh as if I plucked the oranges out of the tree myself."

"If she wanted orange juice," Dalal retorts, "she would have asked for orange juice. If you don't have pineapple juice, just say you don't have it."

"But it's all sweet, it's all fruit. I promise you it's just as good."

"Is this what they pay you for, to snoop and argue with clients? Do you want me to call your manager?"

"I'm just here to take your order, madam."

"Then take it!"

"Forget the juice, get me a Turkish coffee," I say. "Medium sweetness."

The waiter tells me, "Maybe you can explain to your friend that I wasn't being rude, just waiting to take your order."

"She's my cousin," says Dalal.

"It's okay, no harm done," I say, hurrying to defuse a situation that could call unwanted attention to us. "Give him your order, Dalal."

"The problem with the help is that they think that just because they work in a five-star hotel filled with tourists, they can *yak-yak-yak* away with the clients."

I frown at her. "Tell him what you want!"

"A beer!"

"Right away," he stammers, and escapes to fetch our order.

"A beer? Since when do you drink?"

"Sometimes I do," says Dalal.

"But it's *haram*."

"Lots of things are forbidden," she says, fixing her eyes to my face, suddenly seeming eager for a quarrel. It is pointless to talk to her when she is like this. So I shrug and ask her about her meeting with the composer. "Haven't you been listening? I haven't met Sherif Nasr yet. But when I do, I know he will be so taken with my voice that he won't be able to resist signing me on." She looks up at the sky as if she owns it. "A perfect voice, yes, and a body to match."

I wince when she traces the exaggerated curves of that perfect body in the air. "Yes, yes," I hurry her on, "so what happens next, once you meet him, I mean?"

"Well, he arranges for a performance, I think."

"Where?"

She doesn't answer, just lifts an eyebrow to mock my sheltered upbringing.

"A nightclub!" The thought fills me with trepidation. I use all my power to imagine her rising to stardom in a respectable way, but the images that flash in my head are grotesque: smoke-filled rooms with big-bellied men, dimmed red lights, and groping drunks.

"I know exactly what you're thinking," Dalal says, "but there's nothing to be worried about. Nightclubs only look seedy in films. In real life they are stages for talent, that's all. You know, so many of the great singers began that way."

The waiter returns, and once he places the coffee and beer on the table Dalal looks up at him and nods a cordial thank-you. It is as if she had not scolded him earlier. The waiter withdraws as noiselessly as an apparition and she continues, "Of course, it will be a while before I have songs written specially for me. In the beginning I'll have to sing the popular songs of other artists. I won't even need to practice that much. I know them all by heart."

I nod. Dalal has been singing since she was a little girl, trilling all the famous songs like a bulbul bird when she was happy and dropping her voice into a warble of laments of lost love and country when sad. And in between, there were always the tunes she made up. She never mumbled them into her chest; she always sang to an invisible listener. "Definitely, you don't need much practice," I say as she holds the glass of beer to her lips. I don't show it, but it pleases me when she takes a sip and makes a face, as if she'd swallowed bitter medicine. I hide my worry, too, that if she keeps asking for beer, she might start liking it. And that would most certainly lead to heavier spirits. Then she would need alcohol all the time, just like her father craves it: the forbidden pleasure of his secret night hours.

Ammi Majed thought his whiskey drinking would always remain as safe as a yolk in a cradled egg. The only ones who knew about it were his few close friends and Dalal's mother, Zohra, who was his other big secret: the second wife who'd made things more complicated by having a child. But then everything changed.

That Zohra Mahmoud: pretty and petite, but so very daring. She had marched into his villa in Al-Wuheida, where his "real" family (that was what Ammi Majed called them) lived. There, she simply let the egg fall to the ground.

"So what did you want to tell me?" Dalal asks.

She catches me off guard. I look at the ground and frown as I consider the best way to tell her about Adel. What can I say? That I am attracted to him? It sounds so trivial, when I want it to sound special.

"Well?" She is glancing over her shoulder, slouching, maybe looking for the waiter so she can scold him again—anything to chase the boredom away. Then she sits up, suddenly alert. There are two girls in her line of sight; they are trying to convince their grandmother to go up to her room to rest. I chase her gaze farther. And there is Adel, looking straight at us.

In a fit of confusion, I turn to Dalal. Her mouth has swollen into a bud; she examines her fingers, as though measuring their length. When she looks up, she catches his gaze and raises her eyebrow in what could only be an invitation.

I'm not sure how he snakes his way between the tables toward us so quickly. I am still grasping Dalal's secret signals and the unlikelihood of his being in the same place as we are when I hear him say, "Mariam? I thought that was you."

"Bih." A nonsensical word, delivered with a friendly smile.

He shifts from one foot to the other. There is nothing I can do. I make the introductions.

"Ah, your cousin?" he says. "You look nothing like each other."

"Cousins, not twins," Dalal says with a light and airy laugh. He smiles, obviously charmed, and waits. She grins, showing too many teeth, and waits.

I am expected to invite him to join us. If he sits, we'll be forced to stay longer. If that happens, he might fall head over heels for Dalal—before I get a chance to win him over. I cannot believe the tumble of such thoughts in my mind. "It's late!" I say, covering Dalal's objection with the noise of my chair grating as I push it back. "We have to leave now." I pull her away from him before she can say anything else, but Adel calls out to me: a reminder of tomorrow's study session.

"Yes," I call back. "Tomorrow."

4

MAJED

ç

"You'd think there would be a little coolness with all these clouds," my youngest son, Badr, says as we exit the mosque after the Friday prayer. Heat-dazed into listlessness, Badr squints at the sky: a glaring white sheet holding a furious ball of sun. "It's still January, and suddenly it gets so hot? I told you we should have taken the car, Baba," he says, fanning his face with both hands, his arms slack as if there were no bones in them.

A haze hovers over the tarmac at the end of the small road; the palm trees stand stiff, their fronds dull with desert dust. No birds and no wind. Dots of perspiration collect on my forehead, and I scowl at the humidity. The weather changed so abruptly the people in the mosque couldn't stop talking about it. "When I was young I walked everywhere, summer and winter, and never complained." I pause to bid peace to some men leaving the mosque, and then continue. "The sand burned the soles of my feet, the sun singed my face. You listening?"

Badr nods with a smile and crouches to uncover our sandals, strewn among the pile of all the sandals belonging to the worshippers.

"With every breath, the heat collected and got trapped up my nose, turned to steam."

"I'm just saying, Baba, an air-conditioned car would have been more comfortable." Badr has a lisp. The tip of his tongue pops out with every word. Right now, it's an added irritation to the fact that he's right. It will take us no longer than fifteen minutes to walk to our house, which is three streets away. And yet by the time we get there, we'll be wet through. And then the blast of air-conditioning will make us shiver and get sick. "The body has gotten so weak with all this modernity," I say, envying the men getting in their cars and driving away. "And you, you children are the air-conditioned generation; you can't even handle a little walk under the sun."

Badr chuckles. "I'm hardly a child, Baba," he says. "God willing, I'll be finishing school this year." He has located my sandals and kneels to position them in front of me. Despite the glare, he looks straight up at me; his lids are slightly hooded and his lashes are so thick it looks like he's wearing kohl. Yes, we have the same eyes; the difference is that there is no restless hunger in his.

"You said that last year," I grunt and start walking. We are the only people on the road. Under my kandora, I am swathed in soggy, hot air. No matter how many times I pull it loose, my wizar creeps back into the cracks, kneading its way into my bottom and clinging to the back of my knees. Ahead is a municipal garbage bin, silver and gleaming under the sun. We cross the road to avoid the stink.

"No, really, this time it's true," says Badr, and he goes into detail about this or that teacher who has it in for him. I lose the thread of his chatter and think of my other unmarried son, Khaled, who normally joins us for the Friday prayer. But he's disappeared, went fishing with his friends for the weekend—or so his mother told me. I don't think he's catching fish after the incident that took place last Monday. I imagine that Khaled must be moping by the shore, using the excuse of a chipped heart to write more of his useless verses. Aisha did not bring up his recent predicament, even though I could tell she was troubled by it, what with all her shuffling about the house with that taut face. Khaled is her favorite son, after all, and he is in pain.

He'd set his eyes on the daughter of Diab Al-Mutawa. He called her a beauty and declared that it had been love from the moment he'd spotted her in the mall. I'd had to hold back a snicker as I listened to him, but in the end I'd nodded my approval, all the while thinking that it was about time he settled down. I had lost patience with him, the sensitive poet who could never get enough pampering from his mother. There was no reason to stand in the way of such a match. The Al-Mutawa family has always been prosperous and held in high esteem by society. What could be better? I congratulated him on his choice wholeheartedly. But then the girl's father refused.

"You hear what I'm saying, Baba? This time I really will graduate," Badr says, jolting me out of my thoughts.

"It's not studies or age that turns you into a man. It's how you handle difficulty," I say in a stern voice aimed at concluding this talk that does nothing more than irk me. "And since you haven't had any—difficulties, that is—you won't mature further." In the silence that follows, my mind drifts off to two nights earlier.

I'd arrived at the Neely agitated, eager to find out whether my friends had heard anything about Diab Al-Mutawa's refusal—by that time I regarded it as an insult to my family's good name. But instead, I'd ended up hinting to them that the drink didn't seem to leave my body as it used to.

"Age plays tricks on the body," my friend Saeed said to me. There were a brown sofa and two beige chairs in the living room of the Neely, but, as always, we were more comfortable settled on the ground around the rectangular coffee table, on which were placed the usual bowls filled with olives, nuts, and chips. Between Mattar, my banker friend, and me sat Saeed, one leg bent underneath him, the other held to his chest by his arm—a Bedouin's typical position of comfort. "You are wiser with age, and you notice that," he continued, mischief lighting his sharp eyes. "You feel fine, you feel young. Whiskey still relaxes you, and you enjoy it. But age is busily changing all that." With that, he clapped my shoulder and guffawed. It felt like being whacked with a plank of wood.

"What rubbish," I said, kneading the sting out of my shoulder. We are close in age, but his small frame has remained hard and sinewy, with muscles and veins that bulge like thick ropes under his skin.

I'd met Saeed nearly thirty years ago, soon after I'd moved to Dubai to work for my brother. Saeed was a regular at the bar of the Saba Hotel, a rowdy place with lots of noisy conversation, smoking, and puking in the bathrooms. Most important, there was no risk of being spotted, because it was not a place anyone I knew went. We'd stay at the bar until midnight, then head out to Mohammad Ali Kebabi, a dim cave of a restaurant deep in the heart of Sharjah's souk. Bread, kebab, and raw onion: there was nothing better to dilute the alcohol.

"Let me say my piece," Saeed said, swaying slightly and rubbing his unkempt beard. He refuses to dye it black as Mattar and I do, and under the bright ceiling light it looked like it'd been sprayed with salt. "I know what I'm talking about. You don't realize what's happening to everything in your body, all those parts you can't see: bones, guts, blood. So maybe you ought to consider giving up whiskey and taking up wine instead."

"You suggest that, huh?" I cuffed his neck just as he took a thirsty gulp of his third glass of whiskey, causing it to spatter out of his mouth. "Do I look weak? Do I look like a woman? You really fart from your mouth after a few!" Both men fell back, roaring with laughter.

I would have liked a simple and straightforward answer for why I feel the way I do; and I thought about bringing up the vile dreams that have been sneaking up on me, leaving me with a numbing sense that some violent death awaits me. But worries like that would be perceived as a sign of personal weakness. Being unable to manage our emotions, whining like women? For men like us, that wouldn't do. So with cleverly disguised words we try to steer the conversation toward whatever is making us anxious, and hope someone will inadvertently come up with a solution. I got no answers. What I did get was the dreadful sense of growing old.

Once the mirth abated, I declared, "Khaled decided to propose."

"What? *Masha'Allah*, God willed it!" Mattar exclaimed. "Khaloodi?"

"You can hardly call him that now," Saeed said. "He's a grown man. What is he, nearing thirty-one, thirty-two?"

"Something like that," I said.

"*Mabrook!* Congratulations," Mattar said.

"About time," added Saeed. "By the time I reached that age, I already had six children. I don't know why you didn't arrange a marriage for him early on, like you did with your other children, and like your father did for you."

"I tried. But he didn't want to do it the traditional way—he said he wanted to choose his own wife."

"Well, anyway, he'll put down roots now. Wonderful news, my brother."

"That's what I thought, too," I said, reaching out for the sweating glass in front of me for my first sip of the night. "The problem is that the girl's family refused."

My friends were baffled. "What? Why?" Mattar asked, cupping his whiskey with both hands.

"Whose daughter is this?" Saeed flung his arms into the air in exasperation. "Don't they know what a privilege it would be to hook your son?"

I merely shrugged, but Saeed could tell I was boiling inside at the insult of this refusal. He bowed his head slightly to show me that he was a good friend and a compassionate listener who would like to hear more. I tapped his back and continued, "The womenfolk, my wife and daughters—even my sisters, who came all the way from Ras Al-Khaimah—did their duty and visited the women of the girl's family to let them know of Khaled's interest and intentions. My wife said it was an auspicious meeting. She came back with nothing but praise for the girl, who apparently had excellent manners. Aisha couldn't wait to seal the arrangement. If it had been up to her, she would have called as soon as she got home to set up the next meeting, for my sons and me to visit and make a formal proposal to her father. But I told her, 'Hold off for a few days. Don't make it seem like we are desperate.'"

"Wise, wise," said Mattar.

"Aisha agreed and waited a few more days before calling them. Do you know what they told her?" I picked up my glass and held it to the light, watching the amber liquid swallow up what slivers of ice remained. "Her father said, 'The girl wants to continue her studies.'"

My friends groaned at this infamous excuse: a polite yet definitive refusal.

"But who are these people? What family is this?" Saeed asked, and when I told him, he became thoughtful. This was a gracious and respectable family, after all. Khaled is a good boy; only the most serious of reasons could make them change their minds. I watched Saeed rub his hooked nose, and I guessed that the very same thoughts were filling his head: *What could it be? Does the old man consider his family better than mine?* I wanted to know. But to go to Diab Al-Mutawa as the father of the proposed groom and ask him outright would have been mortifying. Saeed knew this and announced, "Well, my friend, I will wait a few days and then go see the old man. He won't tell me right away, of course. But I'll talk to him in a most clever way." He tapped his forehead with his index finger, and a spark of shrewdness lit his eyes. "I will suck the information out of him without his realizing it. Leave it to me. I'll unravel the riddle."

Mattar sighed, and I nodded. That's what the Neely is for: it is a place where we can share common enjoyment and camaraderie, take pleasure in one another's good-humored nonsense and take a man's stand whenever it is called for without being asked. We recognize that we are all saddled with pressures—work, family—and this makes the gatherings at the Neely vital for our serenity.

༄

There's a light-blue Audi parked outside the house. The engine is on; Mustafa, my right-hand man at the company, dozes behind the wheel. I'm puzzled that he's here on a Friday. It's the one day that my whole family assembles for lunch. As Badr and I draw closer, I spot the fifty or so threads of hair on the top of Mustafa's head standing and quivering from the force of the air blowing out of the air conditioner. Mustafa straightens up in his seat as soon as I knock on the window, flattening the hairs to his scalp before rolling down the window.

"Why are you sitting out here?" I ask, squinting at him under the dazzle of the whitewashed sky.

He jumps out of the car and rubs the creases out of his shirt before answering. "Well, *bey*, I didn't want to disturb you on a Friday, but I couldn't wait until tomorrow to give you this news." I instruct Badr to go on ahead and to notify the family that Mustafa will be having lunch with us. But Mustafa insists he does not want to inconvenience us. "My wife would never forgive me," he says. "She has cooked *molokhia*." In this muggy heat, I can almost smell the slimy green broth these Egyptians can't get enough of. My instruction to Badr is the expected etiquette, as is Mustafa's refusal to enter our house, the private sanctuary in which his employer resides with his wife and unmarried children. So we head to the men's *majlis*.

It's a one-story structure to the right of the main house. There's a large sitting room that opens onto an even larger dining room. There's a kitchen and a bathroom, and next to it a row of sinks for the guests. Once a week, I receive visitors who arrive after the evening prayer to socialize and exchange news. Between the house and the majlis there is a lawn with a marble fountain in the middle, dry for the moment because the water is still turned off. Two weeks on, and the plumber still hasn't finished his work. My kandora is glued to my back as we walk over the grass. One of the cooks scurries past us, hugging four bottles of water. How many times have I told him to serve *limboo*, chilled lime juice with lots of sugar, when it's hot? It's the best way to get heat out of the body. I want to call him and scold him, but that would mean another minute under the sun. So I quicken my pace, and Mustafa does the same.

We walk up the three steps to the heavy teak door. The foyer is round, with colored glass fitted into the ceiling. Light shines through them, and Mustafa's face turns a luminous green. I indicate that he should wait for me in the sitting room while I splash water on my face.

"They don't go out in the morning," Mustafa says as soon as I settle next to him, "only in the afternoon: four, five, six o'clock. *Keda*, like that. They don't come back until late: nine, ten, eleven o'clock. Keda. They always dress nicely, with makeup and styled hair. They take the microbus—maybe because they can't afford taxis."

"Of course they can't afford taxis."

"Well, that's when my man always loses them—until this time, that is. Yes, he took a chance and got on the same microbus, dangerous as that was. I mean, what if, what if?"

"But they don't know who this man is."

"True, but if they saw him there and remembered his face from another place, and then keep spotting him? They might solve the puzzle and form a picture."

"We're the ones trying to form a picture, not them. Now, Mustafa, will you get to the point and tell me what you found out?"

"Yes, yes, exactly." Mustafa clears his throat. "Anyway, my man—and I won't tell you his name or where he lives, for your protection, of course. The last thing we want is people saying that Majed Al-Naseemy is spying on his daughter and her mother."

"What did you find out?"

"They got off in front of a building near the embassies in El-Dokki. It's an old building, gray or maybe beige, I'm not sure because of all the dust and diesel fumes. You know, in Cairo buildings are never washed."

"Mustafa!"

"Sorry, bey," he stutters. "Where was I?" He interlaces his fingers, then leans back and thrusts his hands out to produce a mighty crack. "It seems they are looking for a composer."

"A composer? What is that supposed to mean?"

5

DALAL

A pinch of what feels like mildew clings to the back of my throat. I cough it away, and the dryness that takes its place signals the start of another day. Something pokes my bottom—another loose spring in the mattress—and I cry out a bit too dramatically before rolling off the bed, all the while scowling with the certainty that I'll never get used to this place.

My waking moments never feel fresh. In my room, the air doesn't move. It's as if a hundred old men slept around me, snoring, belching, and farting all night. The lingering staleness that is the hallmark of our dark, dank apartment always seems worse in the morning, and it makes me rush to slip into my dressing gown and step out onto the balcony off the sitting room. It's not much better out here, overlooking an alley so tight that any trapped breeze fizzles to nothing before it can reach me. The balcony is so small that I'd have to stand sideways if anyone joined me. Alone, I have enough space to take one step to the right or left. A pencil of light falls just beyond its edge. I clutch the iron railing and lean over to bathe my face in it.

I live with my mother on the fringe of the densely populated Imbaba slum in a building just a couple of streets away from Sudan Street. I can't see the road, but I can hear it. The persistent honks wrapped in the hollow drone of traffic is a daily reminder of how close I am to Sudan Street, that just by crossing it I'd be strolling in the more affluent Mohandessin district.

I hear a call from a balcony below me in the facing building. "Don't get too much sun, or you'll turn black." It's Salwa, a sweet-faced mother with five children and a brutish husband. She has pulled up her cuffs and is hanging her washing on a line secured to poles that jut out of her window ledge. I peer down at her briefly and look back up at the sun, taking notice of another woman two balconies above her who is preparing to do the same with her laundry. It pleases me that there are no bruises on Salwa's pale arms, that she is cheerful for a change. Her husband must be in a good temper. I wonder whether it's because their children are doing well in school, or if he's had a recent promotion at work. I have to force myself to stop, to pull myself away from the details of our neighbors' lives. I don't want to start caring. Then I might not try as hard to break away from this soul-destroying place.

Two weeks on and still we haven't managed to see Sherif Nasr, the composer. My limbs feel heavy at the thought of trudging into his office again later today. Once more, Mama and I will step into the rumbling elevator that will take us to the seventh floor. I don't look forward to that windowless waiting room, full of other hopeful mothers and daughters. Sometimes the secretary sends us away because he's not in. If he is, however, the biggest struggle is remaining patient and pleasant during the long wait.

"And more important, don't fall over!" Another voice comes from the building facing mine, but one floor above, on the sixth floor. This well-fed neighbor is called Tafida, and her husband works in the sanitation department. She is grinning, but her eyebrows furrow as she concentrates on the stuffed brown paper bag she is holding. Her plump hands press it firmly, as if willing it to magically turn into a ball. Once satisfied, she steals a look below and lets go.

I watch it crash to the ground and disintegrate in an explosion of potato and carrot peelings. I've seen this many times before. It lies alongside two other garbage bombs. Cats tackle the fish skeleton that peeps through one burst bag, trying to free it from the threads of pulped sugarcane. The other ripped bag looks alive with clumps of flies, which hover and stick to bits of soggy bread on a spill of watery yellow mush. It could be lentil soup or vomit—hard to tell. After the cats and flies are done feeding, whatever is left will lie there. People will skirt the mess until some brave soul, hopefully with old shoes, kicks the guck along the street to a gutter or rubbish heap. Perhaps Tafida's husband's people will pick up the mess. But it has been more than a week since I last spotted any sweepers or garbage collectors on this street.

I want to ask Tafida about this, inquire whether there is a strike, perhaps make a smart comment that poor streets are just as important as tourist roads. I want to tell Salwa that her clothes will never dry if she keeps hanging them right under other people's laundry. Instead I smile at the women and say, "Good morning to you both."

They giggle; it's 2:00 p.m. But all hours that don't require a bulb being switched on are morning hours to me. They, on the other hand, have been up since dawn to prepare breakfast for their husbands, feed and clothe their children for school, make the beds, scrub the floors, wash the clothes, and cook the food for the rest of the day.

I laugh along with them, but all I can think about is my singing career, which is proving to be so much harder to attain than I'd predicted. I passionately crave this career. I dread the possibility of becoming one of these women, enduring a life like theirs, being unimportant and apathetic. I have been in Cairo for ten months and I am still stuck in this wretched alley, where rats grow fat and roaches don't scurry to hide.

I step into the apartment as the sun moves on to shine on someone else's balcony. My mother is in the sitting room, stretching the sleep out of her limbs.

"How long is this going to take? How many more times must we go to Sherif bey's office?" There is the whine of a starving cat in my voice, which she ignores as she plods to the kitchen to make some food.

I follow her and sit on a stool at the small wooden table. She fills a medium-sized pot with water and a smaller one with milk. She lights the gas stove and places the pots on burners. I slump on the stool and watch her pull butter and cheese out of the fridge—three wedges in paper wrappings. There is a mechanical efficiency in her movements. She reaches for three small plates, two cups, and a bunch of mismatched knives, forks, and spoons from the cupboard and drawer, arranging them in no particular order on the plastic covering of the table.

My mouth is a pout of disappointment as I peel the paper wrapping off the butter. "I mean, I really thought this would be easier, and the whole process is getting me down." My voice rises over the tumble of fava beans she pours into the first pot as the water starts to boil. She is making *ful*, the humble first choice of Egypt's masses, popular because it's cheap and filling. "How many people have we talked to in the studios? How many phone calls have we made?" I hold a hand to my ear and deepen my voice. "'Yes, we are interested. Yes, we want to meet. No, don't come yet. Wait for our call. We'll call you tomorrow, in a couple of days, in a week at the most. Yes, yes, for sure. *Wallah al-azeem*, by God!' They sound so excited and get us excited along with them. And then, *poof*!" I snap my fingers. "Zero! No one calls, not a soul follows up, nothing happens."

Mama lifts the heated milk off the flame and turns to look at me. She says, "Well, and a good morning to your complaining."

"Then, finally, we think the great Sherif Nasr will see us. But that cow of a secretary won't let us in. Really, Mama, how does anyone get famous here?"

"Well, what did you expect? Did you think people would take you straightaway?"

"Yes," I say, like a child denied someone else's slice of cake.

"Just because you managed to come in second on *Nights of Dubai*."

I flinch. More than a year has passed since I appeared on that show and still the humiliation of failing stings, like a spattering of lemon juice on grazed skin. If I'd come in first, I wouldn't be here, struggling to get a break. The station pays for the composing, recording, publicity, and distribution of the winner's very first song, but I'd had to settle for second prize: a generous seventy-five thousand dirhams, the money we're using to live here. "Second is not so bad," I mumble, unconvinced.

Mama doesn't answer, only takes four eggs out of the fridge. I lay my head on folded arms on the table and let my mind fill with images of the multicolored lights that had raced over my face and the billowing smoke that had curled around my feet as I stepped into the silver bubble of a spotlight. I was wide-eyed with excitement. The stage was egg-shaped, with an orchestra on one side and three judges on the other. It felt natural being there. It felt right. Cameramen whirled around me. The audience never tired of cheering and clapping every time they were signaled to do so by a man wearing headphones.

Nights of Dubai was the first program of its kind on Dubai television: a battle of talents directed by legendary star maker Simon Asmar. The Lebanese man had launched the careers of the great singers Majida Al-Roumi, Ragheb Alama, and Nawal Al-Zoghbi, to name just a few. Why couldn't he do it for me?

From the moment I saw the television promotion inviting all Arab talent "from the Gulf to the Ocean," I knew I had to join. I was accepted right away and decided it was better not to delay telling Mama. As expected, she showed no interest and remained on the periphery as I rushed to the rehearsals. But that changed after the first two live episodes aired. And it was all because of a phone call.

His words were harsh and his threats daunting. "A Naseemy girl on television? The shame!" My father had demanded that I drop out immediately. Strangely, his reprimands filled me with a sense of importance. He was finally taking notice after having neglected me for so long. Mama did not bother with charm. She spoke to him in a mundane voice, as if she were talking about what she needed to buy from the fruit and vegetable market. She pointed out that we were not his responsibility anymore since he'd divorced her, that he had no say in our lives.

Once she hung up I'd become aware of a chaotic flapping in my chest. All I could think of was what he would do to us. She didn't answer when I asked her, just reached for her makeup bag. She would be joining me at the studio. I watched her line her eyes, the color of blue ice, with a steady hand. I watched them turn to steel.

I hear the spattering of hot oil. "They wanted a winner from a different Gulf country," I say, sitting up straight. "They had to choose someone who was not Emirati so people would not accuse them of favoritism. I came in second only because of politics. Everyone said so."

"That's not the point," Mama says as the eggs pop and sizzle. "Even if you had come in first, it might not have made things easier now. You've got to understand that you're not the only one trying to get famous. There are many like you out there."

"Politics," I repeat, nodding vigorously. "That's what it was."

"Much as you want it to, life doesn't work that way," Mama says, picking up a plate and sliding the eggs onto it. "There are other young ladies all over Cairo who feel just as you do and, let me tell you, have just as much talent." Her voice has grown louder. She waves the spatula in the air while she scolds me. "And they're probably sitting in the kitchen feeling sorry for themselves, useless as can be, moaning away while their mothers do all the work to put a morsel of food into their mouths."

There's blame in her voice, as if I were the cause of our worries and sorry predicament. But who can blame her? She's the one who's had to deal with my vindictive father and his cruel control tactics. He forced us into that dilapidated *shaabia* house—subsidized government homes built in compounds and available to every Emirait citizen—and made sure we were always in need of money. An overflow of guilt at voicing my grievances turns my skin so hot I can almost smell the burn in my cheeks. I take a yawning breath, hoping to convince her that my grumbles were no more than small talk to pass the time, to while away the minutes as we get ready for our day. I don't look at her, only pick up the cheeses and start to unwrap them: a hard yellow Roumy cheese and a soft white Baladi cheese. I place each on a separate plate and try to arrange the cutlery the way Clara used to. I wonder what happened to my Filipina maid. Does she remember me? Does she ever think of the apartment she lived in with Mama and me, which I called the snow palace?

I lived there until I was eight years old. Mama called it modern, with its lacquered tables and cabinets, sliding aluminum balcony doors, and light curtains with pink swirls that reminded me of strawberry ice cream. But in my young mind, it was a snow palace. The couches were a stark white, which Mama kept protected from dust and stains with a see-through plastic covering. The whole apartment had wall-to-wall carpeting, plush and cream-colored, which I would often lie on. I would rub my cheeks on the furry softness and pretend I was cleaning my face with snow, which I had seen only in pictures.

The apartment was in Deira, with a sprawling view of Dubai's creek. We had a ritual, Baba and I, of leaning over the balcony to watch the men unloading crates off the dhows moored at the dock. He told me they came from Iran, Pakistan, India, and even from as far as Africa. There were *abras*, too, water taxis that chugged back and forth from one side of the creek to the other, always crowded with passengers. I can honestly describe those as happy days, even though, if forced, I would probably be able to count more outbursts and sulks than times of laughter and contentment. Now that I think about it, maybe I was only happy because I always got my own way.

Clara had a sweet voice that often grew croaky at the end of the day as she tended to my incessant demands. Whenever she felt a tantrum brewing, she would burst into song at the top of her voice. There was a desperate force as she drove the melody out. She ended up sounding wounded, as if she'd stepped on spikes. One day my father shouted at her, accusing her of scaring me. I liked that he did that. I thought it showed his love for me.

Baba visited us at the snow palace every other day. He would always show up after the evening prayer. Many times, he entered our apartment with his arms folded behind him. With a glowing smile, he would ask, "Who is the most beautiful girl in the Emirates?" I would hardly be able to contain my curiosity as I lunged to the right and left to catch a glimpse of the hidden surprise. How big was the toy? What color was it? How much fun would it bring me before I flung it into the basket full of other toys I'd grown bored of? "Stop jumping up and down, you little monkey!" And I'd have to force myself to stand still, with a silly grin that hurt my face. "You still haven't answered me," Baba would say, looking around with a confused expression on his face. "Maybe this is the wrong apartment. Is this the eighth floor? Is this flat number 815? Is this the right place?"

"It is! It is!"

"Are you the most beautiful girl in the Emirates?"

"I am! I am!"

"Ah, thank goodness. For a moment I thought this was the neighbor's place. A kiss, please?" He would bend down so that I could kiss him on his right cheek.

"Another one."

"Baba!" I would object, but hurry to place another kiss on his left cheek.

Satisfied, he would straighten. "Now, what could it be?" He would look up. His eyes would narrow and he would move his lips without making a sound, as if counting stars. And then, with a dramatic twirl, he'd swing his arms to the front and hand me the gift.

A doll, crayons and a coloring book, a jump rope, a LEGO set, anything to keep me occupied so that he could be alone with my mother. I would grab it and rip open the package, then hop off to play with it in my room as he settled on the couch with a glass of what he called "apple juice for grown-ups." Foul smelling, it soon got him slurring his words.

I want to talk about our past, when Baba treated us like queen and princess at the snow palace, but I curb my nostalgia. Mama probably doesn't want to hear anything more come out of my mouth. Her face is fixed in a frown as she picks up a fork and starts crushing the ful into a paste. Once more, our day is about to begin with a meal that is both breakfast and lunch: fried eggs, mashed ful, and bread and cheese, all washed down with two cups of strong, sugary tea.

6

MARIAM

❧

The chair is hard. I relieve the stiffness of one crossed leg by uncrossing it. I stare at the tiny specks of dust that have collected on the table, which I'd wiped with wet pieces of tissue as soon as I'd arrived. Even though the study rooms at the Emirati Students' Club are cleaned every day, it's impossible to keep Cairo's pollution outside. It floats in. It leaves behind a sticky film on the metal grid of the window and collects as black grime on the beige shutters and windowsills.

We sit at the edge of the large rectangular table. Adel fidgets and looks around. There is nothing to call his attention away from the lesson: no television, no view through the window, no pictures hanging on the walls.

As always, I have left the door open. I speak loudly so that curious people outside the room know we are studying, and nothing more. "Pay attention to this here," I say, pointing, and Adel straightens up. He takes a long breath, and his eyebrows furrow as he focuses on the text. After no more than a minute his gaze strays once more. I follow it and spot the haphazard movements of a pair of flies mating at the other end of the table. "Pay attention," I repeat. The echo sounds louder than my voice. I feel as if I am talking to myself. And I am— talking to myself, that is. The flies detach and take to the air. Adel narrows his eyes and follows their flight.

It is our third session, and Adel has proven to be an erratic student. Sometimes he arrives with an incredible ability to concentrate, swallowing the lessons with as little effort as he would guzzle down water. Other times I have to go over the same point again and again. Whatever mood he is in does not take away the warm tingle I feel just from being near him. Always, I convince myself that it's nothing more than that of a committed teacher whose student is showing progress.

Adel is wearing a blue shirt tucked into jeans. His face is narrow at the forehead and broadens into a well-defined square chin. His mustache and beard are neatly trimmed in a *gofel*, the lock design that traps his long, thin mouth in its center and leaves the cheeks bare. He seems to have lost the thread of the flies' progress. *Daydreaming again*, I think as I pitch a sidelong glance at him. He raises his hand and runs his fingers up and down along a strand of his soft, black hair, which is always swept to one side and falls in a glossy tumble just over his collar. I look away. It is clear that he will not absorb much in today's session. "Maybe we should stop now."

His hand swoops down and bangs the table. I flinch, thinking I might have insulted him—until I spot one of the flies stuck to the base of his palm. "Got it," he says, flicking it to the floor. "Sorry. What did you say?"

"I just said that maybe it's better to stop for today."

He is suddenly alert. "Why?"

"Well, it seems you're finding it hard to concentrate. It's all right to end the lesson if you don't feel like continuing."

"No, no, no. I don't want to have had you come all this way for nothing."

"Don't worry about it."

"No, please. What you're teaching me is vital, and I appreciate all your help." He leans closer to me and I catch his scent, fresh and antiseptic—talcum powder and Lifebuoy soap. "You're right, though. For some reason, I am finding it hard to concentrate today. But I must, I must." He puts his hand on my cheek, then quickly drops it and gives my hand a soft squeeze.

It's the first time he has touched me. Instinctively I pull away and glance at the open doorway to check whether any prying person might have chanced to look in. There is no one. Awkwardness settles between us. Before I can think of how to respond, Adel suggests that he go down to the canteen to get some refreshments, something to get his head working again. "Yes, juice is a good idea," I mumble, running a finger through the new dust on the table.

As soon as I'm alone in the room, my hands start shaking, and I busy them by tapping the edge of the table with my thumbs. My heels follow, clicking on the floor. What was that touch? How was I supposed to react? I should have slapped his hand away immediately, but it happened so suddenly, too quickly for me to react.

Was there a secret signal in that touch? The tapping and clicking grow louder. Was there some infatuation in it? How bold of him! I should have said something smart to put him in his place right away: a strong "How dare you?" or even a slightly quizzical "What do you think you're doing?" accompanied by a tilt of the head for extra emphasis. That would have been the right reaction. That's what the daughter of a respectable family would have said. That's what I should have done: slapped his hand and scolded him. But I'd done nothing.

I stop all movement and stare at the textbook in front of me. A sense of confusion and vulnerability washes over me and I start turning the pages slowly, deliberately, while I try to retrieve the leonine self-assurance I'd had so long ago. The more I think about it, the more I realize how much I've changed. I used to be a lanky girl with a confident stride: big, brash steps and strong, swinging arms. I'd believed

I was special. My tongue was sharp and my spirit free. That was when my father was alive.

"My miracle child." That's what he called me.

When my mother died giving birth to me, my grandmother came to live with us. Not yet seventy, she was a strong and obstinate force. Mama Al-Ouda—"the big mother," as the family calls her—was unflagging in her efforts to weave some feminine restraint into me. She was quick to lose her temper and slow to let go of a grudge. Whenever I made a cheeky comment, she'd swoop in as fast as she could to slap some discipline into me. But she was a heavy woman. I could bend, twist, and hop out of the way before she had time to swing her arm.

Over and over, she took her complaints to her eldest son, my father. "What gentleman would want her? She mocks me and respects no one. I tell you, Hareb, the heart of a man is growing behind that girl's ribs."

Mama Al-Ouda found no sympathy in my father. He was my safety net. As far as he was concerned, I could do no wrong. When she accused me of being presumptuous, he insisted that it was the desirable attribute of courage. If I asked too many questions and she told me to stop being nosy, he countered by saying I had an intelligent curiosity. And so it went: if I sulked, it was a natural shyness; if I made too much noise, I was acting as any normal child would. There were steady bursts of squabbles over my constitution and development. She said *skinny*, he said *athletic*. She said *lazy*, he said *deep*. Knowing he would always take my side, I became fearless, and my spirit grew plump with self-importance. After all, I was the child he thought he would never have: the miracle child.

Throughout his two marriages that preceded the union with my mother, my father watched his younger brother's family grow from one to four children strong while he remained unable to produce any of his own. Even after my mother became my father's third wife in 1960, Ammi Majed's family kept expanding—another boy, then a girl—while my mother lost two through miscarriages, the second of which came with some added unhappy news from the doctors: a stern warning that another pregnancy could pose a threat to her life. She did not die with her third miscarriage, but she lost enough blood that the doctor declared further conception to be impossible.

So my parents gave up. My father could have divorced my mother and married another woman, just as he'd done with his first two wives. It was the conventional action by men with a longing to have children, accepted in Khaleeji societies by men and women alike. But Baba was older; he'd grown settled. Besides, he cared for my mother deeply, and for a long time, my parents settled into a life pattern of acceptance. Their yearning for a child dulled as they put their trust in God's decision. But then my mother was with child once more. "A miracle," my father declared. The doctors were baffled. They pleaded to my parents' common sense, to consider aborting lest she lose her life during the pregnancy. But Baba would hear none of it. It was God's will, after all, and what right did a mere human have to question His supremacy?

This time my father decided to take my mother to Bombay for the full term of her pregnancy; he was convinced that the doctors there would do a better job. The labor was long and ate at her strength without mercy, and I entered the world moments before she exited.

Adel's laugh outside the room brings me back to the present. I realize that my shoulders have risen, stiff and stuck to my earlobes. I loosen my neck. It makes a cracking sound and he says, "Oof! Don't do that," as he peers through the doorway. "You'll damage that delicate neck."

What am I supposed to say to that? There was a time I would have been able to come up with an answer that was both sharp and graceful. Instead, I stare at his empty hands, as he eases onto the chair. "You said you were going to bring us juice. Where are they?" There is accusation and aggression in the tone of my voice.

With his quick wit, he makes light of the situation. He lifts up his arms in surrender. "Before you kill me, let me explain."

This time I follow his lead. "No explanations for a dying man."

"All right, then—a wish?"

The charade continues, and I cross my arms as a judge might. "The law specifies that a dying man must have his last wish."

Adel rises. "And are you a follower of the law?" He bows his head and indicates the open doorway.

"That I am," I say.

                                       ↄↄ

It sounds like a crowd has gathered, but there are only five students downstairs, their chatter amplified by the echo that bounces off the club's walls. They are waiting for their private tutor to arrive. The television is on, but no one pays attention to it. "Poor things," Adel whispers. "They have to start their private lesson when we've just finished."

"Well, actually, we haven't finished anything," I correct him. "We're just ignoring today's lesson. Technically, that is."

"Technically, huh?"

Heat rockets to my cheeks over my lumbering choice of words. Thankfully, Adel is too excited to be leaving to notice. His car is a four-door silver Hyundai that has fared well on Cairo's roads, with no more than a series of feather-light scratches on the sides. The lethargy and distraction that filled him during the study session are gone. There's an odd glint of intensity in his expression that does not suit his light mood as he keeps joking about all the other wishes he might have if he were a dying man. He shifts gear and reverses onto the road. I keep my eye on him as I sit curled into the door with my arms crossed tight, hoping he does not touch my hand (or face) again, wondering why I agreed to accompany him to Farghaly, a blatant flirting hot spot. The Khaleejis will be arriving soon, once the sun dims, leaving behind the shadowy thrill of all sorts of possibilities. *It's still early, though*, I think; it's only half past six.

After a few quick turns, we reach the brightly lit juice shop on the corner of the bustling Arab League Boulevard. There's an elaborate arrangement of fruits running the length of Farghaly's curving glass display. Above is an empty space through which I catch the staff's flitting eyes as they go about their business of peeling, chopping, and blending the fruits.

Six beggar girls, their ages ranging from five to nine years, appear as soon as we arrive. They hop around the car with palms pushed flat out. A boy in his early teens plods over to my window with a tower of about twenty thick books cradled in both arms. To keep them from plummeting to the ground, he hooks his nose firmly over the top book while trumpeting the titles: "*The Ottoman Empire, Interpreting Dreams, Akhenaten, Healing Through Herbs and Plants.*" The group disperses when the waiter shoos them away. Adel and I don't bother reading the menu, which is a giant, brightly colored wooden slate hanging by the door. He raises his hand and calls out their signature juice: "Two fakhfakhinas!"

Feeling comfortable with the evening so far, I sit up straighter and uncross my arms. Despite the murmur of traffic, the bursts of car honks and bicycle tinkles, and the sounds of shuffling people—talking, shouting, hawking—I say, "It's so quiet." I've never seen the juice shop so empty. Adel agrees, with a weary groan that makes my voice sound too cheerful. He seems to be waiting for something to happen. I follow his gaze to the beggar girls and consider whether I am boring him. Huddled on their heels in a semicircle at the side of the shop, they seem engrossed in a game that involves pebbles and dirt. But they're quick to look up whenever a car stops, to calculate whether there's an opportunity waiting.

The fakhfakhinas arrive in long, narrow glasses, each with a straw and fork. They brim with chunks of banana and strawberry packed with other fruits in an exotic slush. For a while, there is only the clink of metal on glass. When I look over at Adel, I notice he is taking his time. With a deliberate twirl of the wrist, he forks a cube of pineapple and closes his mouth around it. He does not chew, just waits for it to melt on his tongue.

I hear an Egyptian song I do not recognize as a gray Honda edges in front of us; the girls in the car are Khaleejias, their shaylas wrapped loosely around their heads. Adel reverses to give them space and continues to back up, making way for a second girl group arriving in yet another car. He stops at the far edge of Farghaly, and a third car, a black Nissan, lunges into the gap between the girls' cars, braking with an abrupt screech.

The girls scream, and Adel lets out a wicked laugh at their panic. I giggle, too, at the boys' bungled attempt to attract the girls. The Nissan blasts the brazen lyrics of a song that demands, "Come to me, come to me, before I lose interest."

"Those boys must be Kuwaitis," I say.

"Why would you say that?"

"Because Kuwaitis are always foolhardy and impatient."

"Oh, really?" Adel looks at me, amused. "Why couldn't they be Bahrainis?"

"Too polite," I say, adding quickly, "anyway, that's what I hear from some of the girls at the sakan."

"Why not Qataris?"

"I don't think so. They tell me that the Qataris are too sweet, too accommodating. They would never be so offensive."

"Kuwaitis, huh?" He is more interested in this bit of information than any of the dental lessons I've given him. He looks away with a crooked grin. "How do you know so much?"

"I don't really know anything for sure. Like I told you, it's what I hear." I utter the lie with a straight face. I could add that Emirati boys conduct the flirting game with frightening seriousness, and that Saudis may lead it to the point of obsession. But I hold my tongue. I don't want him to know that I often join the sakan girls (and even Dalal) for a bit more than juice at Farghaly. Our flirtations have all been innocent, of course. But Adel might not understand that. If I tell him, he might lose respect for me.

"Kuwaitis!" Adel straightens up and rests his chin on the steering wheel. His curiosity is piqued. "Look at them, thinking they can bulldoze their way into the girls' hearts."

We are sufficiently close to watch every detail of the unraveling scene, yet far enough away not to attract attention. Comfortable in this spot, I watch the girls in both cars shout at the boys, accusing them of reckless driving and uncouth manners. The boys respond with nonchalant sarcasm. It is clear they are taking the taunts in their stride, turning their heads coolly to the right and left, from one car to the other, while every now and then alarming the girls by stepping on the gas to produce a sudden *vroom*. The girls screech. The waiters scuttle from car to car, trying to restore calm with sweet words, in stark contrast to the biting threats they direct at the circling beggar girls, who have doubled in number as more cars pull in for juice or a light seduction that might lead to a sweet escapade.

"I haven't seen a fight for a long time." Adel stuffs his mouth with three chunks of banana all in one go while keeping his eyes fixed on a scene that has suddenly grown chaotic. There is a constant stream of new arrivals. Some drive on, to try their luck again after a turn or two around the block. Others start parking closer to where we are. The ease I have been enjoying dissolves, and I suggest that we leave.

"Now?"

"Yes, now," I stammer. Feeling exposed, I pull my shayla lower over my forehead. "You know, move out of the way. I mean, look at all these people." Although making space for others is the least of my cares, I dread the possibility that someone might see us. There are many excuses I can come up with for being there—taking a break from studying; thirst—but who would bother to ask? Any person who might chance to recognize me would most likely choose the swiftest and most damning conclusion—and spread it. I become aware of my shoulders tightening as I imagine the scores of restless tongues: "I saw Mariam Al-Naseemy in a car with a boy." That's how it would bounce off the first tongue. "They were drinking juice and doing who knows what else." That's the tongue that would inject suspicion. "They were even holding hands." And finally, fiction would be turned into truth, into a report that would inevitably reach the ears of the cultural attaché, who would not hesitate to inform Ammi Majed.

"Look, look," Adel says. A young man in a Toyota has flung a folded piece of paper out his open car window. We know it contains a telephone number, and perhaps a suggestion for a meeting somewhere private. The paper flies in a straight course but misses its target, bouncing off the hood of a maroon Fiat that has slowed to a halt just in front of us. Adel snorts with glee. "Hopeless, just hopeless."

I start fidgeting. "I have to get back, Adel. The sakan curfew will be in effect soon."

Adel sighs and looks down at his juice, and I think, *Finally, he'll get me out of this place.* But then he dips his fingers into his glass and pulls out a soggy slice of mango. Holding it up to his face, he starts licking the juice that trickles down his hand. My mouth is a hoop, but no words come out. His movements are slow and deliberate, and when he turns to look at me he curls his lips into a half smile, paying no heed to the juice that sinks into his beard and dribbles down his wrist.

What trick is this? I look away and start examining the smudges on the glass of my half-open window with a compulsion that feels silly. "I need to get back," I mumble. "I can't have people seeing me in the middle of this pickup place."

"This is too much!" he shouts, and drums the steering wheel with his hands. I wince and look back at him, to find he's reacting not to my request but to another note that has fallen short of its target. "They miss again," Adel says. "And they actually took the time to fold their paper into the shape of a boat. *Hah!*"

The note has rolled somewhere beneath the car, and the interested boys direct one of the beggars to fetch it. She scrambles under the car, and once she retrieves it, the boys call out, "Give it to her, Asma." Asma starts to hand it to the driver of the Fiat. But the boys wave their arms with exasperation. "Not her, Asma, the other one."

"Can you believe these guys?"

I click my tongue. "What rudeness! That poor woman driving; she must feel horrible. She won't be able to face them out of embarrassment."

Embarrassment does not rob the driver of her voice. "Shame on you!" she hollers at the boys. "How would you like it if someone did that to your sisters?" Although she is wearing a shayla, I can tell she is Egyptian from her accent.

Little Asma is no older than five or six—too young to know what she should do. She clutches the boat-note with one hand and tugs at her dusty plaits with the other. "Go on," the boys instruct her. "Hand the note to the girl in the passenger seat, the beautiful one, the princess."

"Go home and let your father teach you some manners," cries the girl in the driver's seat. "How would you like it if your mother . . ." The girl in the passenger seat, the princess, shushes her before she can go on. She turns her head to peek briefly at the boys. I crane my neck to get a better look, but her shayla covers her profile. I manage to pick out the tip of her nose and the glimmer of her pearly complexion. Her arm floats out the window. There is a subtle elegance in the way it moves. The wrist twists and the palm flattens. She holds it up like a mild-tempered policeman stopping traffic, a signal to the boys not to make a scene.

There is no need. The boys are in a good humor, even when their note is refused. Asma cries out to them, "They say they don't want to be bothered, that you should leave them alone." The boys seem amused. The driver of the Toyota leans out the window and pounds his chest. "Now, why would you do that? Don't you realize my heart is burning here?" He slips some money into Asma's open hand and motions to her to go back and plead his case.

Back by the Fiat, Asma says, "Take pity on him." She mimics his stance with her fist glued to her ribcage. "His heart, God protect it, has burst into flames." She takes note of the girls' response and skips back to the Toyota. "The girl in the driving seat says you should drink a bottle of water to put it out."

"Tell that big mouth that my messages are for the princess. You must make her understand that nothing can quench the fire in me."

And so it goes for the next few minutes, until the boys start sending songs. Once more, the mouthpiece is Asma. With a squeaky voice filled with the murmur of the lovesick, she sings of the boy's burning desire in a melody she creates right then and there. The princess laughs, and this time she turns her head fully, flashing the boys a smile filled with the suggestion of intimacy. She really is beautiful. It's Dalal!

I know her actions are all in jest, but what does Adel think of her? I don't dare look at him. "That's it, let's go."

"Soon."

"No, now."

He raises his hands. "Remember the dying man's last request?"

"No more requests, no more joking." Stern, unsmiling, I stare ahead. "I have to get back to the sakan immediately."

❧

Adel drops me off at a safe spot a few streets away from the sakan. Just as I open the door, he grins and says, "By the way, wasn't that your cousin back there?" I don't answer, just slam the door and forge ahead blindly without a thought spared for direction until I find myself lost, standing in front of a café I've never seen before. There are a few out-door tables under an arching trellis covered with vines. It's quiet and I pause for a moment, listening to the soothing gurgles of the shishas. I fix my sight on the smoke hovering in slowly dispersing clouds and touch my cheek with the same pressure that Adel had. Instead of smiling with the memory, I scowl.

He was cool, curious, passionate, intense, playful, and unpredictable all in one evening, his mood flying in different directions like a leaf caught in a crazy wind. His behavior confuses me. Previously I had thought he was a sensitive man, but after he licked the mango juice in that suggestive way I don't know what to make of him. He seemed to find pleasure in seeing me fidget and squirm. Why? The questions shuffle and shift in my head. And what about Dalal? Did he recognize her straightaway?

I do not need the complication of Adel in my life. I'll make a list of everything that has puzzled me today and ask him. Once I get the answers, I'll never see him again.

7

MAJED

෴

With the plumber still working in the dining room, Aisha has set up lunch in the family room. I hear the racket before entering, and even though I know what it will be like in there, somehow it seems that the children have become noisier, more boisterous, since I saw them the week before. "*Wee-wah, wee-wah, wee-wah!*"

A long time ago I decided it was important for the family to congregate for lunch every Friday in my house, so that I could get a sense of fullness, pride, and achievement over this other kind of wealth: eight sons and daughters, five of them married, who have bequeathed me with twenty-one grandchildren. Standing frozen at the door and watching the chaos in front of me, I'm filled with a longing to reverse that decision. But that would be very un-grandfather-like.

No one notices me until I raise my voice. "These . . . these monkeys! Why doesn't anyone control them?" And then my children and in-laws hurry to greet me with handshakes and kisses on the forehead.

"They're just excited to see you, Baba," says Nadia, the third eldest of my four daughters and the only one who is somewhat timid.

Maybe I only think that because she does not make as much noise as the rest.

"So excited, they haven't noticed me standing here for the last few minutes?"

My second-eldest daughter, Amal, orders the kids to get up. "Say hello to your grandfather."

Only the older children rise. Their faces are long and their voices full of the moping boredom of their teen years, or perhaps they are sulking because they'd rather be somewhere else. The little ones keep running in circles around the three palm-frond mats Aisha laid on the floor. "Wee-wah, wee-wah, wee-wah!"

"Why can't they sit still with a book in their hands, use all that energy to get educated?" I complain.

The mothers laugh, and my eldest daughter, Mona, explains, "God bless them, they're too small to be thinking for themselves."

"I don't need you to tell me that," I say to her. "You talk to me as if I haven't had children of my own, as if I haven't watched over you lot." I like to say this even though we all know I left most of their upbringing to their mother, who was more than efficient in keeping them away from me. I pretend I don't notice the shrewd smiles that Mona and Amal exchange as they drag the smallest children, kicking and hollering, toward me. No sooner do the children place their hurried kisses on my cheeks than they rush away, grabbing all the cushions on the couches for a rough thrash and tumble. Two of the little ones whack wooden swords just as Aisha, carrying a bowl of what smells like fish curry, hurries by, barely missing them. This time I ignore them.

I turn to join the men, my sons and sons-in-law, at the far end of the room, but I catch sight of Aisha's sister, Shamma, seated with them and arguing a point with my eldest son, Saif. He is red-faced with annoyance, hardly hearing her as she lectures him about something to do with the need for more housing for the less fortunate, as if she were Mother Teresa. Why can't she go discuss recipes and children (even if she doesn't have any) with the women? Saif's debating skills are artless and unexceptional, and I can tell he's losing ground. He would already have unleashed that flaming temper had it not been for the interjections of my second-eldest son, Ahmad, who puts to good use his canny skills at playing the role of appeaser.

Shamma's is a rare visit that clouds my mood. I spot her bare neck as she turns her head and adjusts her shayla, her hair cut short just like a boy's—no doubt for the purpose of being inflammatory. "*Marhaba, Ammi*," she says in greeting, shrugging the argument to one side and rising to shake my hand. I sniff and nod my hello back at her from a distance, deciding not to get pulled into the discussion because, simply, she has no business being on this side of the room with the men.

It was in the early 1980s that, after a couple of years of marriage, she divorced her husband with the excuse that he was a lazy drunk, indifferent toward her. To the chagrin of her family, she didn't go back to live with them. Instead she rented an apartment and sought employment at the Ministry of Public Works. Then she took study leave to get a degree in architectural engineering (a most unusual vocation for a woman) at the Emirates University in Al-Ain, and returned to the ministry once she was done to work as an engineer in the Tenders and Contracts Department. What business does she have sticking her nose in a man's world, as if she were his equal? That's what I'd like to know.

I'd hoped I would be able to reflect on what Mustafa just told me in the majlis, but that will have to wait. The spacious living room suddenly seems too small, with all these people in it. And here comes another one.

With stick in hand, my mother trudges into the room, looking weighed down, wearing all that heavy gold in traditional designs. Through her burka she keeps her eyes fixed to the ground like a grazing sheep. "Mama Al-Ouda!" the children sing, and frog-leap to hug her, diving at her knees like a giant wave and nuzzling their faces into her ankles.

"Get them away," she grumbles. "Do you want me to fall and break my bones?" Mona yanks them off and marches them all the way out to the kitchen to be fed by the maids.

Amal says, "We can proudly say you're the only woman of your age who hasn't broken any bones."

"*Tuff, tuff,*" Mama Al-Ouda lets out, and fake spits into her burka to ward off wicked spirits. She waves her hand in front of her face and rubs her fingers for extra protection. "*Hib-hib*, salt in your gaze to remove the evil eye."

"Say 'masha'Allah,'" Aisha says, carrying in another bowl, which smells like shrimp curry.

"Masha'Allah!" everyone chimes, and we take turns greeting Mama Al-Ouda.

Two of the older children carry in a chair and a side table for my mother, who at eighty-seven suffers from nothing more than stiff joints and slight loss of hearing. The rest of us settle on the floor. In the middle are two large trays of rice mixed with meat, and a tray of plain white rice to be eaten with the three varieties of curry and two types of fried fish. Placed along the edges of the mats are plates of radishes, Indian pickles, and dates. Cans of fizzy Coca-Cola, 7 Up, and Mirinda sit to my side, as do two jugs of limboo and a bottle of Tabasco.

Bending forward over the mats, we scoop rice and meat with our right hands. The room is quiet, as if someone had flicked off a switch that was responsible for the ruckus of moments earlier. We are like a pack of wolves. Only Aisha eats slowly, tipping her burka discreetly to one side with every mouthful. There is some civility, a dignity I might say, to the way she twirls the rice into marble-sized balls, dirtying only the tips of her thumb and the two fingers closest to it.

With our tummies filling, an animated discussion starts. There's the plumber's failure to locate the source of the leakage, and our two new maids, hired to replace one we had to send back to the Philippines. "I just don't know," says Aisha, shaking her head, "how I'm going to manage. They're proving to be nowhere near as efficient or clever, impossible to train." Any conversation among the women about the help is bound to bring out every dogged opinion, and the discussion could carry on until the end of the meal.

With the exception of pleasant-faced Nadia, my daughters are not easy on the eyes: their eyebrows flit up and down like bat wings, their mouths are pinched, and their eyes are scrunched and wrinkly like prunes. They have hard faces with voices to match, an undertone of spite and vindictiveness, a viper's hiss, as they spit their words out. I don't look at them. I gather a handful of white rice and pour chicken curry on it, stirring the mixture to the right consistency: not too dry and not too soggy.

"Mother, I think you were too good to that maid," says Amal. "You gave her money for her mother's gallbladder operation, for her children's schooling in the Philippines; you even fixed her rotten teeth."

"Yeah," says my youngest daughter, Nouf, who is Mariam's age but like her twin, Badr, is still struggling to finish school. "They were yellow and black when she arrived, and she left with a set of white fangs."

The teenagers laugh as I finish molding the lump of softened rice. It fits like a ball in my palm. Hunched over the mat, I cram it into my mouth in one quick move while glancing at Shamma, who has lifted her finger and is about to chide them over their lack of sympathy toward the destitute. But Amal cuts in, "And the clothes! So many dresses you gave her . . ."

"Slippers, too," Mona adds, her face reddening at the memory of the treacherous maid. "And then what does she do—what does that sneaky girl do—to repay us?" She pauses for effect and skims the bewildered expressions around her, even though it's a story they can all recount backward. "She gives favors to men, and in her quarters at the back of the house, too. Right under our noses!"

"I just don't understand why she did this to us," says Aisha.

"Because she's a snake," says Nouf, laughing like a maniac. No one else reacts, and there's a lull as the verbal slaughter abates. The only sound is my mother's teeth crunching ice, a habit she developed the day she discovered ice. She's been quiet; her practice is to filter information, squirreling away the bits that reinforce her beliefs and chucking out the rest. And when there's a comment to be made, she'll make it in a voice of self-proclaimed wisdom. Her bangles clink as she shifts on her chair.

"It's always better to have a stupid maid than a clever one," she declares. This opens another discussion, but I can't follow it because they are all speaking at the same time. So I busy my head with what Mustafa told me earlier.

"A composer," he had said, "means that someone wants to be a singer."

"What do you mean, someone? Stop speaking in riddles and tell me!"

The hairs on his head were starting to rise. He dipped his fingers in his glass of water and smoothed them back in place. "Your daughter Dalal."

"How can that be? Doesn't she know the scandal she would cause? What's she trying to prove?" Then I asked Mustafa a question that was both pointless and absurd. "How can her mother allow it?"

Ah, that Zohra! She had been a neglected child. Orphaned at fifteen when her parents died in a car accident, Zohra had been taken in by her reluctant maternal grandparents. They fed her and clothed her. They did their duty in providing a roof over her head. And in case she didn't notice, they made sure to point out their sacrifices daily. I took her away from all that.

"I don't think you should panic, bey," said Mustafa, his voice barely audible. "You know what the chances are of getting into that business."

"No, I don't."

He looked at me. "Well, they're small."

"How small?"

"Very, very small. Tiny. I'd say a dot."

"Just as tiny as getting on a television program, right here in Dubai?" I punched the cushion on my lap and Mustafa jerked his head back toward the door as if someone had knocked. "She managed, didn't she?" Dalal Majed: that's the name they'd used on the show. I suppose I should be thankful they didn't use my family name. Still, I had felt exposed. And it did nothing to console my injured pride at having been disobeyed. "It went on for three months. Every Thursday night she kept appearing on that show. Disgraceful!"

"Please, bey, calm your nerves," said Mustafa. "*Insha'Allah*, this whole situation will fizzle to nothing."

"How can I calm my nerves?" I barked, and crossed my arms in a huff. I watched him stare at his feet, twiddling his thumbs as he waited for the moment to pass. But my head was brimming with Zohra.

She was a blind kitten; that's what she was. I taught her to open her eyes and command a view of the world. I had gathered her to my chest and built in her a confidence that she is now using to hurt me— to exploit our daughter. The insult of it!

Zohra hadn't even panicked when I found out that my daughter was singing on live television. When we spoke, there was a bored rasp to her voice; I was sure she was holding back a yawn. She had said, "You can't tell us what to do, I'm not married to you anymore," or something of the sort. I was livid, and at that precise moment I made the decision to stop sending her money. Every day I looked forward to receiving her apology. I imagined her groveling and promising never to go against my word again. The days passed and I waited. Nothing happened.

My mind ticked like a dysfunctional clock as I tried to figure out when exactly Zohra had lost her respect for me. It was as if there was no history between us, as if that was not my daughter on the screen under those bright lights, on display for any man to watch and dream of in that lustful way that only men can.

Then, months later, Mustafa told me that she'd taken Dalal and left the country, that they were living in an apartment in Cairo.

"How are they managing? There's rent, food, clothes, transportation. I haven't sent her a dirham for over a year."

"Well, I can check about that."

I tightened my lips and fixed my eyes on Mustafa's bowed head. "Listen to me: we cannot let them get out of control."

Mustafa snapped to attention and stood up like a capable soldier. With his skull in the path of the air conditioner, his hairs started leaping and shuddering like battery-powered stick men. He stepped out of the current of air and smacked his hair back to sleep. "We must control them, bey."

"Yes, we must keep an eye on them," I mutter to myself now, and absentmindedly rub my temples with food-smeared fingers. Grains of rice cling to my head and a stream of curry trickles down the side of my face. My family freezes but, realizing I am deep in thought, says nothing.

It's my mother who breaks the stillness. She raps a bone on her plate. When the marrow does not slide out, she pokes the bone under her burka and sucks. The noise is like water pulled down a drain. Aisha rushes to the bathroom to bring me a moistened towel, which I use to wipe my face. The chatter resumes, as if my blurting out some vague statement and dirtying my face were the most natural occurrence. This time they talk about Mariam.

"Why does she get to study abroad?" moans Nouf.

"Because she's cleverer than you," says Badr. "If you get the same marks, then you can go abroad to study, too. You don't even know what you want to study."

"Not true," says Nouf. "The thing I want to study can only be found abroad, in London." She lifts her hands to her face and shapes a square around her eyes. "I want to be a photographer, and work for one of those magazines that sends you all over the world to places untouched by humans. The other day I saw a picture of the most beautiful jungle. There was light coming through the trees—only someone with a photographer's eye would notice that—and I thought, *Yes, that's what I want to be.*"

"You know that jungle mud can't be wiped off with makeup remover?" Badr says. "You'd have to use bathroom cleaner. But you'd have to be careful, because it might strip the skin off your face." Nouf touches her cheek. "And what kind of heels would you wear? Pointy or platform?" Badr snickers.

"Heels? Makeup remover?" I say. "What talk is this? How do you know about such things?"

Nouf sticks her tongue out at him and attacks him with weak slaps. Instead of holding her at bay, his hands twist and wilt in a fruitless defense. When he spots my glower he coughs and tries to hide his foolish grin.

"Will you send me to London to study photography, Baba?" asks Nouf.

There are sardines in front of me. I pick one up and start peeling the skin off the flesh.

"It's pointless to ask our father such a question when your grades are so low," says Ahmad.

She ignores him. "Will you, Baba?"

"*Chup! Chup!* Shut up!" Saif says. "We don't send our women away to study."

"Just like we didn't send Mariam to Cairo?" Nouf says. "You think she's clever and I'm stupid, don't you. Say it, all of you!"

My mother groans with this second mention of Mariam's name. She raises both hands to the sky and says, "Oh God, bring her back to us safe and sound." Her voice is as soft as a raindrop. "Keep Satan away from her. Allah, shield her from his evil." She burps and, with a sudden rush of force, says, "Majed, enough modern ideas—sending girls away from their families to live alone, with strangers around them. You must bring Mariam back to us right away!"

"No," Shamma exclaims, shaking her head. "That would be so cruel. Masha'Allah, Mariam has so much potential."

"Girls belong in the home," Mama Al-Ouda insists.

"It's not like before," Shamma says to her, with a sighing irritation at the old woman's folly. "Women are out there today, working side by side with men. They are proving they can stand on their own two feet."

Aisha nods, and this makes me wonder what other rubbish her sister feeds her when they are alone. I don't like Shamma's influence on my wife, poisoning her thinking, and I make a mental note to speak to her about it later. I won't forbid her from seeing her sister. But I'll make my wife understand that her seeing her displeases me.

"We must accept that a woman can be productive in the workplace as well as keep the home in order and bring up the children."

How like her to be muddling up the role of women. I'm about to berate her, but Saif beats me to it. "With respect, auntie, how would you know? You don't have any children." His bluntness shuts her up, and I have to stifle the chuckle at the back of my throat as I reach for a second sardine.

"Well, when will you bring her back?" Mama Al-Ouda says.

I hold my temper and ignore her persistence; she is my mother, after all.

Mona says, "She did two years at the dental college here, at Ajman University. I don't understand why she couldn't just finish here."

"Yes, Baba," Nouf says, bobbing her head with zeal, her eyes flitting over my face like a fly over a festering wound. "Why did you send her to Cairo?"

I'm not sure why they want Mariam back. It's not as if they'd paid her any attention those years she'd lived with us after her father died. I shrug. "It's the only thing she ever asked me." All that time, she'd been nothing but a brooding presence. How do I tell them I agreed so that I wouldn't have to look at that stony face and those eyes, always so filled with accusation? "Besides, she has always been top of her class," I say, glaring at my mother to make sure she understands that that's the end of this particular discussion. Through the slits of her burka, her eyes narrow as if she is pained by my insensitivity. "She's doing well there," I add. "She'll come back when she finishes."

Ahmad consoles Mama Al-Ouda with a sober nod. "Our father knows best. You must leave the family matters to him."

Mama Al-Ouda's eyes snap open. She picks up the bone on her plate and holds it up like a stick. "Well, I think she should be here," she grumbles, and scans the faces around her for a response. When no one answers, she sighs and raises her head. Her eyes are lost to view, drapes rolling down a window of scrupulous condemnation. "God keep all that is evil away from her," she moans, and then, with a tired voice, she recites a prayer for my dead brother, Hareb. I keep my expression blank. Once she finishes, she thrusts the bone to her mouth and slurps what's left of the marrow with the breath of an athlete.

The noise is a signal, and my grandchildren get jittery as their mothers start discussing their toilet habits, with particular interest as to who has problems with constipation. No one mentions Khaled and the rejected proposal. That is left for another time. Badr whispers something to Nouf. This time she punches him without mercy. I ignore the high-pitched cry that comes out of his throat and try to find comfort in the familiar fuss and bickering, the lunacy and pettiness, the hypocrisy of this family. Everything is as it should be, harmless and under control, in the privacy of my home and out of society's judging sight.

8

DALAL

Imbaba pounces on you with its undiluted air of exaggeration, its streets thick with a constant stream of babble and protestations. A gold-toothed man complains about the price of gas as he waits for a mechanic to change his car's oil at an open-fronted auto-repair shop. To the side of the blackened walls a gang of boisterous little boys plays, ramming one another's shoulders and making loud noises, trying to drum out the squeak in their voices.

Mama glides by them without so much as a glance. She looks clean and neat and out of place in her navy suit: a buttoned jacket hugs her slim waist and a skirt reaches just below her knees. She keeps going, past a half-finished building and a makeshift teahouse at the corner of the road: three low stools are arranged to the side of the brew bubbling in a pot, which sits on a slapdash gas stove planted on a cement cube that juts out of the pavement without logic or sense. For atmosphere, a small transistor radio blasts one of those popular upbeat songs, people music.

I follow her, in a huff at the prospect of waiting for hours for an appointment that won't take place. A bus rumbles by. It is packed with the usual jumble of squashed limbs and faces pressed to the windows, with an overflow of people hanging out the open doorway at the back and crouched on the roof. The back hood is left open so the engine doesn't overheat. It farts a black thundercloud of fumes over a man with a cartload of radishes, heaved forward by a sweet-faced donkey. There's an urgent tinkle and I turn to see an older boy on a bike racing toward me, his head balancing a tray holding piles of fresh Egyptian bread. The front wheel swerves to the right. He bumps me to the side as he shifts his upper body to the left so the tray does not tip over. Before I can react, he curses at me without stopping his bike.

"Shut your mouth, you animal," I shout back, shaking my fist at him. But he's gone, threading his way through the shambling pedestrians, hollering vendors, and rolling mule carts. I spot a gangly boy who always wears the same striped shirt. I've seen him now on three different occasions: twice in Imbaba and once outside the composer's building. Who is he, and what does he want? When I mentioned him to my mother, she told me to stop being foolish. I'm about to point him out, but he disappears into the crowds.

The microbus is just to the side of Sudan Street, ready to set off on its route. Five people stand by the front passenger door, but the driver won't let them board because he's saving those precious seats for us, just as he has been doing for the past week. I hasten to catch up with Mama.

Hassanain, the driver, is an unnerving presence. To block the door he simply pushes out his wrestler's chest, leaving the waiting people scared to do anything more than appeal to his better nature, begging to be let on and whining about their urgent need to reach their particular destination. He does not back down. "The seats are reserved," he barks. Even though it's supposed to be a first-come, first-board policy, no one argues this point. The rejected passengers shuffle to the side and scan the road for another microbus as we hop gingerly to the front of the line.

My mother seats herself next to the driver and I'm by the window, which I keep pulled down to blow away the stench of stale sweat and curdled breath. Hassanain greets us with a timid smile and then, his fingers curled tight around the steering wheel, he drives on in silence, pretending he doesn't notice the way my mother's arm bumps into his every time the bus dips into a pothole. It's a short trip, and another shy smile cracks Hassanain's lips as he bids us farewell, his eyes shining with the anticipation of seeing us again when he comes to collect us later.

❧

The secretary has faded blond streaks that match her ashen complexion. She looks up at us with an open mouth, as if we'd disturbed the flow of a complicated thought that was forming in her head. On her tongue spreads a puddle of pink bubble gum. She nods at us, indicating that we should take a seat. It's as if she hasn't seen us before.

As always, the odor of nervous anticipation lingers in the still air, and I sigh at the dull wait ahead. Maybe I shouldn't let my mind wander and grow plump with glowing images of on-the-spot recognition, of instant renown. Every now and then, a hopeful candidate is called in with her mother. The minutes gather and drag, and I call on my store of patience. Still, there is some comfort in the fact that this composer spends so much time with each girl. Sometimes there is a grand expression of victory on the faces of the exiting mothers, even though the daughters always look dazed, as if unsure how the interview went. Most times, though, mother and daughter leave distraught, which makes me wonder what the composer told them.

Once more, Zohra puts on her educated airs and tries to convince the secretary of my talent. "My daughter Dalal's voice really is something special. There is a rare quality in it that a great composer like Sherif bey will immediately recognize." She chuckles softly. "Of course, first he has to hear it."

The secretary is unimpressed. She blows a neat balloon. It pops, and she laps it back into her mouth before it can stick to her lips.

"My daughter has that same rare quality, too," a mother with a peasant's accent says.

"Not this rare," Zohra snaps at her, and turns back to the secretary.

"Look," says the secretary, "I only follow orders here. You may think he does nothing but sit inside, waiting for you. But Sherif bey is an *artiste*. He has his composing to do, too. It's his work, and he does it at the same time that he takes appointments. So, in short, he's a busy man." She grins. "But you can wait if you like."

I glare at Sherif Nasr's secretary, wedged behind her corner desk. She isn't making it easy, and for the hundredth time I wonder whether she is holding a grudge over a comment I had whispered to my mother on our first day of waiting: I had called her a lazy cow. Her droopy eyes have a blank expression and her lower lip stretches all the way down to her chin and back up as she chews her gum. She didn't react at the time, but now I'm sure she'd heard me and decided to make our lives difficult. She has been sending us home, rejecting us, for nearly three weeks now. None of Mama's efforts to win her over has worked.

First my mother tried charming her with light jokes and kind words. Then a gift: two small jars of Kraft cream cheese, part of a supply of edible treats that included Mackintosh chocolates and Danish butter cookies brought especially for this purpose from Dubai. (Many people in Cairo are convinced that anything that comes from abroad is of better quality.) There was a flicker of suspicion in those cow eyes as the secretary held the jar up, but my mother quickly explained that the cheese was fresh, delivered just the day before by a relative visiting from the rich Khaleej. "And look," Zohra added, picking up the other jar. "Once you finish the cheese, you can use the jar for water, or even tea." She had tapped the rim. "Good, strong glass."

I sigh and pull out my magazine, flipping to the glossy center, where Monica Fayyadh poses in a two-page spread. She is hugging her knees, wearing a flowing baby-pink dress, her mouth pouting, full of desire and promise. I stare daggers at her tiny nose, rubbing the slight bump that breaks the straightness of mine. Mariam gasps every time I tell her that it's the first thing I'll fix once I've made enough money.

"Character!" she'd exclaim. "It gives you character."

And I'd laugh and say, "Poor-girl character, pretty one. What I want is rich-girl character."

"But you mustn't touch what God gave you, which looks fine, even if a little imperfect," she'd insist.

I'd always answer her, "No flaws for the rich and famous!"

"Lebanon's Bomb: Monica's Painful Childhood." That's the title of the article. At three, she was plagued by nightmares that made her wake up in a sweat; at seven, she fell off a ladder and broke her arm; and at ten, a terrible incident! Her parents lost her for a full hour somewhere at an open-air restaurant on their way for a weekend in the mountains. The more I read, the more I mock the silliness of these episodes with clicks of my tongue. Where is the pain? Where is the tragedy? Why can't they write something useful, like what steps she took to get famous?

I slap the magazine shut and slump on the chair, frowning at the other people in the plain, rectangular room. We are seated facing one another on chairs that are arranged along the walls. There's a fat woman quietly knitting, and a pair who leaf through newspapers. The rest do nothing more than stare ahead, their eyes brimming with dreams, in a state of admirable patience.

I lean close to my mother and whisper, sharp and quick, "Why do we have to sit for the whole time in one place?"

"What do you suggest we do?" Her mouth barely moves. "Go back to Dubai with our heads hanging, a pair of failures?"

"No, I mean, why can't we try other composers at the same time?"

She shakes her head. "Look how long it took us to finally get here. Sherif bey has more clout than you can imagine, and we will win him over." Mama has so much faith in him, this composer to the stars who hasn't produced anything worthwhile in the past fifteen years. She doesn't seem to care that he has resorted to creating jingles, which have proven to be a lucrative diversion while he waits for inspiration to take hold of him.

I sigh and whisper, "There's no hope, Mama, really. I can't sit idly and wait anymore. I should be doing something else." I don't mean it, of course, but I wonder if this might get her to think of some better solution.

"There's nothing of value that you can do," Mama says. "You didn't even finish school."

Not for the first time, I want to burst through that door and demand that he hear my voice. But that is not the way it is done. Like every other expectant soul in this room, I need someone to speak for me. I must keep alive the apparent innocence of my doe eyes and play the role of a dainty gazelle to draw out the composer's protective instincts, while my mother works her charm to instill in him the desired admiration and interest. It might work, and it might not.

I watch the only young man in the room; an Adam's apple the size of a plum protrudes from his weasel-like neck. He looks odd in the midst of the throng of mother-and-daughter teams. Every so often he leans forward, rises halfway, and, hovering just over the seat, does a light jiggle, as if he's fearful that the chair might stick to his bottom. It makes me giggle, but only a little. Then it's back to the fidgety boredom of waiting.

The door to Sherif bey's office swings open and a mother pushes her daughter out, obviously enraged by the outcome of their meeting. I straighten up with expectation and look at the secretary, who is scribbling on the paper in front of her. "I think it's time we went in," Mama says to her. "You do know how long we've been patiently waiting . . ."

The secretary holds her hand up. "You are not the one to make that decision."

"Yes, but you will agree that this whole situation has reached ridiculous proportions," says Zohra, with an airy chuckle. "All these weeks—it's completely unheard of."

"I don't count time, madam," says the secretary.

"Well, maybe you should, madam," I say, rooting my fists to my waist.

"You, young lady, should learn to hold your temper," warns the secretary, poking her pencil at me.

"She's right, though," says one of the mothers sitting at the end of the room. "You must respect our time."

"It's easier to get an appointment with the president," complains another mother, who has only put in six days of waiting.

"Well, maybe you should go see the president and find out if he can help you," the secretary retorts.

"Ladies, ladies, calm down," the young man says, and in one synchronized motion the women grunt and cross their arms to their chests.

Closing time is drawing near, and the masticating cow has already started preparing us for the disappointment of another wasted day by shuffling the papers in front of her and arranging her files. It's a ritual she follows once she's ready to close the office. Her final act will be to run an index finger along the rim of her desk, quickly inspect the accumulated dust, and dilute it with spit before declaring, "We're closing now. Sherif bey won't be able to see anyone else today."

Despair constricts my chest. I say, "You won't let us go in there, will you? Even though there's no one there. You're going to send us away again."

She frowns at me. "I've already explained the way things work here. You don't have to come if you don't like it."

"We come because we need to," says the peasant mother.

"A person in need should never complain," says the secretary, rip-ping a thick wad of paper for emphasis.

"There's no call for rudeness," Mama says. "Obviously this woman has traveled from a distance to see the composer."

Suddenly the fat woman who was knitting surprises us by jump-ing off her seat and, with incredible speed, marching to the desk. She waves the whole bundle—wool, needles, and pink-and-blue patch—at the secretary and declares, "I've had enough!"

It's the spark that lights the blaze, and before I can think, I am up and joining the mob of squabbling mothers and groaning daughters, leaving Mama behind. Even the young man is galvanized. Standing at the periphery of the group, he altercates in a voice many notches shriller than the rest.

I push to the front and bang on the secretary's table. "How about you knock on that door and tell him we will not be turned away again!"

"And if you don't, we will." The fat woman pokes her needles in the air.

"All this will get you nowhere," the secretary says, and shields her face as she retreats toward Sherif bey's office.

"I say we all push into that room and demand that he grant us an interview. Now!"

And that's when the door bursts open, and Sherif Nasr steps out.

᳄

It is my mother's legs that get us into Sherif bey's office. Even though I'm not able to make out his eyes, half-hidden behind the umber tint of his thick-rimmed glasses, I can tell he has trouble looking away from them: one crossed over the other, pale and shining through the light glitter of her stockings. He simply waves the secretary's complaints to the side and decides he will see us right away. I stick my tongue out at her as I follow Mama into his office.

Shafts of light peppered with tiny floating dust particles spill through the glass of two lofty doors that open onto balconies. The room smells slept in. I disregard the lingering stench of cigarettes and old kebabs and gawk at the high ceilings and fancy curlicues. Sherif Nasr is somewhere in his midfifties, with a pencil-thin mustache, hair molded into soft hills with Brylcreem, and a triangle of white handkerchief in the top pocket of his toffee-colored tweed jacket; it's as if we'd taken a big hop back to a bygone era.

Yes, his office brings to mind the homes of the romantic rich in all those black-and-white Egyptian films. But that's where the similarity ends, for crowding this room is the largest batch of mismatched furniture I have ever seen. An old-fashioned table with gold corners that curve like commas stands on four fragile legs between two flesh-colored sofas. Lampshades frilly with lace are propped on modern smoked-glass side tables. It's as if each piece had been collected from a different house.

He drifts to the other side of an oversize wooden desk. He's not a heavy man, but the swivel chair hisses when he slumps into it. Rooting his elbows firmly on the desk, he says, "I don't like to interview anyone if my sisters aren't with me. We make decisions together, you see, because they have a knack for these things. It's easier for them to spot what I am looking for. But today they had to leave early."

Mama and I look at each other with the same questions in mind. *How is that possible? How could they have left without our seeing them?* He sniffs and motions to us to take a seat, as if irritated that we haven't done so already. We are swallowed into the doughy sofa. My head tips back and pulls the rest of me with the surprise of it, but Mama is quick to shift to the edge. By the time I pull up, she has already leaned forward and safely bonded one well-shaped leg to the other. There's a dainty smile on her face. She's set to start.

Sherif Nasr's thin eyebrows lift up over his glasses. "Yes, where was I? In fact, I was about to leave. But then, well . . ." He squints at his watch and coughs. "I have a little time, and . . ." His gaze drifts to one of the balconies. While Mama remains focused on him with the delicate smile she reserves for such people, I turn around as discreetly as possible to find out what caught his attention. The only thing of interest is a male pigeon trying to impress a female, with much fluttering and acrobatics. There can't be any novelty to it, what with all the other pigeons out there. I hear a scratching sound and look back to find him jotting something down with his pencil. Ah! Inspiration.

We watch him. We don't say a word. Instinctively, we know we must stay quiet and wait. It takes a long time for that inspiration to be translated into musical notes. Every now and then, there's that faraway look again, aimed at the light dimming outside. Soon I get bored and fix my eyes on the large glass cabinet behind him that displays his various accolades. On the shelves are medals, plaques, certificates, and even a crystal trophy in the shape of Nefertiti's profile. There are photographs, too, showing a much younger, quite handsome Sherif Nasr posing with some of the Arab world's music legends.

He is caught in half profile looking at the ground in a picture with Abdel Halim Hafez, as if the camera might blind him with its flash. With Umm Kulthum, the symbol of Arab music, unity, and identity, he manages a timid smile, but he holds his shoulders too high, as if worried she might bite him. In many photographs, it looks like he wasn't ready when the camera clicked. He stands next to many singers—all great, all dead.

He pauses to rap the desk with the nail of his index finger, kept long for strumming the *oud*. When I look back at him he is staring at us, but I know he doesn't register our presence. We smile at him anyway, just in case. He grins and makes a noise that is half hiss, half grunt, and focuses on his notes once more. "This is how the musical mind works," Mama whispers to me, her eyes watery with admiration. "This is what they mean when they say *genius*."

"Freakish!" I whisper back.

"*Shh.*"

He scribbles furiously, making clicking sounds with his mouth, which I'm sure is the beat he's composing. Suddenly the phone rings, and he stiffens and glowers at it. "What?" he barks into the mouthpiece. The woman's voice is nasal, slightly broody. Since everyone knows he's single, I immediately guess it's one of his sisters. Sherif Nasr breathes deeply and says, "No, I didn't mean to shout. It's just that I'm busy right now." Pause. "Yes, I know you're waiting for me. I'll come as soon as I can." Pause. "Fine." Pause. "Yes, fine." Pause. "Fine, fine, I'll eat my dinner cold." He hangs up and brushes the papers in front of him to the side. "So," he says, pulling out a cigarette and sticking it into a plastic filter, "what do you want?"

"Well, we can start by giving you our background," Mama says.

He looks at his watch and seems about to dismiss her suggestion when she begins to praise his talent and legendary status. Then Mama follows with the account I have come to know by heart: my talent, my perseverance, and the star quality of my performances all those weeks on *Nights of Dubai*. I could join her in a duet. I know where her speech speeds up and where it slows down. I could even put in the pauses, strategically located to leave room for contemplation. But I have my own part to play: nodding or shaking my head at key moments. There is a shy smile on my face that I mastered in front of a mirror; it accompanies a slightly lowered glance to the side as my mother ends her presentation with praise for my good fortune at having not just beauty but also a voice that would make a bulbul jealous.

There's a lot of information, but her account is quick—an exact seven minutes, practiced and timed—to ensure that his attention does not drift. She holds him captive through her storytelling skill and her legs, which he peeps at every now and then between puffs of his cigarette.

"Well, this is all good, Madam . . . er . . ."

"Zohra," says my mother.

"*Sitt* Zohra." He nods. "As I said, it's all good, this, this life of yours, and the talent you bring with you." He leans back in his chair. "But I hear this kind of thing every day."

"Of course, you are right. What was I thinking, telling you so much at this first meeting?" Naturally, this part is rehearsed, too.

"And anyway, I can't say anything until I've heard the young lady's voice." He waves at me with the long fingernail.

"Dalal."

"Yes, Dalal. Beautiful name. Beautiful meaning, too: to be doted on. And I can tell that you are a mother who thinks the world of her daughter."

"You're too kind."

"Hmm." He stares at the balcony doors again, and I wonder if his inspiration is coming back when, with a sudden thrust, he leans forward and puts out his cigarette. With finality he says, "Really, Sitt Zohra, I'd rather you come again when my sisters are here. Then we'll give you the most thorough appraisal." He narrows his eyes at his watch. He is ending the interview—without having heard my voice.

Mama unexpectedly claps her hands; it has the effect of a thunderbolt on a sunny day. I flinch and Sherif Nasr jerks. "Up, up!" she orders. She is already standing as I rise. Poised behind me, she grabs the tops of both my arms in a rather painful squeeze. *This is not part of our drill*, I think as she jostles me to the side of his desk. Sherif bey is struck mute, his lips tightened into a line that runs parallel to his mustache.

"Now, Dalal," Mama says. "Sing!"

9

MARIAM

～

The clinic is on the fourth floor of the dental building. I thread my way through the throng of patients in the dank waiting hall. The students work on volunteers; they get dental work done for free and we get rewarded with experience. The men sweating in their shirts might be taxi drivers, civil servants, or construction workers. Those wearing Egyptian *galabias* could be doormen or farmers who might have traveled on three or four buses to get here. There are three bawling infants and other restless children, hopping around or fidgeting alongside their parents. The lucky ones have occupied the benches; the others stand where they can.

A man shakes a plastic bag in front of my face. It's the tooth seller. He says, "Forty pounds for three." He sells teeth to students so they can practice root canals; because my shayla is smoothed around my face and bunched neatly into my dental jacket, he recognizes that I am a Khaleejia and has automatically quadrupled the price he would have quoted to an Egyptian student. But root canals will come in my last year. For now, it's fillings and extractions.

There is an informal first-come, first-served policy, even though some of the patients have appointments. Whenever there are bullies, the shy patients end up waiting longer than they should. Today the provocation comes from a burly, turbaned farmer who insists I treat him right away. "Let me go in first and see what's happening," I tell him when he blocks my path and jabs a finger into the back of his mouth to show me the decay. It is only once the security guard yells at him that he steps to the side.

The familiar clean-and-dirty odor of the clinic, a mixture of Dettol and nervous sweat, hits me as soon as I enter. It's a bright room with fluorescent lights and mustard-colored walls. A jungle of pipes dips into the various dental units with their waist-high aluminum partitions. With more than fifty third-, fourth- and fifth-year students drilling, filling, and extracting, the clinic is clamorous with the slurps of suction, hisses of the compressor, clanging of instruments, chattering of students, and clomping of heels. Every now and then a patient screams; the students never fail to stop what they're doing and look up to see who it is.

I ask the clinic manager for my patient's file. Seated behind a wooden desk by the entrance, the manager leans back against a wall with a framed picture of Hosni Mubarak. He indicates that my partner, Ghada, has already picked up the file. I spot her straight ahead and make my way toward her, past dental chairs occupied by open-mouthed patients, each attended to by a pair of students. Under the lights, one probes, drills, or fills while the other assists.

"My turn to practice today. Your turn to support, but since you were late I went ahead and got everything ready." Ghada's frizzy hair is tamed into a pair of tight plaits. Sucking the end of one, she points at the gleaming dental equipment—handpiece, mouth mirror, explorer, tweezers, drill—that she has sterilized and arranged on the desk. I turn to the sink and as I start scrubbing my hands under the tap, she continues, "The problem is, I can't do anything because he refuses to open his mouth."

He is a wiry young man with a thin face. His arms are crossed high on his chest, as if daring us to pry them loose. He looks like an enraged child, his lips sealed in a line so severe that his cheeks are hollowed into craters. "He says he has pain in the back." Ghada directs her comments to the man. "He probably needs a filling, but I won't be able to tell him anything until he loosens that mouth of his!" Her tone sharpens in a burst of testiness.

"I told you, I won't let you work on my teeth until there's a proper doctor here," he mumbles, opening his mouth a crack so the words can come out. "You two are students, for God's sake. What do you know?"

There is a burst of sharp yelps. "*Eyah, eyah, eyah!*"

"Hear that? I don't want to be in that situation."

"We won't do anything until the professor checks first," I say, and look around the clinic to locate him. Instead I spot Adel. His gait has the light hop of an untroubled person as he strolls into the clinic. He pauses to chat with the manager before joining his partner in a booth just to the side of the entrance. There's the easy grin that makes his eyes crinkle. It softens his face and hardens mine as I try to figure out how I'll be able to sneak out of the room without his noticing me.

It's hot. I loosen my shayla and raise my head toward the ceiling fan. It groans and creaks. It ruffles my bangs but does little to take the edge off the heat. If our unit were at the far end, I would have been able to catch a breeze through the open window. I pull off the shayla and fluff my hair before pinning it into a bun and covering it with a surgical cap—cooler, and easier to blend in with the other students. Adel's gaze travels in my direction and continues. He doesn't notice me.

I have managed to avoid him these past couple of weeks simply by changing my routine so that it didn't intersect with his whereabouts. I had stalked him for so long that I had memorized his wanderings on the university campus. I knew his schedule and, before that strange and ridiculous evening at Farghaly, the knowledge had served me well: I'd casually appear wherever he would be.

There were late Thursday afternoons when I used to settle under the jacaranda tree that rose a comfortable distance away from the pitch where he played football. In the lecture halls, I'd slide into the long wooden benches a row or two behind him: a subtle nearness that got me a view of the back of his head. Whenever the room grew stuffy with heat, he would doze off. His hair would grow damp and stick to the back of his neck. But that did not disturb him while he slept, a well-rehearsed habit in which he kept his back straight and his head only slightly askew.

It was never hard to find him; and then how easy it was to avoid him, to turn invisible in a university of sixteen thousand. Between classes I would blend into the swarm of rushing students, let them bump me along through the smoke-smelling corridors to wherever they were going. If I knew he would be going to a lecture I had to attend, I'd wait until he entered before settling into the last row.

But a couple of days back he'd found me just as I was leaving the library, the only place where I'd drop my guard because of the near-zero chance of his appearing there. He looked relieved to have located me, as if he'd been searching all over Cairo. After the usual niceties, he asked why I had stopped the lessons. "Perhaps you should get a private tutor like everyone else," I suggested. I was proud of how my face remained blank as I said that. He scrunched his mouth in a half smile, looking puzzled and amused at the same time. He waited for me to elaborate, but I turned and walked away.

"Wait, there's more," says Ghada, her head swaying with scorn. "Why don't you tell my partner here your other requirement?" She glowers at our patient, and her bulging eyes look ready to pop out of their sockets. "He won't open his mouth until we guarantee that there will be no pain."

"That, too." He snorts.

"I've had enough of you," Ghada says, and waves to the professor, who, after hearing her account, solves the problem by grabbing the patient by the collar and yanking him out of the chair.

Our next patient is a brave lad, no older than sixteen, who stretches his mouth as wide as he can. His eyes are stained yellow and he keeps them focused on the ceiling as the professor warns us in English, "Take every precaution. I think this boy is jaundiced—hepatitis C, maybe."

Ghada steps back. She insists that I examine the boy.

"But it's your turn," I say to her, looking at the professor for his backing.

"I've had more hours as the main than you have," says Ghada.

The professor makes the decision. He claps his hands. "Mariam, check his teeth."

Turning away from the patient so as not to hurt his feelings, I double my protection with a second pair of gloves. With goggles secured to my forehead and surgical mask pulled over my face, I peer into the boy's mouth, with the dental mirror in one hand and the explorer in the other. I poke, and the boy grimaces. "Patient has a lower-right second-molar decay," I announce with authority. The professor keeps his eyes fixed to some point over my shoulder and hums his agreement. After more probing, I decide he needs three fillings and maybe an extraction of that molar because it's so decayed. Examining the X-ray, the professor confirms my prognosis and gives me permission to proceed, then moves on to check on another team.

Ghada chats with the students in the unit behind us about the dress she wore to her cousin's wedding as I inject anesthesia into the patient's gum. While I wait for his mouth to numb, my gaze drifts over to Adel. He is assisting, and carrying on conversations with three other students in three different units. When will he ever learn to concentrate on one thing? Will he grab my arm as I rush out through the clinic door? How should I react in front of all these people? Suddenly he stops talking and looks around, stretching his neck over the partitions. He's looking for me, I'm sure of it. And this sends a shiver of delight through me. I save the image for later, to be cuddled along with my pillow.

"I feel like there are ants crawling in my mouth," my patient says.

I tear the sterilized pouch and remove the high-speed drill, attaching it to the adapter. My hand is steady as I guide the drill in a controlled rotation over his tooth. Spit and water sprinkle my goggles. The rot is soft and starts disintegrating too quickly, so I relieve the pressure. With the drill's sustained drone, I remember my father, when he was as self-assured as I feel right now. He watches me, and from behind my mask I smile with the image. What would he have thought, seeing me like this: so poised, so sure, on the way to becoming a real dentist. He would have cocked his head to one side and opened his palms to the sky, whispered a *masha'Allah* to show appreciation for my accomplishment. Then he'd make a joke about how he won't be able to open his mouth anymore because his daughter would spot the bad teeth and miss the smile—or something like that.

The decay is deeper than I'd anticipated. I'm not sure whether I should continue. What if the tooth cracks? I can't see, because the patient's mouth is full of water. "Suction!" Ghada holds the pipe in the boy's mouth at an awkward angle. She leans over as if being pulled with a rope and keeps her head turned away. I turn off the drill and instruct the boy to rinse. Sliding my chair back, I snap at Ghada, "I can't work like this. You're supposed to be assisting me, not drifting to the other unit to gossip. You need to be near me." I pay no attention to her reluctance as she takes a tiny step closer. "Anyway, I need your opinion. I've drilled two millimeters, I think. Should I continue?"

When she, too, can't decide, we call the professor, who reaches for the spoon excavator and scoops out a gooey decay. "Switch to low speed on the handpiece till all the decay is gone," he instructs.

The pitch of the buzz is lower and Ghada edges away again to chat with our neighbors, this time providing a detailed review of a new cake recipe she came upon. There are so many other students like her, bringing the noise and chaos of Cairo's streets wherever they go. "Maybe you would be a little more useful," I call out to her just as she finishes listing the ingredients, "if you start giving our young patient here a bit of information on hygiene. If we don't educate them, they'll just keep coming back. Why don't you demonstrate how he should brush his teeth after every meal?"

"I don't think he's in the mood to hear anything I have to say," says Ghada, strolling back. "Look at the agony in his face."

The boy mumbles and I pull the suction out of his mouth. He says, "I don't have a toothbrush."

"There you go," says Ghada, raising an eyebrow as if she'd just won an argument. "There's no point talking about something he doesn't have, is there? Anyway, there's no time for advice. You should get this filling finished quickly so it's not a completely wasted afternoon." Ghada pulls an amalgam capsule from the drawer and hops off to mix it in the machine.

The session is drawing to a close. Students pack up and start shuffling out, turning over their used dental tools to the attendants at the sterilization area and handing in their patient files to the clinic manager. I can't see Adel, but Ghada is on her way back with a light skip in her stride. She sings, too. I shake my head at her unseemly conduct; what patient would trust a dentist who sings? She empties the capsule into a glass bowl before loading the amalgam carrier and handing it to me.

After dispatching and condensing eight loads, I pause to examine my work. It's neat and professional. Now I only need the professor to tell me so. I am about to look up and call him when I sense a heavy breath behind me. I swivel around and drop the amalgam carrier, startled to find the bullying farmer from the waiting room staring at me with hard eyes. He must have slunk into the clinic when no one was looking. Ghada scurries to the corner with a squeal when he starts waving his arms and yelling, "You said it wouldn't be long. That was over an hour ago!" He looks ready to strike.

I am frozen in my seat. I want to scan the room and find the professor so that he can rush over and pull the farmer away by the collar, but I don't dare move. A crowd gathers around us with bewildering speed. All the students still in the clinic leave their befuddled patients behind, their mouths filled with instruments, to bunch around my unit. Two of the male students stand on one side of the farmer and try to wheedle him into calming down, but the farmer is raging like an injured bull, accusing me of lying to him. A third student twists the farmer's arm in an attempt to force him back, but the farmer whacks him down, and I hear a thud and a clang.

I am still in my chair and gripping the handles so tightly I've lost sensation in all my fingers, when someone pushes through. I blink repeatedly when I realize that it is Adel. He grabs the farmer's mouth and squeezes with all his might. And the walls catapult the echo of the bully's wail. Defeated by the pain of a rotten tooth, he is dragged out by the guard.

It happens so quickly. I'm hardly aware of the professor as he assures me that the danger is over. A girl flaps the air in front of my face to cool me, and another dabs her handkerchief, which smells like an old kitchen, to my forehead. "We are exposed to violence," Ghada says, who, having decided it's safe, jumps out from her corner.

"But there is security—two guards at the door. Where were they?" someone says.

"Two is not enough. We must send a petition to the dean demanding that he increase the number of guards in the waiting room to prevent something like this from happening again," Ghada goes on. Encouraged by the wave of heated agreement around her, she continues, "We need more security in this place!"

The professor has had enough. He barks at the students to get back to their patients and finish. Gazing at their reluctant retreat, I look for Adel. But he's disappeared.

10

MAJED

It happened again. A dream from which I awoke shivering. This time there were no women, only my brother, Hareb. His *ghitra* was folded in the old style, a messy heap on his head. He wasn't wearing his kandora, just an undershirt that was stained with mud, and a *wizar*, gathered between his legs and looped into a knot at the waist. He looked exactly as he had all those years back when he worked in the palm grove, using the farming tools of an ancient age: a knife with a blunted blade for trimming the palm tree's fibrous trunk and a *yirz*, an ax with a small, sharp head, for breaking rocky bits in the soil. He looked as though he were about to loop a jute rope around a palm-tree trunk and strap it around his torso so it would hold his weight while he climbed up to prune the tree's crown. I can't remember anything he said in the dream, only the expression of deep disappointment in his eyes.

Why did I dream of Hareb in those days before we had money, when the extended family lived together in my father's house in Ras Al-Khaimah? Stuck in traffic, this is the question that occupies me. I tap on the steering wheel and mutter a curse at the long row of cars in front of me. I'm convinced that the traffic lights at the intersection have been programmed to stay red three times longer than green. There is roadwork on the two other routes from my house in Al-Wuheida to the office. So, 9:45 a.m. and here I am, stuck on a road jammed with cars heading to too many busy destinations: Deira's souk on the right, Sharjah on the left, and, straight ahead, the other side of the creek, Bur Dubai. Even though it's past the morning rush hour, this junction remains packed.

"Move slowly." That's what Hareb used to say. "Weigh everything from every angle before jumping in." I'd always nodded out of respect toward my older brother, even though I did not agree. His advice would have been solid if this were a sluggish city, but Dubai has proven to be anything but that. It's 1995, and I wonder what he would have made of the new hotels, shopping malls, public gardens, and water parks, the mushrooming office complexes and apartment blocks, the influx of expatriates in an anxious rush to find wealth or security or both. It seems that it all happened after his death seven years ago, the explosion of world-class sporting events—tennis, golf, snooker, motorboat racing—as well as the exhibitions and back-to-back trade fairs that bring a steady flow of people from all corners of the world. Hareb caught a whiff of it, but he did not live long enough to witness this new and sudden escalation.

There is an overpass at one end of Al-Maktoum Bridge, and plans for more at various points in the city. Sometimes I get lost on the sprouting new routes. Ahmad told me the other day that there was talk of an ambitious plan for six-lane highways to ease the flow of cars as the city expands. When he noticed my vexed expression, he added, "But it's good, Father. It means there will be more people coming here, bringing more opportunity."

"What do you need opportunity for?" I said in a voice curt with annoyance. "I've done all the work; you're all set." As I think about it now, it seems like something that an old man, reluctant to embrace change, would say. I slide my sunglasses down to the tip of my nose and scrutinize my reflection in the rearview mirror. It's a hard face, one that looks much firmer than its sixty-three years. Three deep lines appear on my forehead when I lift my eyebrows, but otherwise the skin is thick and full-blooded, with none of the scratches of old age. My eyes are brooding, that darkest shade of brown rimmed with a couple of barely visible rings of blue, which I inspect to see if they have eaten up more of my irises. I can't remember them in Hareb's eyes. But then his were much lighter, the color of the thick mountain honey of the *sidr* tree. His daughter, Mariam, has those same eyes, clear and spirited. When she was a girl, they sparkled with a million expressions. Then she grew up, and whenever she sets them on me they are heavy with blame.

There's a photograph of my brother and me, taken at my father's farm. We stood posed the best way we knew how, stiff as the palm-tree trunks surrounding us, in front of the gushing water pump that was emptying groundwater into the cement reservoir. There's a date on the back, and as I try to remember it, my gaze drifts to the other drivers sealed behind their rolled-up windows, jaded and staring ahead with the air-conditioning blasting at high on their faces. If honking were not against the law, they would certainly make noise.

Why can't I remember the date? I was the one who jotted it down, after all, since Hareb learned to write much later. Was it 1959, or later, once Hareb had created his company in Dubai? The light turns green and a taxi driver tries to squeeze in front of me. I don't let him, and when he keeps trying to nose in I honk, keeping my palm pressed on the horn. The blare jolts the other drivers. They must suppose there's a medical emergency, because they steer their cars to the side to make way for me. The light switches to red. I pass through anyway.

I circle the Clocktower roundabout, still puzzling over the date. Was it just before the water pump broke? I know that was in 1963, because that's the year my father sent Hareb all the way to Dubai to fix it.

My brother had paid a fee of two rupees to join fifteen other passengers in the back of an outmoded Ford Model T truck, miraculously kept in service through the innovation of its owner. Hareb settled in between the passengers' goats and sacks of green limes. They had to wait until the tide was low before they set off along the shore for a journey that would take six hours. The sand was thick and slushy. Whenever the truck got stuck, Hareb and the other passengers would dismount to help free it. They shook the vehicle and wedged chinko, the indispensible perforated steel sheets, under the trapped tires before pushing with their full weight until the truck rumbled forth like a beast out of a swamp.

Hareb returned three weeks later. As soon as he arrived, he unloaded my father's repaired water pump, along with six brand-new pumps. An Indian businessman he had met had asked whether he would be interested in making a sale in Ras Al-Khaimah. A week later Hareb had sold all six water pumps and was planning his next trip to Dubai to bring back more.

I'm heading east on Airport Road, my head filled with Hareb's tales about Dubai and its enterprising creek back then, which brimmed with gliding dhows delivering goods and rowboats transporting people from one side to the other. Neighboring farmers and friends joined us to hear about the traders who arrived in Dubai with wares from India, Pakistan, Iran, and even distant Zanzibar. With the rat-a-tat noise of the newly fixed water pump in the background, they'd settle on palm-frond mats in a well-shaded part of the grove and snack on the dates piled in a bushel in the middle. I served them *gahwa*, Arabic coffee, in the usual custom—no more than three mouthfuls, poured into tiny bowl-shaped cups—as we listened to Hareb speak of the town's maze of sandy alleys, hardened through the constant shuffling of buyers and visitors, and of porters pulling heavy loads on wooden carts that rumbled ahead on two wheels. The shops were open-fronted and packed with merchandise ranging from canes, daggers, and brass coffeepots to sacks of rice and fabric bolts. There were spices smoothed into pyramids and shimmering gold displayed in glass showcases, and rows and rows of food in tins.

Since I had never been to Dubai, I longed to join my brother on one of his trips. But I had a job: collecting customs duties from the few ships and small boats that docked at Ras Al-Khaimah's sleepy port. The English company in charge of the customhouse employed me. They paid me well and installed me in a small office at the back of the company's bungalow headquarters, which I shared with my boss, David Dudley from Sussex, a place of green hills and lots of rain in the south of England. Working under David, I learned to speak, read, and write in English. He taught me how to calculate gains and losses, and I kept them listed neatly in a ledger.

When I asked him if I could take a trip with my brother, he said, "Dubai? Do you know how unpredictable such a trip could be?" Under his feathery eyebrows, his eyes narrowed until they turned into sharp green dots. "If you went with the intention to stay a week, you might end up getting stuck for a month—the truck that travels there might simply break down completely. Happens all the time, you know." He clicked his tongue and sucked in air through his teeth, as if in pain. "You do agree, I think, that it wouldn't be wise to undertake such a journey, in view of all your responsibilities here." And I had nodded, eager to accommodate his common sense.

That's how it was with the English. Instead of refusing your request outright, they made you feel as though you were making the decision. Even with this realization I still felt privileged to be around them, so clever and educated they were, so unemotional and organized. David often invited me to join him at the small bar that was part of the compound where he and the other British expatriates lived. The bar smelled of dog because there was always a pair of salivating bitches sprawled beneath the wooden tables. Hareb once asked what I did with all those English people, and I explained the game of darts to him. Naturally, I didn't mention the lager we drank that made the game all the more entertaining.

An airplane rumbles overhead and I realize I have missed my turn. I have passed the airport. The city is behind me and the desert stretches on either side of the two-lane road: clean humps of pale dunes. Another thirty minutes and I'd reach my farm in Al-Khawaneej, with its nine hundred palm trees that produce five of the finest varieties of dates: khenaizi, barhi, lulu, sukkari, and khalas.

I would have liked to continue, skip the office altogether. I could easily miss work for a day, but Saeed will be coming in later to tell me what he found out in his meeting with Diab Al-Mutawa, the man who rejected my son Khaled. Mustafa will have news from Cairo about Dalal and her mother. And I have to look for that photo. I know it's in the office, but I can't remember where I put it. I keep my eyes focused on the road, looking for the next U-turn. What year was it taken?

11

MARIAM

❧

For more than a week I searched for Adel. I scanned the lecture halls and clinic, and trailed around the government-style buildings on the university grounds. I made sure to linger longer than I needed to in the library in case he was looking for me, too. Here I am again, poised behind a desk with open books and plenty of diagrams of all shapes of teeth spread in front of me. I sigh and pack up. The driver will be arriving soon to take me back to the sakan.

Outside, the sky is a cerulean expanse with the odd cotton ball of cloud. There is a grassy patch in front of the library, its edges fringed with stunted trees whose leaves are trimmed into neat squares. I cross it, keeping an eye out for Adel, and move onto the main path, which is broad, with crouching sphinxes on either side. In my mind I have played out various scenarios of how I'll approach him. I shall walk up to him and say hello. Then I will thank him for his heroic intervention and congratulate him for reacting so quickly. If I am able to keep my voice from shaking, I might even praise his sharp instinct in grabbing the source of the farmer's pain. And then we can be friends.

As always, there are groups of students socializing or going over their notes on the lawn, drawn together through nationality and shared interests. A cluster of Sudanese girls, their heads wrapped loosely in colorful hijabs, giggle together. Farther down, a group of rich Egyptians and the fashionable set from the Levant—girls and boys—slouch in a loose circle, projecting a world-weary demeanor. They set themselves apart by the conviction that they're a notch above the rest simply because they've embraced a Western style of living. In between their light flirtations, they look up with nonchalant glances. Their deadpan faces reflect boredom with a dollop of scorn. They smoke, too. And it's not just cigarettes. I catch a whiff of weed as I hurry past them.

Ahead sits a large group of boys from the Khaleej, mainly Saudis, Kuwaitis, and Qataris, with a sprinkling of Bahrainis and Emiratis. Then there's another mixed Khaleeji girl–boy group, bunched slightly to the side, where the conversation is carried out with alert formality and studied behavior. One too-familiar word or gesture could set tongues wagging so hard they'd whip the air into a mighty wind that would carry news of inappropriate behavior all the way back to the girl's home. So every act remains proper in this public place. The girls are huddled together, standing stiffly or sitting on benches; the boys try not to look too interested. There is a visible space between them that every now and then is filled by a courageous girl stepping into it to compare notes with a male student.

I join them briefly so that I'm not labeled a snob. Curiosity sits in their eyes. I can tell that they are waiting for the right moment to ask me about the attack at the dental clinic, but just in time I spot the driver pulling up to the university gate. Another girl from the sakan, whom he has picked up before me from a different university, is in the backseat. Just as I say my good-byes and turn, Adel pops up midway between the group and the car. My rehearsed lines abandon me and I let out a puzzled squeak. How could I have been looking so hard, only to miss him?

Come with me! The message in his taut face is clear. Why does it have to be now, in front of this bunch, their eyes twitching to snatch a hint of improper behavior? I'd wanted to find him so desperately, and now I wish he would just vanish. *Poof!*

I teeter from one foot to the other, trying to decide what to do. I finally decide to make a break for the car. If Adel gets in my way, I'll knock him down.

"Mariam, I need to see you."

He says this just as I glide past him, quickly approaching the sakan car. The girl in the backseat is leaning forward, about to spot me, but suddenly I change direction, cutting across the lawn. Every step takes me farther away from the car. Adel follows me. I don't hear his footsteps, but I know he is behind me.

❧

He takes me to one of the open-air cafés in Giza, along the banks of the Nile. Its splendid name, *Casino La Brincessa*, is on a faded board that hangs askew from a hedged trellis. A discreet entry down a narrow path carpeted with artificial green turf leads to the river.

Adel was quiet in the car, eyes fixed ahead as he maneuvered the vehicle through Cairo's traffic. I had stared out the window, stroking my bangs, dumbfounded by my offbeat behavior yet, strangely, wallowing in the thrill of it. What was it that made me change course so abruptly without weighing the consequences? I did not turn back when Adel overtook me, just followed him to his car. How long would the sakan driver wait for me before heading back and reporting that I was missing? Yes, missing!

I did not think twice. Spontaneity led me, just as it used to when I was a girl, confident in the knowledge that no matter what mischief I got up to, my father would be there for me, the iron spine that held me up. That was before his first stroke.

There's an atmosphere of neglect at Casino La Brincessa, in the chairs pale with age, the lusterless peach plastic table covers, the stubby lampposts riveted into the earth at a slant, the gaze of ownership that sits in the eyes of lazing cats. I don't mind, because what is important is that it is a well-chosen place: far from the tourist track and little frequented by Khaleejis. There are no persistent little girls selling necklaces made from ambrosial *full* flowers, young men armed with cassettes of romantic songs for sale, or photographers insisting on snapping eternal memories.

I'm not sure why this is called a casino, since there's no gambling at the riverside cafés. There is, however, the notion of romance; they're places where a lover can gaze at the Nile and compare his amorous sentiments to its vastness. They are respites from the congested city. The norm is to take your time and not rush things, although there's always a maître d' hovering around the tables, weighing conversations' progress and making sure to cut in with a question or comment at every crucial moment of tender articulation, tormented declaration, or intimate profession of love.

I guess that this one has been pestering the six couples already sitting at tables, because there is relief on their faces when the maître d' diverts his attention toward us. He leads us to a table by the river, and the couples focus on each other again. I can tell that they are all in the spring of romance by the way they lean their shoulders forward with heads tilted to the side, their ears perked to catch every whispered word and every rustle of a gesture, their eyes bright and wide, registering every mood and expression.

The maître d' delivers our order of black tea in tulip glasses, along with a large bottle of cold water. Settled by the riverbank beneath a tree with a plastic tube of light snaked around it, we blow at the steaming tea. The air feels cold and damp. I loosen my shayla and air my bangs. I don't know what to say to break up the curdled silence that has settled between us since we left campus.

I have so many questions to ask Adel. I want to know whether they interrogated him as they did me. First it was the professors, then university security—two men who took down notes—and finally the cultural attaché, who arrived from our embassy to hear my statement and then made a formal complaint, demanding more security at the university. So much to talk about, and then there's the matter of thanking him, too. I must not forget to thank him.

We're halfway through our tea when the maître d' returns and leans over the table, as if about to divulge a deep secret. "We have cold lemonade, soft drinks, and the best Turkish coffee. Or anything else you might desire. Can I get you anything, bey?"

Adel shakes his head, and when the maître d' retreats I say, "It seems many of the students have been complaining about the lack of security at the college. Have you heard anything?"

Adel shakes his head just as the maître d' butts in again: "And shisha, too. I forgot to mention the water pipe. There's honey or any other flavor: apple, mango, licorice."

This time Adel gets up and rests a brotherly arm over the maître d's shoulders, leading him a few steps away. I can't hear what he says, but I do spot the *baksheesh* that Adel slips into a handshake. One of the couples sees it, too, and the girl frowns with disapproval. She hisses a comment to her partner—she's probably saying that Khaleejis think they can buy the world! But what else could Adel do when privacy has turned into a luxury that can only be bought?

"Apparently he was a madman," I say once Adel is back.

"Who was?"

"The farmer. I heard he was charged and sent to jail. No one knows for how long. Did they call you to ask questions?"

"Why would they?" The expression on his face is serious. "Are you sure you saw what you think you saw?" There's the hint of a roguish smile, which he suppresses with a sniff. "I'm sure you were mistaken. That wasn't me in there."

"Well, thank you for not being there," I say with a nod. I intended it to be light and jovial, but it comes out thick, like the air around me, which has completely stopped moving. I turn to the river and gaze at the fading line of sunset. Even though I feel the awkwardness returning, I mutter, "You must have gotten lost in the chaos."

Adel lets out a hearty laugh, and with it comes a sudden breeze. It's as if the weather was waiting for a signal from him. Undulating gusts spin around us, triggering the leaves to rustle and inspiring the cats to prowl all at once, intent on some cat-and-cat games. Adel calls the waiter over and orders a shisha. Then he grows chatty, which suits me fine.

He is from mountainous Fujairah, the only emirate of the UAE whose coastline is solely on the Gulf of Oman. He is from a middle-class family; his father is employed as a government accountant. Out of his six siblings, he is the second eldest and the only boy. He leans back in his chair and, between drags from his shisha, tells me that he is the first in his family to study abroad. He tells me they're proud of him, and I'm overwhelmed with tenderness toward him when he expresses his fear of letting them down. I insist we resume our lessons to make sure that doesn't happen. But Adel has already moved on, describing his apartment in Mohandessin, which he shares with two other students. "Sometimes we get up to no good," he says with a wink, and takes a sharp inhale that makes the shisha gurgle furiously.

I'm not sure what he means, and I don't ask. Instead I grunt softly, and my mind drifts; I consider how simple and straightforward it really is to establish a comfortable rapport between a man and a woman when there are no expectations. This is the way it ought to be.

Dusk sets in and the river slaps and sloshes, as if readying for a night of rest. The sun idles low in the sky, ready to pull back its light. I watch as its last vivid ray, a ruby streak wobbling on the Nile, disappears before turning back to the café to see the maître d' hassling another couple. He takes pleasure in being too available. He calls the waiter to empty the ashtray and wipe their tablecloth; when they don't pay him to go away, the maître d' decides he must adjust the table's wobble. "Right away!" he insists with a flourish, ripping paper out of his notebook and folding it into a thick wad to insert under the table's leg. When the woman considers out loud whether she wants another lemonade, the maître d' snaps his fingers to confirm the order before she has a chance to change her mind. Then he strides victoriously over to another table to bother them.

"It's your turn now," says Adel, leaning forward. "Tell me about yourself."

He catches me off guard. "Me? What is there to tell?"

Adel tilts his head back and blows a long breath of honeyed tobacco. My vision follows the smoke as it eddies to the side and over the low wall that separates us from the river. By the bank, it's the color of dirty dishwater. I spot twigs and grasses delivered by the current; collected in a recess in the wall, they form a nest on which bobs a gray rag, an empty bottle of soda, a sodden piece of cardboard, and a bright-yellow plastic bag.

"I mean, why did you choose such a difficult subject? Why didn't you choose something easier, like art or history? True, you can make a lot of money as a dentist, but it's not as if you need it. You're rich already. You don't need to work. You can just sit back and do nothing." His tone is gentle. There is no jealousy in it, only curiosity.

He doesn't know that my personal wealth is not in the millions, just enough to get by. My father intended to put some properties and land in my name, to secure my future. But by the time he got around to it, it was too late.

Some strange emotion catches me by the throat. My chest tightens and I start fiddling with my chair, picking at the damaged zipper of the cushion under me, pulling it this way and that, trying to force it to close over the nibbled sponge filling. Adel is conscious of having struck a sensitive chord. He puffs at the shisha and watches me intently. I am touched by his solicitude when he says nothing more.

Some of the girls at the sakan have asked me these same questions. They had already calculated the amount of money my family has, based on snippets of society's various estimates of the Naseemy fortune. In response, I would play down the importance of money and launch into a lecture on the significance of serving the community and repaying our generous government by getting educated and bringing home vital skills. It's a dull explanation, something you'd feed a reporter or a government official. But it served me well, because they'd stopped asking. To Adel I find myself uttering, "I need to feel self-worth."

Adel flinches. There's a break in the steady, rhythmic bubbling of the shisha's water, and I look for something to focus on. There's the steel sugar bowl. Picking up the teaspoon, I chip at the hardened sugar crusting its sides. My mind roils with disbelief at what I've just said.

Adel puts the pipe on the table and leans forward. He wants me to open up, but how can I with all this self-blame, this guilt that runs as deep as the river to my side, as thick as the silt at the bottom. I was there. I watched it all. I said nothing. I let it happen.

The images rush through my head: the hospital bed where my father, propped up on a couple of cushions, was recovering from a fall after his stroke; the worry beads unmoving, as still as the hand that was holding them; the open mouth and teary eyes, so grateful to Allah for sparing his life, to his brother for caring so much; the paper in front of him and the court notary asking him, "Do you understand with your full sense what this means?"

I know we should leave in the next few minutes if I want to arrive at the sakan before nine, but a heaviness holds me down. My head drops to my chin and I avert my gaze. A mosquito fires its sharp drone somewhere around my forehead as the moody air turns still once more. It bites. I pay no heed to the itch. I dare not meet Adel's gaze.

One word, one look from him might slacken my tongue and cause all that is held back to gush out.

"So," he says. "How is your cousin, what's her name? Dalal . . . yes, that's it, Dalal. Is she your best friend?"

I am so grateful for the shift in subject that I answer him immediately. "Yes, she is."

"Were you close when you were growing up?"

"Oh, yes," I say, and as he returns to his shisha, my mind drifts back in time and I think about how our unlikely friendship came to be. The first thing that struck me about Dalal was her impertinence. I was with Nouf in the school's playground when Dalal sought her out and told her that there was no escaping the fact that they were sisters. Dalal stood before us with her fists stuck to her hips and bragged about it. We were speechless with disbelief.

She was an odd-looking little girl who did not look like us at all. Her curls had expanded with the humidity and spilled out of the two pink hair clips on either side of her head. One of her eyes refused to open fully and her nose was so flat that, in the morning's glare, I could not make out the line; only two dots emerged in the middle of her milky face.

There was quite a commotion at Ammi Majed's house when Nouf later reported the incident, and this spiked my curiosity. Was she really my uncle's secret child? Where did she live? What made her suddenly want to slip into our lives?

Nouf called her an imposter and demanded that I never talk to her about it. I kept that promise, but that didn't mean I couldn't speak to Dalal directly. Our friendship developed slowly (we were so different), but flowered after my father had returned from his recuperation in Germany. It was a turbulent time in my home as my father tried to deal with his brother's betrayal. He had no time for me—and I ended up seeking out Dalal. We had united in our misery. We vented our anger and frustration on the man responsible for all our woes, my uncle, her father, vowing to get back at him one way or another.

This is how far back my thoughts have wandered when I become aware of Adel tapping the table with his water pipe, pulling me back to the moment. "I just asked you a question," he says. "Three times!"

"Sorry. What is it?"

"Your cousin, Dalal, what is she doing here in Cairo, anyway?"

"She wants to be a singer."

"A singer, huh?"

I nod. "She does have a beautiful voice."

"Maybe we can get together with her sometime soon. And she can sing for us."

"She would love to," I say. "The problem is that once she starts, you won't be able to get her to stop."

Adel chuckles and puts the pipe back into his mouth. He sucks in a deep breath, making the water explode into mighty bubbles. It is a happy sound that makes me think of a merry group of babbling women. The maître d' saunters back to our table. It seems the privacy gained from the baksheesh has expired. An order of two more teas satisfies him and he leaves us, while we settle back to chat about Dalal and her antics.

12

MAJED

Through the showroom's glass walls, a tractor gleams. As I enter Green Acacia Ltd., the office boy picks up a rag and starts wiping its hood with urgent strokes. It is a demo utility tractor with a front loader, bright green with yellow tire hubs. Parked on the glaring white tiles at a slight angle, it faces a tomato-red chisel plow. On the right side of the showroom is a reception area where Mustafa usually sits and where, near closing time, I often join him and watch the passing cars outside on Airport Road. I catch sight of him by the stacks of plastic mulch and rolls of tubes used for drip irrigation; he is busy with a customer.

It is the same large showroom that Hareb bought soon after registering the company, but it never looked like this when he was alive. It used to be dim and dusty, the paint on the walls in uneven shades of beige, the flooring kept dull in its original cement base, the employees crowded behind metal desks that were fringed with towering masses of truck tires and heaps of spare parts. My brother placed little importance on modernizing or neatening Green Acacia.

When I took over, I rearranged the company. I separated the offices, installing them in the back for privacy. Now I pass a row of work spaces with glass partitions, filled with accountants—Egyptians and Indians—who straighten up when they become aware of my presence, looking up from their sheets, ledgers, and newly installed computers. Their starchy faces break into humble smiles of respect. I nod back my greeting and turn the other way, passing a large room we use for storage and pausing at the open doorway of the first office. Saif is slouched in his rotating chair with his back to me. The phone receiver is propped on his shoulder as he murmurs into the mouthpiece. He is talking to a woman, and it's not his wife. I can tell because his voice sounds amorous.

Ahmad is in the next office, engrossed in his newspaper, but he spots me and jumps to his feet like a soldier, with an expression that he's ready to accommodate my every wish, as he recites a list of the latest developments—a few queries from interested companies, a couple of updates on the various contracts we have going—that have taken place since he arrived at eight o'clock sharp. "Hasn't your brother gotten over his broken heart by now?" I ask, frowning at the other desk in their shared office, which has been vacant since a fortnight ago, when Khaled suddenly packed up and left for Bangkok without telling me. Ahmad shakes his head, sighing to show his empathy. When I grunt, he calls out to Saif, who rushes to our side, clutching a green file to his chest. As always, my sons have an idea they would like me to approve. I've already delayed the prospect of hearing out this latest one for too long. So I signal them to follow me, with one thought: to get it out of the way quickly so they will leave me in peace and I can search for that photograph.

My office, along with my secretary's, is at the end of the corridor. It has a seating area that looks sunken because it's so much lower than the imposing desk. Whenever I have visitors, I join them on the soft leather seats so I don't look down on them; that would be disrespectful. I don't bother to do this with my sons. No sooner am I settled behind my desk than Saif pulls what looks like a thick contract out of the green folder. He hands it to me. It is typed and bound, and seems a most tiresome twenty-page read. "What's this?" I say, balancing it like a dead fish on the palm of my hand.

He clears his throat and says, "This is our proposal for taking this company higher, to the next level."

"Oh? Closer to heaven, you mean?" I chortle at my pun. Ahmad smiles, but Saif just blinks, as always ambivalent toward that thing called humor.

"There's an analysis of the market," Ahmad says, looking deep and thoughtful with his hands clasped loosely, the index fingers tapping each other. "You'll find some good ideas in there."

"Really?" I put on my reading glasses.

Ahmad is about to continue—his buttery voice might have been able to hold my attention—but Saif, with his rampageous disposition, spoils it all. "Yes, Father, really," he says, his voice gruff with impatience. "There are suggestions of what we should do to expand the business when the market is up and broaden our scope when it is down." I don't appreciate his tone; it borders on impertinence. It sours my mood right away.

"That's easy. When it's up, we make money; when it's down, we hold firm." I scoff as I flip through the pages. "Is this what they taught you in those business courses you took? You should have asked me instead of wasting time—the company's as well as mine—by making up this nonsense."

"But this is all scientific. It's based on sound business principles. In it you'll find the market trends, and predictions, too."

I laugh. "So now you can tell me what will happen a year from now?"

"Please, just read it!" It's a demand, not a request.

I settle on a random page filled with multicolored graphs showing the market analysis that Ahmad had mentioned. I flip two more pages before slapping the proposal shut. "I can't look at this now," I tell them, pulling off my reading glasses. "I have too much work. I have to review our transactions, for one thing: what we spend dirhams on and how much we save and what goes toward your salary, so that you can live well. That's what I am prepared to tire my eyes over: the money coming in and going out. Not this encyclopedia you've brought me."

Saif's face darkens. He looks at his brother, who shakes his head in a *you-failed-horribly* sort of way. Some might say that I should give my sons more say in the company, but there's too much hunger in their eyes, two pairs of torchlights always shifting, always restless with greed. There is a knock, barely audible. I guess it's Mustafa, and when he peers through the doorway I wave him in. "Mustafa! The boys have ideas—again!" I slide the proposal to the edge of the desk and lean back in my chair. "Give it to Mustafa to look through," I tell Saif. "He can tell me whether it's worth considering." I glower at his baffled face. "Anything else?"

"No," he mumbles.

Once my sons have left the room, Mustafa dawdles at my desk and says, "He's not happy with that joke you just made, bey." With an edgy grin, he caresses his scalp in an east-to-west direction.

"It wasn't a joke. You will read what's in that file and tell me about it."

"Yes, bey." He plops down and is swallowed by the sofa, his legs and back folding into an awkward bend, and starts relating the latest goings-on in Cairo, as reported by the four young men he has assigned (working in shifts) to follow Zohra and Dalal. Mustafa opens a small notebook and reads the detailed notes he has jotted down. He tells me that the spies have confirmed that for the past nineteen days Zohra and Dalal have been seeing the same composer. "It's nights now," he says with bulging eyes, "late nights."

"And what's that supposed to mean?"

"I don't know, bey." He leans back, looking defeated.

Lots of descriptions and no conclusion, I decide, considering whether it might be best if I traveled there to see for myself. I'm curious to find out what their living conditions are like. Zohra appreciates comfort. How is she managing in the middle of Imbaba's muck? I picture her dainty feet skirting piles of rubbish on the streets, her fine nose twisting every time a cloud of exhaust blows in her face. The images fill me with a cool glee. Yes, she probably regrets the day she left Dubai and the shaabia house in Al-Mankhool.

My shaabia was in the middle of a maze of narrow sandy paths, well trodden and hardened to a dirty gray, with an opening every so often—an empty plot of land where boys played football. The house was built too big for the plot, the courtyard no more than a tight square with a *ghaf* tree squeezed in the middle of its cement floor.

For many years my shaabia was rented to an old woman, a widow who couldn't afford to maintain it. It had peeling walls and leaking pipes, ant-strewn cracks in the floors and threadbare carpets, old air-conditioning units that roared but did not cool when the heat shot up in the summer. The widow passed away at a most convenient time: just as I decided to send Zohra to live there as punishment for what she'd done.

The best years with Zohra were the first few. After that she lost her sweet demeanor, replacing it with a haughty sarcasm that made me want to break her, the thankless creature she'd become with her unrelenting demands. It wasn't just that she wanted me to make our marriage public, which I'd always assured her that I would do at the appropriate time. She'd also started insisting that I leave Aisha and move in with her. The nerve! Then one day she announced that she was fed up of waiting and would announce our marriage herself. It was a threat I did not believe, but it was a threat all the same, and it had the effect of pushing me away. I turned cold. I stopped visiting her. And then she came.

It was the eve of Eid Al-Adha, the celebration of the Big Feast. I was watching Aisha as she arranged the sweets and nuts, pouring them into bowls as part of her preparations for the stream of visitors that would fill the house for the next four days. The doorbell rang, and the maid went to open the door. I didn't recognize Zohra as she entered; she was wearing a burka and abaya. She must have thought that would add credibility to what she had to say. It was Dalal—around eight at the time, with her big head and wrists so skinny it looked as though one might snap in her mother's tight grip—who shook me into an awareness of the catastrophe that was about to take place.

Zohra hollered, "He's a coward! He's a drunk!"

Aisha had turned to me and asked, "Who is this woman?"

"This woman?" Zohra said, jerking Dalal forth. "You should ask him who this little girl is!"

And then something strange happened. Zohra's voice started to shake, the words falling out in a jumble. Perhaps she suddenly felt intimidated by the grandness of my house, or even by Aisha, who was staring at her in a disconcerted panic. "What's that?" she kept asking. "Who are you? What is it you're trying to say?"

There was no time to lose. I made a big noise; I waved my arms to intimidate her. I raised my voice so high that Aisha, in her distress and confusion, plugged her ears. I dragged Zohra and Dalal out of the house by force and ordered my staff to send them off in a taxi. I still can't comprehend how I was able to compose my features so quickly. I'd put the fury in me on hold and marched back into the house to face Aisha. "Madwoman," I said to her. It was hard to judge how much she had absorbed, whether she believed what she'd heard, but I wasn't about to investigate. "Where do they come from, these beggars? Who lets them into this country?" I might have gotten away with that argument if fate had allowed it.

A week later, my daughter Nouf stormed into the house with the news that there was another girl at her private school going by the same family name. "She came right up to me and said we were sisters! Ask Mariam, she was with me. We'd never seen this girl before; she's two classes below us." Nouf was overwrought, choking on her words. "Sisters? How is that possible? She looks nothing like us and talks with an Egyptian accent."

I hadn't realized they all went to the same all-girls school, and this time there was no escaping the connection. Aisha understood. I remember that her sister showed up at the house more often during that time, no doubt begging her to walk out on me. I kept expecting to come home and not find my wife. But Aisha stayed, quietly withdrawn, unapproachable with that blank face. It was hard to guess what was going on in her head.

Not so with my sons and daughters—four of them were older and married and therefore presumed that they had the right to make demands. Saif and Ahmad hardened their expressions and kept asking, "What now?" Mona and Amal, on the other hand, made a racket with their protestations and declarations of the hurt and anguish I'd caused. They dragged the other girls, Nadia and Nouf, into tears and hysterics, which I knew I could have ended if I confessed, admitted my mistake, shown some remorse, even lied to make up for the betrayal: "It happened in a moment of weakness. She was a seductress who lured me into a marriage I did not want. She must have used magic, blinded me with it. Then the child came—and that must have been planned, too, so that she could shackle me. And no, no one else knows about it. And yes, of course I'll divorce her." That's what they were waiting for. That's what the whole family expected, but they should have known that I would never have allowed them to bully me and force a confession, real or made up.

At first, I really meant to divorce Zohra right away, but their reactions chased that resolution away. What business did they have judging me? I kept the whole lot of them guessing my intentions. And that included Zohra, who had to endure a long drawn-out torture until I finally severed our relationship. I think back on that time with cool satisfaction. After moving Zohra into the shaabia, I cut back her finances slowly, a monthly reminder of how lucky she had been to have had me in her life. Ultimately, she couldn't afford to keep Dalal at the private school and had no choice but to move her to a government school. I prolonged my family's mental anguish simply to reinforce the fact that the decision was mine alone.

At the time, in the heat of the moment, I had thrown the blame back at them, accusing them of driving me away, and in the end they did the only thing they could: let it go. Normality returned a few weeks later. And nothing was ever mentioned again about that other wife and child.

۞

There is a knock, and Saeed enters. I expect he'll tell me that Khaled was deemed too old for the girl, or perhaps that the girl's father had decided that his daughter must marry a cousin, make sure the money stays in the family—all expected, all reasonable, really. It would have been better if Khaled had let his family choose the girl for him— just as we did for his siblings, just as my marriage to Aisha had been arranged—instead of searching for a love match. That would have been best: easy on the mind, gentle on the heart.

I rise to greet Saeed with a kiss on the nose and a warm handshake as Mustafa slinks out of the room. Once we're settled on the couch, Saeed taps his head and says, "I saw the old man, and he's quite mad." He snickers. "So you shouldn't take anything seriously, because his mind is not sound and he has started imagining things."

I clear my throat and tell him to start at the beginning.

"I made four visits, and even then, even after using every skill to approach the matter without arousing suspicion—I mean, who am I, after all? Neither the groom's father nor his brother—I walked out with nothing."

"Then what?"

"I went again yesterday, and this time I got him talking about all the various businessmen in Dubai—you know how these old men love to talk about how these people made their money—and that got him in the right mood. Finally!" He works up quite a laugh, sounding like a rusty machine. "What an imagination! Such a wild story! Barely worth repeating."

"What did he say?"

"Yes, well." He rubs his face. "We chatted, all friendly, just harmless talk, which I made sure led to the various distinguished families here in Dubai, and I mentioned you to see if I could provoke some sort of comment."

"And?"

"First he sniffed."

"Sniffed?"

Saeed nods. Through his teeth, he frees a hiss of apprehension. "You know, he has this medical stick that replaced the cane he carried when his legs got weaker from the diabetes. Well, he clutched that stick and started pounding it on the ground."

"Why?"

"He told me that your son wanted to marry his daughter and he swore he would never allow it."

"Why? What has the boy done?"

"That's what I asked him. 'It's not the boy,' he said, with that rudeness you're obliged to forgive just because he's an old man. 'It's the father. I cannot give my daughter to the son of a man who is responsible for his brother's death.'"

For a second I'm not sure I heard him right. "Why would he say something like that? Everyone knows Hareb died of a stroke." I shift on the couch to quiet the outrage that has gripped me. "The crippled shit! Why does he spread such malicious talk?"

Saeed dismisses the whole episode with a swoop of his arm. "What does it matter, anyway? Who is going to pay attention to the blasted tongue-lashings of that grizzled fool? His brain is shriveled like a bad nut."

There is heat, a slow fire in me that settles in the stiffening veins of my neck. I want to be alone, and as if he's read my mind Saeed glances at his watch and gets up to leave, with the made-up excuse that he is late for an appointment. The door closes behind him with a soft thump.

People talked when I took ownership of Green Acacia. With Dubai's small, close-knit community, it would have been naïve to presume that the episode would go unnoticed, especially since Hareb voiced his outrage to anyone willing to listen. I wasn't one to ask for details, but I knew many debated whether I was right to do what I did.

Still, after any seismic shift, things cool off and settle. I was sure this was what happened, convinced that my well-guarded reputation and good standing were not seriously affected—until now, when that crusty old Diab Al-Mutawa blamed me for my brother's death.

My gaze drifts to the cabinet in the corner, and suddenly I remember that that's where I'd put the photograph. I'm up and pulling open the drawer at the bottom. Slouching on folded knees, I sift through old bills, receipts, and other scraps of paper thrown in and forgotten among the paper clips, blunt pencils, and dried-up fountain pens.

The photograph is lodged between the pages of an old copybook. I satisfy my curiosity first, nodding at the date on the back. It was 1963, right after Hareb made that first sale. The likeness was striking in our youth: we both had broad shoulders and strong, straight backs. Later we'd grow the same belly, too, a firm padding that spread to the sides of our waists. David took the photograph and I recall him suggesting that we stand with the palm grove behind us, but Hareb was so proud of the repaired water pump that he insisted we stand near it. Behind us is the metal pipe, curving up at an awkward angle, its mouth emptying a surge of water into the reservoir.

I wipe the surface of the photograph. Although Hareb was nine years older than I, we look close in age: able-bodied men with pride-filled chests pushed so far out that the bottoms of our kandoras hang just above our ankles. David told us to smile, but not knowing how we'd look with our teeth showing, we had decided on manly frowns.

He was the popular brother, friendlier, more talkative, and it was only because of his good relationships with people that he'd managed to secure those big contracts in Abu Dhabi and Al-Ain. With the country's boom in greening projects, the timing was right, and the contracts fell right into his hands. Yes, he started this company, and he was lucky enough to secure its assets, but I'm the one who launched it to the highest level. It would be fine if it is only Diab Al-Mutawa who thinks that I caused Hareb's death. But what if there are others, all those businessmen and acquaintances who have never once shown anything less than the highest regard for me?

I examine my brother's face, looking for the anguish I had dreamed was in his eyes. It's hard to tell. His ghitra is slanted too low on his forehead, casting a shadow over most of his face. And with that I conclude that the bad dream was the result of nothing more than indigestion, to be expected after last night's heavy supper of kebab and onions.

13

DALAL

~

At the start of every meeting, I sing a few lines from one of Umm Kulthum's songs to get Sherif bey's creativity flowing. He clicks his tongue as an accompanying beat. Squeezed between two fingers, his cigarette leaves behind a wavy line of smoke as his hand glides in the air from side to side. My voice fills the room. His head sways with rapture.

It's a ritual he insists on. He is a "true artiste," Mama insists every time I complain about the futility of what has begun to feel like a sacred tradition. His glasses are on the desk, and without them his lids look unprotected, as if they might lose their definition and melt into the rest of his face. They slacken and conceal his eyes, dark as watermelon seeds and slushy as the juice. His lashes flutter like moth wings as he takes careful glimpses of my mother.

Tonight she does not lean forward, her chin resting on her knuckles, to watch me. There is no giddy appreciation in her face, only a forced smile of stretched patience. Her legs are crossed and she jiggles her foot. Every now and then she exhales with a force that indicates that some deep annoyance will soon explode. My voice strengthens with anticipation and I hurry my performance along.

"Bravo! Bravo! Excellent start to the evening," Sherif bey says, slowly swiveling toward the wall to reach for his leaning oud. Hugging the instrument to his tummy, he plucks a few strings and embellishes them with a chord.

"Yes, my Dalal is consistent in her performances," says Mama, "but you . . . well. It seems it is not in your power to facilitate our way." After weeks of gentle prodding and encouraging hints, all aimed to hurry him along, she has decided to take the straight path to the source of our frustration.

Sherif bey flinches. It's the first time she has spoken to him that way. He sets aside his oud and rubs his eyes before shielding them with his glasses. "Are you upset with me?" he asks.

"I'm just wondering whether this . . . all this . . . is going anywhere."

"I'm not sure what you mean, Sitt Zohra," he says carefully.

I march to the couch. "She means it has been a month now and we still haven't gotten anywhere," I say, plunking myself down next to her.

"Dalal! Stop it! All I'm saying is that I am deeply distressed that I feel we are not taken seriously." She utters the words to me with unhurried precision in a whisper designed to be heard by Sherif bey.

He reacts immediately. He jumps up from behind his desk and hops over to face us. "Sitt Zohra, your words hurt me. How can you say such a thing?"

"You see, Dalal," Mama continues without so much as a glance at him, her voice even, "the sight of us in this hopeless situation—me a divorced woman, you with no father to protect you—makes people disrespect us."

"I don't disrespect you," Sherif bey says.

"Well, what do you call this?" I interject with a wave of the arm. "All this time and you haven't thought up some measly tune for me, or opened any doors for us. You must know everyone in this business. Why haven't you introduced us to them?"

"Ah-ha-ha." It's a deep-throated chuckle, but there is no humor in it.

"If he introduces us, we can get the right exposure," I persist, turning back to Mama. "Look at us, meeting like this in the middle of the night, wasting our time—and for what?"

Sherif bey waves a finger at me. "That's quite a tongue you have for so young a lady."

"He's right, Dalal. I didn't bring you up to talk that way," says Mama.

"You listen to your mother, little girl," Sherif bey says.

"It's true, Mama," I moan. "He knows all the right people. They have parties he can get us into, make introductions. But he doesn't."

"We are instructed to come at this awful hour," says Mama, nodding with resignation, "and expected to stay behind these closed doors. After all, there's no one out there asking after us."

"That's exactly my point, Mama. He doesn't care about us."

"One thing you must understand, Dalal, is that this is a business full of insincerity. Wherever you turn, there are people who you might think are looking out for you. But no, it's all an act. They're all the same, putting your noble interests to the side and taking advantage of you."

"Don't talk like that, please," he shouts. "You make me sound like a brute."

She looks up at him, and their eyes lock. All is still. All is tense. I get bored waiting for it to pass, and I gaze at the wooden screen standing in the far corner of the room. Behind it is the other entrance, the alternate route that he uses to get to his office without having to pass the secretary. It's the door we slip through when night sets in.

Finally Sherif bey looks away in a huff. "Yes, it's hard to be patient, and I know how hard this life has been for you. In fact, I can't sleep at night thinking of the cruelty you have endured out there in the Khaleej."

"You mustn't have sleepless nights over us," Mama says. A quiver of vulnerability—so convincing I want to salute her—rattles her speech.

He flings his arms in the air. "I can't help it. An artist is always too sensitive for his own good!"

She nods. "It's not fair that we should ask for more. You have been too kind already. But now I think we must part."

He sniffs and mutters, "So be it. Everyone has a destiny to follow."

She sighs and says to me, "What hurts me, daughter, is the disrespect. But we have our dignity, after all. We should get going now, Dalal."

All this time wasted! How much more can I handle? I can't hide my distress. "No, Mama, we must not be hasty," I begin, but she has already risen and is sidling through the various bits of furniture; she disappears behind the screen. I expect him to rush over and plead with us to come back. He does not. I expect my mother to turn back with some clever excuse. She does not. She's already by the elevator, tapping her foot as if her impatience might speed it along.

"It's too early to leave," I protest. "Hassanain won't be here yet." Although it is convenient to have the microbus driver pick us up every evening and drop us off at home in the late hours, after yesterday—when he made a vow to protect us if ever need be—the thought of seeing him makes me groan. He's just like the others, the helpers and facilitators, the people of the street who want to be a part of our lives. How many of them have claimed to know someone in the world of the stars who is that VIP ticket to success?

Not too long ago there was Abdo the butcher, who set out on a thorough investigation. In between his gifts of flesh and bone, he went out of his way to make sure we understood that he was trying his best to help us. "I called, but the man has left town . . . I met his assistant (you know how it is, they all have assistants) and he says it's as good as done . . . Soon, soon, I'm this close." It's not the charade that I mind. What bothers me is that Mama reveals our life to them, with uncalled-for details, and they feel they have a claim to it.

Abdo the butcher wanted her. A couple of months back, just before she gave him the brush-off, he called out to me as I passed in front of his shop. Standing between carcasses hooked on railings, he grinned broadly and waved toward another complimentary provision to nourish the dainty divorcée. "See how tender and marbled it is?" he said, holding up the supple piece of meat for me to see. "It comes from the rump!" He slapped it with his other hand, as if it were a woman's buttock. "It will make you strong, and your mother, too." Of course, I pretended to be interested, which was difficult with the damp, meaty odor and the pestering flies. "How is she, anyway?" he continued as he wrapped paper around the meat and tied it with string. Then he lowered his voice and scrunched his eyes at me. "Why didn't your mother remarry? Has she rejected the idea completely?" I shrugged, and he patted his heart with his right hand to illustrate his humility and kindness, following the gesture with a downward gaze to demonstrate his good intentions.

Later, when I told Mama, she wasted no time getting rid of him. The next day she handed him a five-pound note as gratitude for his efforts to help us. He would have objected with the vulgar outcries typical of someone of his class, but Mama had caught him by surprise. Before he could react, we had strolled out of his shop. He doesn't talk to us anymore. He stares at us with dagger eyes whenever we walk by. We have learned to enjoy chicken since then.

We're out on the street, and a breeze blows the smell of greenery from the neighboring Shooting Club. I have not given up hope. I'm convinced this must be some ruse to send panic into Sherif bey's heart. Surely she will linger at the building's entrance to give him a chance to rush down and beg us to come back. I hurry after her as she marches through the treelined streets, bewildered by her bold steps. After all, we are walking away from "the genius of the music world, the artiste among artists," as she has repeatedly described him. Sherif bey composed the music of her youth, the tunes that turned her head sodden with romantic reveries. Surely she won't give up on him so quickly.

I am not the only one who is surprised by her early departure. The spies my father sends to watch us—there are two of them tonight—are caught off guard, too. As Mama breezes past them, one is quick to pretend he is looking for some important item in his pocket, while the other drops to the ground to tie his shoelaces, even though he is wearing sandals. What a clumsy duo!

We end up on Wezarat Al-Zeraa Street. It's 9:30 p.m., and dust and fumes ride on gales whipped up by zooming cars and rumbling buses. "What was that all about?" I shout over the noise.

"We'll talk about this when we get home," she says, craning her neck as if anxious for a taxi. A few slow down, but she ignores them.

I am aghast. All the effort, all the time, all the hope—what was it for? "I want to know now!"

"This is not the time or place," Mama says just as a taxi jerks to a stop. She takes a step back, then forward, as if trying to remember what she was about to do. When she opens the door, I refuse to get in.

"Now, Mama, now," I insist, stomping my foot on the pavement.

"You will not talk to me like that in the middle of the road," she scolds.

"We can't keep wandering from place to place, always getting nowhere," I whine. "I'm tired. I can't do this for much longer."

Her grip tightens around the door's handle. "You can't do this for much longer? Have you ever bothered to think about me? Huh?"

I look away. One of the spies has crossed the road, rendering his position useless since he is too far away to hear us; the other is closer, once more tying his imaginary shoelaces. I reckoned that the taxi driver would wait a little, pick up pieces of our argument through the open windows and add his own spoonful of wisdom. But he is not interested. He yells at Mama to shut the door and zooms off with a screech. What a night of volatile tempers! And then there is a honk.

It's a Mercedes, a well-kept old model, ivory-colored with a burgundy interior. The uniformed chauffeur waves his gloved hand at us, and through a curtain of cigarette smoke in the back we see Sherif bey's anxious face peering through the window. Mama and I refuse his offer of a lift and walk away, ignoring his pleas to talk things over. The car follows us as we backtrack onto a smaller street; the pair of spies trails us.

It's a glorious moment when Sherif bey hops out of the car and dashes toward us. Elated by this welcome twist to the evening, I hide my smile as best I can and watch him, plucked out of his cocoon of an apartment and looking disoriented in Cairo's streets. I suddenly realize that he is besotted with my mother. He begs her to be reasonable, to come back to the office so we may talk like adults.

Mama looks as cool as the moon as she accuses him of taking us for granted, thinking we'll always keep coming back. I want to raise my arms in a cheer when she demands: "No more hiding us. Introduce us to all the important people in the music business so they can hear Dalal sing."

"Yes, and after that you needn't bother with us anymore," I say, glancing over my shoulder at the spies, making sure they hear me well and proper. Finally they'll have something worth reporting to my father. "We can take it from there."

"No, Dalal. You're wrong," Mama says. "This is a journey, a long one, which I, for one, would feel privileged to share with Sherif bey."

With that, Sherif bey's lips curl in a lopsided attempt at a smile, and I feel sorry for him—but only for a flash.

14

MARIAM

"Feeling better? What did the doctor say?"

I prop myself up on the pillow. That's enough of an invitation for Tammy, a first-year student and one of my two flatmates, to tiptoe into the room and settle at one end of the bed. The curtains are drawn and the room is dim, bathed in the cool blue of morning light. Still, I spot the inquisitiveness in her impish eyes. She senses there's more to the story I made up after arriving at the sakan just before midnight last night.

"The doctor says it must be some virus," I say, and pat my head, which is slightly warm. I suspect that the injection he gave me triggered an allergic reaction. "It might be contagious," I add, hoping this will make her go away.

Tammy acts as though she's immune to germs. "How could it be that you fell asleep in the library? And doesn't the staff check to make sure no student is left behind before locking up?"

"I really don't know, Tammy. But when I woke up, I realized I was in a corner that could easily have been overlooked."

"Hmm." She curls her lip at me with obvious disbelief, and I find myself wishing she had never discarded the veil that used to cover her entire face. But Tammy had sought a transformation as soon as she arrived in Cairo, and she started with her name: she changed a somber-sounding Fatima to the lighter Fatami, and later, with the playfulness of a wink, altered it one more time, to Tammy. Because of the new freedom she's found being away from her father, brothers, cousins, and every other male relative and neighbor in the tiny oasis village of Nahwa (deep within the mountains of the northern Emirates), she has taken to dressing differently, too. For her morning classes at the college she wears a satin shirt, bloodred and stretched a little too tightly around her chest. Tucked into a long black pencil skirt, it's belted just under her ribs with an eye-catching rhinestone buckle that draws attention to her slim waist. Her shayla, which she used to loop twice around her neck, has long since loosened and now sits as no more than an embellishment over yellow-streaked hair that's parted on the side and falls like a horse's tail down her cheek. "How come all the noise of people leaving the library didn't wake you up?"

I feel like I've turned into a creature of intrigue under her gaze. I shrug with a helpless sigh. These are the same questions Abla Karima asked me. *Amm* Eid, the doorman, was pacing up and down when my taxi pulled up in front of the sakan door. His relief at my safe arrival was immediate. I was the missing resident, and his hands had shaken as he raised them to the sky to thank Allah for my safe return.

"Where have you been, Sitt Mariam? We were worried sick," he said. I did not answer him, only shook my head with puzzled exasperation. Slow-thinking in emergencies, I had already prepared a few excuses, but I couldn't decide which to use. He unlocked the sakan's door, metal with opaque glass for added privacy. "Abla Karima is worried sick, too. Every ten minutes she pops out here and asks me whether you have arrived yet."

I was slightly relieved at the mention of this particular matron. She is the most docile of the lot. "Did she telephone anyone?" I asked. One call, that's all it would take to end my studies in Cairo, my planned career and independence.

"Not yet. But she wanted to, many times. She threatened to make a call if you didn't get here by midnight."

I blessed her under my breath. Out of the four ablas, she is the only one blighted with indecision when things don't go according to protocol. If it were Abla Taghrid, she would not have hesitated to report me, and I'm sure the cultural attaché would have been waiting along with her, his arms crossed, his foot tapping the floor with extreme displeasure that this most sacred of rules had been broken. Amm Eid followed me through the entryway and to the next glass door, which has a beautified plastic covering showing swans gliding on a river. No man is allowed through it, and Amm Eid stopped in his tracks and looked around as if lost. On the one hand, he knew he should go back to his post. On the other, his ears were burning to hear my account.

He was in luck. The swan door burst open and Abla Karima waddled down the steps. Long necked with a beaklike nose, she always makes me think of the storks wading in the Nile's tributaries. Her hands fluttered with agitation and she rattled off a full list of questions, pausing only when her breath ran out and she had to replenish it with a massive gulp of air. When I told her, "I fell asleep in the library, I don't know how," she flapped her hands some more—maybe to cool the heat that was building in her—and launched into another set of queries. "I'll have to report this, you know," she warned. And that's when I staggered to the side, leaned against the wall, and said, "I think I have to see a doctor."

Alunood ambles into my room with a pair of sandals dangling from her fingers. She is my other flatmate, a second-year fine-arts student. She has heavy eyelids and large downturned eyes that brim with gloom. "You know you have probably been reported," she says, and parks herself heavily next to Tammy.

"No, she hasn't," says Tammy. "Otherwise the attaché would have been here already to find out all the details and punish her."

"It's early yet." As always, Alunood's voice is flat, with a no-nonsense quality to it. "He'll be here soon enough." With that, she bends over and starts strapping the sandals to her feet.

"It doesn't matter," I say. "I had no control over what happened. And if he doesn't believe me, there is always the doctor's report."

"What exactly did he write?" asks Tammy, as if anxious for the pronouncement of some exotic disease.

My eyes grow heavy and I close them. Maybe it's the nagging guilt over making up so many lies. But what else could I do? Tell them about my secret escapade with Adel?

I suppose Dalal would have been proud of my performance. I acted as best I could, even though all the while I was convinced that everyone could see right through me. The doctor had shined a tiny torch into my open mouth and peered into the back of my throat. Then he pinched my nostrils to check for inflammation. He seemed unconvinced. So I said, "My head feels light."

"Dizzy?" he asked.

"Yes. And there is pressure in my eyes. And I can't breathe properly, either." I stammered with the mention of every fabricated ill.

The stethoscope emerged.

"My stomach hurts, too."

I suppose I had described a few too many aches, each having nothing to do with the other, because the doctor hummed and scratched his head.

Tammy's eyes light up. "Maybe you fainted! Maybe that's what happened in the library."

I nod weakly. There is a tingling sensation in my limbs, and this makes me worry once more about that injection. What was in it? Perhaps the doctor was trying to teach me a lesson for pretending I was sick. Maybe he was insulted by what I did next but could not resist accepting what was offered—for the first time in my life, I slipped him a bribe for a forged diagnosis.

It wasn't easy with so many people in the room, but it helped that they were in perpetual motion, opening the window for fresh air and closing it when the night air chilled the room too quickly. They rushed to the kitchen to prepare what remedies they could for all the ailments I complained of. There was thyme for my sore throat, mint for my stomach pain, and chamomile to slow my palpitating heart. In the midst of the pandemonium, I slid a hand into my handbag and pulled out a wad of notes I had no time to count. The doctor raised his eyebrows with surprise but quickly slid them from my palm as he took my pulse. I did not need to say anything else; he understood completely.

A sudden fatigue washes over me and I yawn. The girls decide it's time they were off to class and leave me to fall into a dreamless slumber.

ॐ

It's early evening, and dusk's light is no more than a gray glow at the edges of the curtained window. It is quiet, and, stretching the sleep out of my limbs, I gaze ahead. A broad yawn finishes in a smile as I think of Adel.

I scratch the back of my head and finger my thick amber hair, letting it spill in a fan onto the pillow. I get goose bumps as I reflect on all the different expressions that played on his face last night. My palm slides over my nightgown to cup the suppleness of my chest. The other hand joins and I squeeze, feeling the pleasure warming me, lighting me from inside out. My tummy dips into a tight hollow and my ribs rise up, as if some hurdle for my roaming hands. They have snuck under my nightgown, and for a while my fingers run up and down my ribcage, letting my imagination change the feel of them to something stronger, sturdier, rougher, even: a man's hand, his hand.

My skin heats with every stroke. My wandering fingers grow bolder and travel lower, as though searching for hidden treasure. There is noise coming from somewhere in the building. I close my eyes against it as my breathing turns impassioned. He cannot resist the feel of me. I am a writhing piece of dough, to be shaped and played with. The thought lights a powerful flame. Desire seizes my breath in rolling waves as I twist and jerk under a spell of sweet and agonizing quakes.

Spent and splayed like a starfish, with the covers in disarray, I grin at the ceiling before realizing that there are voices just outside my door. It is an argument, animated whispers between Tammy and someone else. There's an abla out there. I can't tell which one, but she is insisting that she needs to see me, and for a moment it puzzles me. The ablas don't come to our apartments unless there is a man around—doctor, electrician, plumber—and then they make sure to warn us to cover up or get dressed, since we often traipse around the rooms in our robes, pajamas, or nightgowns.

I hear Tammy snap at her, telling her that she can't go in because I am resting. Like all of us in the sakan, Tammy considers the apartment her private domain and shields it with zeal. One case of easy access, and the ablas will gladly form a habit of nosing into our affairs.

To fortify their position, or out of sheer frustration, the ablas are forever bossing around the rest of the staff: their assistants, the dadas who run their errands and clean the building's communal areas, the security men, the drivers, the doormen. Their demands are never-ending, and they insist on knowing every detail of the sakan's go-ings-on: who said what, who came by, who went where.

The girls' squabbles with the ablas are mostly over car bookings. Whenever a student wants to go out, whether to classes at the university, shopping, errands, or recreational visits, she has to fill in a request form the night before with departure and return times, which is then handed to an abla for coordination. The ablas map the drivers' routes for the next day and group students in cars according to their timings and destinations. And that's when, without fail, the bickering begins. These are like territorial catfights, quick screaming bursts and threats that are settled quickly so that peace can return—until the next night. Arguments with the ablas are a daily occurrence, a part of life at the sakan.

Some of the ablas are more lenient or deal with problems by brushing them to the side, but not the one outside my door. Now that she is speaking louder, I recognize the voice as that of Abla Taghrid. She wears a skirt that stops three fingers under her knee to show her modernity and takes solid steps in a pair of closed black shoes with a slight heel to indicate refined practicality. Abla Taghrid is shrewd, with enough spite to create mountains of problems. In the five years she has been working at the sakan, she has gotten three students evicted.

"The well-being of every girl in this sakan is my responsibility," she says. She is right outside my door. Any moment now, she'll burst through and flick on the light switch so she can catch me looking the image of health. I pull the blanket up to my neck and kick my legs to generate heat.

"Okay, I will tell her to come down once she wakes up," says Tammy.

"I have to make sure she is fine," insists Abla Taghrid.

"I told you, she is sleeping!"

"She has to wake up now. I have a message for her from her uncle."

This piece of news sets jitters rushing through the length of me, and it takes every bit of restraint I have not to toss off the blanket and jump out of bed. I usually call the family about once a week just to let them know I am okay. Ammi Majed has never called me before. Could word of last night have gotten to him already? What could it be?

The door opens a crack and a pencil of light spills in just as I burrow under the blanket, pretending to be asleep. "Are you awake, *habibti*, my darling?" I thought she might linger for a while by the door, but she's right by my side, her voice sounding as sweet as if it were dipped in honey. The ablas would like us to accept them as second mothers, the protectors and guiding voices of experience. It's another way of cementing their position and setting themselves higher than the rest of the staff. Some, like Abla Taghrid, would like to get more involved in the girls' personal lives, always on the lookout for opportunities when one of us might be vulnerable enough to reveal a secret or two. That's nearly impossible, because we've labeled her captain of the moral police. Even new students are warned off as soon as they set foot in the sakan. "How are you feeling?" she asks.

I groan as if just waking and slither out from under the blanket. I avert my gaze (better she not see what's in my eyes) as she touches my head. It's hot, and she pulls back her hand in surprise. "Your uncle called," she says to me. "I told him that you were a little ill and asleep in your room. So he said he'd call you later."

I wait for her to tell me more. But Abla Taghrid just stares at me, stretching her thin mouth so that it runs parallel to her square jaw. In the faint light, her round eyes shine like wet pebbles. High above them are tattooed eyebrows, two thick dashes, giving her an expression of perpetual astonishment. "Did he say what he wants?"

"No."

This makes the hot and the cold rush through me at the same time, and once again I wonder whether a real fever is coming on.

"Right!" She slaps her thighs. "I'll let you know if he calls again. Otherwise, come down yourself and telephone him."

She'd like that, I'm sure. The communal phone on the ground floor is close enough to her quarters that she can hear every squeak and breath. If that were not enough of an intrusion, there is another curious ear: the operator who places all the international calls. Every few minutes there is a click as she checks whether the call is still running. Sometimes she even interrupts the conversation and, with her flute-pitched voice, warns us of the cost so far—as if the expense were coming out of her pocket! Not for the first time, I long for the convenience of my Dubai mobile phone. But it doesn't work here.

"And just to let you know, he did mention that he was coming," says Abla Taghrid as she makes her way to the door.

"H-h-here? W-w-when?" I stutter.

"I don't know," says the abla, and she closes the door behind her.

I claw at the blanket. I am transported back to the hospital room where my father, having two months earlier suffered from a stroke that affected his right side, lay recovering from a fall in which he'd broken his good leg.

He had turned unpredictable in his misery. I couldn't figure out which I hated more, the savage emotions that suddenly seeped out of him or the bouts of cloudy-eyed listlessness that lasted for hours on end. And then there was his vulnerability on that particularly sticky November day in 1987. He was blubbering, his body convulsing under the force of choke-filled sobs, when Ammi Majed walked in and calmed him down with talk of sending him to Germany for a faster, more efficient recovery. And then they began talking about problems at the company.

The sakan room feels hot. I hurl the blanket to one side and sit up. Not for the first time, I tell myself there was nothing I could have done. I didn't understand what was going on, and even if I did, what could I have done to prevent the grievous outcome? Spoken up? Who would have listened to the objections of a babbling eleven-year old? But no matter how many excuses I make, the fact remains that I failed him. The shame of it sits like a noose around my neck. It suffocates me.

"Cash flow, that's what worries me," Ammi Majed had told my father. "We might need to sell a building because of this Iraq–Iran War that's dragging on. All those attacks on tankers in the Gulf—well, let me just say it's affecting all the businesses, and the banks have grown more careful. They are not giving loans."

My father groaned. "How serious is it?"

"Well, import and export is affected, too. But if we act quickly, we can control the situation, or at least minimize the damage."

It was at this point that I got bored. My thoughts drifted toward my schoolbag and the diversions it held. I reached for it and pulled out two large-headed miniature gnomes from the side pocket, along with a half-consumed tube of Smarties chocolates.

"You must understand, brother," Ammi Majed said, "I'm here for you. I just want you to concentrate on getting better. With your permission, I will do what is best for the company."

"You have my permission."

"Signatures."

"What?"

Ammi Majed cleared his throat and shifted his gaze to the ground. "Well, you see, I would need the authority to sign," he mumbled. Then, with a breath filled with resolution, he added, "I am talking about full authority, so that I can inject some life into the business."

"Of course, of course," said my father. "You have it. We are brothers, and I know that all you do is for the good of the family."

"The permission would need to come from the courts. There are papers you have to sign."

"Yes, yes. God bless you. Get it arranged."

Ammi Majed shifted on his feet, looking a little unsure as to what he should do next. "He is right outside."

My gnomes were violently quarrelling, but I paused my playing and gaped at the door. It surprised and embarrassed me that there had been a person waiting in the corridor all this time. Did he hear my father's outburst, the wailing sobs from earlier?

"Who?" my father asked.

"The court notary."

There were five men. I knew Mustafa from the office and I'd seen Ammi Majed's lawyer a few times, but the notary and the other two men, who were presented as witnesses, were strangers. I thought the notary was being funny when he asked my father, "Are you Hareb Al-Naseemy?"

"Who else could he be?" I said, bursting into a giggle that was cut short by the nasty look Ammi Majed directed at me.

The notary didn't seem to mind, though. He was a young man with steel-rimmed glasses. His eyes twinkled at me as he curbed his smile. Then he repeated the question, to which my father said exactly what I did: "Who else would I be?" Thinking my father agreed with me that it was a silly question, I was about to laugh again when I noticed that he was staring at the man with impatient eyes. This was grown-up talk, with all its riddles and mysteries, and I returned to the gnomes. "You want a Smartie, do you? I'll show you," I muttered into my chest. The second gnome picked up a Smartie and squished it over the first gnome's head. The red shell cracked, and I smudged the chocolate filling over its face.

"As per procedure, I need you to answer me," the notary said.

"Yes, yes, you can see that I am," said my father.

"Do you, in your full mental capacity, give power of attorney to your brother, Majed Al-Naseemy?"

"You know, I've broken my leg. All I want from this world is health."

"You understand that he'll be the person who will solely make all decisions related to the company—buying, selling, and the like—as he sees fit?"

"I have to go away to get better. I ask you, *ibn al-youm*, who is going to take care of the company?"

"I need a yes or a no, sir."

"What have I been telling you all this time, young man? Don't you know to respect your elders?"

The gnomes were finished arguing. Both faces were smeared with chocolate, which I started licking off while sneaking glimpses of my father's reddened face.

"I'm sorry, ammi," said the notary. "It's just that we have to do things according to the rules. And that means you have to actually say the word in front of me, in front of these witnesses."

"Yes, yes, yes!" yelled my father. "That's three times I'm saying it. Is that enough?"

Ammi Majed had to placate him again before they could proceed. In addition to the signature granting power of attorney, other signatures were needed on documents from customs and bank authority papers, all of which were contained in a file that Mustafa had brought along. Ammi Majed spread them in front of my father. And my father signed them with his good hand.

15

DALAL

و۶

I sit cross-legged in front of the mirrored closet door with half my hair in rollers. My mouth rounds into an alluring pout and I try out several facial expressions, mixing surprise with different degrees of innocence. "I don't understand. Could you explain it to me again?" My lips broaden a little. "So kind of you; I would be quite lost without you." It's the perfect pitch, and, graced with that hint of a smile, it is enough to produce the illusion of warmth and compassion.

I take a deep breath, and even though my routine practice of matching vocal tones to facial expressions is over, the glow on my face remains. "How well things are going!" That's what my mother keeps saying. Sherif bey now takes us to private parties, which he says are filled with all the right people. He calls them career makers, so I had expected them to hunger for a talent such as myself, or at least show a little more interest. He's introducing us to his sisters this afternoon. Mama calls to me to hurry up just as I begin to tackle the other side of my head. I've barely zapped three strands of hair with heat and wrapped them into rollers when someone starts banging at the door.

"We want to speak to the sitt, the one they call Zohra!" It's an order, not a request.

"Open up!" That's another voice.

"Mama, can you get that?"

The raps grow louder.

I shove the rollers to the side and barge into her room. My mother looks like a shy bride. She is wearing an ivory-colored suit with a matching chiffon carnation pinned over one ear. There's an unspoken command for a moment of privacy, for silence, as she sits on the edge of her bed, slowly twisting open a tin of Nivea cream.

"Didn't you hear me call?" When she doesn't reply, I wave at the door. "There's someone there."

"Well, go see who it is," she says.

"How?" I exclaim, waving both hands at the unfinished shape of my head. "Besides, it's you they're calling."

She takes her time rubbing the Nivea into her hands despite the ruckus at the door, which sounds like hundreds of pounding fists. "There's nowhere you can go, Sitt Zohra," someone calls. "We know you're in there, and we won't go away. You have to face us."

"What have you done?" I say, suddenly alarmed by the realization that it's the neighborhood women out there. They have made snide remarks at my mother before, obviously feeling threatened by their husbands' attentions toward my mother. But that was on the street, and Mama had brushed their animosity to the side and marched ahead. Now they are here with clear and dangerous intentions, it seems.

She waves her creamed hand in front of her face. "What are those stupid women thinking? That we'll be in this stinky neighborhood forever, that we're interested in stealing their good-for-nothing husbands? I want you to go out there and handle the situation."

"What do you mean by . . ." I can't finish the thought. "No, no, no, no." I imagine opening the door to women spraying spit through their gnashing teeth, their thick hands and fingers ready to rip. "Do you hear them? They are ready to draw blood, and it's you they want." Then a thought occurs to me. "Is this a test?"

"Test?" In her gray eyes, there's a flare like a mirror caught in light. "This is life!" I shrink back when she chides me. "If you can't tackle a bunch of loudmouthed vultures, what hope do you have in the world of music?"

I nod with resolve. There must be no hesitation when I deal with them. After all, this is life. With a brusque swing of the arm, I yank the door open and snarl at the women, "What? You've woken up the dead!" I must be a frightful sight with half my hair puffed up and frizzed, tangled like a fisherman's net. With the element of surprise to my advantage, I act before they have a chance to overpower me. "Don't you have any shame, banging on people's doors like this?"

The woman at the front is the glaring constable of the group. I recognize her as the wife of Abdo, the butcher. She steps back, nudging the group into retreat. I'm about to end the confrontation when someone pushes through. And then my father is in the room, a concrete force towering over me. My first reaction is to run away. I scurry past him, but there's a man blocking the door. He kicks it shut.

"Enough stupidity!" says my father, his voice barely audible, and he gets a grip on the untamed side of my hair, tugging at it as I cower and make mousy sounds. "I've had just about enough of your antics." He forces me onto the sofa just as my mother comes out of her bedroom.

"Oh," she says, tapping at the carnation in her hair. Out of nervousness or disbelief, she speaks to him as if he were some regal guest who has graced us with a visit. But she can't quite finish her sentences. "How did you . . . ? When did you . . . ? What are you . . . ?"

"Sit!"

We sit side by side, the sofa swallowing us as my father castigates us for our blatant disregard for his good name, our reckless and selfish behavior toward the family. He doesn't need to shout or strike us. The sight of him is enough: all that blood filling his face, the thick purple veins on either side of his neck. "So, you've decided that you are special?" he growls. "I'll tell you the truth, the both of you: you're not. You're as ordinary as they come!" He aims his fiery eyes at me. "But it's not your fault. It's mine, because I made the mistake of choosing your mother—if you can call her a mother, filling your head with such dreams, bringing you to this filthy place. Oh yes, it's my fault. But that doesn't mean I'll stand by and let you ruin all that I've built!" Mama keeps her gaze fixed to her hands, shiny with cream, accepting all that he says without demur. When he commands us to drop everything and go back home, she nods her head in agreement. Crushed under an abrupt flood of thoughts that spell defeat, the best I can manage is to emit a tiny whimper. This is the end, the end of something that never quite began. I look away and sob quietly.

And then, a pause. I suspect he's gone quiet so he can hear my sniffles. Time ticks, and in the silence I imagine he's gloating over my sorry state, my mother's shaken haughtiness, the strength he still holds over the pair of us. When I finally look up, however, he is quite changed. His face has lost the color of moments ago. It's ashen, as if gripped by shock. He frowns at the ground as he holds on to a chair with one hand and clenches his other hand repeatedly. Then he says his final words, and I find out that the force of earlier has not abated: "Heed my words, the two of you, or by God I promise you: there will be consequences."

With that, he turns and stomps out of the apartment. The neighborhood women are still lingering at the door, shifting on their toes and murmuring their curiosity at what ill wind has just blown in with this stranger from the Khaleej. Mama flings the door shut in their faces and starts pacing the apartment. "Go wash your face," she says to me. "And make sure to fix that hair. We don't want to be late for our meeting with Sherif bey's sisters."

16

MAJED

❧

The minutes crawl by. I only have to endure this dutiful-uncle act a little longer before I can drop Mariam back at the sakan. We are on the upper level of Casino Qasr Al-Nil. As always, this grande dame of casinos, featured in the movies of old, is brimming with Khaleeji tourists. Like most of the cafés by the riverbank, the seating is arranged as if on the deck of a large ship. The Nile runs just below us on one side, and on the other there's a decorative wall of turquoise tiles.

It's chilly by the river. I wear a jacket over my winter kandora, dark gray and woolen, and shoes instead of my habitual sandals. I gaze at the water and feel my nerves finally settle after the encounter in Imbaba. I had been sitting in the backseat of the car, bewildered with disbelief that Zohra would live in such an appalling place and that she would drag my daughter there, too.

She appeared just as my gaze had drifted up the facade, stopping at the fifth-floor balcony. I wasn't used to seeing Dalal from this distance. I had stared at her, discomfited by the change in her. She no longer had that caricature face, the too-flat nose and wide-set eyes, the too-big head sitting atop the skinny frame. That little girl had looked like she was made up of the spare parts of different engines forced to lock into one another. And now she'd blossomed into someone wonderful to look at, shapely, with the glow of polished marble in her face. The observation passed quickly as I shifted in my seat, filled with disapproval at the sight of her in her bathrobe. Her hair was wet and dripping, like the sagging lines of laundry fixed to the ledges around her. I recall having muttered a curse aimed at Zohra for allowing her to appear on the balcony looking like that, for not raising her properly, and for dragging her all the way here toward a future that will lead to no good.

The driver remained silent as I sat in the backseat, my eyes fixed to the sight of her. I was tempted to tell him to drive off, but, having grown fed up with Mustafa's feeble reports, I'd decided it was crucial to fly out to Cairo and do something about those two. It was important that I be perceived as more than a bodiless threat. And with the necessity of taking charge, a tangible force that rumbled along the length of me, I was out of the car and marching toward the building, mildly aware of the driver hopping at my heels.

The lively music from a passing Nile cruiser pulls me back to the moment, and I take a deep breath while attempting a fatherly smile at Mariam. Reaching for the wallet in the inner breast pocket of my jacket, I ask her if she needs anything. She shakes her head and says, "We don't need any help here, Ammi Majed. The government scholarship program provides us with more than enough." My gesture is rendered useless and I pull out my handkerchief instead, dabbing my forehead, even though the air is cool. Her refusal feels like she's lowering my worth somehow, which is bizarre because even though the air between us is thick as always, there's nothing I can hold against her. She addresses me with respect, her manner as cordial as always.

The waiter delivers our order, and in the silence that follows I decide I must be imagining things, my perceptions still jittery because of all that took place two hours earlier at the apartment in Imbaba.

Something happened in the middle of my confrontation with Dalal and her mother: a tingly sensation, as if a colony of ants were spewing out of my joints, accompanied by a cold sweat, which thankfully stayed hidden under my layers of clothes. I remember thinking it was a fleeting moment of agitation, most inconvenient. But then, more alarming was my pulse started racing, which got my head spinning. I'd clutched the chair for fear that my knees might buckle under my weight—what a catastrophe that would have been!—and gathered all my strength to make sure that did not happen. I'd overpowered them. I'd broken them and slashed their resolve. I was in a position of advantage over the pair, and I wasn't about to let the whole encounter fizzle to nothing.

While I wait for my mint tea to cool, I decide to test Mariam's tone once more. "How are your studies?"

"Fine."

"Tell me about your days at the university."

She stirs the juice in front of her until its many colors mix into a dull yellow, then pulls the straw out and takes her time running the length of it between her lips before answering, "There's nothing to tell. It's all fine." This time there's no mistaking the defiance in her tone. I narrow my eyes at her as she sticks the straw in her mouth and starts twirling it like a baton from side to side. It's a taunt, and a very unladylike gesture indeed! This is something new, and I'm not sure where it's coming from. I clear my throat and harden my eyebrows at her, frowning. This makes her stop, and I cross my arms and look away. I know she thinks I had no right to take over the company—she probably blames me for his death—but what does she know! In fact, she should be thankful I've provided for her all these years since her father's death.

Hareb treated me like a brother as far as the company was concerned, but he did not think to make me a partner. And yet, despite the sting of it I worked with unparalleled devotion and commitment.

Mariam doesn't realize that I made Green Acacia versatile, so that it became worth more than just tractors and mulch, landscaping and agricultural commissions. Its prominence as one of Dubai's most successful companies is all because of me. I added land and property through both my sharp business sense and Saeed's shrewd skills of persuasion as my broker. It was a side venture, and Saeed and I were cunning and aggressive, true innovators in our dealings. We would buy low using bank loans or company money and sell high, returning the profit to Green Acacia.

I take a sip of my tea and contemplate what has come over all these young ones with their inflammatory behavior suddenly turning bullheaded with disrespect toward their elders. There's Dalal, flouting the rules of conformity, and Khaled, who left the country and escaped his responsibilities at work. Last month I contacted him, demanding he return immediately from Bangkok. What does he do? He writes me a letter brimming with self-pity. He was rejected by the woman he loved; so what! This was my thought as I crumpled the paper and hurled it at the wall. "*Tfoo* on you!" I had said out loud, mimicking the spit of disgust.

Mariam makes a ghastly noise as she sucks the last of her juice through the straw. With her tall glass drained, there's nothing else in front of her to rouse her newfound impudence.

I mull over this change in her and wonder whether it's wise to keep her here, so far from the family's supervision. It must be this place— this Cairo—that is making her so. Mama Al-Ouda has always been adamant in her opinion of educating girls: "She learned to read and count in school. And that's enough. Why would she need to go on and waste her youth by learning more instead of getting married and bringing us the blessing of children?" I watch Mariam chew the end of her straw to bits and think, *It's time that she got married and became someone else's responsibility.*

17

MARIAM

Here it comes, breaking the silence in a spirited melody of flutes and tambourines on loudspeakers. Over the roaring propeller rise the rhythmic claps of the passengers, keen to get the most out of their twenty-minute excursion on the Nile. The music is cheerful and the motorboat is gaudily festooned with flashing lights and disco strobes.

Here it comes, and I am thankful for the diversion, a distraction that will make the minutes tick faster until this pretense of family cohesion concludes. A massive eagle of flickering red neon is perched at the front. It looks as though it would have taken off had its wings not been too small for its body. The two dolphins, on the other hand, are of the correct proportions. Positioned on either side of the back of the boat, their bodies light up in different colors at different times.

Just last Friday Adel and I had boarded one of these chugging crafts, squeezing among a group of Egyptian countryfolk who had come to the city for the day. Adel and I have been growing steadily closer ever since that evening at the Casino La Brincessa three weeks ago. There was fun and frolic on that boat trip, an afternoon of unabashed laughter and joy. My heart felt light and playful, a feather held in a breeze.

Afterward, without intention or plan, I told him how my uncle had tricked me out of my rights and caused my father's death. At first he seemed unable to concentrate, but this was not one of my tutoring sessions, and soon he was sitting still. I knew he was intrigued at hearing it all, the treachery and pathos of the tale. For the first time, my throat did not choke with rage as I described the shock stamped on my father's face. My eyes did not mist when I told Adel about how my father couldn't stop expressing his disbelief over how his brother could betray him, first to his friends, later to the lawyers who arrived at our house with thick files and long-winded explanations.

During those black days, I kept away from my father as much as I possibly could. He'd turned unpredictable. He became so preoccupied with retrieving the company that he had no patience for me. He snapped at me if I as much as uttered a word. I'd retreat to my room with my homework or take refuge in the kitchen, helping the maids peel fruits or bake cakes. On the days I thought I might explode, I'd make the driver take me to Dalal's house. And after my father's death, I was horrified. He would not have had a stroke if not put under so much stress by my uncle. I was strangely methodical telling all this to Adel, as if opening locked drawers in a cupboard and emptying them one at a time.

Adel did not speak until I was done. Then he asked, "Why do you have to bend to his rules? What can your uncle do to you, anyway?"

"He is the head of the family," I said. "He controls everything."

"No, he doesn't. You have a government scholarship. So you don't need him. Once you graduate, you'll work and build your own future. You won't need him then, either."

How simple and feasible, how painless it all sounded. "But he can just pull me out of college," I said, "right this very moment if he wants to."

Adel had dismissed this. "Why would he? What would he gain

from that? Listen," he said, leaning forward. "You are your own person, Mariam. And it's time you realized this."

Never mind that his attention had drifted again right after that. His words were what counted: the most commonsense argument I had ever heard. I nod at the memory and look up from my straw, the teeth marks indistinguishable from too much chewing, at Ammi Majed.

I don't need you!

That's the thought that flashes in my head as I lock my gaze on his in defiance. There is heat in his thick-lashed eyes. My heart thumps, but it's a beat that's filled with bravado. I don't need you or your wife, your children or your mother, to look after me. I am my own person!

My uncle shifts in his seat with obvious displeasure. *Outright disrespect!* That's probably what is going on in my uncle's mind this very instant. He busies himself by adjusting his red-checkered ghitra, even though it sits in perfect symmetry on his head. When he snaps his fingers for the bill, a sense of victory bursts in me. Through my quiet rebellion, I have shown him that I do not care to grant him what he sees as his rightful esteem. I will tell Adel about it—Dalal, too, the next time she joins us.

We make a jolly group, the three of us. Adel always suggests that I call her, because he enjoys her spiced-up tales. His dark eyes glint like water at the bottom of a well as he listens to her. I watch him as he watches her, the way he cups his chin with an ear directed toward her so as to catch every piddling pun. This time, I'll be the one with the exciting account. I know Dalal will enjoy hearing about the way I got under her father's skin.

I'm grinning by the time we're in the car, my thoughts far away. It's once the car makes a jerky halt that I snap back to the present. Ammi Majed orders me out before I have a chance to get my bearings, and he herds me past the secretary sitting in the foyer of the offices of the cultural attaché. My mind whirls as I struggle to understand his intentions.

The cultural attaché half jumps up from his seat as we barge into his office. "You are making our girls turn defiant and discourteous!" Ammi Majed hurls the accusation at the young man.

I can't tell whether it's fear or a foolish need to speak up that makes me attempt to defend him. "That's not true, ammi."

"Shut your mouth!"

My face feels like a lump of burning coal. I hug my arms and sense that I've lost control over my vision as my eyes zip across the floor and up the walls. I end up blinking at the ceiling for what feels like an eternity.

"What is it that you're teaching our well-mannered girls at the sakan? Did you know that you're ruining them with your careless supervision?"

"Please take a seat, ammi," says the cultural attaché, who has hurried to the other side of his desk. He places a careful hand on my uncle's arm and indicates the black leather couch. "It may be exactly as you say, ammi. We may be doing something wrong, but we can talk about it, find a solution." Like a diplomatic shopkeeper intent on keeping a mad customer happy, he speaks with an apologetic, concerned tone. It does nothing to mollify my uncle.

Whatever pent-up rage he had buried comes out. He starts raving like a common man, promising to complain to the embassy and the Ministry of Higher Education, even threatening to make a case against the poor young man. A cloud of dread keeps me frozen in place as I try to work out what all this means and where it will ultimately lead. And then he says it: "I'm pulling my niece out of your care. She can finish her studies back in Dubai."

I slap my mouth with both hands and shake my head. I collapse to the ground, my face inches from my uncle's feet. The secretary yelps, and the cultural attaché hollers at her: "Water! Tea! Juice! Immediately!"

18

MARIAM

ᝌ

"They're both unmarried and they live together because no deserving suitor ever came by. And since that was their fate, their life's mission became to pamper their brother. 'The little one'—imagine! That's what they call Sherif bey because he's the youngest, but not by much, I don't think. A pair of fatties, those sisters are! Rice, stuffed pigeon, and macaroni with béchamel sauce—that's what they eat every day, I can bet you."

We groan, and in mockery Adel puffs his cheeks and recedes his chin until it doubles. Dalal laughs, looking very fresh with her rosy cheeks and cozy in her puffy baby-pink jacket. Its collar of feathers plays around her chin. "So there they were," she continues, "pretending they weren't interested in finding out more about us. The younger sister, Sitt Faten, leafed through a magazine while the other one, Sitt Magda, pulled out her crocheting."

"She must have been trying to send a message," I exclaim, raising my pitch so I duplicate some of the adventure in Dalal's voice, "that you should take a woman with needles seriously." It's a fruitless attempt to pull Adel's attention away from her. The only compelling tale that could cast Dalal's account into shadow is the one I would rather forget. I can't tell either of them about that!

Two weeks later, and still I struggle to swallow the indignity of it. I had reacted exactly as my uncle had wanted, collapsing at his feet in desperation and begging him to let me stay in Cairo—so distraught so theatrical, so unlike me. Why couldn't I have stayed aloof? I should have regarded the sight of him, red-faced and absurd, with contempt.

My first assumption was that he knew about my attraction to Adel, and all our secret meetings. What if someone had seen me and reported back to him? But he would have confronted me eyeball-to-eyeball on such a matter.

The cultural attaché had implored my uncle not to be hasty. "Mariam is an ideal student," he said, "intelligent, with nothing less than top marks in her college." My uncle had answered that that was not the issue. I knew I looked pathetic. In the back of my mind I knew that I should get up, but I couldn't find the strength to do so. As I think back, I realize it must all have happened very quickly, but at the time it felt like I would never stop pleading with my uncle. My voice weakened to a hoarse warble and my tongue felt swollen in my mouth: too large, too dry, an overstuffed parcel of wretchedness no longer able to produce a word. It was a humiliation that clearly pleased my uncle, because he suddenly changed his mind and said I could stay. This set trains of alarming thoughts rumbling in opposite directions in my head. What did it all mean? But when I looked up at him, I understood.

There he stood, a statue of power, arms crossed, neck stretched, mouth hard; his eyes were cold pebbles sparkling with cruel triumph. Throughout me spread the sobering realization that no matter what I said or how I acted, Ammi Majed would always be an unbeatable force, the formidable master who drew a life plan for every member of the Naseemy family.

He'd aimed to shake me, to break me. And he did. He crushed me, and I let him.

Dalal is still talking about the sister with the crochet needles, and Adel seems to be absorbed in every dispensable detail. A runaway gust flings pink feathers into her mouth, and Adel quickly brushes them away. She withdraws, feigning embarrassment, and I try once more to get his attention with a joke that doesn't come out as one: "Maybe she should have used the needles as a weapon, poked your mother where it hurts."

"She can poke wherever she wants to, but she won't be able to deter my mother." Dalal nods with imperious haughtiness. "She is determined and devoted—to me, that is. She'd do anything for me."

At this point I lose patience, because the one thing I know about Zohra is that she and love don't mix. I snort. "You don't think she's thinking of herself as well?"

"What do you know about a mother's love? It's not as if you ever had any."

Heartless! I am stung and mortified that she would say something like that, and in front of Adel, too. I tighten my lips and glower at her, waiting for an immediate apology. When none comes, I stare past her, focusing on our sailor. His galabia flaps along with the sail, which he draws and releases while steering the boat with his foot.

It started as a blustery day, and Dalal, with her usual impulsiveness, decided it would be fun to sail on a *felucca*. She dragged us to a boarding point in Maadi, a part of the city where there are no bridges to interrupt the feluccas' cruising. All the owners gave us a flat refusal, citing the unpredictable weather, except for a ruddy-faced man called El-Rayyes. He pointed to his small boat with its single sail and space for no more than six people and told us that he would take us, on the conditions that it would be a short trip and that we'd pay three times the normal rate.

"Girls, girls," Adel says. "We're here to enjoy ourselves, not bicker like a pair of parakeets." There are two benches running the width of the boat; I'm seated facing Dalal and Adel, whose backs are to El-Rayyes.

"Yes, indeed," Dalal says, and aims a playful jab at his stomach. The boat tips to the side and her knuckles brush the area under his navel. His face colors, a rush of crimson. Why does she have to embarrass him so? I fold my arms and look away, narrowing my eyes at the swaying line between river and land, softened to a blur in a stretch of fog. The wind has quieted, and the small wooden boat bobs over the gray water like a floundering piece of cork.

Dalal jumps to her feet and rocks the boat. Lifting an arm to the sky, she exclaims, "Ah, the sense of freedom on this rapturous river!"

"Sit down!"

She flashes me a grin. Even though her eyes differ in size, they glow equally with daring. I lunge forward. She yaps like a frisky pup and dodges my reach just as the boat tips to one side. She tumbles and would have done a belly flop over the side had Adel not reacted so quickly. He grabs her wrist, and my fantasy of fishing her out of the water—a soggy, trembling pink ball grimy with wilted river grass—is defeated. I've moved to their bench. I glare at her wrist, which has turned limp in his grip. Adel flops down on the middle of the bench and plants her on his other side.

"What are you trying to do?" It's the first time El-Rayyes has raised his voice. "I won't have anyone falling off my boat and drowning."

"No harm done," Dalal snaps back at him.

"Why do you want to play with your life like that?" El-Rayyes hollers. "You fall in, and I'll be the one blamed."

This time Dalal ignores him. She neatens her feathers and declares, "Ah, isn't this nice, the three of us together side by side."

El-Rayyes has not finished. "You think you're indestructible just because you're young? Do you want me to tell you how many youngsters this river has swallowed?"

Adel turns around. "Okay, ammi, we understand. Nothing happened. So let's just enjoy the rest of the trip."

"The rest of the trip?" El-Rayyes says scornfully. "I'll show you what's left of the trip." With that, he steers the felucca around . . . and then pauses. A wily patch of mist has crawled over us and enshrouded the boat. He cannot get his bearings.

19

DALAL

The felucca smells of rust and rotting wood. It—and everything else around us—has long since lost its charm. Everyone is quiet. The fog travels in sheets so thick that when I stretch out my arms, only my fingers are visible, looking like knobs of dough in the mist. My fingers dance: now you see them, now you don't. I do my best not to think about my father and how he had materialized at the door.

His voice had the intensity of gunfire, even though he wasn't making much noise. A numbing fear had spread through me as he bored through my confidence and ridiculed "this absurd amusement, this game of becoming a singer." I could do nothing more than cower in silence, as if my existence depended on it. "You make sure she stops this nonsense," he told my mother, "and removes all thought of ever becoming a singer. It won't happen. I won't allow it!" In the back of my mind I hoped that once he left I could still figure out a way to get what I wanted. But that vanished when I spotted my mother nodding her agreement. How would I be able to manage without her? With every bob of her head, I felt my dream of walking into that bright spotlight of fame shrinking. Even now it baffles me that she'd hid her intentions so well.

"You let them think what they want," Mama said to me once my father had left, "let them feel good about the conviction that they've won. Then you do your own thing."

My father's visit is not yet a distant memory. I would have liked to talk to Mariam about it, but nothing about her encourages me to do so. Even the fog can't soften her hardened face. The ghostly quietude remains, and to fill the void I start humming the catchy tune of a commercial about falafel. It's one of Sherif bey's most successful jingles, and I wonder whether, along with his youth, he has lost the ability to compose real songs.

"*Wah!*" Adel growls, finally deciding to spin some humor over our sodden little group. His face bursts out of a pocket of fog that envelops us, like a decapitated head, so close I smell the river's damp on him. Even though he hasn't startled me, I delight him by springing to the side with a whoop of alarm. I push his face away and then yip when he aims a peck of a kiss on the flat of my palm. He bursts out laughing. Then, noticing Mariam's unchanged surly expression, he kills it abruptly. And then there is only the sound of the gurgling water and El-Rayyes, grumbling and cursing into his chest.

He is lost; I know he is. We are rolling in a capsule of moist air. "It's either this way or that," I complain to Adel. "Why is he making it so complicated, turning the boat here and there? If he sticks to a straight line, we're bound to hit land." Beneath us the water sloshes and slaps the sides of the boat, and above us the sail flaps like wet laundry on a line. I look around once more, eager to catch sight of the horizon, a familiar rim that's gray with the city's pollution. Failing, I close my eyes and strain to pick up the hum of distant traffic. There is no sound, and I consider how impossible it is—how eerie!—that Cairo can suddenly turn noiseless like this. As the boat continues to rock over a river that has become more like an open sea, I feel betrayed by the city.

Adel growls again in an attempt to cheer me up. But my humor has dried up. From the moment we boarded, he has been flitting between Mariam and me like a merry bee unable to decide which flower is plumper with nectar. I order him to find out what's happening with El-Rayyes. As he slips away to the back of the boat, I casually slide closer to Mariam, confident that it's just her nervousness at being stuck in the middle of the river that has made her so gruff with me. She is stroking her bangs. "Stop it," she hisses when I tickle her under the nose.

"Come on, cousin, what's wrong with you? Just relax. We'll get back safe and sound."

"I'm not worried about that!"

"Well, what is it, then?" Not for the first time, I wonder whether she might be attracted to Adel. "Do you like him?" I whisper.

"Don't be ridiculous," she scoffs, and turns away. "We're just good friends."

Do I detect some hint of embarrassment, a little smile, perhaps? I scrutinize her face. "Come on, Mariam. You know you can tell me anything," I purr, shifting closer and nudging her with my shoulder.

"Sometimes you are unbearable," she snaps. "You had to get us into this predicament, didn't you. You had to pull us onto this boat in such weather. And now we are lost. Everything is about you. You are so selfish." She pushes me. "Go back to your side and leave me alone."

I slide away and lean over, running my fingers through the water. The mast breaks the wearisome drift with heart-joggling rumblings, as if the wood is about to crack and come tumbling down on us. Suddenly, *thwack!*

We shriek. Victim of the fog, the ibis did not expect to encounter a looming piece of lumber as it skimmed over the water. It drops between us like one of those garbage bombs in Imbaba. Shocked and shivering, it kicks its reed-thin legs as if they might pump some air through its dangling windpipe.

I yelp and blow on it, as if that might give it enough life to flop over and fly away. Mariam reaches out for it, and I do the same. We grab the bird at the same time. "Leave it," she says, but I hold on tighter. It's a fishy-smelling creature. The kicking stops and is replaced by an ominous shiver, as if the ibis's soul were rising in objection. I imagine it pecking us with that scythe-shaped beak. When it dies in our hands, we stare at it as if it double-crossed us.

Mariam pulls, and the skin ruptures. I yank at it, and a joint cracks. It's only when tiny insects start crawling out from between its sticky plumes that we throw it overboard. The bird vanishes in a glob of fog. Under the smack of the sails, I don't hear the splash.

⟡

It has been a month since I last saw Mariam on that foggy, soggy afternoon. We had ended the day with stiff nods and insincere promises to get together again soon. There were smiles just like the one that stretches my face at every party I attend. We couldn't very well part in a sulk, at least not in front of Adel.

He seemed to have been entertained by the quibbles and the bird drama. It's as if he'd looked forward to our taking it a step further, perhaps reaching the point of pulling each other's hair. But really, if I had to tell the truth, at the end of the day Mariam and I had reached an unspoken understanding: we would avoid seeing each other anytime in the near future.

I blow my frustration into the air, making sure not to disturb my smile, which shows just the faintest glimmer of teeth (Mama says you can never tell who might be watching). One glance at this medium-sized party is enough to convince me that the guests are interested in nothing more than the food and political blah-blah-blah. Tucked away in the corner is the unfortunate musician, ignored as he plucks at the strings of his oud.

Whatever harm had been done between Mariam and me can be fixed at a later stage, I suppose. Better to be cool for a while. That's an American expression Adel likes to use whenever I get restless or irritated. "Be cool." I whisper it under my breath, puckering my mouth the way Adel does as he stretches the word, always letting his hand glide in a straight line in front of him; it's a gesture that's meant to seem offhand, but it fails to obscure the intensity that sits in his eyes as he scrutinizes my every twitch.

That look! There is rawness, a dollop of the animal in it. It's not as if I've never seen it before. The first time I spotted it was in the eyes of a youth in Dubai. It was a few years back, soon after the straight lines of my girl's body filled and curved. The boy was nowhere near as handsome as Adel. He was a puny creature, the stubble of his beard covering too little of his hollow-cheeked face. He'd show up at the end of every school day as I made my way out through the gate. He always had the window of his Ford Mustang rolled down, even in the searing heat. The car was a mousy gray, with red seats and a powerful vroom to it. Two stickers bearing the logo of Al-Ahli football club were positioned on either side of the license plate.

With his sunglasses clinging to the tip of his nose, the boy would hook his elbow to the door so that he was half leaning out as he neared me. For a long time, I ignored him as he tried to lure me with those predatory glances. Then one day he changed his tactics and held up a cassette, twirling it between his fingers. When he threw it at me, it was a direct invitation for me to take the initiative: he'd jotted down his telephone number on the cassette. To his dismal luck, the supervisor caught him in the act, frowning at his effrontery. He blew me a kiss and zoomed off; she reported him.

There was the usual injunction, and the more humiliating punishment of having his name printed in the accident-and-legal page of *Al-Bayan* newspaper along with a head shot in which he looked like a convict. I never saw him again, but I'm sure he kept his car window rolled up for good after that.

We see each other, Adel and I, every so often, and even though I'm not sure what it will lead to, I do enjoy flirting with him. There's something liberating in it, a distraction I look forward to. But I couldn't resist asking whether he had seen Mariam. He dismissed my query with a wave of the hand. "She's a *zameela*," he said, and his nostrils flared as if the scent of rot had touched them. "Just a fellow student, that's all."

This party is so dull that I find my thoughts drifting to Mariam again. I miss her. Perhaps it's because we went through so much together as girls, trying to understand the pain of losing our fathers—whether in life or through death—and dreaming of the futures that were stolen from us. In the past, whatever quarrels took place between us could be ticked off as trivial, necessary to cement a lifelong bond. I could tell what her exact thoughts were while they were running through her mind. I could anticipate what she would say and how she would react to every situation. But she surprised me on the felucca; it was the first time she had been unpredictable.

The mood had soured so quickly that I hadn't gotten a chance to tell her about the songs I've been singing at some of these parties (all with the wrong crowd, it seems, since they have not led to anything), or about my first acting role, soon to be filmed. My mother met the director at one of these parties and somehow convinced him to include me. Who would believe it? But who would believe that Mariam and I would fight over a dead bird?

Whenever I remember those insects crawling out of the feathers, my hands feel dirty and I'm overwhelmed by the urge to soap them. That nasty lump of feathers and flesh, warm on my palms: the bird's death separated us like a barbed-wire fence. What were we trying to prove, tugging at it like that? I resist the temptation to rush to the bathroom and wipe my hands on my skirt. I shake the thoughts out of my head, because everyone knows that too much thinking doesn't benefit a soul.

"Ah!" There's my mother, ushering the director toward me. Sherif bey trails a couple of steps behind, wagging his head at the ground like a goat sniffing dry grass. He doesn't approve of my debut film role and warned us that it would do more harm than good in the long run. Mama didn't give him a chance to elaborate. She shut him up with an acid stare.

I rise. My smile broadens, and excitement propels me toward the director. Although it is not my aim to be an actress, Mama said it's a stepping-stone that might bring us closer to big fame. It's a tiny part: the hero, distraught by a misunderstanding he has had with his fiancée, goes to the beach at Maamoura. Heartbroken, he roams along the shore—when a beach ball accidentally hits him. And that's when I make my entrance. I'm playing the role of a beautiful young foreigner who runs into the scene to retrieve the ball. She is so grateful that when the hero hands it to her, she rewards him with a kiss on the cheek. Of course, the hero's fiancée sees all this, and that causes more problems for him.

"Ready for the big day?" asks the director.

"Of course she is," Mama replies. "This week she'll be on boiled chicken and vegetables. And only water, the day of."

"Absolutely," says the director. "Her tummy must be flat in the swimsuit. She has to look convincing as a European tourist."

Mama and the director laugh. "How should I enter the scene?" I ask, determined to get it right. It may be a minor film role, but this undertaking might just catapult my career. "Maybe a flirty jog?"

"On set, my dear, all will be revealed on set," says the director, and Sherif bey groans, obviously not happy at being left out. The director looks at him, amused. He cups Sherif bey's neck and says to my mother, "It seems like your fiancé is the one with nerves. *Ha-ha. Ha-ha-ha.*"

A middle-aged woman appears, insisting that she must introduce the director to her son instantly. As she leads him away, I cock my head at Mama. Fiancé?

"So why is that man always with you wherever you go?" the woman sitting next to me asks. "What is he to you?"

I know what I am supposed to say. I have memorized the line and can recite it in a single uninterrupted breath: Sherif bey, the esteemed composer, is a close family friend who has put his work to the side in order to accompany me and my mother and make sure we are not taken advantage of. Instead, I answer honestly: "I don't know."

There he is, Mama's absurd choice of a husband. The smile on my face stays fixed in place as I disdainfully watch him lurking by the buffet. He shifts the steel covers one by one and sniffs at the food. Is he to be my new father? The woman clicks her tongue. "Really," she says. "He's such an old pickle, isn't he?"

"Yes, he is," I reply without further thought. "And he'll be my stepfather soon."

"Hmm," she says. "I don't know whether that's a good thing, Dalal. For your career, I mean."

"My career?" I turn to look at her for the first time, and I can't help but stare, because there is so much to take in. She is a heap of a woman, with a bust like a pair of soldiers standing at attention. Her eyes are the size of buttons, but unlike plain buttons they are a yellow green and they glow. Her brocade hijab—a bronze color a few shades darker than her complexion—can hardly be considered religious; her full neck is showing! She's swathed in a turban that rises into a tilted mountain peak; a fancy knot at the top is held in place by a tear-shaped turquoise brooch that matches her dangling earrings. I shake my head and ask her how she knows me.

"I know more important things than your name, *habibchi*." She squeezes her teeth together so that the *t* of *habibti*—"my darling, my beloved"—turns to a *ch*, an enchanting twist to a word so versatile it can be used to express intimacy, friendship, sarcasm, or scorn just by changing the tone. "I know, for example, that you have a voice and flair. And your background, half-Emirati, half-Egyptian—ah! Dazzling!" She flings her arms to her sides as if opening the curtains of a stage. "Let's just say that you could become quite the shooting star."

"Have we met before?" Her flamboyant gestures inspire in me a mixture of irritation and unease.

"*Ah, ha, ha,*" she muses, grabbing my face in her palms like it's a melon. "Habibchi, ya habibchi, you don't need to know me. The important thing is that I know you, and your potential." With that she lets go of my face and makes a dramatic retreat back into her seat.

"What are you talking about?"

She shakes her head. Her face scrunches up, as if she's just taken a swig of cold, too-strong coffee. "What they are making you do—well, all I can say is *beware.*"

By this time, I have lost tolerance for this guessing game. In a fit of pique, I snap, "Who *are* you?"

She sighs and looks at me as if I am the dullest person on earth, then digs into her purse and pulls out a business card with her name on it. "Nivine Labeeb," she says, handing it to me, "but you can call me Madame Nivine. That's how I am known in the *bee-zee-ness.*" She uses the English word, stretching each syllable equally. I scan the card for her occupation; it isn't printed.

"Which business?"

"The fame business, of course. I make stars."

My eyes widen at this revelation. I make sure not to miss a word as she raps on about her expertise in the field of managing rising talents. By the time she has finished, I'm mesmerized by this woman.

"You see, *hayachi,* my life, you may have people around you who tell you they know what they are doing, that they're following the perfect path to get you to the top. But I bet that deep in your heart you know that something's not quite right. *Hmm?* I mean, with your talent, shouldn't you be famous by now?"

"You're right. I should be famous already." I'm not smiling any-more. A need for sympathy grips me, and I look to Madame Nivine. She is quite the opposite of my mother. With a face as broad and bright as a sunflower and that prominent bosom, she looks like a formidable source of protection. I want to nuzzle up to her. "It has been so diffi-cult, all the waiting, all the hoping. I'm like a yo-yo. One day I'm up, next day I'm down. Sometimes I feel I might lose my mind."

"Yes, habibchi, yes. I understand that you have put in so much energy already, and the only thing you are getting is disappointment."

"So much disappointment," I moan.

"Yes," she drawls, and pauses as if satisfied with the success of a hypnosis session. "My point, hayachi, is that I have experience and that all-important business sense—both qualities I can proudly say I've had since birth, in the genes, you might say—and when I see some-thing that might destroy potential, I have to speak out. And here it is, my bit of free advice: do not appear in that film in a swimsuit. The people, the public, will hate you. You'll kill whatever chance you have of a singing career."

20

MAJED

&

Saeed doesn't hear me as I let myself into the Neely an hour earlier than our usual meeting time of nine p.m. Bent over, with the sleeves of his kandora rolled up, he is emptying one of eight cartons of Heineken, part of our monthly supply of alcohol. He shoves the first load of cans into the fridge and then lets out a raspy laugh as he becomes aware of my presence.

"Welcome! Welcome!" he says, and rises to greet me with a nose press and a pat on the back. He is overjoyed; it's our first night together since my return from Cairo. It feels like a celebration that's long overdue, and Saeed launches into an account of what to expect tonight.

On Wednesdays we normally order from one of two restaurants: Yamal Al-Sham or Automatic. Mustafa places the order and delivers it around midnight, by which time we are badly in need of sustenance. We usually get a main dish of kebab or tikka (always with extra grilled onions), and all the accompanying essentials of a Lebanese spread: stuffed grape leaves, hummus, *mutabal* eggplant dip, *tabbouleh* and *fat-*

toush salads, and bitter black olives and bright-pink turnip pickles. But tonight our friend Mattar has insisted on cooking.

"You know how Mattar loves to cook," Saeed says. "He'll arrive smelling of Old Spice and leave stinking of kitchen. Right here!" Saeed bangs the table. "He'll take his drink with him and sit right here with a knife and a cutting board. And once he starts chopping those onions, he'll cry like a woman." It's a sight that never fails to improve our mood, and we burst out laughing just thinking about it.

"But never mind all that," Saeed adds with a conspiratorial wink. "I've arranged a surprise for later." He taps his temple and sways his head slightly with dreamy eyes to indicate high satisfaction. "Yes, you'll be happy as a camel lazing by a well."

I have a fair idea of what he's talking about, so I nod, still chuckling, while Saeed begins to brief me on the problem he's having with the cousins from Goa, a hotelier and a senior accountant. They provide us with a regular supply of alcohol; liquor licenses are issued only to non-Muslims, with a limit set according to salary bracket.

"Thomas is fine—and generous, maybe because he's surrounded by drinks all day—but Diego, well, he's all jittery that the police will find out he's supplying alcohol to Muslims. When I saw him he writhed like a worm, as if to say, *It's okay to get upset at me, but don't beat me up.* I said to him, 'Don't worry, man'—those Christians from Goa, they all pretend they have European blood, and they think *man* makes them sound white. Never mind that you can't see it in their skin color: soot!" He snickers. "Anyway, I tell him, 'The police have more important things to do. Don't you know that accountants are the most boring people in the world?'" Saeed lets out a hearty guffaw. "His face curdled, as if I had insulted his mother. And then he got sulky and refused, simply refused."

"So what did you do?"

He pulls a cigarette out of his pocket and lights it. "I insulted his mother, of course. After that, his sister, and then I slapped him with this." He kicks his sandal off his foot, and I grunt, shaking my head at the thought of a grown man cowering under blows from a sandal. "Not too hard, of course," he hurries to add, with a smirk. "Just enough for him to understand that I do not take kindly to people breaking an agreement."

"Did he hit back?" I ask, even though I know the near impossibility of a shy accountant—a foreigner at that, one who is an Indian even if he does believe that his heart is pumping liters of European blood— hitting the brash local bully.

Saeed's mouth warps as if there were dirt lodged between his teeth. "*Ykhassi, sibal*, he wouldn't dare, the monkey! The bastard was trembling with shock. He shrank and curled to the size of a football, and I had to hold back the urge to shoot him." He lifts his head and directs three hoops of smoke to the ceiling.

It's not his action that repels me. It's his lack of control. These modern times—when girls can defy men—make me fume, but I rein in my anger and use it constructively. I'm filled with a quiet glee when I think about the way I handled both Dalal and Mariam. I flung stone-hard words and gestures at them, stirred their fear, and broke their resolve, without resorting to barbarity.

Dalal and her mother will pack up and come back to Dubai, no doubt. Mariam, well, I'm now convinced that Cairo has brought out nothing but the worst in her. I'm still confounded by the way she tested me. What was she thinking? I suddenly decide to bring her back and marry her off before year's end.

I shake my head, emptying it of all thought to make space for gaiety. My gaze settles on the heavier spirits, the twelve bottles of Black Label whiskey that crowd in a group on the counter. "Well, you managed to find someone else to get our supplies, didn't you," I say. In addition, there are a couple of bottles of vodka and another two of gin—the preferred drink of the women who occasionally join us.

He chuckles and pours me a drink. I take it, and leave him to finish whatever he still needs to do in the kitchen. Settling on the couch in the sitting room, I inhale deeply. There's the familiar powdery scent of carpet cleaner and flowery air freshener. I feel youthful and robust. *All settled with that lot in Cairo*, I think as the ice cubes clink in my glass.

I pull a cigarette out of the box of Marlboros on the table. Unlike Saeed, who finishes a full pack every day, I only smoke at the Neely. Kicking off my sandals, I light it and take a long drag, rubbing my bare feet into the carpet, which is a deep navy color (the better to hide spills). The walls are a few shades lighter; we're surrounded by blue. More than once—when I'm particularly light-headed with drink and stumbling over the furniture—I've quipped, "I'm seasick." Every time, without fail, the fellows let out a boisterous laugh. *Good times tonight,* I think.

"All fine out there?" Saeed calls. "I'll be right with you."

"No hurry," I call back, and rub the glass's cool rim along my lips.

❦

Their eyes are half-closed, their mouths frozen into pouts of seduction. Arms stretch toward the ceiling, and hands twist. Chests jiggle and hips gyrate. But then they start bouncing on their feet with the same lack of grace as a camel's awkward trot on asphalt. We hoot with laughter at the girls' hopeless attempts to follow the rhythm of one of Mehad Hamad's older songs.

Saeed twirls his fingers at me to find out how I'm doing, and I answer with a cocky tilt of my head and a raised thumb: "Number one!" It's early still, and already this is turning out to be a wonderful evening, filled with snatches of touching and groping and nuzzling and fondling. Mattar is in the kitchen preparing *foga*, an Emirati dish of meat and rice cooked all together, not strained—or so he never tires of telling us—and mixed with tomato, onion, garlic, dried limes, and a special Khaleeji mix of Indian spices. Our friend Thani sits next to me; he's not a Neely regular, and only joins us once in a while.

Mustafa was here earlier, but he only stayed long enough to brighten the mood with a bit of clowning around. He left once the girls arrived. We have shed our ghitras, keeping our balding skulls covered with only the head caps. We slip off the couch to huddle in a semicircle around the coffee table, where we joke with the pair of dancing girls and cheer them on.

"What's so funny?" Mattar calls.

"Come join us and see for yourself," Saeed yells back.

One sniff and my stomach growls like tires on gravel. "What is that wonderful smell?"

"Only the best: cumin, turmeric, cardamom, cilantro, black pepper, red chiles!" Mattar calls out each herb and spice as if declaring the winners of some competition.

"Who cares?" says Saeed. "Come out here."

"Nearly done," Mattar says.

"Is same!" Zoya whines, stifling a giggle so that she can pretend to be upset. "*Pukka-puk-puk! Pukka-puk-puk!*" She has white-yellow hair, parted in the middle and so fine that her pink scalp shines every time she shakes her head. "No change in this music, habibi. You no get bored?" Her words are thick and slurred, a consequence of her Ukrainian roots and three glasses of vodka.

The other girl is called Galina. Emboldened by Zoya's complaining, she begs us to put on some Western music. Her mouth is as red as a ripe strawberry and her eyes are as blue as a sapphire. With such an appealing combination, men should find it impossible to refuse her requests. But there's a hardness in her voice that no woman should have—a hardness that I think must be linked to years facing blustering winter winds in her native Russia—and it makes me wince.

Recently we've had an influx of girls from the cold climes of the north. Before that, the girls Abu-George sent—he's Saeed's Syrian friend who works in a lingerie boutique—were from neighboring India or Iran, or farther afield, from the Levant or even the Philippines. Whoever they are, they come by taxi and we welcome them at the Neely.

They wear jeans and tight T-shirts that creep up their bellies every time they raise their arms, revealing skin so soft, so white it's as if they'd been rolled in baby powder. It's a refreshing change to eye the pair's luminous complexions and uninhibited Western ways, even if they are still rough around the edges and lack the kittenish grace of their Eastern counterparts. Long-limbed and lovely, they do what is expected to amuse us, to make us feel special—and they make no effort to mask their hunger for a quick profit. After all, they want the money that makes a better life.

Mattar emerges from the kitchen and topples next to us on the floor in a fit of joy. Thani hugs his folded knee to his chest with one arm and uses the other to whack the rhythm in the air, trying his best to instruct the girls, to somehow make the tune lose its foreignness to them. "*Dum-baka-baka-baka! Dum-baka-baka-baka!*"

"*Pukka-puk-puk?*" the girls insist, and we burst out laughing again. With tears in my eyes, I wave a finger and declare their request granted. Zoya hops like a happy schoolgirl. "*Da, da,* English music!"

Thani changes the cassette. But to Zoya's dismay, it's another Arabic singer, this time Abu Bakr Salem with his warbling voice. The girls let out a dramatic groan but are dancing again in no time, trying to swivel their hips like belly dancers.

"Hopeless!" shouts Mattar, rising off the floor on shaky legs and holding a glass at a precarious angle. I wonder whether we should let him back into the kitchen, with all those knives around. He reaches into his pocket, pulls out a couple of ten-dirham notes, and puts one on Zoya's head and the other on Galina's. I grin at his bravado; Mattar is the shiest of our lot. They retrieve the money as it slides down, and stare at it. "This means I like your dancing," he explains to the bemused girls. He has a silly grin on his face. "This is how we show appreciation to traditional dancers at weddings."

Galina holds the paper note from the corner as if someone had pissed on it. She wags it and says, "So little appreciation." A cruel smile deflates the plumpness of her strawberry mouth. "You big, you old, you rich. Why so miserly?"

He lunges away from her, spilling some of his drink on the carpet. He is embarrassed at her slight—and in front of us, too! He mumbles something about its being nothing more than a gesture of fun before hurrying off to the safety and solitude of the kitchen.

"What do you think you are doing?" Saeed springs to his feet and raises a fist. Galina recoils. But Saeed does not strike her; he knows that hitting a woman is cowardly.

"I no do nothing. I make joke," says Galina.

"It's okay, it's okay," says Thani, eager to keep the peace.

"No respect!" Saeed grabs her arm and drags her into the kitchen so she can apologize to Mattar. We steal glances through the open doorway; she does so willingly, and even sits on his lap. Our mild-mannered friend pats her on the back to indicate that all is well. Once they return, the group does its best to recover the revelry of earlier by playing some upbeat Bedouin music by Samira Toufiq. Thani leaps into the air with renewed gusto. He grabs one of the bamboo canes stacked in a bin next to the cassette player and twirls it between his fingers while dancing to the beat. Saeed joins him, reaching for another cane, which he holds between his thumb and index finger. Together they perform the traditional *Ayala* dance, swinging their canes to the right and then to the left in a gentle sway while bobbing their heads as if in a trance.

This should be enough to lighten my mood, but I look back at Mattar. His droopy eyes hold the expression of an abandoned dog. Slumped in a chair, he looks around the kitchen, seeming confused as to what he should do next. Obviously he is still shaken. This makes my blood boil, and I think of all the women who find pleasure in playing with my emotions: Zohra, Dalal, and now Mariam.

I had my eye on Zoya, but I decide to conquer Galina instead. I will not be gentle. I'll take her to the bedroom and ride her until she can't walk. I'll pin her down and take pleasure in hearing her gasp. When she struggles, I'll pull her hair. When she squeals, I'll press her head down with my open hand until she's choking on the pillow, until she learns her place, until she begs me to let her go.

The music blares on, but Saeed and Thani freeze, puzzled at my swift and sudden launch into their midst. Galina's wrist is bony in my grip, and I jerk her toward the bedroom. Saeed breaks out into a raucous cackle that I can hear even after I've slammed the bedroom door shut.

The heat that builds in my loins is volcanic. I fling Galina onto the bed; I expect to hear her cry out in protest. Instead she closes her eyes and mews, stretching every limb, every muscle, like a cat sprawled on fresh grass under the sun. No matter!

For a moment I see two of her. But a tight blink fixes that, and I reach for her T-shirt, removing it with a violent tug that musses her hair. I pull back and take a sharp breath that doubles the size of my chest. (Surely she will cower.) Her chest is bare. When she unbuttons her jeans and kicks them off, I waste no more time and flop like a plank of wood on top of her. Finally she squeals. But there is no fear in it. Only lechery.

It's not the way I imagined it. But this is just the beginning. And break her I will.

I force her head into the pillow. She starts sucking my fingers.

I pin her down with my weight so she can't move. She wriggles. Then smiles.

I squeeze her ribs. She giggles. Then grins.

I pull her hair. She screams. Then laughs.

What creature is this?

There is but one thing to do. And that's when I realize I am still fully clothed, swimming in swathes of fabric. She is positioned and ready. My elbow digs into her chest as I prop myself up to wrench up my kandora and kick off my wizar. And then I am in her.

My eyes burn. Little rivers of sweat trickle along the sides of my forehead. Every thrust is coupled with a hoarse grunt that seems to explode from somewhere deep in my belly. I ignore it all.

Her tiny nose quivers, and I wedge two fingers into her nostrils. My other hand grips her neck. "Let this be a lesson!" She doesn't understand Arabic, but nevertheless she does her best to respond: a gasp and a squeak burst out of her trembling lips. Strangely, they are turning the same shade of blue as the Neely walls.

She kicks. I hold her ankles in place. Smothered under the mass of my body, she feels as flat, as lifeless, as a piece of cardboard.

Just as Galina's eyes start rolling in their sockets, some hellish force erupts in my head, flashing images of my daughter, Dalal, pinned under vulgar old men. I cry out in my head. And somehow, I am heard.

Hands are all over me. Like the tentacles of an octopus, they slither under my armpits, grip my wrists, hug my tummy, and tug at my ankles. I am pulled off the bed and pushed to the side. I punch the air, and the effort makes me dizzy. My head hits something, and as I crumple to the ground, my vision darkens.

A hoarse, persistent cough brings me back. I squint at the bed: Saeed, Mattar, and Thani huddle around it. There's that other girl—I forget her name—with the white-yellow hair, too. She screams and points a finger at me, and this makes my head throb. Thani blocks her, but she pushes him to the side and jumps at me. She slaps me, spits on me, before Thani pulls her away.

So many things happen around me, and so quickly, that I cannot make sense of what is going on. I am about to object, to demand to know why my friends have burst into my moment of privacy, but a sense of foreboding washes over me. Something significant has just happened.

21

DALAL

I have been waiting the better part of the day to act my part. I have endured not just the early wake-up and morning flies, the sticky sand and midday heat, but also a heavy feeling of dread about what the director will say once I tell him that I won't be wearing a swimsuit in my scene. There's my mother to deal with, as well.

All week long I have wanted to tell her about my agreement with Madame Nivine. My plan was to wait for her to defend her choice to marry Sherif bey. Then I'd simply produce the signed contract. And she would have to accept it; after all, she was the first one to make a secret decision. When days passed and she still had not brought up Sherif bey, I decided to just tell her anyway. I convinced myself there was nothing to it; I filled my lungs with resolve. But, sadly, my courage proved to be less solid than I had anticipated. The result: half-witted mutterings and an increasingly deflated sense of daring, things I had never expected from myself. And now it's too late; I've run out of time.

I try to make myself as comfortable as I can, but I'm wearing jeans so tight they could be a second skin. I'm sitting on a blanket next to my mother, watching the filming from a distance. I yawn and ease back onto my elbows; my foot knocks the empty lunch box. This sets off a long growl in my stomach. Mama had given me an apple earlier but, without a second thought, handed the sandwich and Qaha guava juice to a member of the crew. The sandwich had had a stale-looking bun, turned moist on the inside from the squished tomato slice that sat on top of the chunk of dry Roumy cheese; a wilted piece of lettuce peeked out the edge. I wasn't hungry then as I watched him devour it. But thinking of it now makes my mouth water.

Even though we are in the shade of a leafy tree, Mama wears a red large-brimmed hat that matches the sunglasses that cover most of her face. She sits with her back straight, prim, her legs folded beneath her and to the side. "This is the most boring day of my life!" I joke. It's an attempt to break her stillness, but it comes out as a whine. I wait for a response, a softening of that rigid spine, an indication that she might want to chat. It would be the perfect introduction to what I have to say. She doesn't answer, just stares ahead at the director and the crew.

They've been shooting in the same spot all morning. The crew cordoned off a square of sand using yellow caution tape. It looks like a crime scene from an American detective series. The director has been barking his instructions into a loudspeaker, making the hero (balding and unknown) and heroine (insipid, also unknown) repeat their lines more times than I can count.

Even though the director found an area far from Maamoura's crowd, some small boys sniffed him out and made a game of dipping under the yellow tape. They were delighted when even the youngest members of the crew were not able to catch them. That was many hours ago, back when the thought of making a movie was fresh and exciting for all of us.

It's late afternoon and finally a breeze picks up, tumbling waves in a hiss of slaps along the shoreline. The sun's light glows warmer. Even I can recognize that the light is changing. "Isn't my scene supposed to be happening in the middle of what they've been filming all day? I mean, look, Mama." I hold my arm under the sun's tangerine tinge, so different from the glaring rays of earlier. "I mean, who would believe..."

"I made the very same point to the director this morning," she says. "'Won't the viewer notice?' He said, 'In my experience, Arab viewers don't let such tiny things bother them. They have been conditioned to overlook such discrepancies. They just fill in the gaps.'"

She coughs up a chuckle, and it's as much incentive as I need for my confession. "You know, Mama, I've been thinking quite a bit this week, and maybe it's better if I don't wear the swimsuit for this scene."

She slides the sunglasses to the tip of her nose. "What are you talking about?"

Someone calls me from the shore. It's the bodybuilder extra whose role is to throw the beach ball that goes astray. He waves at me to indicate that they'll be filming my scene soon. It's the fifth time he has done this. I ignore him and focus on my mother. "Well, I've been asking around, and this is the kind of move that could come back to haunt me once I'm famous. Reporters are always looking for a scandal. Imagine the headlines, Mama: 'The Great Dalal: Naked,' or 'The Great Dalal: Is She the Right Role Model for the Arab Youth?' Or 'The Great Dalal: Something, Something, Something.'" I pause. "Well, that's what I'm thinking, anyway."

She pushes her sunglasses back up. "How many times have I told you, Dalal? You shouldn't waste your time thinking; this requires a special kind of intelligence. Why are you picking on such small details when there is a bigger picture to see, when you have me to depend on?"

My mouth dries up. It hurts that she never wants my opinion. I look toward the shore, where it seems that this time the bodybuilder extra was right after all. All those countless takes of heated arguments between the hero and heroine have finally produced a noteworthy performance. The director seems satisfied. He has stopped barking instructions into the loudspeaker. The crew claps, and he raises his arms and jogs around the inner boundary of the yellow tape as if he's just won a boxing match.

"Well, get up," she orders. "They're calling you."

"It feels wrong," I say, staying where I am.

"Look," she says, "your hesitation must be because you're nervous—who wouldn't be, hmm?—but it's a lovely swimsuit, with flowers and frills." She removes her hat and sunglasses and glares at me. "And you're going to wear it."

❧

"Every song that comes out of your mouth will increase the bulge in her pocket." It's been an exhausting day, but Mama's fury shocks the fatigue out of my limbs. She waves the agreement in the air like a fly-swatter before shoving it so close to my face that I can smell the ink. "Did you bother to read what was written here? It says that seventy percent of all the money you make in performances will go to her."

"Yes, but at least there will be concerts and soirees, private and public. Look again, Mama. You're missing all the good bits, everything she is required to deliver: three albums, and three video clips of the primary songs." I create a mental picture of what I'll wear and how I'll move in those music videos, which will be repeated often on all the satellite television channels. I'd like to dwell on the image, let it blossom, but this is the wrong time. Mama jerks on her feet, looking like a sparrow caught in sticky mud. A hard blue vein pops out of the middle of her forehead. I haven't seen her this agitated since my father dismissed her as his wife and put an end to any hope of comfort in our lives. "And don't forget," I add with a surge of passion, "she'll manage my life, introduce me to the right people, build my career, too."

"You are to pay thirty percent of the cost of production of each album. Where are you going to get that money?"

"That's easy. I'll manage." It's something I haven't thought about.

"Listen to what I am saying, Dalal. Eighty-five percent of the profit from the sales of the cassettes will go into her pocket."

I was convinced I had signed a fair deal, but Mama is getting my head all muddled as she keeps throwing big numbers at me. Was I too hasty in signing the three-year contract? Surely Madame Nivine couldn't have taken advantage of me. Where is Mariam when I need her? She would be able to give me a fair analysis. I roll my eyes and mumble into my chest, "At least there will be cassettes."

"What was that?"

I consider pointing out that Madame Nivine's share is high because she is the expert, the one who will be doing all the work; that's what my flamboyant manageress kept telling me at the party. Once I had nodded my agreement, she'd pulled two sheets of paper out of her purse as naturally as one would reach for a hankie. I must admit I didn't look at the neat letters as carefully as I should have; I was satisfied by her explanation of the main points. My blood pumped at double speed and the tips of my fingers felt fat with opportunity when she handed me a gold fountain pen to sign with. The very next day we met at the registration office at eight in the morning—ooh, so early!—to make it all legal. Two witnesses were grabbed off the street, and the official signed and stamped both copies in a faded but nevertheless attractive shade of blue-green ink. How simple it all was. And what pleasure I got by making such a bold move, and, more important, by the thought that I had gotten back at Mama for getting engaged to that shriveled-up Sherif Nasr without telling me.

"And who is this Nivine Labeeb woman, anyway? What do you know about her?"

It is late, and my head is dizzy with all her questions. What a day it has been! I had upset Mama when I held fast to my decision not to wear the frilly bathing suit. And then I had to face the director's displeasure, though that only lasted a few minutes because he was concerned about losing the light. In fact, he understood my point once I explained it to him. Mama didn't, though. And right at the end, just before we boarded the bus back to Cairo, I told her about the contract.

On that dim yet lively bus there was a sense of lightness and pleasant fatigue that only a day by the sea can produce. One of the crew members pulled out a *tablah* as we began moving. Hugging the drum under his armpit, his fingers twisted along the edges to release a string of raps. Then a second drum, a tambourine, materialized. Its owner, slumped a couple of seats behind the driver, held it up and shook it to add an accompanying jangle. The metal jingles along the rim looked like golden fish shimmering on the surface of an inky sea.

The duo prompted the first burst of song. "*Salma, ya salama*, we went and came with *salama*." The passengers clapped and swayed. The rhythm was irresistible, and every now and then the driver would add honks from his horn. It took all my effort to resist joining in, but there was my mother, sitting next to me at the back of the bus, staring out past her frozen reflection into the starless night.

Snacks and soft drinks surfaced between songs and were passed from hand to hand. The wind blowing through the open windows carried the smell of eggs and *libb*, roasted pumpkin seeds. Mama would not eat. I didn't eat either, swallowing my saliva instead as I concentrated on breaking her stillness. I fancy I acted maturely as I made light talk about Madame Nivine's bubbly character and promised to show her the contract once we arrived home. But Mama remained silent for the entire five-hour trip through the desert.

It wasn't a good sign. This was the first time I had disobeyed her, after all. I could have left her and joined the others, singing and dancing and clapping and snacking. I'd hardly eaten a thing all day, and my empty stomach growled. But I stayed where I was, a daughter tugging at the thin string of hope that her mother might sigh and say, "Whatever you feel is best, dear." Or perhaps she would pat my shoulder and offer me a kindly gaze filled with the special admiration only a mother can have for her child—all sentimental fluff, really.

"How can you trust her without knowing what sludge she's molded out of?" Mama blathers on, but I picture Madame Nivine's face, so bright and open, and some of the doubt dissolves and is replaced by a new wave of defiance. I would like nothing more than to charge out of the apartment and not come back. Ever. I'm sure Madame Nivine would take me in. After all, she is now officially my partner, which makes her my protector, too. But a retreat would be perceived as defeat. So I stay put.

Mama's eyes have paled to the color of melting ice. It's unsettling to look at them. "Congratulations," she says. "For the next few years, you will belong to her."

Crossing my arms, I direct my stare at the wall and wonder why I am not feeling the satisfaction I had expected from seeing Mama so alarmed, and from proving to her that I can make decisions on my own.

"How could you do this?" she hisses. "How could you throw away everything we have worked for?" She waits for an answer, but my lips stay tight. This enrages her further. She shouts, "What were you thinking?" She flings the contract in the air and marches out onto the balcony.

I am surprised by my self-restraint, which has exhausted her, and a little proud of it, too. I decide right then to perfect an emotionless face by practicing it in front of the mirror. I will need it when I am famous. If one of the reporters—doubtless there will be many who will want to interview me—decides to get bold and asks a question I don't want to answer, I can just summon this statuelike expression. My prolonged silence, my sour face, would be enough to kill every curious cell in him. *Hah!*

Well, maybe not. At some point in the middle of my reverie, Mama has crept back in, rejuvenated by the foul air rising from the street below. "How can you be so selfish? I've put all your needs ahead of mine so you can become successful and live in comfort in the future, so you are not at the mercy of your father, so you won't need anyone anymore."

I blow up. "That's a lie! How can you say something like that when all you want is to share Sherif bey's bed? You didn't consult me when you decided to take him as a husband, did you?" I picture their bodies snuggled, their shapes curving into a precise fit, like two spoons one on top of the other. "It's disgusting!"

She raises a hand and I wait for it. I tilt my head to one side so that the full surface of my cheek is open, a dare to what may come. A thought hisses and grows, with the urgency of a screaming kettle: If she slaps me, I vow never to talk to her again. I'm not a child anymore.

But Mama rounds her knuckles into a fist, as if deciding that a slap is not good enough, that a punch might be more appropriate to dent her daughter's outburst. What would that do to my face? Could I become famous as the singer with the bulbul voice and broken front teeth? Madame Nivine said that for the best result in the world of fame and music, an enchanting voice must always be partnered with beauty. Alarmed, I drop to the floor and stay there, curled up like a tortoise.

"Oh, get up."

"No."

"You are even sillier than I thought."

I don't look up. I'm sure she is waiting for me to reveal a soft spot. The next thing I hear is her bedroom door. It closes with a hard thud.

22

MAJED

The Neely stinks of cigarettes, booze, and onions. Saeed had insisted that I stay put and let him take charge. My head spinning, I'd passed out on the floor. He should be coming back soon. I open the balcony door and groan at the lingering ache in my head. Peering down below, I half expect Saeed's Nissan Patrol to veer into the parking lot, for him to hop out with a broad and reassuring grin that heralds his success in taking care of last night's unsavory business.

Noon. What is taking him so long? A flood of impatience has me dialing his cell phone number repeatedly. (Ah, where is the man!) When it keeps disconnecting, I stomp back into the apartment, still shocked that things had gotten so thoroughly out of control.

Some bizarre fit—that's the only word for it—takes hold of me: a bout of weakness and shivering that propels me to the bathroom, where I throw up. Galina's strawberry lips had turned blue. How could I not have seen it? She was struggling. She was choking. How could I not have heard it? I splash my face with cold water, then stare at it in the mirror; it is stripped of its color, like a dying leaf. I curse

Satan's water for having blinded me, for having dulled my conscience to the point that I'd nearly killed the girl.

Back in the living room I frown at the empty glasses and cigarette ash on the table, at the pillows strewn on the floor and the sticks we'd used for that ridiculous dance. There's something else, too: a string of amber worry beads that Hareb gave me. I pick it up and flop onto the couch, wondering who had retrieved it from the cabinet drawer.

My brother bought the beads sometime in the early 1970s, when the company first started making real money. He paid a grand sum of two thousand Indian rupees to a merchant in Bombay. It was the first time he had bought anything expensive. And he chose to give the gift to me.

"Because we are one," he had said. Judging by his expression, he believed it to be a profound truth, impossible to dispute, and I had found myself nodding vehemently, convinced of our sameness. After all, we were brothers brought up in the same household, part of the people of the palms.

As a boy I'd often helped Hareb at the palm grove, removing the dead leaves and debris from the dug-up water channels or pruning the trees. We'd secure ropes around our waists and scramble up the date palms in a competition to see who was faster. It didn't matter to him that I almost always won. But on the occasions when he won, I would sink into a dull, black mood. He'd slap me and tell me not to be such a sissy. Then, as if remembering the age difference, he'd pinch my cheeks until they turned red: a demonstration of his love for me that was no less painful than the slaps. I was ten; he was nine years older.

Lost in the memory, I'm hardly aware of the beads sliding between my fingers, clicking in a fluid rhythm that eases my impatience. I'm pulled back further into that past shared with Hareb. Under a dome of sky that traps a harsh light and the burn of the sun, we hold our heads up to catch a whimper of a breeze. There's the *seih*, strewn with umbrella-crowned desert acacias. How many times did he drag me along the broad expanse of the valley to hunt for honey? With a wide-mouthed earthen jar hugged to his waist, Hareb enjoyed the search, and after he'd nicked the honeycomb from the bees and stored it safely in the jar under a muslin cloth, he would insist on sharing it with the neighbors. With a grand smile, he would watch my face sour as I divided the find.

I smell the dry dust. Barefoot on the scalding earth, with tattered kandoras and sun-bleached wizars pulled up and knotted securely at the waist, we would dart on the balls of our feet from one patch of shade to the next, moving in zigzags to avoid the dried-up plant pods, spiral-shaped and prickly and the scatterings of half-buried acacia thorns. Once, trotting back home along the seih after we'd found a particularly large nest, I stepped with my full weight on one of those needle-sharp thorns. I remember squealing like a woman as I fell back, and I raised my foot so that Hareb could pull it out.

Along with a few stray bees that followed the scent of their honey in a dizzy pursuit, a cluster of buzzing flies zoomed around the jar. They changed course upon scenting the blood on the bottom of my foot. I cursed them. I cursed the thorn. I cursed the tree.

In that moment, as payment for my injury, I decided I would no longer distribute the honey equally. The burn, the sweat, and the throbbing hole in my foot: they were enough to convince me that I should keep as much as I dared from a honey jar that I considered mine by right. I did so with no guilt, and over time I grew bolder, held back a little bit more, always ready to argue my case if Hareb ever discovered that I'd kept more than my share. He never did.

I search for a hint of sameness. I'm mulling over how my brother and I shared an upbringing but not a way of thinking when my phone rings. Saeed has arrived.

He steers the car out of traffic and onto a relatively empty road. He offers me a cigarette and I light it, pulling in three long, deep drags. Smoke enters through my mouth and exits through my nose. The nicotine shoots to my brain, but it fails to satisfy me. "Tell me."

Saeed rubs the stubble on his cheeks. "Well, we brought the doctor."

"What?"

"Don't worry. He's a discreet old man who Abu-George uses to deal with all kinds of medical issues concerning his girls. Nothing broken, according to the doctor—just some bruising here." He strokes his neck.

This should relieve me, but the scowl that's been plastered on my face since last night's incident stays put. The questions loom in my mind like barbed wire. "Stop trickling information! What does the bitch want?"

"She's completely on edge. She would have gone to the police had we not taken charge right away," Saeed says. "Abu-George and I warned her to think before she acts, because she's in a conservative Muslim country. A girl in an apartment filled with men—especially a girl who is selling her services—would not be believed! We told her that the first thing the police would say is, 'What were you doing there in the first place? You asked for it.' We told her she'd be thrown in jail and, once she'd served her time, deported."

A police report—and that could lead to a court case! It would be her word against mine. Even if it all went against her, there's no guarantee that word of what happened would not get out. Society is fickle. All it takes is a single scandalous whisper. I would be branded. It wouldn't affect my success as a businessman, but it would discredit me in the eyes of my peers, make me a laughingstock: Majed Al-Naseemy, notorious for assaulting whores.

"These Western types," Saeed says, "love to make a big fuss out of everything—no respect for discretion. I talked to her like a kind father, gentle, you know, explaining that that's not the way to resolve a small problem. And, stupid cow that she is, she blew up." He sighs through his teeth. "I guess it's because she's shaken. Yes, very upset."

Right now, the last thing I care about is how shaken or upset she is. "Yes, yes, of course she has to act like she is," I say through clenched teeth. "This whole drama is nothing more than a neat little deception. Isn't that how these girls are, always acting this role or that?"

He opens his mouth, but one glance at my bulging eyes and he fixes his sight back on the road. He's driving toward my house. He says, "Abu-George—he stayed with her—had the doctor give her some sedatives. So she's calm, in a better state to listen to him. Let's just wait and see what happens. Don't worry, everything will be solved, insha'Allah."

"Solved? What, angels will descend and make this go away? Did you offer her money?"

"She won't take it."

"Why not?"

He takes a sharp breath through tobacco-stained teeth. Every minute drags as I wait for an answer. I suddenly understand. He has failed.

My agitation is a worm in my gut. It slithers; it pauses. And when it bites, I pound the dashboard. "I should have dealt with the situation myself! This is all your fault, you know," I say, "you and that bastard Abu-George. Bringing such girls to the Neely!" My tone is fierce, relentless. "The most you can handle is keeping the Neely stocked. Anything beyond that is too hard for you. Have you ever done anything right?"

"Now, wait a second." He looks hurt, but knowing Saeed, it's certainly an act. "I—"

"*Chup, chup, chup!* Shut up! No, you listen to me. You are going to take me home and wait for me while I freshen up. Then you will take me to the slut so I can put an end to this mess."

At the house, I am beset by a brooding anger as I shower and change into a fresh kandora. I grab a wad of hundred-dollar bills from the safe and slip them into my pocket. Aisha arrives home from an outing and finds me in the kitchen, gobbling down the last bite of a sandwich.

"Your eyes look like someone poured kerosene in them," she says. "And why is Saeed waiting outside? The doorman told me he brought you here. Where is your car?"

"At the garage."

"What's wrong with it?"

"How should I know? Do I look like a mechanic?"

"I mean, what happened?"

"It broke down."

"Did it happen last night? Is that why you didn't come home?"

"What's wrong with you, woman? You want to know about the sore and its medicine?" my voice thunders, silencing her abruptly.

❦

I drive Saeed's car. He sits next to me and indicates the way. My grip on the steering wheel is tight as I cross Al-Maktoum Bridge and head toward Meena Bazaar in Bur Dubai. Once we reach the Ramada Hotel, I make a U-turn and enter the first of the smaller streets behind it. The buildings here are medium-sized, rising no higher than ten floors. We pass one that has been turned into a hotel. I miss the name but catch the sign at the entrance: VALET PARKING WITH DRIVERS.

It's 2:15 p.m. A school bus in front of me keeps stopping at curbs and corners. I want to finish this business with Galina the Russian as soon as possible, but I don't overtake the bus, just stare at the bundles of noisy children hopping off. The delay gives me a chance to think.

Much as I'd like to break her neck as soon as I see her, getting physical would only inflame the situation. She will be angry; of that I am sure. She will probably curse me. I decide I must rise above all that and deal with her using words only—strong words, and perhaps, if she is sensible, a few gentle words, too—as I urge her to take the money. It's the sight of the dollars, clean and crisp, that will tame her.

"There, right there." Saeed points to a mud-colored six-story build-ing with cement troughs for balconies, and suddenly I can't wait to con-front her. I honk the horn, and the three cars behind me do the same.

The elevator smells of coconut hair oil and stale sweat. Saeed presses a button. The second-floor corridor is broad and dim. Lunch-time noises seep from behind apartment doors, along with the pun-gent whiff of fried onions and heavily spiced Indian curry.

Her apartment is three doors down, and Abu-George is outside, punching numbers on his phone as he waits for our arrival. He wears a striped shirt with the top buttons undone, showing off a thick gold chain nestled in chest hair. His jeans are so tight—his flab is pinched into a tube around his waist, his crotch squished in a trap that looks so painful I find I'm jiggling my hips to make sure all the equipment between my legs can move freely—that I wonder why he needs that cowboy belt to hold it up. He puts his phone in his pocket and tells me that the effect of the pill the doctor had given her has worn off. "Now, it won't help to lose one's temper," he adds with some hesitation. "We have to be calm."

"Of course," I say, giving him an icy stare.

"Right," he says, and rakes his hair—shiny and slick with oil—back with his hand before turning toward her apartment. He knocks, but to our surprise the door across the way cracks open in response. We turn around and see a small girl with a red thumbprint bindi on her forehead. She stares at us with big black eyes that brim with dis-trust. I crouch to her height and scold her in Urdu. "Who called you?" I hiss. "Get back inside." The alarmed girl retreats just as cold air blows on my back.

None of us is fast enough. The Russian slams the door before we can slip in. "I no want to see heem," she yells from behind the closed door. "You go away now."

Abu-George shakes his head. "They are so stupid sometimes, these girls." He pulls out a chain clanging with keys and tools and inserts one into the lock. With a few pokes and twists, he unlocks the door. And we're in.

Galina is not surprised by our successful entry. She stands with her back to the window at the far end of the room, holding a phone. "You move to me and I call polices."

Instinctively, I motion to Saeed to go down and wait by the car so he can warn us if any cops show up. Abu-George tries to reason with her. "Come on, Galina," he says. "What do you think? We're here to hurt you?" He touches his heart. "We are friends."

Looking at her, she could be any Western tourist. She wears a long summer dress with bright flowers. A scarf is tied around her neck, and this makes me wonder how severe the bruising is. As if reading my mind, she pulls it off. The bruise is the color and texture of a rotten date. "He keeler." She spits out the accusation and adds strength to it with a string of Russian profanities. "He try keel me."

"I'm here only to talk," I say, taking out the money and counting it note by note. "I am here to tell you that whatever you want, I am ready to help."

"You no can buy me," she shouts, pointing the phone at me as though it were a pistol. "Dirty man!" Her mouth is warped with scorn, and I puzzle over how I ever compared it to a strawberry.

She is ludicrous. And here I am, forced to bear her insolence. Stuffing the money back into my pocket, I shake my head to keep from losing my temper and glare at the beaded curtain to her right that must lead to the bedroom. It quivers and clacks with every gust blown by the noisy air-conditioning unit.

"Galina, habibti," says Abu-George in a voice filled with boredom, "put the phone down." She hesitates a little before plunking it on the windowsill, within her reach. Abu-George takes a few steps toward her. "You are here on a one-month tourist visa. Why do you want to go and ruin your stay? Come on, Galina. You don't want that."

He goes on mollifying the girl. I have no interest in this petty rapport between pimp and prostitute. But I'm obliged to wait for the outcome. My gaze drifts around the apartment. It's a no-nonsense place filled with furniture that looks little better than a laborer's— probably somebody else's discarded goods placed next to the city rubbish dumps for collection. She has a stained pale-green couch, scratched-up plastic chairs pocked with cigarette burns, and cheap wobbly lamps swathed with flimsy crimson scarves. A pile of thin foam mattresses is stacked against a wall; the crumpled sheets on top indicate that the apartment either is shared by a number of people—girls in the same line of work, no doubt—or is a place of business, a pleasure den.

"I promised our friend in Russia that I would protect you," Abu-George says to her, "but I won't be able to do anything if you go to the police and they throw you in jail. What would he say if I told him how unreasonable you are being, hmm?"

She stiffens at the mention of this friend. (Who is this person?) "I tell Sergei he want keel me," she mumbles into her chest.

"Come on, there's no need for so much talk. We can end this right now. All I'm asking for is a little help from you." Abu-George makes a pinching gesture with his fingers. "Small-small only."

"No small." She turns to look at me. Her eyes are as hard as pellets of blue ice. "Thees beeg theeng."

"He good man, Galina!" Abu-George waves his arms in exasperation. "You want breaking his house? He have wife, childrens, grand-childrens."

"Yes, why he not be with them? Because he feelthy old man."

The hangover has not gone away completely. I feel it acutely in a surge of heat that explodes in my head. I frown and rub my forehead.

"Listen, Abu-George," I say through clenched teeth, "I think there's no point in continuing." I turn to the girl and attempt a magnanimous smile, tightening every facial muscle to lock it in place. "I'll say what I have to say just one more time: I didn't mean to hurt you. I'm prepared to make up for that." I pull out the money and fling it in the air. My smile evaporates as the banknotes float to the ground. "Now take it! And get the hell out of my life!"

"I no want your dirty money," she screams. "I want you to walk to me on knees. I want you put head on ground next to my feet. I want you to beg I forgeev you."

What patience I had left has depleted. In an attempt to control my aggravation, I clap my hands. The suddenness of it makes her jump. She grabs the phone and dials. "Ello, polices?"

I react just as swiftly, lunging forward and knocking the receiver out of her hand. It falls to the ground, where Abu-George stomps on it as though it were a scurrying rat. She swings an arm at my face, but I shift to the side. She is hysterical! I make a grab at her from behind and secure her in a powerful grip. She struggles but is unable to lash out. From the corner of my eye I spot Abu-George with his mobile phone glued to his ear. His face lights up. He says, "Hello? Sergei?"

I don't know who this Sergei is, but the mention of his name has an effect on Galina that is nothing short of a miracle. Moments earlier she was tight-limbed with hysteria, spitting curses at me. Now she turns wobbly like jelly, and I let her go lest my grip leave dents in her bones.

"He wants to talk to you," Abu-George says to her, disregarding her obvious distress as he shoves his mobile phone into her hand.

I am riveted in place, unable to take my eyes off her as the color drains from her face and her voice lowers to a whimper. From wildcat to rabbit: I am baffled by the transformation. Who is this Sergei, and why is she so scared of him? Engrossed in the conversation, Galina drifts toward the window, looking like someone shouldering a heavy burden. I turn to Abu-George, who is busy cooling off. He dabs the sweat off his face with a starched handkerchief, then ruffles his shirt, whipping a breeze through his springy chest hairs. Once he spots my confusion, he signals me to follow him out into the corridor.

The snoopy little girl with the bindi isn't the only one who has heard the ruckus. Every other occupant of this damned floor—clusters of Asian families, including a shrunken gray-haired granny—peers out from their apartments. Abu-George waves his arms and yells at them to get back in.

Once we're alone, his voice lowers, as if the walls might have ears. "Sergei is their protector in Russia," he says. "I know him from when I was studying in Moscow in the early '80s. For a long time we weren't in touch because he got involved in a number of shady dealings. But now, well . . . with this new demand for Russian girls, what can I say?" There must be a disapproving expression on my face, because he quickly adds, "I'm not close to him. I'm just a service provider—strictly entertainment, nothing more. No drugs, no money laundering, no black market, no bribery. That's not me." He sniffs. "It's only recently that we reconnected. I arrange the visas. He sends the girls over to work for a month. Then I send them back. That's all."

"So, he's their pimp in Russia. And you're their pimp here. But what hold does this man have over these girls?"

"He doesn't say, and I don't ask."

"And why didn't you call him right away instead of letting all this . . . this . . . inconvenience drag on?"

"I did. I've been calling him since the . . . inconvenience began. I just got through to him now."

"Well, you tell him it's not enough for him to reprimand her. Explain to him that I am ready to pay whatever amount to get her out of my life. I want her back in Russia—along with that other bitch with the white-yellow hair. You hear me?"

"Absolutely."

I suck in a lungful of air and let the relief spread. Here is the end of this agonizing ordeal. "So, what will he do to her once she gets there?" It's an afterthought, curiosity. "Break her legs? Kill her?"

"Of course not!" Abu-George is taken aback. "Even though these Russians have their own codes of conduct—none of our morals, I must admit—I know Sergei, and he's certainly not a killer." Abu-George pauses and seems to be struck by a wave of panic. "And what would that make me, sending her back to Russia if he were a killer? Well, he's not!" He shoves his fingers into his shirt pocket and pulls out a tiny cross, which he holds to his mouth. He looks up and mutters something to the heavens: a pimp in prayer. "No, he'll just scold her. That's all. Maybe he'll slap her around a bit, but she's used to that. Nothing more."

I don't need to hear any more. We'd kept the door ajar, and now we step back in to find Galina crawling on her knees, picking up the money. She looks up and shifts onto her feet, but she still cowers. She hangs her head and mumbles, "I sorry. I no mean disrespect."

Carefully, as if her neck might break, I lift her chin. "What was that?"

"I say, I very much sorry."

I pause to prolong the moment and look deep into her starless eyes. She may not be repentant deep down, but that doesn't matter. What I see is enough: dread in the face of a dark fate. I picture her and that other girl pissing in their stringy panties once they come face-to-face with Sergei. He will deal with them: a scolding and a few slaps, Abu-George wants me to believe. I don't think so.

"Please tell Sergei you forgive me?"

"Fine," I say, and release her jaw. When she slumps to the ground to pick up a banknote lying next to my foot, I step on her hand. She cries out. "You're not keeping any of the money," I say. "You will collect it and give it back to me."

She stifles a sob and nods.

23

MARIAM

～

The invitation was extended to every girl at the sakan, but, along with a couple of other serious-minded students, I decided not to go to the party. It was arranged by Buthaina, who lives on the seventh floor, to mark the end of the school year. With June around the corner, this is a critical time of year. Even though I've just finished my written exams, I still have to prepare for the orals, the first of which is in a week.

I hear a clattering of utensils in the kitchen. Tammy and Alunood are probably arranging ingredients for the maid, Naeema, who will cook a dish for them to take upstairs. For the past few days it has been mayhem in our apartment as they rattled about trying to decide what clothes, shoes, and accessories to wear. It's as if their summer vacation has already begun.

I sit at my desk, back straight, with a textbook in front of me, and commend myself on my strength of will: not everyone can resist the fun of a party. I flip the pages to the chapter on corrective jaw surgery. Minutes later I'm imagining Adel and me together.

He will marry me; everything points in that direction. He is respectful and caring whenever I am with him, and that can only mean that he is preparing for a life shared with me. I envision the children I will bear him, tumbling on grass or splashing in the sea with his sporty limbs. They will have his long lashes and my full mouth, and their hair will be healthy and thick, glossy under the sun.

I run my finger along the textbook's lines in a renewed effort at concentration. Closing the book, I address the wall, trying to recall what I've just read. I raise my voice, exaggerating every syllable of the medical terms. In the middle of a sentence, I draw a blank. My gaze travels toward the large window, where a male bulbul noisily courts a female on a balcony railing. The feathers on his black head are spiked and his white cheeks expand, making his red spots in the center swell. He is an adorable little thing. He pecks at the aluminum railing and shuffles back and forth. The female is drab and unimpressed. With a shake of her wings, she takes off.

The chair creaks as I get up to block out such small distractions. I draw the curtain, thinking it's just a matter of creating the right environment. But now there's more noise from the kitchen, a slamming of drawers and banging of utensils. "What's going on?" I call, leaning out the doorway. When the girls screech, I march over to tell them off, but the sight in the kitchen stops me in place.

"What a mess." I gape. They giggle. The cupboard doors have been wrenched open and the counter is crowded with every pot and pan we own, along with six plucked chickens and stalks of molokhia heaped in bales. I slam the cupboard doors shut. "What are you trying to do?"

"Here, catch," says Tammy, flinging a chicken at me.

Slack flesh lands in my open palms, a jolting reminder of that wretched ibis. Dalal and I had clutched it as if it were a lifeline. I'm not sure why I held on, but at the time it seemed important that I did.

Chicken blood drips through my fingers.

"*Eeee!*" the girls screech, and when I don't react, Tammy whacks it out of my hands. It lands on the floor with a plop.

"What did you do that for?" cries Alunood. "That's blasphemous, disrespecting a soul like that."

"It's dead," says Tammy.

"It wasn't dead before. And now it's food. And food must be respected."

Having had enough of their twaddle, I raise my hand. "Look, just do what you want, but keep your voices down, because I have to study."

"But we can't," wails Tammy. "There's a crisis."

"Naeema called to say she can't come," explains Alunood. "Her little boy is sick, and now we're sick, because we don't know how we're going to get this dish cooked and ready for tonight." She speaks in a monotone. Her thick-rimmed glasses sit just under the broad bridge of her nose so that she must lift her chin to see me properly. "You know what our cooking is like." She shrugs, and I grimace at the memory of the one meal they tested on me. Tammy's rice had more water in it than grain, and the hard balls of meat and lumps of salt in Alunood's accompanying curry were equally unpalatable.

"Well, just chop some fruit and make a fruit salad."

Alunood is appalled. "Impossible," she says. "Everyone else will have made something delicious. It is an Emirati custom, after all."

I nod. Certainly it's a tradition to be taken seriously, and I say, "The problem is, I've never made molokhia."

"It's easy," pleads Alunood. "Just cut everything up and put it in the . . . saucepan, or . . . pot, or something like that." She pushes her glasses up and points to the cookbook leaning against the wall, the pages held open by a tub of yogurt and a kettle. "It's all written down, there in Chef Ramzi's cookbook."

"You must help us, please, please, please." Tammy drops to her knees and hugs my legs tightly. Her theatrical tomfoolery makes me chuckle. This is what Cairo does: it brings out the playful and the cheeky in you. Far from her father and brothers, Tammy bursts with exuberance. Far from my uncle and his household of stifling rules and proper conduct, I let her merriment infect me.

With a mischievous grin, I pick up a bale of molokhia leaves and mouth the scientific name to myself: *corchorus*. I'm not a perfect cook, but for some reason, looking at the ingredients in front of me—onions, garlic, cilantro—I am eager to try something new. Besides, considering my ebbing concentration, perhaps it would be better to take my mind off my studies for a bit.

The girls jump up and down in relief. "We'll help you," says Tammy, prancing between the fridge and the counter. "We'll do all the chopping." She pulls a fruit knife out of the drawer.

"Look, just put away all those chickens. I don't need more than two."

Tammy claps her hands and hops up and down. "And you will come to the party, won't you?"

I shove them out of the kitchen and start skimming through the recipe.

❧

Tammy sniffs. "They're burning the expensive stuff."

I press the elevator button with my elbow and look up the staircase. A trail of smoke unfurls, floating down from the seventh floor. On our level it breaks into feathery clouds and disperses. I catch a trace of the beguiling aroma of oudh incense before it is eclipsed by the smell of the boiled leaves and fried garlic in the molokhia I am holding.

"You shouldn't have troubled yourselves," Buthaina exclaims when we arrive. She's neatly clad in a handsome Palestinian caftan, black with tiny arabesque motifs crocheted in brightly colored thread. She takes the pot out of my hands and passes it to her roommate, Nawal, who hands it to the maid. Unlike us, our hostesses chose their heels pragmatically. I feel clumsy bending so low to receive Buthaina's greeting, delivered in the Emirati way: a slack handshake and a series of air kisses that make clicking sounds like a toy machine gun.

"So much food!" cries Nawal, obviously panicked by the arrival of yet another dish. She has opted for a sky-blue Emirati *thoub*, a translucent chiffon overgarment. Even though it is a generous cut, she looks like a fish struggling in too little water as she waves her arms back and forth, swishing the fabric. She cranes her neck to welcome us with the same popping pecks.

Alunood raises her chin and declares, "It's molokhia, that's what it is."

Even though Buthaina and Nawal grin, they are not able to camouflage their apprehension. It seems that my roommates' cooking abilities are infamous. "Mariam made it," Tammy adds quickly, swishing her abaya as if introducing the hero in a play.

Nawal's features settle back into place, and Buthaina releases her breath and nods. Their approval strikes me with a flush of pride that spreads the length of my cheekbones. And I'm glad I decided to come to this party. Buthaina and Nawal are the sakan's only grown-up students; they're in their early thirties. We refer to them as the *kubar*, the older ones.

Buthaina and Nawal are teachers at the Emirates University in Al-Ain; they are on study leave to gain master's degrees in Arabic literature and history, respectively. Both are unmarried, seeming to prefer putting their energy into what they call "the honorable aim of bettering the human mind." And that's why, I suppose, they have been taking their time finishing their degrees. Their extra years in Cairo have given them not just knowledge but also the ability to shift accents. They can go from Emirati to Egyptian and back again, depending on whom they are talking to, with as little effort as flicking a light switch.

"So, Fatima," says Buthaina, "how are we doing with our studies?"

"Tammy."

"Of course, Tammy," she says. "But I have to say that Fatima is such a noble name."

"It's the prophet's daughter's name, after all," Nawal says, rolling her eyes to indicate her boredom with the first-year girls and their immaturity. "And you don't want it. Is Tammy your official name now? Are you going to change it on your passport, too?"

"I haven't given up anything. Tammy is my nickname and I love it!" A fierce glint grazes her tiny eyes, but it disappears as soon as her glance shifts beyond the entrance toward the sitting room. "*Yah!*" She clasps her palms with delight. "Balloons!"

Little hearts trail down from the balloons' ribbons; it's an oddly whimsical decoration, considering that this is the apartment of the academically minded kubar. Tammy and Alunood waste no more time at the door. They dash into the sitting room and start tugging at the ribbons. The kubar grin politely, and, feeling responsible for my roommates' boisterous behavior, I make a halfhearted plea to them to stop. But there are others emboldened by my roommates. The girls who'd arrived before us slide off the couches to join in. Every one of them is in heels (no matter the girl's height, always the heels), some thin and pointy, others thick as bricks. The girls tug down a balloon; once it's close enough, they leap as high as safety permits in their leaden platforms and volley it a couple of times before it floats back up to the ceiling. I clap my hands for attention, but the stomping feet and balloon slaps, the yelps and the laughter continue. I turn back to the kubar with open palms and a shrug. "It's a party, after all."

"A zoo, you mean," says Nawal.

"What I want to know, Mariam," says Buthaina, "is how you, a sensitive and sensible young lady from a distinguished family, manage to keep your sanity with those two around all the time." She pauses to look at Tammy, who is making a display of letting her abaya slide off her shoulders. Her legs are wrapped in tight jeans, and as the abaya slithers down, she hooks it around her foot. With a nifty twirl, she shapes it into a ball and kicks it into the air. The girls clap and Tammy raises her arms, a champion in a body-hugging blouse that shimmers with gold sequins and creeps above her belly button.

I chuckle. "I suppose they're entertaining. And young."

"Not that young," says the crusty Nawal. She sucks air through her teeth as if in pain. "Look at her; she's thinks she's in a nightclub."

"As Mariam said, it is a party." Buthaina's tone silences her roommate. "And a party must have a little noise and laughter." Nawal scowls, but Buthaina pays her no heed. "Come on," she says to me. "I have to check on the food." She folds an arm around my waist and leads me toward the kitchen. She pulls the lids off each of four pots, still warming on the stove, and steps back to evade the cloud of steam that escapes. Her maid wipes down what she can of the counters, which are crowded with food brought by the other girls. On one counter, sitting near my pot of molokhia, are a couple of other Egyptian favorites: a casserole of macaroni with béchamel sauce and a dish of layered meat, potatoes, and tomatoes. On the other counter sit desserts: a shallow bowl of crème caramel; another of cool, milky rice pudding; and a closed pot of what I guess to be *luqaimat*, Emirati crispy dumplings sitting in a puddle of thick date syrup.

"I'm sure you're just being polite and loyal," continues Buthaina, "which is understandable, given your superior upbringing." She winks at me, and this makes me unsure whether she is serious. "But it doesn't take a genius to notice that they must drive you crazy with their silliness day in and day out."

I grin. "That they do."

She chuckles and scoops up a spoonful of hearty soup, raising it to her lips. The maid hurries to her side with a sponge in her hand, and I marvel at the way she has been coached. Unlike our Naeema, this maid has been trained to anticipate spills.

I admire Buthaina for the way she has organized her life, having long followed the path of order and independence. After finishing her studies, she will return to teaching at the university. I imagine her teaching not just what is in the textbooks but also a multitude of valuable life lessons.

"*Mmm.*" Buthaina's moan sounds as though it's filled with appreciation for every blessing in life. When she turns and smiles at me, I think that if I had a mother, I would like her to be just as organized and capable as Buthaina is. She pauses at the second pot and, after tasting its contents, is so exacting in her description of what is missing that I start to worry about the taste of my molokhia. What if it doesn't meet with her approval? I chide my carelessness; I forgot to check that the color was the rich, deep green it should be, or that the water had separated from the finely chopped leaves. There's an essential test that marks a good molokhia, and in my hurry to get everything ready on time I forgot to perform it.

As if reading my mind, Buthaina steps toward my pot. She scoops a spoonful and raises it for evaluation. She nods when the slimy mixture falls in a straight, unbroken line—a sign that my molokhia has passed the test—and glides back to the stove.

"Did you know, Mariam, that from our first gasp of breath, we, as members of the female sex, are at a disadvantage," she says, sampling the curry in the third pot and clicking her tongue. "Lemon, I think, and . . ." She pauses, considering what else it might need. "Yes!" A pinch of cumin and three squirts of lemon later and she's moved on to the fourth pot. "That is the tragedy all across the Arab world. From the moment we start grasping what life is about, we are told that we are the weaker sex, that we cannot do anything on our own, that we must depend on men—whether our fathers, brothers, or husbands—to lead us like sheep. But there is a way to avoid this: by using what's in here." She taps her temple with her free hand. "In the end, it is the mind that is the treasure of our being, the part of us that has to be stimulated and developed every single day of our existence."

It's hardly the subject to lighten a party's mood, and it's a sharp contrast to the noise in the sitting room. Someone has switched on the cassette player, and the Kuwaiti singer Nabil Shuail's willowy voice croons pure and clear, as smooth as butter. It's enough to silence the chattering. When his voice ebbs, the girls squeal.

"Listen to them," says Buthaina, laughing. "You'd think he was in the room with them."

She returns to my molokhia and stirs it while asking after my family, to which I give general answers. "You know, people say your father had a special kindness, a rare quality that made him loved by all." She doesn't wait for me to confirm this. I can tell she detects it in my eyes, which blink now as if flushing out a stubborn lash. "They say he was progressive in his views, too. What a pity that he was taken away from you so early in your years."

"*Al-hamdulillah* for the multitude of God's blessings," I say, overwhelmed by appreciation for this person who seems to understand me so well. I wish I had an older sister like her: smart and worldly, untroubled about what society might think. Her attitude sets her apart from the other sakan girls.

Ah, what a relief it would be to talk to Buthaina about Adel, and how he makes me feel like a puppy chasing its tail. I have to admit that even though I appreciate his cordiality toward me—a sign that he already considers me his future partner—I do miss his cheekiness, which has disappeared. Sometimes, when I am with him, I crave the twangs of electricity that used to travel the length of my limbs, like that time he ran his fingers along my cheek at the Students' Club. Recently I've tried to encourage him. Whenever we sit side by side, I allow my shoulder to bend toward him like a bloom hungry for the sun's light. If I'm facing him, my foot might accidentally bump his in the hope that he might take some initiative, like tapping my thigh or reaching for my hand. But he doesn't, and then I feel foolish. If I suddenly told Buthaina that it's maddening to have the man you love show too much respect, how would she react? Surely she would understand—she must have loved someone this way at some point in her life.

I picture Buthaina as my sister. She would have stood by my side and given me confidence during those crucial years when I grew up in a household that never felt like home. "So what can we do, as women I mean, to become more, er . . . to be more . . ." I pause to find the exact word I mean, the quality that would help me face my steel-minded uncle, that would make me shine whenever I am with Adel. How does one reclaim a destiny that has been snatched away without license? " . . . strong?"

"Self-assertive and competent, you mean? Mariam, Mariam, ya Mariam, this needs a proper sit-down. Sometime when we can talk alone, sip tea together, and discuss all sorts of things. Habibti, you know you can tell me anything, don't you."

It's a statement, and I nod, because she's right: this is not the right setting for a proper talk. She's still occupied by adding the last flavors to her dishes, and her guests are making more noise than necessary in the sitting room. They are now singing along with Nabil Shuail, drowning out his voice yet failing to reach the high notes his talent allows him. They sound like mewing kittens stuck on a sinking ship. It's time for me to rejoin them.

❧

I lean against the wall of the sitting room and watch the girls dance to the gentle beat of Mohammed Abdu's "Ana Habibi." The steps are deceptively simple; the dance exudes cautious sexuality and an uplifting freedom of spirit. It's in the delicate lifted hand, the twirling of fingers just above the head as if letting drop some magic powder. It's in the hips that rise and ebb like gentle waves, and the shoulders that shudder as if responding to a chill that races up the spine. It's in the subtle workings of the neck muscles. Suddenly, as swiftly as a thunderbolt, the head sways, releasing waves of of lustrous hair, while the hand settles on the chest as if steadying a runaway bandit of a heartbeat. This display is not mad abandon. It's a burst of energy that is checked and controlled. Any more would be vulgar. There is a reined-in swell of passion throughout the dance.

Tammy notices me and pulls me into the middle of the group. Even in a room full of girls wholly absorbed in their own thoughts, I feel self-conscious as I try to summon an essential ingredient to dancing attractively: sensuality. I picture Dalal and her ability to move different bits of her body independently, yet with the effect of a harmonious whole. I imagine Adel watching her as I try to imitate her. But my movements are awkward, and my joints make sporadic, clicking protests. As the song draws to an end, I decide that Adel must never see me dance. I am as graceless as a penguin waddling on ice.

Nawal switches off the cassette player and claps her hands for attention. "The food is nearly ready! So sit and relax a little." Swishing in her thoub, she points to the vacant chairs and couches. "That's right, Mona, you can sit there. And Alunood, there you go, next to her." She herds the group of girls toward the corner.

Tammy squeezes next to me on the couch. "Just like her to dampen the mood!" She lets a hiss of air escape through her teeth. "Really! If I wasn't so hungry, I would walk out. Right this minute!" This makes the girls laugh, and they start chattering. There is light talk of the coming exams. Then one of the girls, who will soon be returning to Dubai to marry her cousin, launches into an elaborate description of her wedding dress. This sets off the other girls, who natter on excitedly about how they envision their future wedding celebrations. One describes the romantic lighting and the color of the flowers on the tables. Another focuses on her dream stage, where she will wait for the arrival of her groom. It's a favorite subject, and Tammy leans over me so she can join in.

Nawal glides over from the other side of the room and settles into our midst, snug as a roosting hen. For a few minutes she nods them on. Then, at the first appropriate pause, she launches into a heated speech about Arab society's folly in placing so much emphasis on matrimony and its trappings. She lists every conceivable ill: the high cost of the ceremony; the bride's family's demand for expensive gifts and money, which forces the young man to take out loans and start married life with outrageous debts. "And of course, don't forget the divorce rate; it's getting higher every day."

Whether out of politeness or timidity, the rest of the girls listen, but they make no effort to hide the dejection on their faces. Buthaina emerges from the kitchen with her maid and starts arranging the various plates and bowls of food on the dining table.

"Yes, divorce," Nawal continues. "Remember that word. I'm sure the poor boy won't ever forget it, because all the money he spends on the wedding will have been for nothing." She chuckles. "Look at you all, murky-eyed with illusions! What dreaming you like to do! What a waste of energy."

I want to tell her that dreaming is a beautiful thing, a survival tactic. In the years after my father died, I would curl up in various corners of Ammi Majed's house and let my mind roam, hoping to find an untroubled place where justice and harmony reigned. Even now I flit in and out of dreams that shape a future with the man I love. In one's imagination, anything is possible. There's freedom to entertain rapturous aspirations that are too daring to actually be uttered or acted upon.

Nawal cocks her head to one side and focuses on the girls one by one, as if to ensure that she has dissolved what spirit had quivered in them, before loosening a toothy smile of victory. "Look at me." She slaps her chest. "Do I look like I need a husband?"

I'm about to turn away, but seeing the girls' faces, as long and pale as mangoes sucked dry, I say, "Maybe you don't. But that doesn't mean everyone else wants what you want." I'm surprised by how calm my voice is. "You are right to point out that there are many drawbacks. But surely you are not saying that a girl shouldn't get married."

Nawal grunts. "I'm saying it's not the solution for happiness."

"Not always," I say, just as Tammy pinches my thigh to prompt me to go on. "But many times, it is. Whether we like it or not, marriage brings security."

"Respectability," one of the girls adds.

"A home of your own," says another.

"Children."

"The sharing of a life," I say, and the girls nod. "Besides, who can determine what the solution for happiness is? That all depends on the person."

"Yes," blurts Tammy. "And right now, what would make me very happy is to get up and dance."

Nawal stays focused on me. "Quite the philosopher, aren't you, Mariam?" She blinks with annoyance. "But you are still young, and your experience is limited. When you grow up, we can discuss this further."

"I don't think we'll ever be able to have a proper discussion, Nawal, because you're only interested in imposing your views."

Nawal opens her mouth, but nothing comes out.

The nerve of having silenced Nawal spreads into my very bones. I am on my feet just as Buthaina announces dinner. For the first time, I put my manners to the side: instead of waiting, I march toward her and take the first plate she hands out.

24

DALAL

❧

"Look at you. Look at the way your waist curves just so. Why, you have crescents on either side." I speak to the closet mirror while admiring the new dress I'm wearing. I talk to my reflection because there is no one else to talk to, because Madame Nivine says that it's unhealthy for a talent to be in a gagged atmosphere, and, most important, to chase away the self-doubt that washes over me whenever I am in the apartment with my mother.

Even if we are in the same room, Mama ignores me. At first I was thrilled, convinced that she finally understood how frustrated I was at being bossed around. I thought she would just sulk for a bit and then get over it. But it's been over three weeks, and with every passing day her resolve grows stronger. She shuffles about the apartment as if I were not there. She stares at me as if I were a cockroach.

"And her face, look at that face, so radiant, so thoughtful, so grown-up." I slap my thighs and rise. Opening the bedroom door, I see Mama ambling toward the kitchen. An idea flashes in my head and I overtake her, blocking her way. She shows no surprise at my rudeness, and I half imagine she'll walk right through me. "Do you like this violet color on me, Mama?"

Her face is as pale, flat, and empty as a sheet of paper. She crosses her arms as if bored, and runs her eyes over the length of me. Feeling foolish and insignificant, I realize I won't receive any compliments and that I should probably step out of her way, but I give it one more try: "How long are you going to stay silent, acting as if I'm just a piece of furniture?" She lets out a forceful snort—like the warning sound of a raging goat—just as we hear a shuffling of feet outside the apartment and a great big thump.

Though we both see the same thing when I open the door, we react differently. I stand frozen like a block of ice with bulging eyes, while Mama shakes visibly. I hear the opening of doors, our neighbors peering and giggling, but my eyes are focused on Mama. She sways, and her hands tremble.

The lowlifes who dumped the putrid pile of rubbish at our front door have already scrambled down the stairs, leaving behind echoes of their sneers. If I rush to the balcony, I'll probably be able to yell curses at them before they've escaped down the street. But I stay by Mama's side.

She is in distress. She needs me. She steadies herself against the wall and holds a hand to her face. Her eyes are scrunched tight in anguish. Poor Mama, looking so fragile. I rush to find a chair and place it next to her. When she doesn't sit, I pat her on the shoulder to get her attention. And she eases into the chair while hiding her eyes from me. It moves me that she doesn't want me to see her vulnerability.

I kneel in front of her and grasp her free hand. I'm not sure whether it's the stench or true daughterly love that causes my eyes to moisten. Carefully I place my head on her lap, and there I stay, inhaling the scent of Nivea and decay.

I wait. I wait for her to stroke my head.

I wait. I wait for her fingers to glide through my curls.

What comes is an order to get up and clean the mess.

There are brown paper bags turned soggy with potato peelings, zucchini pulp, old gravy, sodden tea leaves, and sugarcane stalks chewed so thoroughly they look like clumps of grimy hay. I stick to the edges, carefully leaning over the pile so I don't soil my new dress. I use two squares of cardboard to scoop the rubbish into a bucket.

I know I should finish the miserable task quickly, but my hands move in slow motion as my mind processes what has just taken place. Why did I obey her? Why didn't I refuse? Why didn't I tell her that this garbage was meant for her? It was an act carried out by a community she has hurt. This stale bread must be from Mitwalli's bakery, these rotten tomatoes from Shehata's grocery—it's all from outraged people whose feelings she has toyed with, who glare at us whenever we pass by their shops. She must know that the neighborhood pooled its rubbish to deliver their message: that she, too, is trash.

A mother cat, her teats hanging like empty sacks under her bony frame, slinks up the stairway and mewls her presence. I throw her a rib of chewed meat. As she devours it, I realize it must have come from Abdo, the butcher.

I am so lost in thought that I don't realize I have sunk to my knees. Drops of a putrid liquid streak my dress and some sort of unidentifiable muck has hardened, like a dried-up stream, along the blue vein of my inner arm. "Disgusting!" My voice has the force of a cannonball, and it alarms the cat, who scoots down the stairs.

Mama is in the kitchen by the stove, waiting for some Turkish coffee to boil. "Well," she says, directing a cool glance at the overflowing bucket clutched in my hand, "is that the lot?" My scowl is lost on her. She turns away and swirls the pot over the fire, then tames the rising liquid with a spoon. "Get some soap and water and mop the floor to get rid of the smell."

"Revolting."

"Of course it is. It's garbage, isn't it?"

I gawk at the small coffee cup, cream-colored and ringed with delicate powder-blue blossoms, sitting ready in its saucer on the kitchen table. She didn't even wonder if I would want some, and that's what turns my throat dry with hurt. It's about as much as I can take. "Not the garbage, Mama." I cough. Even though the frog croak stays in my throat, I continue. "You."

"What's that you're saying?"

"You, Mama. You have used every person in this neighborhood, and now they hate you. That rubbish out there, in here . . ." I swing the bucket, and bits of soppy newspaper tumble to the floor. " . . . I shouldn't be the one cleaning it up. It's meant for you. They want you out!"

"What do I care if they want me in or out?" She bangs the pot on the table, and dark liquid spews like mud over the sides. "And what tongue is this that's grown longer than a snake? You call yourself my daughter? I didn't bring you up to talk to me like this. Don't think you can be impertinent and get away with it."

This is when I should retreat, even apologize. I should be satisfied by melting that icy exterior long enough to feel the heat of some genuine passion. Daughters never shout at their mothers like this—I never have before—no matter how much of a tyrant the mother might be. It's unimaginable, even in the boldest fight scenes on television dramas. But the sight of that one coffee cup keeps me from coiling back into submission. "This daughter has had enough!" I drop the bucket to the floor. "You sicken me."

❧

Hunkering down in the bathtub, I scrub like a madwoman. I scrub until the loofah turns my skin pink. There is only one thought in my head: to get out of the apartment and away from my mother.

She bangs on the locked bathroom door, calling me an ungrateful animal. I plug my ears, but I can still hear her asking the heavens why she was cursed to have a daughter like me. Then the banging stops and I bend under the tap, feeling as vulnerable as a rabbit as I hurriedly try to rinse the soap off.

I imagine that I will feel better once I am out of the apartment, but when I am, I still feel a rage and frustration that I can't shake away. The cat laps at the residue of muck at the door. I kick. I miss.

I am wearing a flowery top with a bouquet of ruffles that arc around my chest. Out in the street, a gust of wind slaps them into my face. The first person I spot is one of my father's spies, practicing headers with a half-inflated ball. Every few bounces he hits a superheader and, from somewhere deep in his throat, expels the noise of crowds cheering.

I call him. "*Ya wad*, come here!"

He jerks his head, and the ball bounces off his nose before tumbling to the ground. He searches the full street, looking everywhere except in my direction. Clearly this spy has not been briefed on what to do when uncovered. "Yes, you." When I march toward him, he tries to look busy searching for the ball, even though it's no more than a few steps behind him. "I have a message for you."

He holds his hand to his chest. "You must be confusing me with someone else, ya sitt." He is taller than I am, even with his head crumpled to his chest. His mouth loosens into a silly, apologetic grin that I want to scrape off his face with a scouring sponge. "I don't know you."

I scoff. "Fine, whatever you say. But I have a message for you to deliver to the big bey who is paying you to keep an eye on me and my mother."

"Your mother?" He shrugs and keeps staring at the ground.

"Yes, the one you've been following for so long?"

"Following?"

"What are you, deaf?" My voice cracks. He flinches and starts carefully retreating, looking around for someone, anyone, who might tell him what to do. No one seems to care. Suddenly he turns on his heels and runs away. "Come back," I call out. One glance at those spindly legs racing down the street is enough to convince me of the pointlessness of giving chase. But it doesn't stop me from yelling out my message: "She's getting married. Yes, you tell my father that my mother is getting married. Again!"

◦℃◦

It's an inky night. There is a moon, round as a plate, but it hides behind a thick patch of mist. For now, the pyramids take its place, illuminated at the bottom, the peaks lost in darkness.

Throughout the drive, I vent my frustration. Adel keeps his eyes on the road and listens, interjecting brief words of concern or, every now and then, clicking his tongue with disbelief. Whenever my agitation swells, he rubs my arm or playfully pinches my cheek. As always, I push his hand away, even though I find myself smiling. It subdues the pain of being insignificant in my mother's eyes. Each time, it temporarily quiets me, but just for a moment; eventually I start again, gabbling like an agitated goose. I keep certain things to myself. He doesn't need to know that I was on my knees, scooping up trash. Mostly I ramble about my mother and how she treats me like a child.

After my outpouring, I wait for some relief to magically ease the pulse of torment. When it does not come, I take a breath and look around. Adel turns off the main road and onto a narrower one, bumpy with potholes. The road crumbles into gravel and sand. "Where are we going?"

"Somewhere quiet. Isn't that what you wanted?"

My jaw aches from talking too much. I fall silent and consider what made me call him. I had plodded through the streets for what felt like hours, crossing roads crowded with people, cars, and rumbling carts heaved forth by weary-faced mules. I was flushed and breathless as I tried to decide what to do. I first thought to call on Azza, since she lives closest to me, but I quickly decided she was too witless and trivial and would be unable to add insight to what I was feeling. The second option had been to head to Madame Nivine's apartment in Mohandessin, but I disregarded that idea, too. It would not do to burden her with my personal problems—not this early in our partnership, anyway. She might lose focus of the more important task of making me famous. Then, without considering that Mariam might not want to talk to me, I'd found myself hailing a black-and-white taxi to drop me off at the sakan.

Sitting in the backseat, I had been soothed by the thought of seeing her after such a long time. Even though she has never said as much, I know she's never liked my mother. With a little prodding, I could get her to speak up. That's what I wanted to hear, after all: someone criticizing Mama's cruel and unfair treatment of me. Mariam would prepare me a cup of *karak*; I pictured her boiling the tea leaves in a pot of milk and sugar, dropping a pod or two of cardamom into the mixture. She'd serve it steaming hot, and I would have to pour it into the saucer and blow on it. She'd watch me and understand my torment. She'd rest her hand on my knee to give me strength. And if I cried, she would do the same. The shared emotion would make us hug and cry some more. I simply wanted someone to stand by me, to make me feel good again. And it's Mariam who can make me feel best.

I got out of the taxi just as the streetlights came on. This time I did not hide behind a bush or throw stones at the window. I walked straight in and asked for her. She was not there.

Sitting in the sakan's waiting room, I had tapped and hummed, restless as a bee trapped in a jar. I heard arguments in the foyer between the abla and the girls about who needed the car and driver most urgently. It sounded like the bickering would never end, and I lost patience and slipped away to wait for Mariam outside the building. But my nervous pacing had taken me to a kiosk; from there, I called him. And fifteen minutes later, he came. "Take me away. Take me out of the city." The words had dropped out of my mouth before I even got into the car.

Now the car stops. With a deep sigh, Adel eases back into his seat. "There, listen to that."

"What?"

"Peace."

He leans over and slowly cranks down my window. His elbow rubs my thigh. My eyelids slacken. "Yes, peace," I murmur, wondering whether that might be just the medicine I need. Adel jerks back and grips the steering wheel. The moon peers from behind its veil. Under its cool alabaster glow, I sneak a look at his square-shaped hands, the way the wristbones stick too far out, the hardened hills of his knuckles. His chest heaves and ebbs. His breath, I notice, is heavier.

The air is still. It smells of burned hay and horse dung, drifted from the homes of the farmers living in Giza. It warms me that Adel made the effort to drive me all the way out here so that my mind could rest. What's this? A dot of perspiration trickles down my chest. I think I'm a little too warm. I blow out a breath, and the ruffles of my blouse quiver like a bed of butterflies.

"So, you see the pyramids over there?"

I allow a second's peep at them in the distance. Then my glance fixes back on him. How handsome he is. He stares ahead, lips parted and eyebrows puckered with some strong emotion. He looks as if he's ready to break out into a song of woe. He swivels to face me. This must be what they call a moment of magic: the way he looks at me, with those eyes filled with such brooding intensity . . . well, that prompts a rippling sensation in my belly, as if it were filled with a million little fish splashing about.

When he places his hand on my neck, my skin puckers. It's not a bad feeling, and I close my eyes. He kisses them, and my pulse quickens. "Habibti," he whispers. I smile, even though I'm not really thinking about him. It's my mother's face that fills my mind: if only she could see me, sitting in the middle of a vast and empty desert with a man who's absorbed with every part of me. Ah, Mama, I won't be waiting for you to make my decisions anymore. I shall do that on my own.

Adel is bent over, halfway out of his seat. The handbrake acts as a barrier, the hard metal poking him, preventing him from getting too comfortable. This suits me fine, because all I want is to feel desired, even a little precious: a short moment, nothing more.

I must call a halt to this soon, though. As every girl knows, such matters must never be permitted to go too far lest word got out and she be considered easy or end up with a soiled reputation. But Adel is discreet—I'm sure of it—and we are quite alone. A little longer, I think, relishing the way his fingers swim through my hair.

The moon shies away. It's dark once more. His hand follows a rhythm, sliding up and down my waist. When it slips lower, I decide it's time to ease out of his grip. Yes, Mama, from now on I take charge of my life.

I open my mouth but can only gasp, because suddenly my seat flops back. Adel ambushes me. How he managed to roll out of his tight space, I cannot tell. But now he's on top of me, heavy and grunting like a buffalo. He strokes and he gropes. And what's this? My ear is wet with his saliva.

I squirm. I tell him that's enough and order him to get off.

"Don't panic," he murmurs. "Don't worry."

I try to wriggle out from under him, but without success. "Get off, now!"

"I will, I will." He doesn't.

My hands are pinned like fractured wings under my chin. With a mighty effort I loosen them enough to smack his face weakly. He chuckles. He probably thinks it's a game. He raises himself, and my hands are released long enough to plant a second slap. The force of it knocks him back.

It's too dark to see his face, but I can tell he's stunned because he freezes, then retreats back into his seat. He opens the door and tumbles out onto the gravel in a huff. "What's the matter with you?" he says, walking around to my side of the car.

"I told you to get off." I straighten my seat. "I told you, but you wouldn't listen."

"What can I say? I wanted you so badly I couldn't control myself."

"Shame on you!"

"Shame on me?"

"Yes."

I wait for his reply. His sneer brings back the shame of feeling small. He steps away. It's so dark I have to guess what he is doing. I hear him rubbing the sand off his clothes. There are a few long inhales, and I imagine him closing his eyes against the night air. Finally, I hear heavy footsteps that grow fainter.

He has left me in the middle of nowhere. I have the mad notion to drive away, even though I don't know how to drive. I check the ignition, but there are no keys. So I wait, agonizing over what he'll say or do when he comes back. A mosquito buzzes somewhere around my face and I slap at it as it follows an invisible halo around my head. I fidget, smoothing and flattening my shirt's ruffles between my fingers. He is away for so long that I wonder if he wandered off to take a piss. By the time he returns, I have decided it's only right that I apologize.

"Why are you sorry?"

"Because I upset you."

He grunts.

"Look, things just went a bit too far. And I don't blame you for that. Let's just pretend none of this happened and then we can be friends again. Like before."

"Like before? Dalal, you have been toying with me."

"Huh?"

"All this time, you have been giving signals that you wanted me."

Perhaps I did lead him on. "Don't speak such nonsense."

"It's not nonsense. It's what women like you enjoy doing."

I don't quite follow what he means.

"Come on, open your eyes! The day you decided to be a singer was the day you closed the door on modesty, on morals. Everyone knows that a girl who chooses such a career is open to affairs with all kinds of men."

"You should know me better than that!"

"What do you think that that life is all about? No one respects a singer."

"Listen, I'm not some poor homeless orphan you picked up off the street! I have a father. I have a mother."

"Not from what you've been telling me. All that whining about how no one loves you: do you think anyone cares?"

The moon reappears. Adel smirks, his teeth glinting. He is ruthless. He is enjoying hurting me! For once, I am tongue-tied. In the silvery stretch of sand and sky, I suddenly notice that we are not alone. There are six or seven other cars, each parked a short distance from one another. I spot the glow of a cigarette in one; someone stretches in another. This is obviously a lovers' spot. He brought me here on purpose, for one thing only. It's not love he feels, only lust, and I am nothing more than an object to be conquered. The realization turns me cold with contempt. I look at him. I want to scratch the grin off his face. "Take me home!"

"Or what?"

"Or I'll scream—and I won't stop until the men and women in those cars grab you by the neck and bury your head in the sand."

25

MAJED

_c_

You'd think an elephant had grabbed her with its trunk and started shaking her about. That's how petrified Amal's baby looks as I bounce her on my knees. She twists and struggles, looking this way and that for a savior. She's nine months old, and already she knows where she doesn't want to be.

Aisha is at the edge of her seat, a hop's distance away, ready to spring to my aid. On the far side of the sitting room, my mother spews her thoughts on child care, repeating everything twice as if addressing an imbecile: "Don't shake her. Don't shake her. She'll vomit, vomit she will." Her voice is as maddening as background static.

Worried I might be squeezing the baby, I loosen my hold. Aisha gulps, and Mama Al-Ouda warns me—twice—that babies can wriggle out of one's grip without warning and smash their heads on the floor.

I blow kisses at the baby. I am determined to extract a smile, perhaps even a drooling baby burble. I coo at her, but the little one writhes with all her strength, searching for her mother.

"Water. Water. A tiny spoonful of water is enough to cool her temper."

"Mama!" The baby's round eyes water, and the kohl that rings them streaks down the sides of her nose. Her cheeks turn red; her wail is as shrill as a whistle, with a force that pierces the center of my head.

Amal rushes into the room and takes her from me. "I'm sorry, Baba. It's just that she isn't comfortable with strangers."

I can't decide what makes my blood boil more: that I couldn't shake a smile out of the baby or that my daughter called me a stranger. It requires a colossal effort to hold back a stiff retort. But I've turned over a new leaf. I will give up alcohol and stay close to my family, and the strength of our bond will give me peace of mind. It's bound to be difficult at first, but with resolve and time I'm sure I can become a patient, tolerant, and supportive person, an ideal husband and father, a grandfather with a wealth of wisdom, a noble member of the community.

If there's a lesson to be learned from the incident with the Russian bitch, it's this: it's time to straighten a path gone crooked. She's left for good, boarded a plane headed north with her friend. All it took was the one phone call to Sergei. I nod in silent approval and think, *That's that.*

In Amal's arms, the baby collapses into a fit of giggles—all it took were a few tosses in the air (why didn't I think of that?). I ask Aisha, "When will the arrangements for Mariam be complete?"

"Well, you know I had to be very discreet. What would people say if they thought we're looking for a husband for our girl? Everyone knows it's the boy's family that must initiate things. How embarrassing. I mean, they'd think we're desperate!" She covers her mouth at the thought.

"Yes, yes." I roll my hand to hurry her along. "I don't need a lesson in how things are done."

"Ali Al-Mutawa and Atiq Al-Najar both have sons who would make a suitable match. So does the widow of Humaid Al-Rawi."

"Salma Bint-Obaid? She has wealth of her own and only the one son, who's already a bit old—is that not so?" I consider the widow's money—which is just lying there, from what I've heard—and come up with no fewer than three ideas of how she could invest it. First I'd have to convince her, but once I did, I'd benefit from being her partner in a number of ventures.

Aisha nods. "And I'm sure she would love for him to marry Mariam. Her husband held your brother in high regard."

"Good, good. Let it not be said that I ignored the future of my niece. There's nothing worse than depriving a girl of an excellent match."

"There is a problem, though," Aisha says, fiddling with her shayla. "None of them is willing to wait for the girl to finish her studies."

"Who said anything about her finishing her studies?" The force of my voice frightens the baby into sniveling again. Amal quickly bundles her up, and, mercifully, the screech that follows explodes in the hallway.

"I thought . . ." Aisha's mouth quivers. She, too, looks set to start whimpering.

"I said nothing about a long wait, woman! Do you want my niece to end up like your sister—a dried-up old woman with nothing to do but willfully aggravate me?" I cross my arms and look away. Such carelessness! I can't help the sudden flare in my temper because I think of Dalal and her mother. I was convinced that they'd rush back to Dubai after that harsh telling-off. But now, a month later, and it's obvious that that will not happen. My mind is a blank as to what to do next.

"Yes, Aisha," Mama Al-Ouda says, "people won't wait."

Back to the subject of Mariam, and I say, "I want her married and out of this house by the end of the year!"

"Insha'Allah."

"And where are all the children? Don't they know to come here so that we may all have lunch together? Why is lunch so late?"

"I'll go see." Aisha stutters over the last word.

I stop her with a raised hand. "Sit." I don't need to explain anything, but, remembering my resolution to be more patient and tolerant, I do. "You must understand that I don't like Mariam being exposed to so much out there in Cairo."

"Always right," Mama Al-Ouda says, "always right you are, my son."

"We don't know what company she keeps, who she sees, what she does." My voice turns soft—considerate, even. "Her place is with her own people, here, where we can keep an eye on her."

"What use is so much education?" Mama Al-Ouda says, adjusting the tip of her burka.

"Let me finish, mother!"

Mama Al-Ouda doesn't bat an eye. "Too much education for a girl does nothing but make her feel important, so important that she antagonizes her husband."

I call on my patience with a long, drawn-out breath and look deep into my wife's eyes. "All I'm saying, Aisha, is that there's no sense in her being so far from the family. Don't you agree?"

Aisha's mouth gapes with surprise: I don't normally ask for her opinion. She answers wisely, "Whatever you think best."

26

MARIAM

❦

Wafa nibbles her fingernails. Soraya can't stop sniffing. Ashraf is on the floor with his notes spread around him. Ghada mumbles a passionate prayer that she is granted a bighearted examiner who will ask only the easiest questions.

The air outside the examination room is stifling. Smoke mixes with the smell of nervous perspiration and the agitated breath of the twenty students who are waiting to be called in to the first day of oral exams. The session could take an easy five minutes or a grueling hour. Students' fingers tremble; their faces twitch into frowns and they tap their feet nervously.

Craving fresh air, I head toward a window at the end of the corridor, where I watch a gust of air rustle the orange blooms of a flame tree. There's a crack in the window and, in one corner, a large jagged hole where bits of glass have splintered off. I stoop and stick my face out, taking in a long, gritty breath that burns my nostrils. Hot and dry, this is the unmistakable start of a *khamsin* desert wind.

Pulling back, I return to pacing the corridor. I check my watch as I shuffle past the janitor who is guarding the door and watching us with vigilant eyes: it's half past nine. The professors sitting in that room should have started calling in students, in groups of two or three, an hour and a half ago.

"This is unbelievable!" Ashraf flings his copybook at the wall. "How much longer do we have to wait? My nerves are stretched to the limit."

"They'll call you when they call you," the janitor says. His voice has the coarse accent of a peasant. He holds his arms at his sides and glues them to the doorframe, as if Ashraf might jump up and force his way through.

"They'll call you when they call you," Ghada mocks, gnawing her plait. Like the rest of us, she is impatient with the wait.

My notes are hugged to my chest, but the smooth roll of words—dental procedures, definitions, and terms—that filled my head from the minute I woke up flickers into thoughts of Adel. He hasn't come to the Students' Club these past couple of weeks for the intense review sessions I'd planned. This surprises me, since it was our last chance to sift through our textbooks before the orals.

All over the college the corridors are filled with groups like this, waiting to be called in. I wonder where Adel is right now, whether he is as nervous as I am or blessed with his usual nonchalance. How prepared is he for today's subject? Will he pass? My lips slip into a smile. He failed his first year—"Homesickness," he said—and again in his third year—"All these words you have to memorize in English, each as long as my arm and sounding like the one before it!"

I'll be traveling back to Dubai immediately after my exams. I did not even consider asking my uncle if I could stay a few days longer, and I regret my lack of pluck, which means I'll be away from Adel that little bit longer. I'll spend the whole summer thinking about him, missing him, and counting the days until my return in September.

I'm at the far end of the corridor when the janitor calls my name and Ghada's. She pleads for a little more time for review. "Why must I be first?" She shifts from one foot to the other as if her bladder might explode. "Tell them to call me in later."

The janitor bobs his head in sympathy. "I don't make these decisions, ya sitt. They give me the names; I call them out."

I hurry to her side and try to calm her down. "I don't want to be the first to go in," she whispers to me. "I want to go later, when they get bored, when they get hungry and want to go home and have their lunch."

The janitor assumes the stance of a soldier—head erect, chest out—and calls again, "Mariam Hareb Al-Naseemy! Ghada Abdel Azeem Ragab!"

"You don't have to shout, you know. We're right in front of you," Ghada snaps at him. Fearing that an argument might cost us our slot in the examination room, I squeeze her shoulders and herd her in before she has a chance to make a bigger fuss.

The room is bare. I don't know either of the professors sitting behind the broad table in the center. The older man looks to be around sixty; he introduces himself as Dr. Wahid Al-Gamzawi. He has a compassionate face speckled with age spots. He indicates the two empty chairs on the other side of the table, and we take our seats. The other examiner, Dr. Sameh Wahab, must be thirty years younger, with a pointy chin and sharp features that give him the shifty air of a weasel. He wastes no time in starting the examination. "The subject today is Operative," he says in English. There's a hard edge to his accent. "I hope you are prepared." His tone is brittle, and when he points at me I straighten up. "How many types of fillings do we use generally?"

For a moment my mind is a muddle. I look at Ghada, whose finger flickers and pokes the air, a silent announcement that should I fail, she would like this particularly easy question to be passed on to her. "Three types," I say. "Amalgam, composite, and gold foil."

"And what would you say is the main disadvantage of a composite filling?"

"Polymerization shrinkage."

"Meaning?"

"The material becomes smaller inside."

"And how do we overcome this?"

"We use a hybrid type of composite, which is part of the new generation of composites. Also, we can fill it in layer by layer."

The answers stream through my mind, as clear as running water. I don't hesitate, and when Dr. Al-Gamzawi taps his fingers together in approval I can't resist smiling. "Yes," he says, with a fleeting glance at his notes. "You are Mariam Al-Naseemy, correct?"

"Yes, Doctor."

"From the Khaleej?"

I nod.

"Where?"

"The United Arab Emirates."

"Yes, wonderful country. And Mariam, I want to know: what is the composition of mercury after amalgam trituration?"

I open my mouth to answer and manage, "It is . . ." Frowning, I search for this much harder, less obvious answer. Dr. Al-Gamzawi's kindly eyes glow with some kind of bizarre satisfaction. It makes me wonder whether he's gloating over having successfully fooled me with a sympathetic facade. I exhale sharply. It's the only sound in the room.

"After the amalgam has set, what's the amount of mercury left in the amalgam?" He taps the desk with every utterance.

"It's . . ." I turn to Ghada. She looks back at me with a blank expression.

"Well?"

"I think, perhaps, maybe." I pause. "Fifty percent."

No expression.

"Forty-five percent?"

"This is not some bargaining shop in Khan El-Khalili!"

"Forty percent!"

He shakes his head and marks the paper in front of him with a big red X. After that the questions get progressively more difficult, and even though I had thought I was prepared, I fumble through the next twenty minutes or so before being released. Ghada does no better.

Outside, the next pair of students is called in. The rest crowd around us for some insight: how severe were the examiners? Can they be charmed? What did they ask? Ghada's frustration explodes into a hysterical description of what she says is the absolute worst day of her life. I deal with the disappointment more quietly. No one notices me as I drift back toward the cracked window.

The storm has picked up. Swirls of dust spray the flame tree. Its branches tap the glass, as if protesting the concealment of its flamboyant flowers.

There's a doum palm in the distance (the only palm that branches), swaying like a drunk, and a mimosa tree to its right (acacia family, does not bear spines), its yellow flowers shivering and flailing like a horde of hysterical tykes. Why did I not study botany? What made me choose dentistry, a field I am indifferent to? I suppose I saw it as a respectable occupation, one that would allow me to gain independence, to pull away from the family and sever the corroded cord that holds us together.

I'm squinting at the piercing glare of June's mustard sky when I hear someone call out my name. I turn around, and by the time my eyes have adjusted to the dim corridor, Adel is by my side and edging me toward the corner. "What is it?"

"All night I couldn't sleep. All night I thought about things, and I have come to a decision. I must tell you . . ."

"Did you finish your exams?"

"No."

"Then . . ." I want to know why he couldn't sleep. What is it that agitates him so? I want to ask him why he is here when he should be elsewhere, waiting for his exam. But I hold back when I notice that the corridor has abruptly gone silent.

The way Adel looks at me—with the intensity of a heartbroken lover—is enough to wake the imagination of even the dullest of minds. Wafa holds her hand to her mouth, and Soraya freezes. Ashraf's eyes glisten and Ghada stops her hysterics. They all stare at me.

Here is something with a whiff of the hush-hush in it: a possible boyfriend–girlfriend situation that could bounce from one tongue to the next until it bloats and explodes into scandal. Why does he have to act this way in front of all these people?

They wait. I laugh. It's the only way to shrug the nervousness away, to keep all that is tucked in my heart secure. "You are so funny." Without further thought, I grab his wrist and march him down the corridor, improvising a tale to convince the others that he has a habit of misplacing his notes. "Perhaps you left them in the cafeteria. Why don't we check?" I lead him through the door of the stairway, which is out of view and thankfully empty of students. "What on earth are you trying to do, making a spectacle like that?"

"It's just that I know you'll be traveling soon."

"Then why haven't you been coming to the club to study with me? I waited for you every single day."

"I can't face the thought of not seeing you all summer. We must find a way to meet once we're back home."

This is something I haven't even considered. In Dubai's tightly knit society—and living under Ammi Majed's roof—how would I manage it? "Impossible."

"There is a way. There must be a way." He grabs my hands, and my pulse quickens. Before I realize it, I find myself agreeing.

27

DALAL

❧

"Sing to the little birdies, Dalal. Let them learn the song."

It's a strange request, but if she asked me to walk across the room in a handstand I'd agree. It's been just six weeks since I signed the contract, and already Madame Nivine has secured my first recording—a song called "Only Me, Lonely Me," written especially for me—and we're heading to the studio as soon as she has finished getting ready. She's in the bedroom of her apartment in Mohandessin; I'm in the sitting room.

I saunter past a cabinet containing a collection of crystal animals and step out onto the glassed-in balcony, where she keeps her plants and parakeets. I turn to the birds—an identical pale-yellow pair—and start to sing. I add my own brand of color to the lyrics:

"It was love at first sight,
Now you wanna take a flight
Just know when you're on that plane
Your sweetheart is aflame

You wanna go?
Then go, go, go.
And stay away.
Oh no, no, no.
On my own . . . that's me . . . yes, me.
All alone . . . only me . . . only me . . . lonely me."

It's not profound, like an Umm Kulthum song. It's bouncy, frisky, like the spring of a squirrel. Madame Nivine says this is necessary to get me noticed. (She assures me that the serious music will come later.) Apparently the public just wants something light and jolly.

"Sing from your heart," she calls out, and I picture her unfurling the turban she has been wearing all day and selecting a shinier one for the evening. During the second round of the song the birds start to fidget, twisting their tiny heads this way and that.

Nivine Labeeb knows so much. Yesterday, the sting of Adel's comments still fresh, I asked her an important question: is it possible for a female singer to become famous and still keep her good name? "Of course she can," she said without a blink of hesitation, "if she has someone like me to make sure no one takes advantage of her." This made me feel warm inside, and I vowed to fling it at Adel if I ever saw him again.

She had then moved on to the subject of Sherif bey and why it was pointless to rely on him: all he could manage in his ripened old age were those tedious jingles for commercials. "He might have been great once, but not anymore. There's good money in jingles, mind you," she added with a wink, "but do you want a career singing tunes that glorify Nido milk or Johnson's baby shampoo?"

"Of course not!"

She had listed all the talented singers, men and women, who had employed her. "I gave each and every one a good shove up that steep ladder to fame. Sadly, none managed to climb to the top. They've all hovered somewhere between the first and third steps." Of course, she had an explanation for this. "You see, habibchi, once they start rising, they think they can find a better representative. And they leave me. So they remain mediocre—or, worse, they dissolve like sugar in tea." She held up her finger and wiggled her nose. Spellbound, I waited to hear more as she shut her eyes and released a colossal sneeze. "Oh yes," she said, sniffing and dabbing her teary eyes with a handkerchief, "many of them flew off to Beirut to find a French-speaking Lebanese manager with a fancy name, like Bierre or Michel or Bascal—what happened to Arab unity and pride, I ask you!—and were taken in by their promises to deliver the stars, and the moon, too. They only realized their folly when they noticed that whatever money they'd made was gone." She pitched a sly glance at me. "You will do the same, too."

"Never!"

She chuckled. "One thing you should know is that if you stay in the middle for too long, you'll only slip to the bottom. You see, you have to understand that people—the public and the fans—all have short memories. And if you don't keep releasing wonderful songs, if you don't put yourself, your very soul, out there, quite simply, they will forget you. So, hayachi, what I am saying is that it's all up to you—and me."

"Nearly ready," Madame Nivine calls now, and I smile with satisfaction. My manager works hard. She secures invitations to some of the classiest parties, the ones that take place in the beautiful old houses in Masr El-Gedida and the posh apartments in Zamalek. There are important people there: television managers and famous film directors, businessmen and influential government officials. As I set about charming them, Madame Nivine woos the oud player into strumming the music of the greats: Abdel Halim Hafez, Mohammed Abdel Wahab, Farid Al-Atrash. The other musicians follow his lead, and before they realize it I am in their midst and singing, to the delight of the guests.

I can't keep still; before I know it I'm once again belting out my song:

"While lovers around me are together,
I'm like a child without its mother.
Dejected, rejected, and all on my own,
My heart is melting. Your heart is stone."

I bring my face close to the birdcage and sing to express my joy in my new partnership:

"I'm your love . . . that's me . . . yes, me.
On my own . . . all alone . . . only me . . . lonely me."

❧

At the studio Madame Nivine leans toward me and whispers, "You know these artistic types—they always want an audience and insist that you be part of the entire creative process." She stifles a yawn. "This must be so boring for you, this waiting."

She couldn't be further from the truth.

The room is dim and full of small lights—red, yellow, green. There are switches and levers, too: a smoky cockpit that's busier than the flight deck of a crashing airplane. My eyes burn, but I unblinkingly watch the sound engineer's fingers zip over the controls. Every now and then he kicks his rolling chair from one corner of the broad mixer to the other so that he can press a button, thread a tape, or plug in a wire. Of course he's showing off for me, the attractive new talent. The musicians wait their turn just outside the control room; they are called in one at a time to play their bit in the recording studio. Ooh, and all for me.

The sound engineer tilts his head back and releases a lungful of smoke, puckering his lips so that it forms a perfect line. I follow it until it hits the low ceiling and disperses into a cloud, and my mind wanders. I imagine my mother staring at the television, the way she does every night. But instead of watching old black-and-white films, it's me she sees, right here, right now, in the midst of these giant machines and professional musicians. There's her face, a clammy knot of despair. I know what she's thinking; her mind churns like boiling water, and she clearly regrets all the times she put me down. Even with the smoke crowding my nostrils, I can still smell the decay of garbage at our door.

In my vision, she wishes she had been nice to me, that she had faked a mother's affection, no matter how insincere it might have been. Her eyes are dark, their light snuffed out, and her lips tremble. Her remorse is too great for tears, and I look at her and say, "You see how well I'm managing without you!" She kneels at my feet and kisses them, a solemn request for forgiveness. I raise an eyebrow and direct a cold stare her way—a copy of the one she used to give me—before crossing one leg over the other, my foot hooking her chin to knock her out of the way. *Hah!*

Our composer, Amro Dahab (whom Madame Nivine also represents), is tireless; he bounds back and forth across the room as if his legs were filled with springs. He has a big head, which jerks every time a new idea flashes in his mind. He makes each musician play every pluck, strum, and tap repeatedly until he gets it "just so." His energy is a sharp contrast to Sherif bey's dismal moods.

"Violinist! Call the violinist." Amro Dahab looks around the control room. Not for the first time, his gaze flicks to me and he scowls. Obviously he is not enchanted by my beaming smile. I'm not sure why, but he doesn't seem to like me.

As soon as Amro has pulled the violinist into the recording room, the sound engineer swivels on his chair and grins at me. He slides a fader: "Y'see, *mazmezain?* One small move, and listen to what happens. Poof! No cymbals. And now . . ."—two more faders are slipped down—". . . only the flute."

I clasp my hands. "Magic, *wallahi*, it's magic!"

"Yes, that's it," Madame Nivine mutters through the side of her lips. "Just act interested." The tea boy enters the control room once more, and she reaches for a black tea—her fourth in the three hours we've been here.

"And now . . ." The sound engineer turns up the microphone, and Amro Dahab's voice, shrill as a pipe as he tries to imitate the sound he wants from the violin, pierces my ears. I make a face and giggle, but Madame Nivine has lost patience.

She gets up in a huff and marches into the recording room. She informs Amro Dahab that he has exhausted the musicians with his needless repetition and that it's time to move on and record the talent—that's me—right away. "She's not an instrument, you know," says Madame Nivine. "Her vocal cords will dry up with all the waiting, not to mention the smoke. And then how will you complete the recording?"

The violinist slouches back in his chair and smirks before digging in his ear for buried treasure. The sound engineer and I listen intently, expecting an argument to explode between an impatient Madame Nivine and Amro Dahab, who insists on getting his composition just right. But then he says, "You promised to get me a name, someone who has recorded at least a song or two."

"I am bringing you fresh talent."

"Two unknowns will not make a hit."

"You may be the one creating the music, but I'm the professional when it comes to making sure your music spreads from one end of the Arab world to the other." Madame Nivine balances her no-nonsense tone with a broad smile. "We've discussed this, and we agreed that you'd concentrate on making music while leaving the rest up to me."

"I didn't agree."

"Your silence indicated agreement."

"You tricked me." He crosses his arms and sulks. But there's more. "And I don't like this tune, anyway. It's frivolous. You know I can do much better. And you won't let me."

Madame Nivine shakes her head. "Not for your first piece."

"My first piece, and you get me an amateur? It will show in the recording!"

By this time, I am quite insulted. But more alarming is the doubt that floods me. What if there's truth to that? As two unknowns, are we set to fail from the very start?

"She's never stood behind a microphone," says Amro Dahab. "I need to make sure the instruments sound perfect so I can cover her voice if it flies another way."

"For God's sake, she's not a bird!" Madame Nivine shoots a dirty look at the sound engineer, and he understands immediately. The control room goes silent. Madame Nivine's face is not quite so jovial anymore; she's hissing something. It's enough to make Amro Dahab drop his head and fiddle with his fingers, like a schoolboy being punished. Even the violinist behaves. With a serious face, he abandons his excavation and waits for instructions.

The room feels cramped; my breath is shallow. I cannot stop thinking about the possibility of failure. I rush out of the room, pass the waiting musicians in the outer office, and make my way through to the empty corridor, where I gulp in air. Will I sound silly, like the presenter of a children's show, singing "Only Me, Lonely Me"?

In the quiet of the corridor, my heels click, as sharp as a knife on a chopping board. Another vision of my mother, one that makes me tremble: this time I'm the one crouched by her feet, a daughter begging forgiveness for having disobeyed her mother.

"Dalal? Ah, here you are."

No sooner does Madame Nivine step over the threshold than I grab her wrists and yank her toward me. "Promise me I won't be a joke." The desperation in my voice startles us both. "Promise me."

She sucks in air through her teeth and wrestles her wrists out of my grip, shaking her head so forcefully that the turban shifts and a lock of hair, secured just above her left ear, drops out. "Easy, girl. You want to break my bones?"

"Sorry. I just want reassurance."

"If you're going to act like this every time you hear something hurtful, I'll tell you right now: go home." It's an order, and she points to the staircase.

"No, no, I promise I won't."

"How many times do I have to tell you it's not all flowers and perfume? The music world is savage. There are people in the industry who will slander you, and there are singers who, if you succeed, will be jealous and hate you for it." With that, she rubs her wrists. "You've left marks."

"Sorry." It's the first time she has scolded me. I shrink into a tight wad of regret.

"And then there are the reporters! They will hound you. They won't just write nonsense about the way you look and what you wear. No, that's not enough to fill the magazines and newspapers. They will actively dig for dirt. If they can't find enough, they will make up stories about you. And the more important you become, the worse it will get. So, I ask you, can you handle all that?"

"I can." (More calmly now.) "I will."

"That's better." She stuffs her hair back into her turban. "I can only deal with one outburst at a time."

28

MARIAM

֎

We pass open-fronted shops packed with car tires and spare parts, and juice stalls surrounded by haphazard clusters of honking cars filled with restless customers. We pass a paint shop, a flour mill, and a parking lot filled with bright-yellow tractors. Later we see a row of workshops constructing house gates in the traditional style: decked with bits of welded metal and painted in bright colors, decorated with flowers, sharp geometric patterns, or the UAE logo. They make me think of Dalal's old shaabia house and how at first she had loved that her gate was adorned with a bright-orange coffeepot—until she realized that it was inferior and reflected the preferences of a common man.

The air conditioner is on full blast. I breathe in Adel's woody, musky scent and sigh. As always, he looks princely in his crisp white kandora with the cotton tassel dangling down the middle of his chest and the ghitra wrapped in a neat turban on his head. He has trimmed his beard close to the skin; it's cut in a clean line just under his chin, thickening slightly where it joins his mustache. Under my abaya I wear a peach-colored chiffon shirt and a loose gray skirt that hangs just above my ankles.

We've been meeting in secret throughout the summer vacation. Some evenings Adel and I have dinner at Caravan, a restaurant by Dubai's Clocktower. There's safety there: the tables are nestled in private rooms with sliding locks on the doors. Other times we drive out to isolated beaches, all the way in Jebel Ali or Ghantoot. Today we've decided to go to the desert. It's four p.m., and to reach our destination we must pass through this noisy, diesel-infused main road in Sharjah's industrial area.

The light turns red, and Adel screeches to a halt. I sink down in my seat, even though I know it's nearly impossible that anyone will recognize me: my shayla is pulled so low it covers the upper half of my face and throws the lower half into shadow. I can't help it. Blended with the thrill of sneaking away is an apprehension that won't subside. What if someone who knows my family spotted me at Abu Hail Center and followed me as I took a taxi to our meeting point in the parking lot of Al-Mulla Plaza? What if some acquaintance happened to pass by just as I hopped into Adel's Mitsubishi Pajero? I thought I would feel braver after so many successful trysts. But no! That gut-twisting anxiety remains.

Abdul Majeed Abdullah sings "Raheeb." Adel raises the volume, and I notice that the man in the car next to us—who moments earlier had seemed bored to the point of dozing off—has turned a curious eye in my direction. I switch off the radio. Adel frowns at the man and then snickers at my silliness. "You don't even know him."

"Maybe he knows me."

"He's not even Emirati." He reaches out, but I slap his hand away before he has a chance to stroke my cheek.

"It doesn't matter," I say. "Maybe he knows my uncle or one of my cousins."

"That's so unlikely." Adel twists his mouth and clicks his tongue before shifting into first gear. The tires burn in a screech. The car jolts forward, and Adel cannot hide his glee. It's not the first time he has acted this way, as if gravity had been pulled from under his feet.

"But not impossible," I insist, and even though I am fully aware that my reasoning is absurd I stick to it because his indifference rubs me the wrong way. "You know the risk I am taking being with you. The least you can do is be discreet."

"Blah, blah, blah." He sticks his tongue out at me and waits for me to laugh and agree that I'm being irrational.

I would have, if this game he enjoys playing had any charm left in it. But the truth is that it has become tedious, to the point that I wonder why he gets so much twisted pleasure out of watching me get flustered.

I look away and busy myself by trying to catch as many names of the various roadside establishments as I can. I make the task more challenging by reading them in Arabic, then reversing the direction and reading them in English: RED FORT PUNJABI KITCHEN; MORNING BREEZE LAUNDRY; SMELL AND SMILE FLOWERS. Later, once it gets dark, the signs will flash in neon or glare through fluorescent tube lights: SIT AND RELAX CAFETERIA; TOPPEST OF THE TOP AUTO BALANCE; SHINE AND RISE BAKERY.

A jolt, and the engine growls as he overtakes the pickup truck in front of us. I glance at him quickly and see that the grin has not left his face. Three cars later, Adel cuts in front of an eggplant-colored Toyota Corolla. The driver, an older woman in a sari, looks straight into my eyes, her mouth warped with the shock of having been missed by a handsbreadth.

I swallow my cry before it escapes. I want to scold him, even slap him, but I resist the urge. That would just feed his need for attention and make him want to scare me even more. I stiffen and continue surveying the shops: COOK OF THE PEOPLES RESTAURANT; THE NUTTY MAN ROASTERY; PARADISE PHOTO SERVICES; MISSION IMPOSSIBLE IRANIAN KEBAB.

There's a shopping bag between my feet, containing two cotton housedresses that I don't really need but purchased as proof that I really was at the mall, shopping. Why do I go through so much trouble for this childish man?

When I first arrived in Dubai five weeks ago, I spent days figuring out the logistics of how I would be able to meet him without raising suspicion. It would have been simple if only I knew how to drive. But Ammi Majed is against that. He will not budge when it comes to allowing the women of his family to drive.

My first plans were illogical and overdramatic. I pictured myself creeping out my second-floor bedroom window and climbing down a ladder, which I would keep hidden behind the tamarind tree. I imagined digging a tunnel to the far corner of the garden. Of course, it was all fantasy, but it gave me time to decide how ready I was to take the gamble of meeting up with him. Then, in a more constructive frame of mind, I examined the workings of my uncle's household: when the family was resting or out of the house; when the staff disappeared into the outdoor kitchen for their meals, or to their rooms for naps. I'm not sure why I bothered taking note of these details, because I couldn't just saunter out through the front gate as I would in Cairo. Although the roads in Dubai are broad, even, and clean, and although there are no hazards at the intersections because cars stop at red lights and wait for pedestrians to cross, a woman alone on foot would draw too many curious glances and trailing cars, and eventually someone would recognize me and feel it his or her duty to let the household know. My solution was simple: one of the house's drivers would drop me off at a mall; from there I would take a taxi to meet Adel.

"You stopped talking, I see."

At the moment I feel very little affection for him. I consider opening the door and getting out. But we are out of the congestion, past Sharjah Airport and speeding toward the desert of Al-Dhaid.

Just before he turns off the road, Adel stops to let out air from the tires so he can drive on the soft sand. And then we're off, following one of the trails plowed by another person's car. To the left I see a settlement of five or six palm-frond huts, littered with roaming goats, and farther along is an oval-shaped enclosure of camels with their young. Scattered between the pristine dunes are plants plump with sap and a scattering of dried-up bushes. Every now and then, in the distance I spot plumes of dust stirred up by other four-by-fours.

As the Mitsubishi sways and rocks, my temper cools with the pleasure of being out in the vast and open desert. Why is it that I cannot stay angry with him for long? Perhaps it's because my time spent with him is limited—and precious. Nevertheless, I do my utmost to remain impassive, even though this becomes difficult when he turns off the trail and onto the dunes.

Up we go, flying off the crest. My abaya slips down to crumple around my hips, and my shayla slides onto my shoulders. I hold on fast, one hand clutching the sling above the car door and the other holding the corner of the seat in preparation for what's ahead.

It's a sea of swells and dips. Adel tears over the shallow dunes of soft-soft sand. With every leap, the breath sticks in my throat. A second later it's expelled with the force of the landing, along with a noise that's between a yelp and a grunt.

He knows I love the thrill. He knows I will soon be screaming from the rush. And I do, when the car stirs up the deeper sand of a high dune. "*Ooh!*" The car growls all the way up to the tip and purrs as it slides down, nearly vertical. "*Eeee!*"

Adel tackles a few more giants before maneuvering the car back to some smaller hilly dunes, where we're hurled from side to side and shaken up and down, back and forth. I grin and grimace at the same time. There is no respite, just terror and exuberance all mixed together until I can't tell one from the other.

He is unwavering in his mastery, sliding the SUV in a wavy line so we don't get stuck, keeping a firm grip on the steering wheel but releasing it when needed, as if in conference with the car.

But then something happens: a miscalculation, a flaw in judgment. He reaches the top of a rise and is startled by what's on the other side. It's steep and narrow. It's a gaping mouth.

We slide down. The car is not as straight as it should be. "Get back up! Turn it around!"

He hears me. I wish he wouldn't listen to me. But the unforeseen hazard has knocked the sense out of him. Adel rotates the steering wheel toward me, and before either of us can react, gravity is pulling us down.

There is a thud. I am as heavy as a sack of rice as I drop on top of him. His cry is lost in the hiss of sand that swallows us. Some part of him—I'm not sure which—is stuck under me at a painful angle. He tries to shift my weight off but manages to do no more than nudge me a few centimeters onto the gear stick, which rattles and pokes me in the belly.

He bellows, and I realize it's his hand. It's pinned to the door under my ribs. I try to move, but my head is as heavy as a cannonball. I want to pull myself up, hold on to something, anything, but my cheek remains glued to the window.

Down, down, down. Every second stretches, and just as I start to imagine it will go on forever the car rocks into a precarious slant. Instinct tells me to jump up and out. Logic slows me down and tells me to get my bearings. There's a groan of metal and a massive thump.

❧

Seated on the slant of a dune, I hug my knees and rock. Still shaky from the ordeal, I mumble my thanks to God for saving us. The overturned vehicle sits in front of me, and I think it's a miracle that the accident wasn't fatal.

Soon after we climbed out through the passenger window, two Nissan Patrols with massive round lights fixed to their bumpers appeared as if out of thin air. They arrived just as I was examining Adel's hand, trying to tell if it was broken. (As if I had a clue about such matters.) Five boys, who looked to be about sixteen on account of their bony frames but were probably older, jumped out. After asking whether we were all right, they examined the car: it lay on its side, two wheels in the air and the pair on the driver's side buried in the sand.

It's the heart of summer, and the air is thick save for a mysterious breeze that suddenly picks up every so often. It's fiery hot and makes a whistling sound as it dredges up tiny twisters of sand around me, as if letting out a sudden fit of hysteria. Sand sticks to my clammy face and turns into a fine paste.

The boys wear baseball caps instead of ghitras—the sporty look. They hike up their sleeves and secure their kandoras in thick knots around their waists. They stand in a row facing the roof and start rocking the vehicle. Adel works with them, but he pushes only with his uninjured left hand. One of the boys drops to his knees and digs. When he is convinced that the wheels have loosened sufficiently, he gives a thumbs-up and rejoins the others. They seem to know what they are doing, and this comforts me somewhat as I mumble into my chest, "C'mon, c'mon, c'mon." The quicker we get out of here, the better. Enough testing fate!

"One, two, three!" They push.

After a few unsuccessful attempts, they decide to rope our bumper to their bumpers and use their cars, one on each side, to yank it back up. This finally works, and my relief is so great that I want to hug them one by one. Of course I do nothing of the sort. Before they leave, one of the boys asks Adel whether he can manage steering in the sand with one hand. "What about . . ." He nods in my direction. " . . . the family?"

"My wife?"

"Yes, your wife. Can she drive?"

"No."

"One of us can drive your car to the main road, if you want," another boy suggests. "Or we can follow you just in case you get stuck."

"Yes, because with that hand . . ." The first boy raises it gently and scrutinizes the swelling with skepticism. "I think you should go straight to the hospital."

"And I will, brother," Adel reassures him. "Look." He raises his left arm and curls his fingers. "The other hand works perfectly." He grins.

Once the boys leave, I get up and peel off my shayla and abaya, giving both a good shake. Sand showers to the ground. The windows were closed, and yet I might as well have been swimming in it—the sand is so fine, it feels as though it has seeped into every pore. It's stuck to the back of my neck and fills my nose and ears, coats my scalp and has even slipped between my teeth. I spit as Adel tests the engine: a splendid purr, as if nothing happened. But as soon as I hop in, he switches it off.

"What's wrong?"

"Nothing."

"Can you drive?"

"Of course I can. But it's too early to go back."

"But after this . . . after . . ." Before I can string the words into a sentence, he hops out of the car and strides up the steep dune. "But you have to go to the hospital and get your hand checked out," I call after him. I try to keep the desperation out of my voice. "It will get dark soon. We must leave!" Adel doesn't even look back.

It's sticky. I let my aggravation out in a noisy puff of steaming air. I would like nothing better than to go back home where it's safe, before anything else happens. I wait a while, and when he doesn't come back I get out of the car to drag him down. I leave behind my abaya but sling my shayla over a shoulder. The warm sand swallows me with my every lunge up the hill. It's like wading in knee-deep water, and by the time I reach the top I'm exhausted.

There he is, sitting cross-legged and staring ahead at the horizon in what appears to be a rare moment of contemplation. I watch him as I recover my breath. It's as if a million holes have been pricked in my skin, and I wipe off the perspiration with my shayla before flopping down next to him.

Side by side, we watch the sun sink low on the horizon. A ball of brilliant red, its rim has gone soft, wobbling and blushing, leaking into the faded sky. He says, "You know, right now I feel terrible."

"Why, Adel?"

"Because I put you through unnecessary risk, zooming all over the place like that."

I wave my arm to indicate that he shouldn't give it a second's thought.

"No, no, no." He turns to face me, and shifts closer on his knees. "Really, Mariam, you could have broken bones in that accident." He shudders. "Or worse."

"But I didn't, al-hamdulillah. And besides, you were speeding because you wanted to give me a thrill, because you know how much I love it." I give him a playful nudge and add a soft rap to his cheek with my knuckles.

He pushes my hand away and blinks repeatedly. "Just let me finish: the fact is, I'm reckless. I never think about how my actions can hurt people." He slaps his chest with his injured hand and cringes. It is swollen around the thumb and tinged a pale blue.

"It's over." A wave of guilt washes over me. "If anything, it's my fault. I'm the one who told you to turn."

"Maybe."

"Yes, yes, it's all because of me. If you hadn't listened to me, we would have been all right."

He shakes his head. "Don't try to make me feel better. I'm no good."

He looks so distressed. Under a curtain of thick black lashes, his eyes moisten. There is a deep sadness in them, I'm sure of it. I hold back the urge to mother him, to hold him to my chest and stroke his hair. Instead, I rub his shoulder lightly to comfort him. But my touch prompts more than it should. He lays his head in the cradle of my crossed legs. What a situation! I try to pretend there is nothing meaningful in the gesture, but it's strange to have his face there, in such close proximity to my crotch.

He stays there, still as a rock, save for the occasional shudder. I suspect he might be crying, but I don't look down to check. (Better to spare him the embarrassment.) I keep my eyes glued to the sinking sun and wait for him to stop, patting his head, expecting him to pull away soon.

But then Adel's head starts to gyrate, nuzzling my navel. I shake him off and move back. He swiftly sits up onto his knees and grabs my face, stretching to plant a kiss on my lips. We've kissed before— tiny playful pecks or coltish expressions of desire, the intensity always monitored and kept in check by my ever-alert mind—so I am comfortable to let him finish before pushing him away. Then we can leave.

But this turns out to be a different kind of kiss: deep and excruciatingly long. It melts my resistance so that when he circles his arms around me in an embrace, I press closer, savoring the hardness of his chest. It's the smallest of moves, but it triggers a wildness in him that catches me off guard.

In one swift lunge, he flips me on my stomach and pins me to the ground. He chuckles, and, anticipating a torturous game of tickle, I shriek and laugh. I try to squeeze out from under him, but he's holding me to the ground so firmly that the only movement I can manage is a few swishing kicks and flaps that lack any real force. He loosens his grip, and for a second I imagine he'll let me go—I have enough freedom to lift up on my elbows. But Adel has a different agenda. His hand creeps somewhere it shouldn't, and in one swift move he pushes up my skirt and traps me once more.

"What are you doing?"

"Don't worry, I won't hurt you," he says as he fumbles with his kandora while still holding me down.

There is movement on top of me: a grinding of his hips, a hardness rubbing at my tailbone. All I can think about is how much of my bottom is exposed. "This isn't funny!"

"Relax, habibti, relax."

My eyes widen; it feels like they'll pop out of their sockets. And yet, strangely, I find his voice comforting. I stop writhing and lie very still.

"Say you love me," he moans.

"I love you."

He strikes me dumb with reassurances—"There's nothing to fear, I'm here for you. I'll protect you, always"—and compliments—"You are too lovely. I cannot resist you, habibti. Tell me you love me again." His murmurs are hot on my neck.

"Hmm."

"I know you do," he says, rubbing and moaning. "Come on, say it."

I look over my shoulder and glimpse his neck stretched taut, his mouth puckered and twisted to the side, his eyes half-open and glowing in the fading, rosy light. There he is, on top of me, caught up in a mystifying knot of rapture.

Sliding up and down now. "Say it." Gaining speed and urgency. "Say it now!"

Before I can oblige, he presses my head down.

I eat sand.

He grunts, and his body breaks into a series of quivers and quakes.

Dazed speechless, I stare at the Pajero's headlights bouncing ahead of us over the dunes. I am numb with shame and a vague sense of loneliness, a physical feeling of emptiness. It's as if some essential part of me—heart, stomach, gut—has been taken away.

It's not until we reach the main road that my lips start quivering, a sign of tears in desperate need of release. In my determination to stay in control—I will not break down in front of him!—I hold them back as questions roil in my head. Is this the way a relationship is meant to develop? If so, why do I not feel special, or even safe? What am I to him? I wish there were someone who could tell me. Where is Dalal? She might know.

"Are you all right?"

I don't say anything.

"Mariam, answer me. Are you feeling all right?"

"Used," I mutter. "That's how I feel."

"We were having a good time. You were giggling, you were laughing. I thought you were enjoying yourself."

Perhaps I was. "You should have asked."

He shakes his head. "I don't know what to tell you. I thought . . ."

"I'll never respect myself after this."

"Why are you so tormented?"

"You'll never respect me."

"That's not true. Right now you are closer to me than ever before."

"I don't think so."

"Why do you say these things?" he groans. "If anything, what happened is my fault. And it must be because I love you more than I can ever express."

"That was love?"

"I know. I'm sorry. It's just that you are so beautiful, and the beast in me took over. I'm sorry. It won't happen again." Adel lets out a hearty sigh. He sounds satisfied, as if he's just had a long and relaxing bath.

"Selfish, that's what you are."

"What?"

I cross my arms and glower. "You heard me: selfish."

"Yes, selfish in my love for you. And that I want to see you every day. I'm sorry for that, *yaani*."

"I don't mean it that way." I narrow my eyes at him.

"Then how? Please tell me."

I don't answer him.

"Look, Mariam, I beg you, don't ruin this day, because it's the best of my life. I'll never forget it. Today your breath warmed me and you heard my racing heartbeat."

"Stop it! I don't want to hear these words, dipped in honey so they taste sweet."

"All right, tell me. What did you mean when you called me self-ish?"

"You don't care about me. All you care about is yourself."

"Myself? What are you talking about?" He sighs and shakes his head. "I'm here for the summer vacation, the hot months, which I should be spending with my family in Fujairah. Once a year, my mother gets the pleasure of having me home. And what do I do? I de-prive her of this joy. I take all that valuable time and spend it with you instead." His words stab the air between us. "After I see you, I go to my friends' apartment in Sharjah and spend the night there, because my house is too far and because I hope I might see you again the next day. Some of us can't afford to stay in a hotel! I could be with my family right now." He punches the steering wheel with the uninjured hand. "I could be with my friends. Right now! Sipping cappuccino at Gerard's or playing cards in their majlis. Ah, how wonderful! So, go ahead and tell me again that I'm selfish."

My lips quiver again, and this time I cannot keep the tears in check; they create rivulets that run down the sides of my nose. No doubt they are tinged a mucky gray with what's left of the kohl after he crushed my face in the sand.

There is no way to stop it, so I try to sob quietly, hoping he'll ignore me. If he so much as utters another word I fear I might start wailing.

He peers at me. "What happened to you? Why are you crying?"

The unexpected concern in his voice pushes me over the edge.

"Don't shake so. Let me pull over to the side of the road for a bit. All right, all right, don't, don't hit me, I won't stop. I'll keep going." Pause. "Hold your nose tight. That will get rid of the hiccups. You don't need to push my face away, I won't look at you." Pause. "Come on, don't bend over like that; you'll make yourself sick." Pause. "You'll just feel worse if you keep everything in. Take deep breaths. Shout if you have to. *Ow!*" Pause. "Okay, don't shout. All I want is for you to stop feeling so miserable."

"Then shut up!"

29

DALAL

֍

"Think sparrow, not eagle." That's what the composer Amro Dahab had said all those weeks back during our first recording, when he was explaining the direction my voice should take. By now, when I've finished recording the last song for my first album, he does not say much anymore. The only thing he tells me once I'm warmed up is, "You shine like gold."

Yes, gold. It's not an original analogy. Nevertheless, it pleases me, and I let it boost my already euphoric sense of accomplishment. Madame Nivine drops me off at home, and once I'm in the dim stairway of the Imbaba apartment I take the steps two at a time. I am ravenous and think I could probably finish an entire stuffed baby goat if there were one cooked and ready in front of me. I chuckle at the thought and decide that a sandwich will have to do.

It's one a.m., and when I get to our floor I see that the bulb is out. Hanging from the ceiling by a wire that's been partially chewed by rats, it has been flickering these past few days. I tap it, which usually gets a tired glow going. This time, however, it emits a second's worth of dazzling light and then pops.

I stiffen. My mind must have played a trick on me. I'm sure I didn't see bloodred letters on the door. My first thought is that someone must have killed my mother. And I can't decide how to feel about that.

I blink and wait for my eyes to get used to the darkness. The word materializes. It's as simple and straightforward as a slap in the face: *Sharmoota*, slut! Upon closer examination, I notice tiny drawings spreading over the doorframe: men and women, stick figures with balloon faces, copulating in the crudest positions. This is some artist—he opted for the leisurely strokes of a paintbrush instead of spray paint. The male figures look different: some have big noses, others have mustaches or beards. The woman is the same, an obvious representation of my mother. I hold my mouth with disbelief. When did this happen? Feeling like a sleuth, I press at a clumpy part of the paint and gape at the glob that clings to my finger.

I plunk down on the stairs and wonder whether my mother is aware of this latest neighborhood insult. It surprises me that there's no sound coming from the apartment; Mama always waits up for me so she can gauge my mood when I get back. She isn't aware that I know she does this. The television is always on, and it illuminates her face with a spill of blue-gray light. She's keen to see me fail. Every time she sees that I'm happy, she tightens her face and stares daggers at me. Sometimes she tries to rattle me with a snide remark or a hurtful comment. But I've grown smart. I never answer her.

I get up and shift on my feet, unable to decide whether to go in or stay out. *Sharmoota!* The word is at a slight slant. I count seven paired stick figures. Whoever did this took his time. Is it possible that Mama didn't hear the strokes of the brush or the shuffling feet and snickering voices? What about the neighbors? Did they laugh so much that they exhausted themselves?

A strange sadness fills me, sadness for my mother. I've felt all sorts of emotions toward her—love and admiration, anger and resentment—but rarely pity.

I close my eyes. What's on the other side of that door? My stomach growls, but I decide to forgo the sandwich. I'll go straight to my room and stay there until tomorrow, and face whatever comes in the new light.

The click of the key sounds too loud. I tiptoe to my room and close the door softly behind me. I don't bother changing or removing my makeup, just slip under the sheet and twist the kinks out of my neck, willing my mind to block out all thought.

The minutes drag. I yawn. I stretch. When sleep does not come, I kick. There is a churning, slow and rhythmic, in my belly. If only I could fill it. I sit up and listen carefully. All is still, so I slink out to the kitchen.

The white cheese looks appetizing. I cut it into cubes and stuff them into the pocket of a Baladi flatbread, along with sliced tomatoes and a sprinkling of pitted olives. I stand with my back to the kitchen entrance and take my first bite. My teeth leave neat punctures: a third of the sandwich furiously devoured. My second bite is smaller but equally satisfying; I savor the mash of different flavors on my tongue. I take a third.

"You're back, I see."

Startled by my mother's voice, I bite my tongue.

"You had me wondering what happened to you."

Is that concern? I swallow the mixture in my mouth in one go and choke. My eyes stream and my face heats up. All the while, my sore tongue throbs. Mama doesn't hand me a glass of water. I get that on my own. She does slap my back, though: hard, like pounding dust out of a carpet.

"Bit your tongue, too, huh?"

I nod and ease into the kitchen chair that she pulls out for me.

There is no iron in her eyes, just a vague look of anxiety. It's a look that warms me inside and out, and I decide it is concern. Not for the first time I find myself wishing for just a little parental worry, even if it leads to a lengthy interrogation, which most girls I know hate. That has never happened to me. I have been given free rein to come and go as I please. Maybe she will ask why I am so late, where I went, whom I saw. If she does, I will tell her everything: how I am moments away from fame.

When I finish clearing my throat, she taps my hand. And that's enough of a prompt for my report to come pouring out. She listens. There is no expression on her face and I'm sure it's because she doesn't want to miss a word, because she wants us to be close. Once I finish I am beaming, expectant, cocking my head like a puppy waiting for approval after performing a particularly clever trick. I make a mental note to scrub away that vile word and those flagrant stick figures, to spare her the pain. I will make sure there is not a trace of red paint left, even if I have to scrape, even if we end up with a door pockmarked with splinters.

"Just remember," she says, "I can only bear so much. When you fall on your face, don't expect me to be there for you."

I start coughing again, as if that sandwich is back in my mouth and going down the wrong way.

"You are building a future that will lead you to the gutter!"

Sharmoota! How could I allow myself to believe that she cares? Again. I get up, slam my hands on the kitchen table, and bend over her. In a voice spiked with animosity, I say, "You might want to go outside and take a look at what's on our door."

She gives me a contemptuous snort. "And you might want to know that I'm not renewing the lease on this apartment."

"What are you talking about?"

"The money has run out and I'm moving." She taps my nose with her finger. "And you, Miss Golden Voice, will have to deal with it."

She sits back with undisguised glee, savoring the effect this news has on me. It stuns me mute. She says, "Since you want your independence so badly—away from the mother who bore the suffering of giving you life—I've decided it's time you got your wish. Now I would like to concentrate on my own future."

"What future?"

"You have two weeks."

Air, I need air! I rush out onto the balcony and lean against the railing, dizzy. How easy it would be to just swing over. The thought frightens me and I look up, scowling at the slit of murky sky.

"That fat woman will destroy you." Her hiss is hot on my neck. "You'll be so indebted to her that when you're unable to pay, she'll take you to court."

Tears collect in my eyes. If I so much as blink, they'll drop. She wants to watch me crumble. I won't let that happen. I take a mighty sniff and slide my hands over my face, blotting the moisture before elbowing her to the side and stomping back in. "It may look rosy now. But mark my words, you'll regret it," she calls.

She follows me through the sitting room, hurling insults. I wish there were somewhere I could hide. I hurry to the bathroom, where I lean over the sink and stare at the mirror. My lids are swollen, and, for once my eyes look the same size: shrunken, small, and hard, like peanuts.

I pick up my toothbrush and start brushing furiously, ignoring the sting on my tongue. I've never seen her this way, so hurtful, so intent on dragging me into a fight. She's still snarling at me. I spit into the sink and turn around. "You can't stand to see me succeed. That's what this is. Isn't that right, Mama?" I wave the toothbrush at her. "And what kills you is that you won't be a part of it. Actually, you'll never be a part of any success. You'll stay the way you are: one big nothing."

When she snorts, I fling the toothbrush. It hits the wall and bounces into the bathtub. I rush to my bedroom and slam the door shut before she can wedge her foot in. "Leave me alone. Why don't you go and open the front door, see what the world thinks of you." I drag the bedside table over and sit on it. There is a loud banging as she tries to force the door open.

"I have only so much patience for you!" she yells. I plug my ears against the abuse that follows. The people above us wake up and start yelling curses. They strike warning thumps that shake the ceiling light.

"Why don't you just go away?"

And then, silence. I'm not sure what to make of it. I find it hard to keep my breath steady. At some point—I'm not sure when—tears begin to trickle down my face.

I hear a muffled shriek, followed by a flurry of footsteps, urgent and noisy. My ear is glued to the door. Yes, she's on the phone, there's her voice. It is muted—a little shaky?—and I can't hear what she says.

Fatigue washes over me. A heavy feeling, like thick slime, settles on my shoulders. It weighs me down. I whimper as I sink to the floor, a trembling wreck of agony and resentment. There I stay, curled like a baby in the womb, with my back pressed against the bedside table. I close my eyes, and three breaths later I am asleep.

∼

It's five days later, and on this morning I awake and smell fresh paint. That's curious; it'll be the first time anyone in this ghastly neighborhood has tried to make his dwelling more livable, more beautiful. Someone in my building must have had enough of the grunginess and decided to freshen up the inside of his apartment.

I sigh at the prospect of another day of boredom. There's a tin on the coffee table. I run my finger around its rim, staring at the drawing on its lid. A lady in a violet gown holds a matching parasol; it looks like she is about to open it. Behind her stands a gentlemanly-looking soldier in a regal red uniform.

I shake the tin, which used to be full of treats. Not many of the Mackintosh chocolates are left; I've been devouring them since I finished the Danish butter cookies. The chunky green candies with the coconut filling were the first to go, followed by the purple variety filled with hazelnuts and caramel. After that, I ate the stick and coin toffees. I pull open the lid and push the sparkly wrappers about, hoping to have overlooked one of my favorites. But there are only creams left, an overly sweet orange and a too-bland strawberry. I toss one of each into my mouth and let the tastes blend as I chew with the sluggish munch of a camel. Drool slides down the sides of my mouth. I wipe it off with my cuff, leaving a muddy streak on the pajamas I've been living in these past few days.

Mama has disappeared. She packed some clothes and left.

At first I was relieved. But then I was overwhelmed by a variety of other emotions. I suffer from fits of restlessness punctuated by long intervals of blank lethargy. I'm quite exhausted with the experience of being alone, but I lack the energy to venture out. I topple back onto the couch and groan, "I'm a prisoner." I don't dare leave the apartment because of what's on that door. I've kept the shutters closed and am careful to move as quietly as a rabbit so that people think no one's home.

Helplessness sucks the air out of my chest. "Too much pressure!" I'm too young to have to deal with so many problems. Besides the effort I'm putting into achieving fame, I have this unwanted responsibility: I need to find money so I can extend the lease. Otherwise, where will I sleep? I need to buy food, too, and pay the bills for the phone, gas, and electricity. They're heaped on the dining table, collecting dust. Yes, too young. I should be in college (despite the fact that I'd loathe all the studying I'd have to do), and my only worry should be passing my exams.

In a burst of frustration I kick the coffee table, sending the Mackintosh tin rolling toward the door. There are footsteps outside, and whoever it is pauses by the door. No doubt it's another nosy neighbor anxious to make sure everything is fine. That's what they say when they knock every day. "Anyone there? Everything okay?" I never answer because I know it's nothing more than vile glee, a need to further ridicule the divorcée and her daughter.

I bite my knuckle and wait to see if the neighbor will knock. He doesn't, but the phone rings, and once I'm sure the encroacher has trudged away, I get up to answer it. Madame Nivine wastes no time: "Should the main song of the album be released before the video *cleep* (that's how Madame Nivine pronounces it) or the other way around?" It's a new trend, a music video accompanying a song, and it has older managers like Madame Nivine baffled over how best to handle it.

I've lied to Madame Nivine and told her I'm sick, because the thought of stepping outside is too daunting. I keep a croak at the back of my throat as I ask, "Why not together?" The phone line is crackly, and I repeat my suggestion.

"I hear you, ya hayachi, I hear you." There's a thoughtful pause.

I sit up straight and fiddle with the buttons of my pajamas, ignoring the reek of damp and dusty potatoes that wafts from the fibers. Any discussion to do with my career calls for my full attention. Madame Nivine has been busy sprinkling her magic powder. Any day now and my song will be released. And then, as can happen in the world of Arabic popular music, things can change for me very quickly.

"Of course, if they do go out together," she reasons, "then we have the added factor of publicity through television."

"That's right."

"But if people hate the *cleep*, that could affect the success of the song?"

She goes around and around over the same arguments. It's the third time she has called me about this, and I still haven't gotten used to the hesitation in her voice. "I suppose so."

"Hmm." Another pause. "And you? Better?"

"Yes." I sniff. "Just this sore throat that's taking forever to heal. Tired, I guess." The rush of excitement melts away and I slouch back onto the couch.

"Yes, well, get some rest. In the meantime, let me think about this a little more, and I'll get back to you with my decision."

For the next ten minutes I glower at the tin and consider how much I hate the remaining flavors of candy. Ten minutes after that, I am splayed on the couch like a wilted star, an arm and a leg dangling over the edge. I am staring at the ceiling with no thoughts whatsoever passing through my head when the phone rings. Madame Nivine again? "So, what did you decide?"

"Hello?"

I shake the receiver. I think I must be dreaming, or else the phone lines must have gotten tangled up, as they often do. One more *hello* puts an end to the confusion. "Ooo, is that . . . ?" I need to be sure.

"Mmm, yes, it's . . ."

We are like infants learning to speak, replacing every word that gets stuck with a hoot, a burble, or a titter. "Where have you . . . ?"

"I'm in Dubai and . . ."

The initial awkwardness passes, and suddenly it's as if we'd never stopped talking to each other. Mariam tells me she's bored and that there's nothing much happening in Dubai. I tell her there's too much going on in my life—Mama's disappearance, the art on the door, the horror of facing eviction—and I don't know whether I can handle it all. She doesn't agree with me, tells me she has never met anyone stronger. Her voice is as fresh as a mint. It hardens my nerves and awakens my senses. I want to take off my pajamas and wash up, put on something bright and colorful. "I'm a hop away from fame," I tell her proudly. "My first song will be released any day now."

"I always knew you'd get there."

The crackles in the line come and go, sometimes giving way to sharp whistles.

"So, are there really actual drawings of couples having sex on your door?"

Mariam's giggle makes me see the humor in it for the first time. "Oh, yes. My mother and many different men."

We laugh after that for a long time. Then we grow quiet at the same time. It's a kind of magic, this harmony we share.

"I miss you," I murmur.

"So do I."

30

MAJED

❦

"So, should I make sure the Neely is ready for a get-together this coming Wednesday?" Saeed asks.

"You ask me this so soon after the Friday prayer?"

He shrugs.

"No," I say mechanically. My mouth is pursed, but I can't hold the expression. My face stretches into a broad grin, and Saeed shakes his finger at me. He throws his head back and lets out a vulgar cackle. I've been so good, so very good and proud of these four months of abstinence. And just now with Saeed's question, a thought crossed my mind: it's not necessary to completely give up drinking, only stick to a moderate intake.

"I thought you'd refuse again," he says, and happily joins Mattar, who sits at the far end of the majlis, flinging handfuls of peanuts into his mouth and concentrating on the advice of a religious sheikh on television.

I stay where I am by the door, jovial inside and out. Everything is going just the way it should. Aisha tells me that the rich widow

Salma Bint-Obaid is interested in a union between Mariam and her son. There has been a surprise message from my son Khaled, too. The envelope—covered in Thai stamps—contained two pages. The first was a short note informing me that he was ready to come back to Dubai; the other contained a poem he had written for me. I skimmed through it twice, and when it still looked like gibberish I crumpled it into a ball and threw it in the wastebasket. He has some explaining to do, that irresponsible idiot.

Weak, that's what he is. Not long ago, I received some disturbing news from a young man who went to school with him. He had just returned from Bangkok and couldn't look me in the eye as he informed me that Khaled was not well, that he has been taking drugs. When I asked what kind, the young man mumbled that he thought it was the worst type: heroin. Once my son returns I shall say nothing to him for a few days, but only for the benefit of his mother, who has been so worried about him. Aisha will want to pamper him. It's her right as a mother, and I'll allow her to enjoy doing so. But after that . . . My thoughts are interrupted by the arrival of the first guest. I bend over to greet him.

Ghaith Al-Yasri is stooped and frail. "Long time!" he says in a mock scold. He was one of my father's best friends, and that means he has the right to pull my ear whenever he feels like it. He does so now, with a surprisingly firm grip. I only let him because I must be civil and honor his old age. Besides, it obviously gives him pleasure.

"Yes indeed, ammi."

"We used to hear news from your family when your brother was alive. But nothing whatsoever, for so long now."

"This is the world now, ammi. Everyone rushing this way and that, forgetting to make time for the important things in life." I try to ease out of his grip, but it's tighter than a clothespin. I have to yank at Al-Yasri's wrist so that he lets go.

He guffaws. "You thought I'd lost my strength, didn't you."

"Yes, ammi," I say, glowering at Saeed and Mattar, who are snickering diabolically from the other side of the room like a pair of irritating children.

Al-Yasri's eyes have fogged with age, but he scrutinizes the majlis and misses nothing. His eyes dart along the plush seating fixed to the walls and the giant television screen. The program has changed; now squeaky-voiced little girls in school uniforms stand on a stage. They arc their arms over their heads as they sing some patriotic song.

Al-Yasri lingers at the doorway. He seems happy to stay right where he is, breathing in the scent of expensive oudh with a grin that confirms that this is indeed a grand occasion. He has come with two of his grandsons, who nudge him along to make space for the other old men who have started arriving, also in the company of their sons and grandsons. They file in and I press my nose to theirs, one by one, in a cordial greeting.

Feeling generous and in a celebratory mood, I had decided to organize this lunch for my relatives and friends from Ras Al-Khaimah, most of whom I haven't seen since Hareb (who'd insisted on staying in touch with people from the old days) had passed away. I had sent my sons to deliver the communal invitation, but I had no idea there would be so many grizzled faces—some I cannot recognize—eager to make the journey to Dubai. Still, it's good; it means that this feast will be talked about and remembered for a long time.

Here they come, with their age-thinned beards dyed black or brightened to orange with henna. Some use their canes to support their weakened gait; others have managed to preserve a surprising amount of the sturdiness of their youth. Their kandoras are starched and hover above their ankles, in the old style. The dashes of kohl on their eyelids have smudged.

They plant themselves on chairs, rigid as statues. Some fidget as they try to get comfortable, unused to the tall seats. They tuck a knee under themselves and try to hug the other leg to their chest, but the seat is too narrow. So they end up settling on the floor; pretty soon the majlis looks like an airport terminal filled with passengers waiting patiently for their planes to arrive.

Some of the guests look peculiar and out of place, these tribesmen in central air-conditioning. A few brought along their yirzes, the small-headed ax of the mountain clans, and two arrived with silver daggers strapped around their waists. Every time they move, the elaborately decorated handles poke their ribs.

The houseboys serve goblets of freshly squeezed orange and lemon juice. My sons Saif, Ahmad, and Badr are here, as well as the grandsons old enough to be considered young men. Everything's as it should be, and I rub my hands with pleasure before mingling with the guests.

I am a perfect host, asking after their health and changing seats every few minutes so that no one feels neglected. Some tell me how they got lost trying to find their way to my house; most complain that Ras Al-Khaimah has become a different place, with too many highways and cars and foreigners and modern thinking. "Before, we all used to live together," says Al-Yasri, who sits cross-legged on the floor, rubbing the thick carpet with his palms as if it were soft sand. "Now, the young want their own home when they marry."

I nod my agreement. "Time has made strangers of people."

From the other side of the room Ibrahim Al-Khadhar calls out, "With this modern work behind desks in offices, they've all forgotten the palms, and what real work, men's work, means."

Theirs are the usual old-man grumbles. I sit in their midst on the floor and listen like a patient sage, inserting a calming comment here and there, clicking my tongue every now and then, or shaking my head sadly so they understand that I have sympathy for them.

"Before, we used to have all our meals together," Al-Yasri continues. "Now we're lucky if we see our children and grandchildren once a week. And if you complain, they tell you they can't help it, that the work hours they have to put in keep them away."

His grandsons are young, probably just starting college; they sit on either side of him. "But now you don't have to go hungry," one of them says, leaning over. "You go to the supermarket and there's any kind of fruit you desire."

"*Shoo ha!*" Al-Yasri pinches the carpet with disgust. "What are these new creations, oranges and apples? I don't need them. Give me dates; that's enough for me."

His other grandson tries to soothe him. "Do you remember, Grandfather, you told me you used to get boils from the heat and humidity? And you'd scratch and scratch? Well, you don't suffer from them anymore because of the air-conditioning." His face is suffused with the familiar smugness of youth. He pats Al-Yasri on the shoulder, oblivious to the temper brewing in his grandfather.

I make a tent with my fingers and rest my chin on it. I stay very still and wait for the outburst that is sure to follow. Al-Yasri slaps his grandson's hand off and cries, "I'd rather scratch until they pop and bleed than live with your conditioner. I'm too stiff to bend properly because of it." His face reddens and he waves his arms to the ceiling. "Majed!" he barks. "Look how they talk to us. No respect anymore."

The grandsons are embarrassed, and I raise my eyebrows at Badr, who understands what he must do. He hurries over and guides them out of the room with a quickly made-up excuse. Rising, I signal to Saif and Ahmad that it's time for the food to be served.

The houseboys emerge once more and spread semitransparent plastic sheets in the middle of the room, from one end to the other. There won't be any fancy foods for this group, like rice-stuffed zucchini or tightly rolled grape leaves; those wouldn't be appreciated. An exotic curry would certainly be regarded with skepticism. No, none of those new foods, either, like hummus, tabbouleh, and fattoush, which have become essential supplements to Emirati spreads. Not for this lot. Meat is king for these tribesmen. Large trays of meat—scattered on generous beds of rice and layered under paper-thin *regag* bread—arrive, the finest anyone could ask for. There are eight stuffed baby goats flavored with saffron, cardamom, and our Khaleeji blend of herbs.

"*Igribou*, get close."

No sooner do I utter the invitation to commence than the group begins a chorus of calls, starting with the name of Allah, Most Gracious, Most Merciful: "*Samou! Samou!* Say the name!" They move to the edges of the sheets and push their kandora cuffs up to expose a generous length of their arms. I do the same and shove my fingers into the steaming belly of one of the goats, extracting the stuffing of onions, chickpeas, cashews, and raisins. The meat is so tender it slips off the bones. Soon the only noise in the room is that of fingers ripping flesh, hands breaking bones, teeth chewing on meat.

Someone laughs, and the sound is so out of place that we all look up at once and follow his gaze to the television. There is a Khaleeji comedy on, with the usual frisky antics. A father is trying to thrash his moronic son, who jumps out of the way and bounces from one couch to the other. The wife yells at her husband to stop, but then he turns and starts chasing her instead. The group bursts out in laughter. I've caught snatches of this program before. There's also a mother-in-law who loves to make problems.

Once the chase is finished, we turn back to the business of feasting. I decide I've had enough and ease back to survey the munching, slurping group. They flick bones out of the way, making small heaps on the plastic sheets. Al-Khadhar busies himself with a goat's head, trying to get to the brain, and Bu-Surour pours so much buttermilk over his rice and goat meat that the mixture looks like soup. He laps it up, oblivious to the pearly drops that get caught in his stringy beard. I watch him and smile. It's good to stay in touch with one's people, and I decide I must invite them all again, perhaps make it a regular event every couple of months or so.

The gorging is fast and passionate. They rise to wash up, and the houseboys start removing the trays and wrapping the plastic sheets over the mess of bones, flesh, and date pits. My gaze drifts back toward the television. A variety show is on now; I see the presenter, dwarfed on a massive purple settee, and try to guess her nationality. She has a flawless local accent, but it's obvious she's not Emirati, because no Emirati family would allow their daughter to appear on television. Her face is round like the moon, and her bangs, under the transparent shayla that sits high on her head, are ironed so straight they fall like sharp pins into her eyes. Moroccan, I decide. She introduces a young Kuwaiti singer I have never heard of, and a music video rolls: a scrawny man who wanders alone along the seashore and croons with a lovesick moan. The injured expression in his eyes reminds me of Khaled, the way he looked before he disappeared, and I try to decide how best to deal with him. Lock him up in a room until he sweats it out? Or . . .

The men return and the tea arrives in thermoses along with bowls heaped with apples, oranges, and bananas. Badr serves gahwa, and soon after that half the group—including the men with daggers and yirzes, their nomadic hearts pulling them away to other places, no doubt—abruptly rise to leave. They raise their hands in farewell, and Saeed, my sons, and I get up to see them out, as courtesy dictates.

When we return, the room has suddenly grown quiet. "What are you all watching?" I ask, pulling my shoulders back and grinning with satisfaction over how successful this lunch has turned out. I follow their gazes. And then I freeze. Only my eyes move; I blink rapidly, as if that will make me see something different. But what is on that screen is unmistakable: Dalal, fluttering her hands like a butterfly, lost in a lurid rainbow sky.

31

MARIAM

〜

The house is quiet. My aunt has bundled Mama Al-Ouda and Nouf into the car for a full day's visit at a friend's house. My uncle and his sons are hosting a lunch in the majlis. Sprawled on my bed, I close my eyes and rake my fingers through my bangs. I can still taste sand. How is it that my feelings toward Adel changed so quickly, from adoration to abhorrence? Was it ever love, or was it something else?

When I spoke to Dalal a week back, I imagined I'd be able to tell her about being pinned into the sand and molested. I thought I'd be able to express my anger at the humiliation, the horrible sense of having been used, violated, stripped of worth. But the whole thing continues to overwhelm me; every time I try to examine my emotions, I get the shivers. Dalal had not sensed my anguish. Why would she? As always, my voice was steady and supportive.

"So, where do you think she went?" Dalal had asked me.

"Who?"

"Who else? My mother, silly."

"I don't know."

"It's not as if she has any friends. Everyone hates her!"

"Maybe she went to that composer friend. What's his name?"

"Ah. Sherif bey. Can you believe I don't have his phone number?" Dalal sighed. "I'd go out and bang on his door, if only I could."

"Why can't you?"

"Have you forgotten the smut on the door?"

I scoffed. "I can't believe that would stop you."

There was a pause. "You're right!" said Dalal. "How hard could it be? It's just a turn of the handle, after all."

"Yes, nothing more than that."

"You know, I'm going to do it right this very minute."

She had plunked the phone down and left me waiting. I remember my steady, even breathing as I waited for her to come back. Hearing her voice that day had returned my sense of composure, which had evaporated the day I met Adel.

What a fool I was, convincing myself that he had feelings for me. Why did I think I could change his volatile nature? So many signs, and I ignored them all. I should have walked away right at the start and never looked back. Instead I let him lead me into a cloud of beautiful dreams. I'd imagined such a future with him—one in which I would be more than a stay-at-home wife. We'd be dentists working side by side, first as employees, later in a clinic of our own. We'd have a house with a lush garden, crowded with my favorite exotic trees and flowers, and exactly four children, who would grow up to be decent human beings because they'd be rooted in rich soil.

Dalal had cut into these thoughts with a whisper that was both sharp and urgent. "You won't believe what happened."

"What?"

"The door—someone painted it red. Some benevolent soul decided to get rid of the drawings."

Now I smile as I picture the bold color; it matches my cousin's daring. My gaze drifts to the small clock on the bedside table, the hour hand pointing to four. There are just ten days left before I fly back to Cairo. What then?

Ever since Adel took advantage of me, I have avoided all contact with him. How will I face him once I'm back at college? I imagine him in the lecture hall or clinic, brashly insisting on seeing me again. How will I deal with that? I practice what I'll say to him: "I'm not interested. Leave me alone." How will he respond? He'll make a scene in front of all the students—that's what he'll do. Just thinking about it makes me jittery, to the point that I jump off the bed and start pacing the room.

Once I'm back at college there'll be nothing I can do but let my studies fill my time—and my head. My exam results arrived, and the grades I received were high, unexpectedly so; I thought they would be marred by my performance on that first oral test. Yes, that's what I'll do, even though I've been wondering whether dentistry is even the right vocation for me.

The closet door is open, and I scan the top shelf. I can't see what I am looking for, and even though I always keep it in the back, I panic, suddenly worried that my father's briefcase is not there. The chair leaves deep lines in the carpet when I pull it over. I climb up, and my hands grope in the dimness. I'm relieved when I feel the briefcase; I pull it out and settle cross-legged on the bed to open it.

My father used to carry the boxy black briefcase whenever he was traveling, and when he came back home he would use it to store important documents. A few months after he passed away, Ammi Majed gave it to me. I know exactly what is in it. For many years after his death, whenever I felt empty or lost, I would sift through the contents. It gave me comfort. I hope it will have the same effect now.

I punch the numbers into the combination lock: three–nine–six, the same as our post-office box number, and spread the items in a fan around me. There's my parents' marriage certificate, and the divorce papers from my father's first two unions. There are two faded airline tickets—Air India, to Bombay and back—and a pair of sunglasses in a broken case. I look through my mother's passport, which expired two years after my birth. It's been stamped in Bahrain, Shiraz, and Bombay. There is no photograph, and printed in its place is the word *muhajaba*, veiled. (At that time, women's faces were not required to appear in their passports.)

There's my father's small red telephone book. I pick it up and leaf through the pages. The handwriting is as careful as that of a child learning to write, and just as graceless. Poor Baba; how hard he tried. In his artless calligraphy, he managed to fit no more than a couple of names and numbers on each page. I used to make fun of the way he looped the letter *ya*, Y, allowing it to balloon and fill half the page; the extra teeth he added to the letters *seen*, S, and *sheen*, Sh, so they looked like bumpy roads; and the runaway letters *ra*, R, and *zein*, Z, skewed long so they were not missed.

Here and there, above and below the awkward handwriting, are dots, sprinkled as if they were an afterthought. And they must have been. I click my tongue as I remember all the times I lectured him about how incomprehensible his writing would look if he kept forgetting where the dots went. "No one can read this!" He would hold his finger to his mouth and look around. "*Shh.*" Then, with a conspiratorial wink, he'd add, "That's the idea. It's a secret way of writing that only you and I can decipher."

"You left me too soon," I whisper with a sigh. I want to dwell longer on the memory of my father, but I hear something big crashing to the floor. It comes from downstairs, and my first thought is that it must be one of the maids breaking a plate. But then there's another crash, and then another. I throw the contents back into the briefcase and rush out to investigate.

32

MAJED

❧

There are fireworks in my head. No colors; just explosions.

This will damage my standing in the community. It's an insult to my integrity, my manhood. Saeed, Saif, Ahmad, and Badr straggle like hesitant street dogs behind me as I stomp out of the majlis. When I reach the house, I holler at them to get out of my sight. Whimpering like women, they beg me to calm down. I swivel around to glower at them. That is enough; they back away, trying to retreat with dignity but failing.

I have often wondered about those scenes in Western movies when a character gets so angry he starts smashing things in the house. Why break something? What satisfaction is there in it? But there is satisfaction. I discover that now.

A large vase patterned with flowers sits on a side table in the hall. The glass is so thick there's no transparency to it. It's the first thing that catches my eye, and I sweep it to the floor. It doesn't smash into smithereens the way I want it to, beyond hope of repair, but my fury abates somewhat. A mad grin bursts onto my face as I watch it break into uneven chunks, silver shards flying in all directions over the marble floor. But then the memory of that video clip comes back.

I had been in the best of spirits, but that blasted song had changed everything. I remember ordering my son, Ahmad, to quickly change the channel. He gave me a blank look, and I had to jab him in the ribs to get him to obey. Saif spotted the remote clutched in the thick hands of a rheumy-eyed old man, and motioned to Badr to snatch it. But he is my soft son, and he couldn't very well pry it loose from those hardened knuckles. Standing as politely as he could next to the guest, Badr crouched and rose repeatedly, as if willing the remote to leap into his cupped hands. When the man wedged it beneath his foot, well, that was that.

I wanted to leave the room, but shock kept me where I was. The camera wouldn't stay still. It kept moving, zooming in until Dalal's face filled the screen, then pulling back in that dizzying technique so popular nowadays. Behind her, garish colors gyrated into hills and hoops, mere frills of ornamentation for the master performer, the star, my daughter.

I couldn't stop watching. Frozen, I felt a spark of regret for having gotten rid of my Cairo spies. (I'd ordered Mustafa to cancel them a couple of months back.) They might have warned me, and then I could have taken action to prevent this mortifying display. What was she trying to prove, wearing that blouse of shimmering armor, with rows and rows of silver sequins that glittered like tiny mirrors? Her arms were bare. I cringed every time she raised them; it was humiliating, watching my daughter expose herself like that. Her mouth puckered into a lascivious pout. I waited for the leering comments. Dalal twisted her hips and snaked her arms in a way no respectable girl should. But when no one uttered a word, I snuck a peek at the group to find out why.

Al-Shamri had shuffled right up to the screen and was ogling her with an open mouth; his missing front teeth made him look particularly depraved. Al-Khadhar's cheeks had darkened like burnt toast,

Bu-Surour raked his wiry beard distractedly, and right next to him
Al-Naqbi gawked at the television while absentmindedly kneading his
small toe. Quite simply, the old men were under her spell, no doubt
fantasizing about the alluring young flesh on the screen.

I no longer felt outraged or embarrassed. Hope crept through
me—I realized that they didn't know who she was. The song would
finish and then they'd leave. They would go home without realizing
that it was my daughter entertaining them and the rest of the country.

Yes, hope! Of course, that didn't last long. At the end of the video,
Dalal's name had appeared on a glittering pink splotch at the bottom
of the screen.

"Al-Naseemy!" Al-Khadhar cried out.

It was as if someone had shoved hot coals into my ears.

Old man Al-Yasri laughed. "From your tribe, Majed!"

Al-Naqbi quit molding his toe and protested. "Shoo ha? It's not
enough that this lowly girl from who knows what backstreet is prancing like that for all to see." He flicked his bamboo cane, as if about to
propel it at a target just past my ear. "She has the temerity to take your
name. Impostor!"

"She's Emirati," said someone's insipid grandson. He confessed to
having seen this video clip just the day before, on another program.

"Impossible! What rubbish you talk!" said his grandfather.

"Our girls appearing on television like that? What father would
allow it?"

I wasn't sure who'd made that last comment, but it prompted
an uncomfortable silence—so long and foreboding, it felt as though
it had been dragged out of the deepest grave. I noticed their eyes on
me all at once, and oddly enough this affected my vision: the room
clouded over. Damn that Dalal! I shook my head sharply and my vision returned to normal. I don't know what expression was on my face,
but whatever it was convinced them that the rumors of a secret wife, a
secret daughter, could be ticked off as truth.

They left in one giant wave after that, forgoing the last ritual of sweetening their clothes and beards with oudh. The houseboys were unsure how to handle such an abrupt departure. They stood to one side of the doorway, their eyes misting with the clouds of smoke that wafted up from the incense holders in their hands.

The guests' mutterings of thanks on their way out felt like pepper on a wound. Oh, there would be much to talk about once they got home. Snake tongues would lash, describing the milky skin and tumbling curls of Majed's daughter, the one he kept hidden. And I was powerless to stop it.

Let me carry on. There's a miniature coffee set, complete with cups and tray: all crystal, all decorative, all immensely breakable. My vision starts to shake. I knock the set over with a punch so powerful it sends me spinning into a wobbly circle. I lose my balance and fall.

Sprawled on the floor with chips of glass and crystal biting into my bottom and my scrabbling hands, I watch the hall warp. My right hand tingles, and when I try to lift it, my movement is slow and labored. Tiny rivulets of pink blood trickle from pin-sized cuts, and for a moment I swim in a muddle, unable to remember what just happened. Someone is watching me from the top of the staircase. I know who it is, but her name eludes me. "Ammi?" she calls, looking hesitant, staying far away. I can't understand why I am not alone in the house. (Didn't Aisha say they were all going out? Where?)

The girl comes down, her face pale as a biscuit—I tilt back my head and watch her move, upside down: light footsteps, as if treading on air. I widen my eyes, half expecting her to grow wings and soar, but my vision grays once more and the next thing I know, she is crouched by my side and pulling glass out of my hands.

"I don't like surprises." I'm not sure why I say this to her, especially since I cannot remember what I am referring to. There's a cushion under my head. (I can't remember putting it there.) It makes me feel like an invalid, and that annoys me. When I try to get up, she presses me back down with a firm but gentle hand. I let her, because I still feel disoriented. "Where's Aisha?" My voice is coarse and muffled.

"I called her, and she's coming soon," says the girl.

When did Aisha meet Dalal? When did they become friends? I shake my head and again see the vase breaking into pieces. There's a reason I did what I did, but the memory sifts through my mind like sand through fingers. Then I catch it, and I glare at the girl by my side, looking soft and lovely and nursing me with feigned concern.

I squeeze her fingers and lunge, swinging at her face with my other hand. I use every bit of strength in me. But Dalal ducks out of the way, and I only manage to leave a barely visible scratch on her chin. The effort is colossal and I collapse back onto the pillow, wheezing.

"You must stay calm!" she commands. When I groan, she adds a little more gently, "It's important you rest, ammi, until the ambulance arrives."

Why does she keep calling me *uncle*?

33

MARIAM

❧

"You call her and tell her she's had enough fun! You hear me? You tell her to stop what she's doing right now, or else she'll have no one to blame but herself for what I'll do to her." It's the first thing he says when we walk into his room in the men's ward at Dubai Hospital. I look at Aisha, Saif, and Amal, but then I realize it's me he's addressing. "Do you know who I hold responsible for my state? Do you?"

I shake my head.

He pokes a finger at me. "It's you. I bet you've been planning this all your life, as a way of getting back at me. It's you—you convinced her to do what she did."

Even though he has looked uncomfortable since he was admitted a few days ago, he'd remained docile while recovering from the minor stroke, mute and obedient as he was poked and prodded during all the routine medical tests. I had expected his displeasure over Dalal's public appearance on television to spill over and include me once he was out, but not while he was still on a hospital bed, and certainly not like this. "No, ammi, that's not true."

"Oh, yes, it is. It's you and that malicious daughter of mine." When *Ammiti* Aisha and my cousins gasp at his mention of this taboo subject, he shouts, "Yes, enough of the hypocrisy! It's all out. I'll say it out loud: she's mine, just as much as all of you." My uncle releases a grand sweep with his hands, which are wrapped in a light dressing where the glass pierced his skin. "And she will get her fair share of the inheritance—the same as the rest of you—when I die." Saif makes a face; my uncle sneers. "Ah, look at you! You can't wait to leave and count my assets, figure out how much money you won't be getting. Am I right, son?"

"You hurt me, father."

"Shut your mouth!" My uncle twists his mouth with disgust. "Just keep all your false blabber to yourself."

I thought he would be weak for a while longer, fearful of his vulnerability. Instead he has suddenly turned into an obnoxious brute, hurling abuse at us.

When Amal tries to placate him, he tells her to deal with her husband instead, and curb his notorious appetite for quick women. Hot tears spill down her cheeks, and Saif has a go at him—only to be accused of falsifying the petty-cash records. Ammi Majed ignores his son's protestations of innocence and decides to attack his wife next, cursing his favorite target, Shamma, and making all sorts of abominable accusations. "It's a fact: it's freakish and unnatural for a woman to choose independence over being a wife and mother. What does that tell us about your dear sister?"

Saif and Amal have had enough. They march out of the room; surprisingly, Aisha stays where she is, with her chin held high, glowering at her husband. This confuses him, and he starts fidgeting with the tubes attached to his nose and wrist. I don't know where I get the courage, but I step closer to his side and smooth the pillow beneath his head. "Ammi, you're not yourself," I whisper. "Close your eyes and rest a little."

My uncle wraps an arm around my waist and says, "Sly little thing, aren't you? Getting up to no good behind my back? I know everything."

"What are you talking about?" I stammer, trying and failing to pull away.

"Yes, what are you saying?" Aisha asks.

"She knows exactly what I'm referring to, don't you, Mariam? You were spotted."

Aisha lets out a frustrated shriek and shakes her head roughly; her shayla tumbles to the floor. "Let go of her!" It must be the first time Aisha has ever raised her voice to her husband—certainly I have never witnessed it. He's appalled. He flinches and shoves me away, as if I'd turned into a blazing coal. "Haven't you done enough damage?" she continues. "When will you stop hurting people?"

"Keep your voice down, woman," he snarls. "They'll think my wife is mad. You want the doctor to come and strap you down?"

I inch toward the door. Perhaps Aisha's newly found boldness— and where it might lead—frightens me.

He spots me. "Where do you think you're going?"

"Home."

"Stay!" They shout the order in one voice.

"You're not going anywhere," he says.

"Yes, I am." My voice is a squeak. I fiddle with the edges of my shayla. "College starts soon, and I have to pack."

"I said you're not going anywhere. Not college, not Cairo, not ever."

What is he saying? I'm overwhelmed by panic, and I babble, trying to force words out of my flapping lips. Aisha taps my mouth and it stills. "What he means is that you'll be going somewhere better. And by better I mean out of his house, so filled with misery."

"House of misery, is it?" my uncle retorts. "It must be because I give you too much money to buy the finest clothes, eat the best food, and travel to London to go shopping. Yes, I can see now how that would make you so unhappy."

"Look around you, Majed." She props her fists on her hips. "Where are your children? You have chased them all away. Khaled will be back soon. He'll take one look at you and walk straight back out and disappear again."

My uncle sits up straight, as if he might jump off the bed. "That weak, spoiled fool. He's lost anyway."

"What are you talking about?"

"Drugs, woman!" Spittle sprays out through his clenched teeth. "And not the soft kind, either. Heroin. Do you know what that is?"

"You lie. Who told you that?"

"I've known for some time now."

He has jarred Ammiti Aisha's nerves. Two worry lines appear in the middle of her forehead. She looks like she is about to faint. I slide my hand into hers. "And you did nothing?" she says. My uncle eases back onto the pillow, looking smug. "You didn't consider going out there and bringing him back so that we could get him treatment? You didn't think to tell me?" Her knees buckle; I prop her up and lead her, staggering, to a chair.

"Like I just told you, he's a lost cause." Ammi Majed lets out a growling sigh and narrows his eyes at Aisha. She hunches on the chair and covers her face with both hands. He waits. He frowns. He loses patience and flings his arms in the air. "And don't think I've lost my strength because I'm lying on this bed. I can give you a lashing for all your impertinence, even from here. You hear me?"

Aisha is on her feet like a bolt from the sky. My uncle is shocked silent by the suddenness of her move; he blinks with utter disbelief at this bold new version of his wife. She aims a reptilian glare at him. He folds his arms over his chest, as if afraid she'll tear the drip out of his wrist. With one defiant move, she scoops her shayla off the floor and wraps it around her head. She extends her hand to me. And I take it.

"Come back! I forbid you to leave!"

The door slams shut behind us. We march down the corridor. Aisha is shorter than I am, but she takes long, stately strides that have me running to keep up. A gurney appears in front of us, sliding suddenly out of a room. Aisha dodges it, but I bump into the metal edge. "Sorry," I whisper to no one in particular.

It's a busy time of day, smack in the middle of visiting hours. Phones ring incessantly at the nurses' station, which is vacant because the nurses are busy wheeling trolleys stacked with evening meals. Visitors arrive in large groups. Ahead, what looks like a full tribe of old men and young boys—I reckon they must be Bedouins from Lahbab or Al-Madam, come to the big city to call on a sick relative—has spilled out into the corridor. A Filipino nurse points desperately at the waiting room just past the entrance of the ward, trying his best to explain to them in broken Arabic that they are not allowed to loiter in the corridor.

They pay him no heed and instead remain, intent on consuming the cans of orange juice spread out in front of them. There are cans of tomato juice, too. These stay untouched; they were brought for the patient, since it's a well-accepted belief that tomato juice increases the body's blood.

We skirt around the bunch; my mind is consumed with whether Ammi Majed found out about my meetings with Adel or if he was just trying to provoke me. And what horrific surprise has he concocted? Where do they plan to send me? I want to ask Ammiti Aisha, but she pulls me along as if I were made of straw. Houseboys hurry this way and that, hugging stainless-steel pots of cooked food and trays of chocolate, carrying coffeepots, dates, and fruits in plastic bags. I expect a collision, but Aisha is sure-footed; she dodges them all and doesn't stop, even when we reach the hospital reception on the ground floor and someone calls my name. It's my uncle's friend Saeed, who has been dawdling by the coffee machine, waiting for us to leave so that he could visit my uncle. He cocks his head and scratches his chin. It's obvious he's puzzled to see us leaving earlier than expected, and with such urgent haste.

Outside, the driver catches sight of us and runs off to fetch the car from the parking lot. The air is clotted with humidity. Under my abaya, a layer of heat fans out over my skin; sweat starts to collect in the dip of my collarbone, in the cracks of my elbows, and behind my knees.

I fan my face frantically with both hands, warily watching this new and unpredictable Ammiti Aisha and wondering what she'll do next. Sweat glistens on the surface of her skin. "I just want to know one thing," she says to me. "Your uncle's ramblings about you being spotted—do you know what he's talking about?"

"No! Don't worry, ammiti, he wasn't himself. He must be hallucinating."

"Or lying." She sighs. "He probably made up all that rubbish about Khaled, too, just to get me riled up." The worry lines between her brows remain, but she nods with relief at this possibility. Silently, we wait for the car.

34

MAJED

❧

Passing stroke, that's how the doctor decided to explain it, after seeing the blank look on my face when he gave me the medical term. I repeat the first word in my head over and over. *Passing*: it has a consoling ring to it—it came, it went. But that other word generates a cavernous discomfort in the pit of my stomach. I try to blot it out of my mind.

I'm fine now. I no longer feel the horror I'd felt the night I was wheeled into the hospital, when I overheard the ambulance men telling the doctor that I'd lost my memory. I believed them, and for days I felt odd. I spent every waking hour quietly reflecting, trying to digest how such a thing could happen to me, while my family watched me with bewilderment and pity in their eyes.

But today has awakened an altogether different emotion: a bizarre yearning to act unreasonably, to shake off caution, to spot weakness and plow to its core. Yes, mine is a capricious mind, and today it has been fueled with menace. Stuck in this room, I can't chase it away, the insufferable irritation. It's no wonder I have to find ways to amuse myself. And once I start picking at the scabs, it's impossible to stop.

When did Aisha become so impertinent, talking back to me? Who has been giving her false illusions of a woman's place in the map of things? I curse Shamma under my breath for always scheming to get my wife to leave me. No doubt she is to blame for Aisha's antagonistic turn. She should have sat back and listened to me speak without so much as a gasp. But instead she confronted me. What was it she said? I strain to recall her exact words and then decide not to waste time with the details. What is important is the fact that she crossed the line. In the days to come, I will show her that I am not a man to be trifled with.

Mustafa was here; I kicked him out before he could so much as ask about my health. (Wasn't he the one who gave me false assurances, promising me that Dalal's efforts would lead to nothing?) Now I wish I had let him stay just so I could lash out at him.

Saeed is here, though. He has given up on cajoling me into a good humor. He sits in the corner chair with one leg crossed over the other like a respectable businessman, flipping through a medical magazine as if it's the most interesting thing he has seen all day. "What, suddenly you want to improve your mind?" He acts as if he hasn't heard me, and I decide there's no point continuing with sarcasm. He's thick-skinned, immune to my provocations. So I complain instead.

"This place is sickening." I look around, and even though there is nothing I can pick on, I am filled with a gnawing bitterness. I'm sure it's this room that has made me so. "They could at least have taken me to a private hospital."

Saeed looks up from his magazine but says nothing.

"Well, it's true. What am I doing here?"

"You were brought in an ambulance. When it's an emergency, they usually bring you to the closest hospital."

"Yes, but you know what these government hospitals are like. They can kill you. Now tell me truthfully, would you trust these doctors? I mean, what do they know." I cross my arms and grumble. "I mean, how do I trust a doctor who can't even speak English?" Just then, my doctor comes in to see how I'm doing. He is Syrian, with a cherubic face, large green eyes, and a patch of yellow peach fuzz on his chin, a sham beard he has obviously been nurturing for quite some time without success. I scratch the stubble on my face and, as he looks over my chart, say, "Tell me again, Dr. Wassef, exactly what happened?"

Saeed intervenes. "The good doctor has told you a million times."

I stay focused on the doctor, smiling at him sweetly. "Well, I'd like to make that one million and one."

"A disruption to the blood flow. A transient ischemic attack."

I keep the smile in place. "Attack, huh? Sounds violent."

"Yes, that's what it's called."

"Small as an ant, though? It came, it passed, am I right?"

Dr. Wassef nods and looks at me with sympathy.

"So why is there a hose in my nose? Why am I connected to these machines?" I see Saeed pat the air, signaling to me to slow down, to compose myself before I get carried away. I ignore him. "Why all these tests?"

"We are monitoring you. There are still risks."

"Oh, just admit it. You don't know what you're doing, so you keep me here." I slam the mattress. "You want to make me feel like an invalid."

Dr. Wassef tries very hard to stay pleasant. "You are at risk for a full-blown stroke, Mr. Al-Naseemy. Do you understand that? Yes, the blockage was small. Yes, it passed. But that just means you are lucky that you got a warning." Saeed shrugs an apology to the doctor, who tells him, "It's all right. Fear makes patients react in all sorts of ways."

I don't like what he says. I fidget on the bed, filled with bitterness and hatred and rage. "Yes, fear," I say, my voice hardening. "You doctors are very good at scaring people, plugging them into beeping contraptions that might stop at any minute."

"The best thing you can do is keep calm, Mr. Al-Naseemy."

"Oh, I must keep calm, must I? Is this what it has come to, a grown man listening to a child who likes to play at being a doctor?"

He looks hurt. "I am a doctor."

"Don't mind him, Dr. Wassef." Saeed hurries to his side and shoots a nasty look at me. "He just doesn't like being confined like this."

"Tell me, little boy, is it hard?"

"Pardon?"

"Do you have to tug at those fine little hairs to get them to grow?"

Dr. Wassef cups his chin. "It's a medical condition, sir."

I grunt and mutter, "Keeping me here this long is ridiculous."

"Sir, you are free to leave at any time. I've finished with the testing, and your report is ready."

Suddenly I wonder whether it's safe to leave. I wave my hands at him. "You expect me to go out all bandaged like this? What about the bleeding?"

"There's no more bleeding." The doctor's tone is not so accommodating anymore. He is rougher than he needs to be as he unfurls the gauze and tugs the bandages off. "See? I'll get the nurse to dab on some disinfectant." He points his chin out at me and sniffs. "Now, if you'll excuse me, I have other patients."

35

DALAL

ع

It's evening, and I awaken to the kind of noise that's kept low so as not to disturb but still has the jarring effect of a school bell. I open my eyes but stay very still, keeping my face burrowed in the pillow. I hear the sounds of chickenhearted footsteps, careful rustles, and jittery breaths. It's my mother pretending to be a mother.

She switches on the small lamp by the door. I keep my back to her and wait, hoping she'll go away. Judging from the soft swishing sounds, I figure she's pulling clothes out of my suitcase, which I had left open in the middle of the room like a book, and arranging my clothes. When she finishes, she tiptoes closer to me, toward the dressing table. There's the ruffle of pages, and this, too, is an action easily guessed. She's opening the glossy copy of *Sayidati* magazine to the page in the arts section that contains my interview. There's quiet now. She's probably staring at my picture, which shows me with my lips slightly parted and a finger held lightly to my chin. There is a quote in bold letters: "My talent comes from my Egyptian blood." I am sure it won me plenty of heartfelt cheer among Egyptians.

Mama doesn't pussyfoot around any longer. "Dalal, wake up. It's seven o'clock."

I release the moan of someone struggling to come out of a deep sleep. "Did the hairdresser arrive? Azza here?" I turn and fix her with a groggy-eyed stare.

"You missed something important yesterday," says Mama, ignoring my questions. "Abdullah Al-Rowaished complimented you on Dubai Television. He said—and these were his exact words—'Dalal's voice is the most promising out there.' Can you believe that? And there's more."

I lie very still, anxious not to miss a word. "Well, I couldn't very well leave the party to go watch the interview, could I?" I say, mocking her to mask my intense desire to hear the rest of what the great Kuwaiti singer had to say.

"The presenter asked him, 'Can you see yourself performing a duet with her?' And do you know what he did?"

"What, what?" There's more air than sound in my voice.

"He hummed the tune of your song." She claps her hands like an excited little girl. "His thick mustache curled to one side in a grin—so cheeky, but sentimental, too. And then he said, 'Only her, lonely her, all alone? We can't leave her like that.'"

To be endorsed by someone as important as Abdullah Al-Rowaished! It makes me giddy with delight. My pulse quickens, and I have to remind myself to feign indifference. If I do otherwise, Mama might see it as an invitation back into my life and career, the opening of a tunnel that would once more burrow deep into my head.

She sits on the edge of my bed, hungry for a detailed account of my first big adventure: last week I went abroad (first class; all expenses paid). Madame Nivine and Azza, who is now my official stylist, joined me, but they had to sit separately because their plane tickets were in business class. First we flew to Saudi Arabia and then Qatar to perform at two weddings. The families were distinguished and treated me with warmth and admiration. They showered me with so many compliments, flowers, and chocolates, I thought I would cry with joy.

Mama pats the sheet gently. "Tonight is important: the recording of your second hit, hopefully!" She certainly knows her business. My first hit, already inserted in an album of mediocre songs (to be released), must quickly be followed with a second hit, which will require another album of boring songs to be recorded. It's the hit that guarantees the sale of the cassette. "You have to wake up so your voice has a chance to warm up."

Yawning and stretching, I whine, "Let me sleep."

She wanted to hear about the trip as soon as I returned to Cairo. I could have told her. Instead I went straight to sleep. And the next morning I went to my next booking, flying all the way to London (business class; still, all expenses were paid), where I performed at a party at the Royal Lancaster Hotel. I sang from 10:45 p.m. until midnight. It didn't matter that I was the B star, the opener for a popular Saudi singer named Rabeh Saqer. The audience lapped up my performance at each and every event. I leaned over and sang, "You wanna go?" and they'd chanted in answer, "Go, go, go!" I got goose bumps every time I replied, "And stay away?" and they hollered back, "Oh no, no, no!" Mama cocks her head to one side, expectation on her face. Yes, she wants the full rundown of my week.

There is a knock at the door, feeble and wary. I don't have to guess who it is. "She up?" Sherif bey asks.

"Don't come in," I cry out, sitting up straight. "This is not a room for men." When Mama's eyebrows furrow, I tell her, "Well, it's true, isn't it? He has no business walking in here, my bedroom, when I'm in my nightgown—or in any other dress, for that matter."

"It's okay," she says softly. "Don't get yourself worked up."

I sniff and look away; she's been working hard to win me over. The suitcase is shut and set against the wall. The clothes, ready to be laundered, sit in neat piles by the door, arranged according to color and type. I should be reveling in the attention. I scratch the sleep out of my eyes as if that would make me appreciate her efforts. Why am I not moved?

We live in Sherif bey's apartment. He is now my stepfather. I would rather have stayed where I was, behind the newly painted red door of the apartment in Imbaba. But I had no money. Mama had wasted no time marrying him, and once the lease on the Imbaba apartment expired, I showed up here with doleful eyes, ready to give exaggerated apologies for all the grief I'd given her just so she would not turn me away. (Where would I have gone?) I had braced myself, expecting long and miserable hours when I would have to bear her needle-sharp taunts. But the taunts never came; she must have realized that I was just steps away from a bright future, one that she could be a part of if I'd let her.

I could almost see the gears twisting in her head as she calculated how she could best demonstrate her affection. She had cleared this room, which Sherif bey used for storage—it had held his oud and sheet music, cleaning products, and an ironing board—and declared it my bedroom. When I stood in the middle of the emptied room, my jaw dropped, and she said, "You must have a space where you are comfortable. I want this to be your sanctuary."

She'd filled the room with new furniture in so many shades of pink, it makes me think of dripping strawberry ice cream. The dressing table has an oval mirror and drawers with brass pulls. The headboard is a giant rose, and there are painted grapevines crawling up the corners of the closet; at the top sit bunches of ripe, magenta grapes. She seemed to delight in buying me new clothes—"You must always look your best"—and I found out that she can cook more than the common egg—"You can only deal with difficulties if you have the right nourishment."

There was the effort of pretend intimacy, too: the lame shoulder squeeze, the failed back rub, and now what looks like the beginning of what might turn out to be an awkward hug.

"Look at you, all upset." She leans forward with her arms floating in front of her, and I wonder if what I've been waiting for my entire life will finally happen: I'll receive a genuine loving embrace from my mother. But just as I expect, Mama has trouble completing the gesture, because it doesn't come from the heart. Once she's close enough to bite my nose, she pulls back like a tortoise into its shell. I feel nothing anymore. No warmth, no expectation, no hurt, no longing: a big, fat zero.

"He tries so hard with you," she whispers. "Don't forget, you're living under his roof. He's paying for your upkeep. So a little consideration is not too much to ask, don't you think? All he wants is to be a part of your life, to protect you."

"Does he want me to call him *baba*, too?"

"Don't be silly, Dalal," she says, keeping her voice soft. She then tells me about a visitor who came by the day I flew out to Saudi Arabia: my father's employee-cum-fixer, Mustafa. "Big threats he brought with him, that one: warnings to stop embarrassing your father. Or else."

"What's that supposed to mean?"

"I don't know," says Mama, "but Mustafa was spitting dynamite. So angry and rude that Sherif bey had to run down and get the driver to kick him out of the apartment. See, this is why you need us around, to protect you. Not that fat manager who you put so much faith in, who smiles and robs you at the same time." Her eyes blaze. "Real family!"

"Hmm."

"It seems your father had a small stroke last month, and he blames you for it." She narrows her eyes and waits for a reaction.

My face is a blank wall. I am in no mood to explain that I'd already heard this bit of news through Mariam, and I hadn't bothered to tell her. "I want coffee." She is taken aback by my indifference, but she doesn't comment. As she gets up to prepare my coffee, I grab her wrist.

"And if Mustafa comes again, you let him talk to me directly. Then I can tell him to go back to my father with the message that he can blame me all he wants—I. Don't. Care."

Alone, my thoughts are pulled back to when Mariam called me with this information. A week later, and she had phoned again with a sadder piece of news, so infuriating that when I heard it my stomach clamped into a fist: the abrupt termination of her education in favor of an arranged marriage to a stranger. She was breathless, distraught, rattled out of her senses, and choking on too many emotions—a side of her I'm sure she's revealed to no one else.

As I spewed out a list of useless solutions—Stop eating! Run away!—that she did not hear, I paced the room. Without registering the senselessness of what I was doing, I pulled clothes out of my closet and threw them into a small bag. I didn't want to waste any time getting to her. How dare they lead her like a goat whichever way they please? Her only wish is to study. But my father is so cruel that he would deny her even this small thing.

It was a quick phone call, a burst of muzzled hopelessness on her part and feverish outrage on mine. It was only once I'd zipped the bag and put a lock on it that a sense of overwhelming helplessness weighed me down. Here I was, dreaming of adoring fans and a spacious apartment (which will come much later, of course) overlooking the river in stylish Zamalek, but I couldn't even travel to be with Mariam in her time of need. Frustrated, I'd flopped onto the bed. What could I do? I didn't have the money to buy a plane ticket.

✌

The blow-dryer whirrs as the hairdresser tames my curls into fine threads. Azza leafs through my wardrobe, looking for the right top. I had told her not to bother because this is simply a recording and not a concert or party, but she'd insisted and said she couldn't have me walking out looking shabby. She added, "Besides, you never know which important artist might casually pop into the studio."

She has a point. I have recently employed her as my stylist, even though it's more for the company than her sense of fashion. She pulls out a striped silk blouse with a bow on the side of the collar. I refuse it. She tries another, powder blue, and I give her the okay signal.

My head sways gently under the heat. I gaze at my reflection, the left eye alert, the right with its lazy lid looking as though it might fall shut at any moment. I lose myself; it's a precious moment when I can lean back and digest my success. Madame Nivine's strategy has been to gain me fame and popularity through a hit single rather than a full album, though my album will be released a few months later, at the end of the year—"too many good tunes will just confuse the listener, habibchi!" It's all part of her strategy of maximizing the hype. And how well that has worked! My first single has blazed through the airwaves like a wildfire, playing over and over on the radio stations, a triumph of the summer. Madame Nivine told me it's the most requested song not just on Dubai FM but also on Bahrain FM, where the phones don't stop ringing from Saudi listeners. It's a station that attracts them because of its great selection of music.

It wasn't just that the tune was catchy. By some massive stroke of luck, the song found its way onto a cassette called *Nights of the Nile*, a compilation of hit songs by famous singers. My name is housed in plastic along with Abdul Majeed Abdullah, Anoushka, and Monica Fayyadh.

There's a little mall stocked with fake designer shoes and handbags at the Ramses Hilton hotel. It's on the circuit for Khaleeji tourists; it's popular because the shops sell traditional Egyptian goods like cotton sheets, towels, and galabias. I try to go there every few days because on the second floor there's a square kiosk that sells cassettes. My poster is plastered to it. A pair of bulky speakers blares popular songs at the entrance. The owner is obligated to mute them whenever the call to prayer sounds on the mall speakers—but only if someone complains.

Azza accompanies me; we start at the café on the ground floor, sipping our coffees slowly to give the roaming shoppers a chance to notice me. So far there have been feathers of recognition; it seems that people are unsure whether mine is the same face as that on the poster. It's only once we stroll leisurely by the kiosk, pretending we are there to shop like everyone else, that they come.

There's always a special light of acknowledgment in their eyes: smiling, nodding, and giggling, they're shy at first. They linger even after they've gotten my autograph or posed for a photograph with me. It's at this point, once there's a cluster of fans around me, that the cassette-kiosk owner presses an abrupt end to whatever is blasting out of his speakers and replaces it with my song. Then I might as well be on a speeding carousel ride—that's the kind of dizzying thrill I get.

My hair is as straight as reeds, as fashion would have it. Azza instructs the hairdresser to pin a large turquoise carnation to add a touch of glamour. Once it's positioned just above my left ear, I move my head this way and that, inspecting the various angles with some skepticism.

"Look how it brings light to your face and matches your blouse," says Azza. "From now on, you need to look creative for your fans, set a trend, you know—a flower here, a bandanna there, face glitter."

I'm not convinced. I blow at the petals that droop like weeds over my cheek. "Isn't it a little too much for going to a recording?"

"No, no," she coos, frowning, obviously taking her role as fashion stylist seriously. "Look at you." She places her hands on my shoulders and leans over so that our faces—mine striking, hers plain—are reflected side by side in the mirror. "You're not just anyone anymore."

She means well; I won't break her spirit. Besides, I like what she says. I raise my head and beam a champion's smile at the mirror. I'll get rid of the carnation once I get to the studio.

✑

At 10:15 p.m. Azza informs me that Madame Nivine is downstairs. She wishes me luck and leaves, along with the hairdresser. Mama makes a snide remark about "that fat crook," which I ignore. Of course Madame Nivine won't come up; Mama would waste no time spearing accusations at her, and that would lead to a heated quarrel.

As I rush about throwing my things into my handbag—keys, money, lipstick, lozenges—Mama and Sherif bey follow at my heels, calling out garbled instructions and opinions. It's maddening. It makes me want to pull at my hair until the curls puff back up. They long to be involved. She wants to be asked to join me for the recording. He wants to give me his professional knowledge, and as the prospect of this happening shrinks, so too does his voice.

"*Bas!* Enough!" I yell.

Stunned into silence, they look at me with outrage.

"You're driving me crazy."

"Is this the way to talk to your mother?" Sherif bey says, rooting his fists into his bony hips.

"She thinks she's so important now," says Mama, "that she's decided she doesn't need me, her own mother."

I could stand still and take it, or I could just walk out. I go with the second option.

"I want money!" That's what I say to Madame Nivine as soon as I get into her *kharteeta*. (In Cairo, *kharteeta*, or "rhinoceros," is the fond nickname given to any model of Mercedes that came out between 1980 and 1985.) It's olive colored, with the usual minor dents and scratches. She stifles a laugh. Tapping her temple, she gives me a probing look, and I tell her to forget the flower for a moment. I calculate that I've made thirty thousand American dollars from the two weddings, the party in London, and the cassette sales of the single. I know there won't be much left once the deductions for the recordings and Madame Nivine's fees are made. Still, I persist. "Not this loose change you give me, but enough money to move out of that apartment."

"And a good evening to you," she says, sliding the car into the middle of the street without so much as a glance in the rearview mirror. "The good news is that there are two interviews booked for you for this coming week: one on a talk show on Egyptian television and the other as a guest in a segment on MBC. And then the world will start talking about you."

"MBC? Really?" This makes me forget about the money for a moment. I imagine being on the London-based Saudi channel, which always looks glossier than the other satellite channels. Then I remember my empty pockets. "So what about my earnings?"

"You'll have to be patient, Dalal. I've told you before, there are a lot of expenses. It's a complicated business, and your rise at this early stage has to be handled carefully, delicately. You hear me, hayachi?" I watch her as she navigates out of the smaller residential streets. She looks cramped; her turban, a glittering green monstrosity, grazes the roof, and her bust brushes the steering wheel every time she leans forward to make a turn. "Don't look at me that way. I don't just pay for the recordings and the video *cleeps*. You don't realize it, but not everyone in the press loves you. Wallahi, you won't believe how many rumors are out there already: she's not an Emirati; Al-Naseemy is not her real name; she worked at a nightclub on Al-Haram Road; she's really nothing more than a backup singer—and everyone knows that for a female backup singer to make it she'd have to either bribe event organizers or find a rich old man with influence to get her to the top."

Much as I'd like to argue with her, she makes sense. "Well, I haven't heard anything about all this—stuff."

"Of course you haven't, because I have made sure it doesn't get out. I've had to butter the reporters with, guess what . . ." She rubs her fingers. "Money."

At a loss over how to respond, I make a hissing sound through my teeth.

She sighs. "Ya habibchi, ya Dalal. I've told them that you are special and exceptional, a unique blend—Egyptian, Emirati—like a fine tea. I tell the Egyptian press, 'She's our girl,' and I do the same with the Khaleeji press. And for now, we are doing well. I must stress, though, that you have to be ready: there's no stopping the stories, the lies that will come out. But it's important that that happen later, when you are established. Right now you're just starting, vulnerable. One wrong move and you could fall flat on your face." She grunts. "And I won't have it!"

There's a burn of passion in that grunt; it suggests her faith in me. I silently mull this over. She knows I'll reach the heights of stardom if I follow the straight path she is carving for me, a path broad enough to fit her buxom form, too.

Nearly there now: Madame Nivine follows a backstreet route as she heads toward the studio. We're somewhere in the middle of a maze of small streets—strangely empty, even though it's near the large and congested Arab League Boulevard—when out of the darkness, a car suddenly appears. It swerves and skids to a halt right in front of us.

Madame Nivine slams the brakes and we're both thrown forward. There's hardly any room for her bosom. It crushes the steering wheel and I cringe at the resulting earsplitting honk. The carnation has loosened, and it tumbles to the ground as I stare at her. Her turban has shifted to one side; it looks like a tall cake about to flop over. Equally befuddled, she stares back at me.

Our daze only lasts a few seconds. Three men with scarves tied around their faces jump out of the car that's blocking us. Before we can think to do anything—curse, crank up the windows, or lock the doors—they are banging on our hood for attention. Madame Nivine shifts her turban back to vertical.

"Who are they?" I hiss, looking around and wondering when

Cairo suddenly emptied. "What do they want?" I sink back into my seat as the men file by my window, glaring.

One of them has a hammer, which he waves in the air. "Leave this path you're following, or we'll break your head." He's shaped like a noodle and is promptly shoved to the side by a second hooligan, who reaches for me through the open window. My hands flutter; along with the quavering squeaks that come out of me, they are a weak defense. In one swoop of movement he has both my wrists squeezed in his grip.

He twists; I squeal.

"This time I'll leave a thumbprint," he warns, his voice gruff and full of menace. He stinks of stale cigarettes and libb. "Next time I'll break your bones."

"Yeah," says the noodle, moving toward the front of the car. "You see this hammer?"

"And what do you plan to do with it?" Madame Nivine had gotten out of the car without my noticing, and she stands facing him, illuminated from below by the headlights and looking every bit like Aladdin's genie.

The noodle turns into a jittery insect when she pounds him in the chest. "She broke my ribs, Yahya," he calls out to the gang's boss, who releases my wrists to deliver a crackling slap that sends the noodle flying to the side. "Don't say my name!" He turns and snarls at Madame Nivine. "Ya sitt, whoever you are, just stay out of this. It has nothing to do with you."

"You swerved in front of me and banged on my kharteeta," she says. "As if it doesn't get enough bashing on the streets every day. And then you tell me this has nothing to do with me?" Her voice starts out firm but turns wobbly almost immediately, and I climb into the backseat, thinking I might not be detected if I slip out through the back door.

Yahya spots her fear, too. Just as I slip my foot out and onto the road, he grabs the hammer and bashes the car's hood. "And does this have anything to do with you? A last warning, you fat pig: keep out of it!"

I'm out and ready to tiptoe away. I desire nothing more than to vanish. But how can I leave her behind with these brutes? I cower by the taillights, unable to take my eyes off Yahya as he smashes Madame Nivine's kharteeta twice more. Emboldened, the third thug—who had served as a lookout up until now—joins the other two, and they form a menacing circle around her, shoving her back and forth.

Poor Madame Nivine. She had gotten out to defend me. Instead, she became the victim of the assault. I twirl my wrists, stiff and sore, and a bubble of rage explodes in me. How can a father do this to his own daughter? Before I can think, I'm rushing into the double spotlight of headlights, striking blindly at the ruffians with all my force. They stumble back with shock, the hammer falling to the ground with a clunk. Every bit of me is alert, stretched like a taut string. When Yahya lunges at me I kick him smack in the groin. He doubles over, howling and cursing.

With their leader out of commission, the united front breaks down for a moment . . . until the noodle picks up the hammer. There's a crazed expression in his eyes. "He'll do it!" I yell, and together Madame Nivine and I start to run away. Suddenly the city comes to life in a burst of illumination.

One, two, three cars roll toward us, all in a row. Like a posse of night angels, they light the street.

"This is not over," Yahya manages to holler, his voice high-pitched in agony. "We'll hunt you down, and next time . . ." We can't hear the rest over the honks and bellows of impatient drivers unable to pass because his car is blocking their way. The brutes are quick to depart, leaving behind the echo of their screeching wheels. Had they stayed longer, the people in the convoy would have gotten out of their cars to investigate—and then, as with any event involving a crowd in Cairo, there'd be the certainty of mayhem, with the delicious chance of their being beaten to a pulp. Such are my thoughts as we drive away.

I am elated by our escape, even though I can't stop trembling. Madame Nivine keeps gulping, making loud popping noises with her tongue. The atmosphere in the car is thick. I clap my hands to dissolve it and say, "Well, that's that: chased them away, didn't we."

"Oh really," Madame Nivine cries out. "You think that was smart of you, coming at them like that?"

"I was protecting you," I say, slighted by her inability to appreciate my valiant rescue.

"Dalal the heroine." She wiggles her neck in an elaborate, low-class display of scorn. "You think they won't come at you another time?" She shakes her head. "Look how they smashed my kharteeta. Look at all those holes in her hood."

"You can fix the bastards. Call that connection you have in the security forces and pay him so that he can protect us."

"My connection has a job, ya Dalal!" she yells, gesturing wildly. "He can't be everywhere. You saw how they appeared out of nowhere. We don't even know what they look like." She sniffs, trying to calm down. "I can't have someone smashing your face in. That would be the end of your career, and I've worked too hard for a disappointment like that."

Instinctively I pat my cheeks, distraught by the thought of my beautiful face all squashed and swollen under Yahya's fists. "What can we do?"

She answers me once she steers the kharteeta onto Arab League Boulevard. "It's time we got you some bodyguards."

36

MARIAM

❧

"It's half past ten. Ladies, tell me: the flower girls—where are they?"

"All set, in the foyer."

"And the musicians?"

"Waiting for her entrance, too."

Having gone through the checklist, the rambunctious widow, soon to be my mother-in-law, rubs her hands together with satisfaction. She's plump, with a receding chin that blends into her neck, a cushiony support for her large head. "Right, time for the bride to make her appearance."

I stand up; immediately, my knees wobble and I drop back into the chair.

There's a gasp, then a giggle. It comes from the blur of women surrounding me. I'm being dressed and made up in a suite at the Hyatt Regency hotel. I hear the swirl of silk and the rasp of chiffon, and the women's every movement wafts the scents of rose, jasmine, musk, amber, and that most royal of essences, oudh. The smells shoot up my nose and fog my head. "Come on, Mariam," my cousin Amal jokes. "You're stronger than that dress. Don't let it pull you down."

Ten kilos: that's the confirmed weight. Add another kilo for everything the hairdresser piled on my head, and I'm carrying about as much weight as a laborer hauling cement. These thoughts are about as far as can be from the romantic sentiments a bride should have, and appropriate for this humiliation of a wedding.

"She looks like she's going to faint!" the hairdresser says, and releases a cloud of hair spray that mists over my face. "Get her some crackers."

"No crackers! We can't have crumbs sticking to her lips," bosses the widow. She complains that she has to get back down to the ballroom, that she can't be in two places at the same time. She asks my cousins whether she can trust them to deliver me in the next ten minutes, and they promise they will. She narrows her eyes at me. They are set close over the generous bridge of her nose, which would have looked fine had her nose been a normal length. But it stops short—it makes me think of an unfinished road—and gives her face the appearance of being somewhat squished. The widow taps her ruddy cheeks and clicks her tongue at me. "Bride's nerves. Nothing to do about it, I suppose," she mutters with a sigh, and clears out.

"Are you feeling weak?" Ammiti Aisha's voice sounds like it is coming from the end of a tunnel. She was not in the suite earlier, and I look around to locate her. Ever since we left the hospital, she has been more attentive toward me, especially since I took to spending long spells alone in my room. There have been days over these past months when I sank into a depression so deep I had trouble eating and sleeping. I mourned an education buried before it got a chance to sprout, a future diverted like an artificial stream, destined to dry up in hard earth.

All my female cousins—Mona, Amal, Nadia, Nouf—would saunter into my room and glower at me, accusing me of being spoiled

and ungrateful. (What girl would not desire such a match?) Only Ammiti Aisha showed me any sympathy, patting my hand with a wistful
smile. Sometimes she would sigh and shake her head in what I was
sure was apology, as if she regretted having actively worked to seal the
union. Other times she would flit in and out of my bedroom like a
noisy bee, trying to snap me out of my despair. I stopped blaming her
after a while. How could she have done otherwise when my uncle assigned her this task? One day she said, "That's how it is for us women.
We are often obligated to do things we don't want to. And the best
lesson you can learn is to stifle the pain." Not a spark of hope in such
talk! And just as I thought that no one could possibly understand my
desperation, she added, "They call us weak, but how can that be when
we are able to bear so much." That was the day Khaled was supposed
to return but didn't. That was the day she found out that her husband
had not lied: Khaled was a heroin addict, after all.

There she is. Through the gaps between the shifting limbs I spot
her. Her burka hides her expression, but I watch her anyway. She sits
on a corner chair, her back rigid as a tree stump, and leans forward as
if rallying her strength.

A woman's bottom blocks my vision, and I shift so that I can keep
my eyes on Aisha. I detect resolve in her position, I'm sure of it. What
can it mean? Maybe she'll display an unexpected burst of courage,
just like at the hospital. She might take a stand against this hounding
army of relatives and busybodies. She might tell them that enough is
enough. Her lips part, and I wait for her to object to this sham of a
wedding.

She'd start a little awkwardly, her voice a sputtering, weak fountain. She'd probably say something like, "Maybe we should wait." No
one would hear her but me. She'd have to cough for attention as she
gathered strength to speak out: "Mariam does not have to get married." And that would unlock the pent-up frustrations and disappoint-
ments she has endured all these years with my uncle.

Someone lights the coals. Smoke curls out of the incense holder. I blink against it repeatedly. When I catch sight of the corner chair once more, it's empty. Ammiti Aisha has deserted me, left me with an absurd fantasy in the middle of this circle of eager faces and restless limbs.

A hand clasps my chin and twists my head back to face the mirror. The makeup artist has worked tirelessly, and has succeeded in making me look like someone else. Caked under layers of makeup, my face has been lightened to the tint of weak, milky tea. The makeup artist blows a hot, frustrated breath. "Rounder, softer, rounder," she mutters, and makes a last attempt to transform my stubborn face. But there is no roundness or softness there. My cheekbones jut high and sharp.

My hands rest on my thighs, palms up, as if I'm holding an open book. An elaborate henna design adorns each palm. Masterfully drawn by the Indian henna lady, they are remarkable pieces of art, exquisite patterns of tightly packed petals. The broad paisley design thins into an elegant swooping curl that ends at the bottom of the middle finger; small vines travel the length of each finger. They twist and sprout dainty leaves along the way. Once they reach the tips, they blossom into peonies.

My bangs are pinned back to join the rest of my hair, which is piled and twisted into a nest of tube curls sitting on top of my head. The hairdresser crowns me with the final touch, a rhinestone tiara from which trails a soft veil.

"Come on, time is rushing," a woman I've never met before says. The others close tighter around me and I sink under their hot and animated breaths. When I gasp in a lungful of air, it's so strained it sounds like a door hinge badly in need of oiling. Mona hears it, too, and for the first time she yells out something useful: "Give her room, ladies!" Then she makes a joke: "A bride is a delicate and nervous flower. Too much moisture, too much sun, too much of anything will cause her to wilt."

The women cackle and fan out. I rise. My dress, embellished with hundreds of pearls, crystals, and sequins, is as heavy as sludge.

"Water," I whisper, and before I can say it again, the hard rim of a glass is touching my lips. I take a sip, and right away the makeup artist is adding another layer of brilliant pink to my lips.

"Enough," says Mona. "Any more color and she'll look like a clown."

Here is a clown who's not laughing. One last glimpse at the mirror: I stare beyond the arty strokes of sea-green eye shadow and the industriously curled lashes, and focus on my eyes. Gone is the hope that once floated on them. Deadened is their soul.

"Move out of the way," Mona commands. "It's time to go down."

37

DALAL

࿐

I am about to snap open my crystal-coated clutch to take out the invitation when the guard at the entrance gasps and then grins. She recognizes me, despite the shayla hanging low over my face. "No need," she says, holding her hand up to her temple in a movement I decide is a salute. "You're the Gazelle of the Desert."

That was the heading written in beautiful calligraphy under my image on the cover of this week's *Zahrat Al-Khaleej* magazine. There are sparks in the guard's eyes, like light on water, a sight that livens my mood even though I've seen the same on the faces of countless other devoted fans. I want to let my abaya slip off so she can see me in full stylish form. I'm wearing a turquoise sequined dress with a crystal beaded halter neckline and a bold V-cut open back. But I hold back and lift the shayla, revealing only my face. After all, I'd promised Mariam to be discreet, to blend in, to attend her wedding with no fuss whatsoever.

"That's my cousin getting married in there," I say, glancing at the ballroom door. It is closed, muffling the throb of music within. "Has she arrived yet?"

The guard shakes her head.

I smile. My timing is perfect. The families of the bride and groom must already have retreated from their greeting post at the entrance to the ballroom. I'm late enough to avoid them, but not too late for Mariam's entrance.

The guard grabs a pen and ferrets out an empty envelope from among the invitations. She holds it in front of me. "Make it to Balquis."

I enter the date: November 9, 1995. With broad strokes, I write: "To Balquis—may your life be filled with joy." I pause before adding: "As much joy as this bride feels tonight." These are the kinds of words my admirers long for. Then I write the signature Madame Nivine had me practice repeatedly while she watched with her tiger eyes. "The stiff *alef* and *lams* will show that you're strong," she explained. "But the *dal* that starts your name, hayachi: you have to curl it just right, like a chile pepper, to show your femininity and vulnerability. Just a little bit of weakness, so that men will want to protect you. That's always a good thing."

Madame Nivine is not with me. It's the first time she has refused me a request. When I failed to charm her into coming (I needed her for support) I'd threatened to look for another manager. Finally I ended up begging her. "As a manager and a friend, I advise you not to go, either," she said. "You're fiery and unpredictable. And given your anger toward your family, you might do something foolish, which the press is sure to exploit."

"You worry about everything."

"I know she's your cousin, your best friend and all, habibchi, but just think: maybe she doesn't want you there. I mean, why did it take so long for the invitation to arrive?"

"Egyptian post!"

"Stop furrowing that brow, Dalal. Don't pretend you're puzzled. And who is this man she is going to marry, anyway?"

"How should I know? His name is on the card. Read it!" Madame Nivine's candor upset me, but I was not about to show it. It's true that

Mariam was tight-lipped when I asked her for details. She skirted my every attempt at probing. She made silly statements that sounded like defeat. I'd finally understood that she'd given up the fight. And that got my blood boiling: they had broken her. When I offered to sing at her wedding, she said, "Dalal, dear, I really don't have much say in anything. You know how these things are, more for the family, their prestige and standing in society, than anything else. They're arranging the whole thing."

"There are weeds in this sea that you are about to swim in!" Madame Nivine had said to me. "Those weeds are your past, and they're going to wrap themselves around your ankles and pull you down."

What rubbish she talks! I toss a sideways glance at my companions. Azza and Hannah, (newly employed as my public-relations manager and added to my retinue) are like schoolchildren trying to win points with their teacher by being attentive. They wait for a request or an order. Azza giggles and bobs her head at the guard. She's still waiting for the signed envelope, which I am clutching a little too tightly. I lean toward her. Handing her the envelope, I whisper, "Look, I don't want anyone to know I am here." Balquis the guard seems pleased to be entrusted with my secret. She tightens her lips and seals them with an imaginary zipper.

Azza swings open the giant door and an arctic burst of air rushes out, plastering the shayla to my face. It takes a few seconds for it to settle. At that moment, the song ends. For a moment it's silent, and I freeze in place, embarrassed by all the eyes on me. Which ones are my half sisters? The only one I might be able to recognize is Nouf because we were in the same fancy school for a while—unless she has changed drastically. What about the others? What will they do if they find out I'm here?

I'm considering turning around and running away, when the next song begins. It has a strong Egyptian beat, and the deafening wail of the singer restores my senses. The singer, along with the rest of the musicians, must be behind the giant curtain to the side of the bridal stage. It is a common arrangement so that the women feel more comfortable. Being in a ballroom filled only with women, those who wear head scarves are free to remove them if they choose to.

I squint through a dazzle of blue and white lights. The ballroom is filled with round tables arranged on both sides of a royal-blue carpet. It looks like any other Khaleeji wedding I've performed at. I let my eyes roam over the heads of abaya-clad women, searching for a remote seat to occupy.

I spot an empty table at the periphery of the ballroom. It's right below one of the speakers, but close enough to the bridal stage that I will be able to observe Mariam without being noticed. It's her wedding, after all, and I must respect her wishes and not attract attention. "Come on, follow me," I tell Azza and Hannah, and I hurry over, all the while considering how strange it feels not to be the central attraction.

Almost as soon as we take our seats, Azza jumps back up. She points ahead and whoops. "Look, look! There's Noosa."

The famous belly dancer emerges from a back door with her arms spread as wide as eagles' wings. She glides between the tables under a spotlight, searching for an appreciative audience, one that will cheer her on and not eye her with disapproval. She singles out a group of middle-aged ladies and shakes her chest, her emerald fringe of beads clacking. It's a sensuous display, and when the women do not cover their noses and mouths with their shaylas, Noosa knows she has chosen the right table and continues to demonstrate her talent.

She starts with a snakelike coiling of the waist, her midriff held firm under a transparent body stocking, and then launches into a series of abdominal acrobatics. Her belly rises and dips, creating mounds and hollows and impossible shapes; there's a roll from the ribs down to the hips and back up again. Her layers of translucent gold chiffon shimmer with each belly twist. The cloth parts like a curtain to reveal her shining alabaster thighs.

Watching Noosa, all glitter and dazzle, reminds me of all the times I've pranced about beneath a luminous moon of light with a microphone in my hand and glitter in my hair. Mariam is my cousin and best friend, and I have to endure the torture of being invisible in the midst of my father's family. I can't help but feel a little betrayed. To distract myself, I settle back and look around.

The wedding has an underwater theme. The bridal stage, looking to have a height of up to my hips, is garnished with white roses and cream-colored starfish; the divan—where the bride and groom will sit—is shaped like a clamshell. Above it hangs a delicate arrangement of softly swaying strips of ocean-colored fabrics. Luminous white balls cling to the cloth: pearls, the most beautiful of underwater creations. To the left is a low platform shaped like a spiral seashell. It has just enough room on it for one person, probably the main singer, who has yet to materialize.

All this must be the work of my half sisters; it's customary for the women on the bride's side to handle the design and arrangement of any wedding. They set the price—no expense spared: a bellowing message sure to score points with the guests—and the groom's side must foot the bill.

Azza's hand drifts over the bowls of starters—hummus, tabbouleh, samosas, stuffed grape leaves—and taps the funnel-shaped glass vase in the middle of the table. It is filled with a variety of seashells. "So pretty," she says, running her index finger along the glass. "How many people do you think dove to the bottom to fetch them all?"

Just the thought of shouting over the loudspeaker to answer her stupid question fatigues me. I sniff and look away, narrowing my sleepy eye at Noosa. She is balancing a cane on her head. The cheering squad of middle-aged women is now sodden with boredom (all those belly bumps do get repetitive after a while), and that pleases me. But Noosa tickles their interest once more when she lets the cane slip off her head and looks toward her three assistants, who lug over a bronze candelabra with no fewer than fifty burning candles. Noosa slaps her chest. Her eyes round with playful alarm at the candelabra, four times the size of her head and a meter tall. She crouches, and the assistants fix it to her head.

"Her neck must be as strong as an ox's," says Hannah, just as the tablah tap-taps the dancer into rising.

"She should be in a circus, not a wedding," I add, smirking.

The beat crescendos, a deafening cacophony of synthesized flutes and violins. Noosa's head dips and swivels; there is awe on the guests' faces. Openmouthed children scrunch their eyes as she tilts to an extreme degree that makes it look like the candelabra will topple to the ground. But Noosa retracts her neck just in time and balances her head with an unflappable bob. Little girls clap and cheer—some of them are my nieces, I'm sure. A jolt of envy rushes through my bones.

I am in the middle of my flesh and blood, and yet I must act like a stranger. No, worse than that! I must be an invisible stranger. Mariam and her weakness! Why couldn't she have shown some boldness and insisted I sing at her wedding?

The candelabra is removed from Noosa's head. Someone passes her a microphone. She holds it to her mouth and wags her tongue in an energetic ululation: the announcement for the *zaffa*, the wedding procession. The bride has arrived.

38

MARIAM

A traditional troupe of women musicians leads the way. They sing, clap, and slap their tar drums. The flower girls follow them, carrying conch shells filled with white petals, which they scatter on the navy-blue carpet. Next is the video crew with their harsh lights. Then it's me.

I am a mermaid.

The dress clings to me all the way to the middle of my calves, where it loosens and fans out to the ground in an elaborate fish tail. In case anyone needs more clarification, nacre fish scales are embroidered to the dress with pearly threads, the shapes fortified with sequins and beads. Like any mermaid treading on solid ground, this one is finding it difficult to walk.

My face glimmers under the spotlight. Little girls gape at me with stars in their eyes. Older girls gaze at me with dreams in their heads. One day soon, they, too, will have their transforming moment and become the bride in white.

The video-recording team, a group of three Filipinas with serious faces, wades backward in front of me. The camerawoman has her eye glued to the viewfinder. She is careful not to make any sudden moves; she doesn't want to bump her head on the light that is raised above her head by the first assistant, or trip over the wires that the second assistant is uncoiling.

"Keep your shyness, but try to look content," Mona says. She struts alongside me, handing out infinite tips. Every now and then her hand runs over the rhinestones studding my shoulders as if they had suddenly grown dusty and needed a polish. Other relatives follow my trail, too. I imagine their eyes on me, radiant with celebration, taking in my extravagant gown. They do not realize that I would gladly give it up and settle for a rag if only . . . if only . . .

"Mariam!" Mona hisses. "No teeth in your smile."

I adjust my smile and continue at a tortoise pace up three steps and onto the catwalk that leads to the bridal stage. There's a seat at the end of it: a clamshell. Could it open up and swallow me?

❧

The folk music group has made the noise it was paid for and left, as has the belly dancer. There's a blissful hush, a signal that dinner is about to be served. An army of waitresses emerges, threading its way between the tables to deliver trays of stuffed baby goat. I spot three types of rice—dill green, saffron yellow, and plain white—along with an assortment of kebabs and curries. It's a brief respite, and I listen to the sounds made by the eight hundred or so hungry guests: the clink of cutlery on porcelain, the gurgle of water poured in glasses, the murmur of light conversation, and the sleepy bawls of the odd toddler here and there.

It's the perfect moment for family photographs with the bride.

Seated on the satin clamshell couch, I watch Amal as she rearranges the scaly tail at my toes.

Mama Al-Ouda doesn't wait for anyone to come get her. She climbs the steps with the help of two Filipina maids, her abaya bundled to her waist so she doesn't trip. Under it she wears a traditional dress made of fine brocade. She lumbers down the catwalk while my cousins struggle with their children. Respectfully, I rise to kiss my grandmother's hand, then give her another light peck on her forehead, over her brand new burka, which shines like a polished bronze shield. She whispers, "Masha'Allah," and cups my face with both hands to give an extra dose of approval.

Mama Al-Ouda settles next to me on the couch, fidgeting, releasing a whiff of Arabic perfume mixed with Yardley English Rose talc. She is bedecked in some of her finest traditional gold jewelry, most of which were gifts from my father when he started making money: heavy earrings; a shimmery necklace that gushes over her chest like a honeyed waterfall; thickly spiked bangles that look like weapons; and more modern gold rings on four of her fingers.

The photographer holds her hand up and says, "Ready, steady." She lets loose an erratic sequence of clicks and flares before saying, "Go!" Alerted by the spray of flashes, the rest of the family hurries to huddle around me. Mona arranges the small girls and boys in two rows according to height and then takes her place. Again, "Ready, steady," clicks and flashes, and the delayed word, "Go!"

I must look the picture of contentment with my bride's smile (no teeth showing). Only Dalal would have been able to sense my agony. I don't bother to look for her, because she would have made her presence known by now if she were here. After all the warnings I gave her, I'm sure she understood that it would be wisest to stay away.

"Mama, Mama! Salem pulled my hair!" Mona's four-year-old, Reem, tugs at her mother's gown just as her mobile phone starts ringing.

"Don't pull her hair," Mona says to her son, Salem, two years older than his sister and double her size. She answers the phone. A pause, then a declaration: "They're coming. The men are coming."

My conjugal life is about to begin.

Reem's incessant tugs turn to furious yanks. "Stop it," orders Mona, and shifts away, blocking her free ear. The music resumes; it's a Khaleeji beat that begins with the piercing throbs of more tar drums. Frustrated, Mona bonds her ear to the phone and shouts, "You can't come now. We're not ready." Little Reem is whimpering and clinging to her mother's knees. Mona ignores her. "Let the singer finish a few songs so there's some dancing. You know none of the girls will dance if there are men in the ballroom."

My conjugal life has been delayed to make time for the girls who want to dance.

"They're tired. They're all tired, these children," says Mona, and winks at me. "Don't worry, Mariam, insha'Allah, he'll be here soon enough." She marches the squirming Reem off the stage, struggling to keep the child's snotty nose as far away from her dress as possible.

I'm not worried, I think. I have sat with him twice. The first time he visited, he was received in the formal sitting room. I was bathed, coiffed, and dressed suitably for the visit, which lasted half an hour. I'm not sure if it was shyness or the awkwardness of two strangers meeting under the gaze of my aunt and her children, but mostly we avoided looking at each other. He asked after my health and I asked after his. We drank gahwa and ate Omani *halwa*. The second time, he visited for lunch, and Ammi Majed was present. I'd felt invisible. The man was certainly more talkative, but only with the other men, my uncle and his sons.

The man is much older than I, just over forty. I call him *the man* because he is just that—the man who will be my husband, who will share my bed, whose children I will deliver. "The older he is, the bet-ter," Amal had told me, "more mature, more settled, more able to take charge." And Nouf had added, "More important, he's as rich as a sheikh."

Just as the waitresses start serving the grand array of desserts, a trill echoes in the entrance, and Budoor proudly sweeps into the ballroom. I see Mona light up at the arrival of the much-anticipated Kuwaiti singer. (She will get the girls dancing, after all.) Budoor begins with an upbeat song that is filled with blessings for this special occasion.

39

DALAL

ೕ

First that vulgar dancer, then the family photographs that excluded its most dazzling member, and now this Budoor, who does not go to the platform that has been built for her. With microphone in hand she winds her way between the tables, swishing this way and that in her many layers of chiffon. They're pale violet and do nothing to lighten her complexion.

The beat is punchy, amplified by the throb of drums from behind the curtain. When the women start clapping, I stab the crème caramel in front of me with my spoon. This just happens to be my opening song: I have sung it at every Khaleeji wedding I've performed in. Someone throws a rose at Budoor, and the crème caramel disintegrates under the force of my jabs. I rise to my feet. Azza and Hannah gawk at me, their open mouths filled with a rainbow of gooey sweet things. "What?! I just want to see better." And I do.

Three tables away, a girl stares at me with wonder in her eyes. She gasps and presses her fingers to her mouth. Her friend scrutinizes me, looking doubtful; they get into a piddling quarrel. A smile tickles my lips. I push out my chin and loosen my shayla, letting it slide off my head. There: no question of my identity now.

And then they come—not just the two friends but a whole group of starstruck teenagers. They compliment my voice, my songs, my pretty face. I play it all down because I know the importance and power of seeming modest. They're close to me in age, but judging from their demeanor, it's obvious they lack my experience and worldliness.

Budoor is four tables away, but she might as well be on another continent. The girls talk over one another, and I wait; I know a crucial request will be made soon. And I'm right: "Won't you sing for us tonight, Dalal?"

"Oh, no, no." I tap my cheek, my forehead, as if I'm burning up. Easing back onto the chair, I cross one leg over the other. I look down at my knee—revealed!—poking through the gown's deep side slit. My abaya sits in a crumpled heap behind me. Azza attempts to draw it up. I slap her wrist—discreetly, of course.

Basking in so much adoration, I understand their insistence. This is a wedding, and these girls want to feel alive. "I couldn't possibly get up and sing. I'm a guest here."

There are heaves and hums of disappointment. Another girl says, "That doesn't matter."

"It's not right. I mean . . ." I lean forward and they huddle around me, as if expecting the disclosure of some great piece of privileged information. " . . . Think how it would look. I'd be disrespecting Budoor, and, after the bride, she's the attraction here."

"She's ugly," says a girl with heavy braces. (How my heart warms to her!) "Come on, we love you!"

"Just one song," begs a pudgy child with plum cheeks and a lisp.

Just as I'm about to refuse for a second time (before agreeing, of course), Budoor makes an announcement: "We have with us a beautiful and famous fellow artist."

By now I am blocked from Budoor's sight and surrounded by a mass of fans, which, it pleases me to note, has tripled in size. Azza and Hannah can't hide the alarm in their faces—tedious, those two—and are unsure of what they should do.

"No, no, really," I say, and allow the throng of girls to pull me off my chair. I'm aware that I am breaking my promise to Mariam. But I can't possibly walk out of my best friend's wedding without dedicating a song to her, can I? It will be quick, just one tiny tune. How much harm can come of that? Then I'll sit down and be quiet.

I continue my objections, but I let the girls drag me toward that big moon of a spotlight. I'm sure Budoor is not thrilled, but she cuts her way into the group and greets me with three sloppy kisses too fervid to be genuine. I don't know how she managed to get a second microphone so quickly, but her proposition that we sing a duet is expected. Graciously, I agree.

It should be just one song, but as our duet draws to a close I feel a tingle in my spine. I do not wait for permission to launch into a second song. I wave Budoor out of the way and launch into Adbel Halim's Hafez's much-loved "Ahwak."

There is no accompanying music; the confounded musicians behind that curtain are no doubt in a panic, scrambling to accommodate this abrupt change in schedule. No matter: my voice booms clear and fine as can be as I drift up the steps and onto the catwalk, a meandering current on which I float, light as a leaf. By the time they join me, my movements have turned fluid—a soft dip here, a smooth nod there, a gentle sway every now and then—as I trap the mood of my audience.

They are enraptured by my delivery of this simple classical tune, its words so familiar, so cherished. To my right a large group of women sways, some with their palms held over their hearts, others patting their chests as if consoling that vital organ or perhaps blocking the escape of some tender sentiment.

Time-honored yet suited more for a small gathering, "Ahwak" is an unlikely choice for a wedding. It's full of nostalgia. The women start clapping at a steady tempo, which I follow. All those eyes on me, all those faces shining with adoration! I could go on all night, from one song to the next; but now, as I finish the last note of "Ahwak," I spot Budoor flagging me to get off the catwalk. She wants me out of the spotlight so she can take back the guests and do what she is being paid to do.

The women clap. I stay where I am, blowing kisses at them. This propels Budoor up the steps. She tries to hide her agitation with an exaggerated grin; she tells me the groom is waiting to march in. I look to the far side of the ballroom, and sure enough, there are men amassing by the entrance, ready to wade through this water world of women. I rush, trying to fit in as many flying kisses as I can before exiting the scene.

The most anticipated occurrence of a Khaleeji wedding is the arrival of the bride. The second most anticipated is that of the groom, whether he appears on his own or escorted by male family members. The women stop their chatter. There's a burst of efficient activity as they hasten to cover up, extinguishing the dazzle of their necklaces and extravagant dresses with their abayas before positioning their chairs for the best possible vantage point.

It's time to leave, but my feet don't move. It would be insulting to have to skulk out like a burglar when I have as much right to be here as any other Naseemy. A thought zaps through my mind: what would my mother do? The idea flickers, then dies. I have stopped caring what she thinks. I see Azza waving at me with one hand and holding my abaya in the other, ready to fling it over me once I get near her. Hannah is by her side, collecting our purses. They skitter back and forth like mice in a pantry, facing the danger of being spotted and then cornered. They are anxious to rush me out, the forsaken family member. Perhaps I should go.

I turn for a final sweeping look at my cousin. My half sisters have just helped her up. One of them dabs her face with a tissue before pulling down her veil. The others fuss with her fish tail, arranging it so that it twirls around her feet just so. Mariam stands very still, waiting for the man who will lead her to her new life. She is like a tree waiting to be chopped, broken in all the critical places. A peculiar ache crawls toward my heart. Perhaps I should stay.

40

MARIAM

꩜

Dalal came after all! The thought screams in my head.

There she stands, so full of fire, doing exactly what I asked her not to do. Strangely, I am not upset at her. I'm surprised to find myself smiling. How is it possible to both admire and dread her daring? To both want it and not want it?

Perhaps it is because she is my best friend, making sure I know she is near me at this difficult time. Maybe it's because she is the only person who dares defy this family. Whatever the reason, I feel a buoyant lightness, even though I know that Dalal's flamboyant display will have consequences.

The cousins hover like wasps, dizzy with rage, as Dalal pairs up with Budoor for a duet: light and night, swan and raven. Mona gets her wish; the girls are dancing. But there is no pleasure on her face. "Look how she shrinks, that Kuwaiti cow. If she backs away and stops singing, woe to her!" she says. "*Wallah*, she won't see one dirham of her fee of twenty thousand!"

For the first time I appreciate the advantage of being the bride, expected to be demure and sit poised like a pretty doll even in the center of a churning uproar. "Who invited her?" Amal demands, narrowing her eyes at me. There's an uncanny glint in them, as if they're filled with shards of glass. "Was it you, Mariam?"

I keep my eyes on the singing pair, a sparkling blue flame and the ash left behind, and answer in a level voice, "Only out of good manners."

Lacking the combination of guts and spite shared by her sisters, Nadia, eight months pregnant, does nothing more than rub her tummy and moan, "Why doesn't she just go?" She has more to lose than the others. Her husband, the only son-in-law who's financially independent, had just days ago threatened to divorce her and take all the children if nobody put a stop to that brazen singer disgracing the family.

By the time Dalal is well into her second song, Nouf has accused me of being a traitor to the family. "Look at Mariam—she's not even pretending to be upset. I bet she did this on purpose to embarrass us," she says, just as chubby Salem scrambles onto the bridal stage once more, pretending to be a train: "*Chi-chi-chi-chik. Chi-chi-chi-chik. Toot, toot.*" Mona orders him to stop and yanks him off the tracks in the middle of his journey.

"Well," she says to me, keeping a tight grip around her son's arm, "it's your wedding, but know this: any embarrassment will affect us all. And God help us if she's still here when my father arrives."

"You did a boo-boo!" Salem cries out, pulling free from his mother to deliver a thump to my knee.

"Control that child, Mona." The group is so consumed with a torrent of questions and blame that Ammiti Aisha's emergence in their midst stuns them into silence. "People are watching. Look at you, bickering like monkeys."

As Mona hands Salem, now so hyper with fatigue that he attempts to bite her ear, to the waiting maid, Nouf says, "Mama, the bride has arranged this fiasco."

"Quiet," says my aunt, seating herself next to me. "We can't stop what is happening without making a scene. So, all of you . . ." She strokes the air. "Stop flitting about and act normal."

That puts an end to the squabbling. My cousins squeeze next to us. "She will sing her song and go," Ammiti Aisha insists, bobbing her head with vigor.

That doesn't happen. Although Budoor succeeds in escorting Dalal off the catwalk, she forgets to take back that second microphone. No doubt confident that things can finally resume to their natural order, the Kuwaiti singer drifts to the middle of the ballroom. And that's when Dalal raises the microphone to her mouth to make an announcement: "I want to wish the bride all the happiness she could ever hope for. She is the kindest and sweetest human being, and I love her dearly." Her voice cracks with deep emotion: an escaping sentiment that takes flight and settles over me like a soft veil. I feel it.

"Look at her," says Nouf, "the insolent bitch! She's half-naked."

"What an actress," Amal huffs, while Nadia fixes her gaze to the far end of the ballroom, squinting at the entrance.

"Let's all throw her out before she makes more mischief," Nouf says.

"You'll do nothing of the sort," says Ammiti Aisha. "She will go now, and everything will get back to normal."

Budoor is ready to sing the verses of blessing and celebration that accompany the men's march to the bridal stage. But the spotlight pivots and lands on Dalal. By the time the Kuwaiti singer has opened her mouth, Dalal is back on the catwalk and strutting toward us. I sit still, conflicted, both wanting her near me and wanting her to leave.

"She's coming here!" Nouf blurts out.

My cousins jump up, pulling their mother with them to form a sort of shield that blocks my view. I part Mona's crisp taffeta gown and the nets of lace covering Amal's silk dress, and peer with amazement at Dalal.

Dalal aims a hard, scornful glare at her half sisters. Then she frees a lopsided grin that's charged with haughtiness. There's a swish of ruffling dresses. Urgent whispers pass between my cousins—what to do with "the half sister, the half-naked singer with her blatant display!"

I am up, standing tall and solid. No one knows that the dress is cementing me in place. Nobody can guess that my gut feels like butter being churned. Questions tumble over one another in my head: how will this predicament end, and what can I possibly do to neutralize it?

My thoughts are sluggish, too slow to catch up with what's happening. I flinch when I realize that Dalal is already in the heart of our group. I don't say a word; I don't know what might spill out of my mouth. She insists on a photograph with the bride: a simple request, but because it comes from Dalal my cousins react immediately with the hiss and venom of tangled snakes. They forget about me and envelop her in a ball of bridled limbs from which escapes the jumble of their reprimands and Dalal's sass: "No shame . . . as much my right . . . call security . . . ruin of this family . . . my family, too . . . leave now . . . not until I get my photograph!"

"They're here!" Mona cries out, and we all realize that it's too late for Dalal to get off the stage without being noticed. So my cousins agree that she can have a photograph if she stays out of the way until the men leave. They huddle around her and shift her to the far side of the bridal stage.

Everything happens very quickly, as if it's a perfect piece of theater. Drums thunder from behind the curtain, and, right on cue, a party of five men enters the ballroom like a band of desert knights without their horses.

Since the groom is an only child and his father is dead, Ammi Majed and his sons escort him. Both the groom and my uncle wear black *bishts*—the formal outer cloak that drapes the kandora for special occasions such as this one—edged in woven gold thread. Focused ahead, they ignore the hundreds of goggling women, taking long, determined strides as if impatient to conclude this duty.

I'm shivering by the time they reach me. The groom takes his position to my right as my uncle places a light kiss on my forehead and steps to my left, adjusting his ghitra for the photographs. He doesn't need to spell out that this is a formality, not a pleasure. His sons follow with their congratulations. Saif, Ahmad, and Badr shake my hand with the tips of their fingers. When the groom's mother appears, Ammi Majed suddenly realizes that his wife and daughters are not with us.

He looks around, squinting against the bright lights, eager to finish this ordeal, and spots them in a cluster at the dimmed far end of the stage. "What on earth are they doing over there?" he asks. "Why aren't they here with the rest of us?"

41

DALAL

I'm supposed to stay hidden and wait patiently until the men leave: that was our agreement. Seven of them are keeping me cooped up—Aisha, her four daughters, and a couple of granddaughters—so close to the edge of the stage that the smallest nudge could send me tumbling over. Staying still is harder than I imagined, because curiosity heats me up: I just want a peep (the tiniest glimpse!) of the groom. My little stirrings ruffle them, and the silks, satins, and chiffons fluff around me like the feathers of a bunch of distressed hens unable to settle down for the night's rest.

But now the seams are loosening, and this puzzles me until I spot my father gesturing for them to join the bridal party. They dillydally, and for good reason: he's a formidable presence. Aisha breaks away first, dragging her feet toward her husband; the rest follow.

A bite of frost zips up my spine, a reminder of my naked back (why did I have to wear such a bold design?). I'm suddenly so self-conscious that I consider jumping off the bridal stage. But my heels are high and there's a possibility that I would break one of my legs, or both. So I settle for the next best thing, and cower.

There's the groom, certainly old enough to be Mariam's father. He holds her hand with the tips of his fingers. I can't tell whether he's shy or indifferent toward her. As my half sisters assemble the family around the stage for photographs, I scrutinize him. His shoulders are raised as if stuck in mid-shrug. His beard is thick. Darkened with too-black dye, it cuts across his cheeks in ruler-straight lines. What kind of husband will he be to my dear Mariam? I search for some sign of goodness in him. But it's difficult with that chest puffed out like an arrogant turkey's. I wait for it to deflate, but it doesn't. *Born that way*, I think.

Someone has delivered my grandmother, who looks weighed down with too much gold, and planted her on the clamshell couch. There's a crusty expression on her face as she watches my half sisters' attempts to impose order on the little ones, who won't sit still. The main troublemaker is a tubby boy who keeps flipping onto his stomach and slithering around on the bridal stage like a lizard. There they are: a family having trouble squeezing together for a photograph. They're not a model family, but the sight of them clumped together makes me feel so alone. Standing at the edge, as always, I am forgotten: so near, but still blotted out of existence. I take a step nearer as emotions swell in me all at once. They're like a broth with too many ingredients; it's impossible to sift through them, or to understand why they are there in the first place.

The family finally manages to get in order: a picture of happiness, which the photographer is eager to snap. My vision blurs. Tears well up, and any moment now they will spill. What happens next dries them up.

The groom's mother, who until now was content to stay on the periphery, suddenly drills her way into the middle of the group. My father politely steps to one side, and she wriggles into the gap so that she is next to her son. She hooks his elbow and weaves her fingers into his. With that, he pulls his hand out of Mariam's—even shakes it, as if he had been holding a filthy rag. There is confusion and dismay in her expression when she looks at him for some explanation of his sudden callousness. He stares ahead with a stony face, and I realize that this man will never make her happy, that she must not walk out of this ballroom with him.

The family doesn't notice a thing; they are too busy putting on their best smiles. I inch closer, feeling useless. My poor Mariam! She tries to hide her humiliation as best she can, but her mouth is twitch-ing and her fingers are shaking. Someone needs to hold her cast-off hand and bring warmth back to her. But then, quick as the snap of a finger, my father spots me. "What's she doing here?" It's a low-pitched growl, but I hear it. I take a futile step back, as if that would reverse the flow of time. His eyes are ablaze, so heated that I imagine the ballroom burning to ashes under their intensity.

I had wandered closer without realizing it. (Every one of them now stares at me.) I look away. Azza and Hannah wave at me with urgency. Whether I walk or run, they want me off the stage. I am tempted to do just that, to get as far away as possible from this fraud of a union. But there is Mariam, and she needs me. I sniff. From behind me comes a whiff of spicy Arabian perfumes, and a viper sputters curses onto my bare shoulder. "Go now, or else I'll call security to drag you out," Mona threatens.

Right then, I make my decision. "It's time I got my photograph with the bride," I say, and elbow her to the side. With my nose in the air and my chin pointed out, I make a beeline for the bridal group. Clutching Mariam's hand, I glower at the lot of them, fish eyed and stunned mute with disbelief. "What?" I say. "Have you forgotten that I'm an Al-Naseemy, too? Now look ahead and put on your best smile."

42

MAJED

ೂ

"Why is the singer here with us?" Mama Al-Ouda asks. When no one answers, she taps Dalal on the calf with her stick and says, "Shouldn't you be out there, dear? Singing?"

Dalal leans over and says, "I'm a singer with special privileges." She waves at my daughters. "Ask them about it."

"Special privileges?" I don't need to see my mother's eyes through the window of her burka because I know exactly what they look like when she's baffled: wet marbles, the watery blue age rings expanding like an encroaching tide. "Well, move to the side with your special privileges so I can see what's going on."

It's strange that I can hear them over the noise, but I do. I bite the inside of my lips and try hard to think of the best way to deal with this nasty twist. "She should not be here," the groom's mother says, sticking her tongue out to indicate Dalal as if I might have trouble understanding her meaning. Soon after Dalal had bulldozed her way through, the widow gave me a grave look—a signal that had us both shifting away from the middle of the group. Now positioned on the periphery, I try to placate her. It's imperative that we maintain a strong relationship; she has agreed to invest a fortune into my various business projects. Even though I'm raging inside, I honey my voice and try to make light of the situation. "Don't let such a small thing ruin the evening."

"Yes, think of our poor bride: blameless," says Mona, who emerges from behind me.

"He's my only child, you understand," the widow tells her, "and it's his happiness that is the most important."

Mona and I nod our agreement. "And what happiness she will give him," says Mona, just as Saif and Ahmad join our small group. "She is ready to give her heart and soul to him."

"Mariam is generous in all ways." I keep my tone gentle and confident. "She will provide you the best company, too. She will serve you with more dedication than if she were your own daughter."

"Yes, I guess you are right." The widow clicks her tongue grudgingly. "I must think of us as one family, I suppose." She crosses her arms tightly over her barrel-shaped waist and gazes toward the groom, who keeps looking over his shoulder back at her. "Still, you need to get rid of that unscrupulous singer right away. And mind you don't make a scene."

I share her exact thoughts, but how she expects me to do that I cannot tell, especially with all those eyes on us. We stand frozen in place beneath the ballroom lights, which are dim now. We're all grinning hard, ideal subjects for the photographer, who clicks her camera with blinding speed. The video-camera woman is just as efficient. She leans from side to side, keeping her tape running, as if in wait for something big to happen. She won't have to wait much longer.

"I will not have my son's reputation soiled because you happened to make such a big mistake," the widow hisses. The humiliation is hard to bear, and I have to force back the temptation to retaliate with a curt response.

How to satisfy the widow? The opportunity comes quickly: a series of mighty ululations erupts like sirens, burning my ears as though hot oil had been poured in them. I am dazed; it takes me a while to realize that the noise is coming from three women I do not recognize, who seem to have appeared out of thin air.

They surprise us all, having managed to barrel their way the length of the catwalk to face the bride without being noticed. There they stand, with their arms raised high. One of them tilts her head and flutters her tongue. The other two follow suit, and out drops an even louder gargle of high-pitched noise. They fling their arms in the air; the contents of their hands flutter down over the group. Owl-eyed with anticipation, Salem cries out, "*Nuthoor!*"

It's the money typically showered over the bride and groom—a messy business. We are bombarded by waves of hard one-dirham coins and crisp five- and ten-dirham notes. Squealing children clamber onto the bridal stage like ants escaping a crushed nest. They jump into the air, limbs unhinged, poking and pinching and tugging, crashing into one another in a scramble to collect as much of the bounty as they can. They crawl on all fours, kicking ankles and stepping on toes, lifting dresses and tugging kandoras.

One of the children accidentally steps on the bride's foot and another pulls at her tail to locate any coins that might have rolled under it. When Dalal lets go of Mariam's hand to shoo them away, I spot the opportunity I've been waiting for. I will extract her from our midst now—who will notice in this mayhem? I must take action swiftly.

It would be better to send one of my sons to take care of this loathsome business while I stay with the widow to keep her calm and reassured. Both Ahmad and Saif await my command. Saif is too edgy and impatient for my liking, and I can't trust him to take charge of this delicate operation. I opt for Ahmad, the more composed of the two. "Discreetly," I mouth, and give Ahmad a go-ahead nod. But it's Saif who lunges ahead.

He cuts through the clamoring children, his ghitra flying on either side of his head like a pair of powerful wings. Dalal latches onto Mariam's hand as though it were a lifeline. He reaches Dalal, and for a moment it looks like he might be able to reason with her. His expression is sober, with just the right touch of intimidation, and even though I can't hear what he's saying, it seems he'll be able to convince her to leave quietly. One glimpse at the guests assures me that they haven't noticed anything out of the ordinary. I will the episode to terminate quickly and quietly. But I realize it's a fool's hope when Saif starts wagging his index finger at Dalal. She eyes it as if it were a worm and shakes her head.

Mama Al-Ouda once more insists on knowing why the singer is not out there singing. Dalal scoffs and leans over to ask the old woman, "Don't you know who I am?"

"Who you are?"

We all hear Saif when he says, "Don't talk to my grandmother. You said your mabrooks, woman! Now, for the last time: walk off this stage and leave us to celebrate in peace. Go back to your people."

Dalal lets go of Mariam's hand and slams her fists to her hips in a bold challenge to his authority. "*You* are my people. Whether you like it or not, I am a part of this family. Your sister—that's right—with the same blood running through my veins."

His face darkens like clouds gathering for a violent storm. "Silence!" he says, the words hissing through his teeth. "If I had a knife I would sharpen it and slice your tongue to bits. You will leave now."

She doesn't budge, and that's about as much as he can take. He lunges, grabbing for her. She whoops and wriggles behind Mariam, bumping her forward. The bride somehow doesn't trip—the group gasps anyway—despite getting her feet tangled in that damned mermaid's tail.

"This is not the way," Mariam pleads with Saif. "She'll go, she'll go now, won't you, Dalal?" Saif's left hand swoops around behind her waist. "And even if she doesn't, what's the harm?"

Saif could easily have snatched Dalal at this point, but he stops short and points a thick knuckle at Mariam. "You shut your mouth!"

"No, you shut your mouth," Dalal says to him, and pokes him on the chest. "How dare you speak to her like that? She's the bride!" And then they are scuttling around the stage, unable to maneuver in the midst of the fidgeting family.

There's a whistling sound coming out of my dry throat. I was just supposed to deliver the groom to the bride, pose for a few pictures, and leave. I hold on to the hope that Saif and Dalal have still been overlooked; observers might assume that the family is doing nothing more than rearranging for more photographs. Until Saif catches Dalal and holds her in a firm grip. He pulls; she resists. Having had enough of the commotion, Mama Al-Ouda launches an adrenalized attack on both Saif and Dalal, poking their thighs and rapping their calves with her stick. I look around for Ahmad or Badr, but they've both disappeared.

"Stop the video," Mona says, rushing to cover the lens with her hand.

"One, two." A flash bounces off the edge of Saif's shoulder just before he yanks Dalal out of the group. "Three!"

"No photos," Amal shouts.

I tighten my eyes and hiss through my teeth; I didn't want this to escalate. In real time, it's seconds; in mind time, it's hours. That cursed Kuwaiti singer and the musicians waver to a halt. In the quiet, I hear what sounds like a million gasps coming from the guests. Some of the women at the tables close to the bridal stage rise and fuss about with their abayas, wrapping them tighter around their bodies. Then they are off, fleeing like creatures who have sensed an earthquake before it strikes.

The widow pinches her cheeks with disbelief. Dalal is leaning back, using all her weight to keep from being dragged off. But Saif is stronger, and he lugs her to the middle of the stage. He'll have to pull her along the full length of the catwalk, all the way to the steps, to get rid of her. That thought jolts me into a reality that now looks impossible to reverse. When the widow wails, I know I cannot stay on the sidelines any longer. I must take action, whatever that means.

The bridal stage has erupted into chaos. Saif drags Dalal farther down the catwalk. Mariam seems to be the only person not moving. I wade through the family with outstretched arms.

"It's an occasion for celebration," Budoor announces in an upbeat voice. "A thousand mabrooks to the groom! A thousand mabrooks to the bride!" She does her best to divert the guests' attention. But it's too late; nobody is listening.

I'm not sure how she manages, but Dalal breaks free from Saif as soon as she sees me. She darts toward me, her feet dangerously close to the edge of the raised stage. With her bright-red fingernails curved like claws, she looks set to scratch my eyes out. I brace myself. And that's when I hear a sudden, ringing wolf howl.

43

DALAL

ॐ

"Wooooooo! Woooooo!"

It comes without warning, a noise so eerie that a hush blankets the room. Mariam stands apart, her eyes aglow, lit from the inside by some obscure madness. Her mouth rounds again: "Woooooo! Enough!" This time it sounds like a lament, a loss, a heart shattered. It brings tears to my eyes; my hands, raised toward her, turn blurry.

"Pull yourself together, girl," I hear my father say to her.

Mariam snaps at him, "Don't you talk to me! I hate you! My father is gone, and it's all because of you. You forced me to be here when all I want is to be as far away from you as possible." She's battling too many emotions. Her voice dips. "Enough pain, enough misery." She wheezes, "Enough."

"I'm coming," I whisper. And just as I'm about to take that first step, I hear a dull thud. I stumble back. It takes me several slow seconds to realize I've been struck, just above my heart. I wobble, teetering on the edge of the bridal stage and fighting to regain my balance.

My father turns around just in time to make a grab for my hands, which flap like the wings of a desperate bird. He lunges but catches only the tips of my fingers; they slip out of his grip as though they'd been dipped in butter. "Baba?" I whimper as I topple off the stage.

&

The first time I come to, I spit out carpet fluff. My arms are tangled under me. I'm aware of cold air blowing up my legs and straight to my crotch. I'm horrified: are my panties exposed? My legs are splayed like a frog's—I'm sure of it—but when I try to lift my head for confirmation, pain shoots through my shoulders. And I'm out again.

The second time I wake up, I'm shivering beneath a blanket and being rolled onto a hard plank. Men in green coats strap me down. It's hard to keep my eyes open. One of them lightly slaps my face as if trying to wake me up. I hear a click and what feels like the jerk of an elevator. I'm moving now, backward, on wheels. A woman hurries along by my side, weeping and calling my name. I'm sure I know her, but what is her name? I try to clear the fog in my head. I hear again the howling cry of a wolf, which brings to mind an image of Mariam in her bridal gown. And there's her voice, growing hollow and distant, as if she were tumbling down to the bottom of a well. "You've destroyed my life! I have nothing. What more do you want?" Where did she go? I need to find her.

I see the bridal stage: empty. Where is she? My head flops back. I'm moving very quickly now between the abandoned tables. Where are all the women? I pass out again.

44

MARIAM

๙

They didn't waste any time getting rid of the lights. Ten thousand green, yellow, and orange bulbs came down the very next morning. They'd lined the walls of the house from top to bottom and spread in sickle-shaped threads along the outer garden wall. They rose in spirals around the tree trunks and sat like luminous sunbirds on branches. It's a customary embellishment in the Emirates: a glowing announcement of a festive occasion so that strangers who drive by can smile, point, and say, "Look, someone in that house is getting married."

I wonder whether the groom removed the lights draped over his house as quickly as my family did. I don't know why I still think of him as the groom, because that's not the case anymore: the marriage is off. It's the only piece of information I have, delivered in one hasty moment by Ammiti Aisha. She whispered it through the doorway and then disappeared. That was yesterday, or perhaps the day before that. I haven't seen her, or anyone else, since.

Under dour instructions from Ammi Majed, they are keeping me locked up in my room. No one has been allowed to communicate with me since my outburst, which had continued even as I was hustled off the bridal stage and into a car that was waiting to take me home. I wailed as I was half herded, half carried to my bedroom.

The room was crowded with people, a family bursting at the seams. I could hear my uncle shouting at Saif for making a mess of things. He stayed posted in the doorway with his sons, relinquishing the responsibility of dealing with the out-of-control bride to Ammiti Aisha and his daughters. The women, yammering like hagglers in a bazaar, couldn't decide whether to voice their outrage or placate the hysterical bride with soft words. Slumped on the edge of the bed, I hugged my chest and moaned, and whenever anyone tried to touch me I screamed and kicked.

I could not stop. It was like water gushing out of a burst pipe. I could not stop.

And then the doctor arrived. The cold stethoscope sent a wave of shivers through me, and he had to pull the thermometer out of my mouth for fear of its breaking between my chattering teeth. He poked it under my arm instead and declared that I had a fever. He gave me a couple of injections, their effect immediate. Then he delivered his diagnosis: severe mental breakdown.

What to do when the bride goes mad? With the warmth of the medicine spreading through me, I laid down my head and the rest of me followed, still molded into my hard dress. I listened to the doctor explain that my state had been brought on by prolonged chronic stress.

"Stress?" Ammi Majed regurgitated the word. Again: "Stress? What mumbo jumbo is this?" The room turned quiet as he pushed through the women. "What stress, Doctor?" he demanded, his voice gruff. "She eats well. She sleeps well." A sweep of the arm, and then, "Perhaps it's the marble she walks on, or the sight of those expensive curtains." Fuming, he shook his head. "Tell me, would living in a house like this stress you?"

My eyes were heavy, but I scoffed at him. He tried to forge a snide smile—an attempt to show that he was still in control—but he was unable to do so: his lips were wobbling like jelly. He glowered at me, but the injections had erased my fear of him and left in its place a feeling of lazy indifference.

"Look at her, she's enjoying this mess, thankless creature that she is," he said, waving his arms in the air. He stepped toward me, bending over until his face was inches from mine, his breath hot on my face. "I know you," he growled, keeping his voice low. "You did it on purpose. All this time you have wanted to humiliate me, this family. Now you've succeeded, blurting out those lies in front of all those people."

I remember shaking my head sluggishly and correcting him with slurred words. "No lies, ammi, only truth."

He straightened up with so much force that his back cracked loudly. "One thing everyone in this room should know: I will not stand for it!" His finger was knifing the air. "You, Mr. Medical Doctor, no more talk about stress. I don't believe a word of it. You go and you find a real medical reason to explain this, because that's the only thing that will save her."

As the doctor defended his diagnosis, I dozed off. I think my uncle stormed out, but I can't be sure, even when I dig through my memory for the details of that night. For the next two days, the doctor came back to check up on me. With each visit, he fed me pills that numbed my mind and turned my limbs pulpy, leading to bouts of much-appreciated dreamless sleep. My only other regular visitor has been a new maid who comes in periodically to clean my room. She also brings my meals, which I only pick at if I bother at all. Her name is Ophelia, and she doesn't speak a word of Arabic or English.

No one tells me a thing. And the beautiful part is that I don't care to know anything—until today.

I am restless. Sitting cross-legged on the bed, I bite the hardened skin at the edges of my fingernails as I wait for the doctor (three hours late!) and his sweet stash of pills. And that's when I hear it: a series of wails that reverberates as if coming out of a deep well. They last until the calls for the afternoon prayer from the neighboring mosques drown them out.

I roll off the bed and race to the door, remembering suddenly that it's locked. "Open this door!" Frustrated, I jerk the handle up and down repeatedly, making as much noise as I can—as if that would make a difference. I can't imagine that anyone will let me out. I had voiced my torment publicly. I'd spoken the unspeakable, shaken the foundation, false and rickety as it may be, of this family.

What did I say? I try to recall the exact sequence of my actions, but it's difficult. Images come in bits and pieces, each disconnected from the others, as if telling a story of its own: Dalal lying unconscious with her hands twisted under her, the widow and her son locking arms and storming off, the way I resisted with every shred of strength when I was rushed off the stage. How long did it last? How loud was my voice? How dare they do this to me!

I yell at the top of my voice, "I don't care!" pounding and kicking at the door.

It exhausts me. Breathless, I drop to my knees and glue an ear to the door. I hear more voices now, and the sounds of people rushing about downstairs. I can't tell what they're saying, but their voices are agitated. I sink farther, a heaviness pulling me to the ground. I lay my head on an arm and pull in my legs, sinking into numbness. Nestled against the door, I let sleep take me away. That's where the doctor finds me; he helps me to the bed before giving me a shot.

Two days later I follow Ophelia around the room, pointing my finger at the ground, mixing pidgin Arabic with English to increase my chances of being understood. "*Inti gooli hag ana*, you tell me, *shoo fee*, what's happening, *tahat*, down?"

Either she's deaf or I've turned invisible. Ophelia stays focused on the job at hand, releasing sharp bursts of furniture spray followed by diligent wipes with her cloth. She scurries from one piece of furniture to the next, obviously in a hurry to finish her work and leave.

When I clasp her wrist to get her attention, she cowers, as if I might strike her. It's obvious that the master's order to isolate the unpredictable bride has inspired gossip among the servants. No doubt they have come up with their own blend of theories on the matter. This one must think I'm violent, so I let go and pat her on the shoulder. This seems to pacify her somewhat. I say, "*Shoo fee bait*, what's happening in house?"

"*Fee mout*, there is death," she whispers, and tiptoes cautiously backward until she bumps into the door. "*Fee mout*," she repeats, and starts knocking at it.

"What?" A house in mourning: that explains why it has been filled with people these past few days. Earlier, I'd leaned out through the window—my legs dangling and my tummy balanced on the sill— for a partial view of the front gate. I had spotted women getting out of cars. Now I understand that they've been arriving to pay their condolences. "Who died?" Since I haven't seen any members of the family, it could be anyone.

Someone unlocks the door from the outside. I take a step toward the maid with the intention of blocking it before she can escape, but I stop short so as not to panic her. "Tell me!"

She gives me a mournful look and slips out.

45

DALAL

⤶

"I was pushed."

"Pushed, fell, it happened, finished. There's no point going over it again."

Saif pushed me deliberately, and I want him to pay for it. For the hundredth time, I tell her I want to take him to court. But Madame Nivine will have none of it. She says, "You ruined their wedding, Dalal. I don't know what drove you to it, but there's no sense in taking your family to court."

"Not the family, just Saif."

"No!" She shakes a finger in my face. She's cross. I lapse into a surly pout on the hospital bed. "You'll spend all your money on lawyers. You'll expose yourself to the press, and they're always sniffing, always hungry to smear a singer's good name. In the end, it's you who will walk away hurt. Didn't we agree we wouldn't talk about this anymore?"

We did agree, but I'm unable to control the heaving sentiments that come in waves when I least expect them to. I must still be shaken about what happened at the wedding. Memories flash in my head and raise a series of unanswerable questions. Here's one: my father, hawkeyed, purple-faced, with his hand stretched out. Was he trying to save me, or was it nothing more than a reflexive action? Why do I care? I take deep, noisy breaths to clear my head, frowning at another memory: Mariam encumbered by that heavy bridal gown, looking miserable.

Azza and Hannah told me that while I was out cold, Mariam had lost her head completely. She had started screaming, placing blame mainly on her uncle. She'd accused him of cheating her father and causing his death. She said he cheated her out of her rights.

I held my hands over my mouth as I listened to the girls' account. My father and the rest of the family were stripped of their dignity, shamed, and scandalized, their secrets shouted out for all to hear. I felt none of the joy I'd anticipated that I would feel after such a public exposure, only numbness. One of us was going to speak up; that was the promise we had made to each other when we were girls. But not like this. How I fear for her! What happened next? Where did they take her? What did they do to her? No one has a clue.

Madame Nivine is shaking her head. "Didn't we decide we have to deal with your accident in a clever way?"

"Okay, I get the message!"

They'll be arriving soon, reporters from *Al-Bayan*, *Al-Khaleej*, *Al-Ittihad*, and even the English daily, *Khaleej Times*. A features writer is coming, too, for an exclusive in the glossy magazine *Zahrat Al-Khaleej*. Madame Nivine got in touch with them so we can neutralize all the rumors and feed them a story of our making. This is how it goes: I had an accident. I tripped and fell while performing at a local wedding. There won't be any mention of whose wedding it was, and we're counting on the reporters not to pry. Madame Nivine says the press here is kinder than in Cairo, the journalists more respectful toward one's privacy, even that of a famous person like myself. I'm to charm them and shift their interest toward my voice and music. I'm to give colorful quotes. In short, I'm to make them love me.

"Now you have to look composed, a real lady, with a touch of tenderness and compassion," Madame Nivine says.

It irritates me that I'm having trouble shaping that particular expression. I've practiced it in front of the mirror so many times it's become second nature—I've used it successfully, too. I've stacked it in my memory, to be pulled out when needed. But right now I can't seem to reconstruct it.

She clicks her tongue. "No, not that face." Her voice is crisp; it demands results. I make another, and she nods slightly but still looks unconvinced. "Slightly better, but keep working at it."

My mother is here, too. She left her husband to his oud and jingles and flew out "to be by your side, my daughter" as soon as she heard. There's an unspoken truce between her and Madame Nivine, thanks to my manager's damage control: she quickly insisted that Sitt Zohra stay near her daughter for interviews, and that the caring mother appear in the photographs as well. Mother (I don't call her *Mama* anymore) welcomed the suggestion eagerly. Now they move about like devoted sisters, trying to make the hospital room look as attractive as possible.

Madame Nivine repositions a flowerpot that holds bloodred roses sprinkled with gold dust. They are arranged in a massive heart with a floppy gold bow at the bottom. Mother shifts a rainbow arrangement to my bedside: flowers curving neatly, one brilliant color after another in the correct order—red, orange, yellow, green, blue, purple.

Azza and Hannah linger by the window, each holding her favorite arrangement. "I love your teddy bear," says Hannah, stroking the toy, which hugs the stems of plump pink peonies.

"Yes," Azza says, "but have you ever seen anything like this?" She raises a silver bowl filled with fruits and a mix of exotic flowers I can't name. Hannah agrees on the selection with a nod and leaves the room to check whether the reporters have arrived.

These are the gestures of love from my fans and admirers. I'd hardly had time to settle in the hospital room when the chocolates, stuffed animals, and get-well cards started arriving. The flowers and balloons spill out into the corridor and put the nurses in a good mood. Even the doctor couldn't keep on his somber doctor's face when he told me I was twice lucky: I didn't hit my head in the fall, and the break in my forearm was minor. "No operation needed," he announced. He still put it in a cast, though, that has to stay on for another few weeks. It starts just below the elbow and encloses my hand and thumb. Already it's covered with hearts, smiley faces, and signatures in an assortment of colors. The signatures are mostly from various visitors who have popped into my room, people I don't know who found out there's someone important—a star—in the hospital and dropped in to wish me a quick recovery.

It's strange that I'm not able to enjoy all this attention. I smile and put on my best show of gratitude. But inside, I feel numb. I can't even appreciate my good fortune in not having smashed in my head or bruised my face.

Hannah peeps into the room. "The reporters are here."

With this bit of news, a flush of heat settles in my cheeks. Then that familiar feeling: a delicious churning of nervousness and rapture. I sit up straight, and when my lips stretch to form the appropriate smile for this occasion, it comes out right.

46

MARIAM

❧

A bolt of lightning slashes the white sky. When a groan of thunder follows, the parrots perched in the massive tamarind tree by my window surrender their camouflaged positions. In a frenzy of screeches and flaps of bright-green wings, they launch the alarm for the impending storm. There's a downpour to look forward to, a rarity that will mark this November day a treasured one, a blessing. That's what will happen outside. Inside, it will remain as still as a grave.

With the mourning period over, the visitors have stopped coming. It's Khaled who died. I finally extracted the information from the maid. He died in Bangkok, I assume from a drug overdose. I'll never know for sure, because no doubt the family has concocted some other story of a natural, less shameful death.

Ammiti Aisha must be shattered. Khaled had a special place in her heart. He was the only one in the family who was open with his affection toward her. Her face always lit up whenever he held her hand or hugged her. Ammi Majed never commented, but it was clear that he abhorred such displays.

Why am I thinking of them? Nobody bothered to let me out for the three days of mourning. But then, why would they? How much longer will they keep me in here? Without the doctor and his pills I am alert, painfully so, and the need to go out is pressing. I've been in this room for ten days. It's enough, I decide.

I march to the door with a raised fist. But, not for the first time, I stop short and consider what would happen if I started pounding. Once more my courage fails me when I mull over the repercussions of my actions, the enormity of what I'll have to face out there. My thoughts turn to Dalal, whose injuries I pray are light. What would she do? I can't decide whether to thank her for saving me from a bleak future or blame her for having triggered one.

Outside, the wind blows, pushing layer over layer of clouds, turning the sky to pewter. Inside, the only sound is the clock ticking, steady, persistent. I back away and pad toward the closet, deciding to sift through my father's briefcase. I need some serenity of mind.

Opening the closet door, I frown at the empty base, where the four locked suitcases filled with bridal gifts once were. They were taken away during one of my deep sleeps. When they arrived, a week before the wedding, my cousins had been so excited. Impatient to discover what was inside, they settled around me in this very spot and insisted I open the suitcases straightaway.

In addition to gold jewelry in a traditional Emirati design, there were a couple of diamond watches, one in white gold and the other in yellow; perfumes, both European and the heavier lingering Arabian scents; and some thirty pieces of exquisite silk and brocade. Two of the suitcases were filled with handbags and shoes, along with four packets of oudh and six bottles, each weighing a *tola*, of the same in its essential oil. Quick to retrieve what I didn't want in the first place, the widow and her son had demanded the return of their extravagant gifts.

Bitterness mixes with helplessness. I pull up a chair and climb onto it. I reach for the briefcase and jump onto the bed, where I unlock it. Snapping it open, I hold it upside down and shake it. As the contents tumble out, I notice something dislodge under a bunching of the frayed felt in the zippered sleeve. Puzzled, I peer into the pocket. Is it possible that I've missed some piece of my father's life? Two photographs had slipped into a tear in the fabric, one stuck on top of the other from the heat and humidity of many years.

I hold the top photo, its colors a faded pink hue, steady in front of my face. This is the first picture I've ever seen of my mother. I know it's her because she is pregnant. She is standing in front of the Gateway of India with my father, surrounded by a scattering of Bombay's pigeons. On their right is a man touting his wares, peanuts heaped on a wooden tray strapped around his neck. In the background is another vendor, dwarfed under an umbrella of balloons.

But it's my mother whom I scrutinize. I look for some clue of her hopes and aspirations, but it's impossible to make out her features behind her burka. She is taller than I imagined, stronger looking, too. It must have been a rare occasion out, and I imagine her in her precarious condition begging my father to take her for a breath of sea air, a request he succumbed to against the doctor's warnings.

I look up when a deafening rumble of thunder shakes the windowpane. And then the rain comes, just as I expected. It falls hard, filled with the whistle and hiss, the crack and roar of life. And all I can think of is my mother, and whether I was worth her giving up her life. My father had called me a miracle child, but how would either of them regard me in this defeated state? It's distressing, and I quickly turn to the bottom photo.

For a second I'm not sure who the little girl staring back at me is. There's nothing prim or proper about her: she leans forward with her arms spread wide over a table. She exudes assertiveness, her lips lifted to one side in a half smile and those translucent eyes staring directly at the camera. Her head is lowered as if she's about to butt someone.

It's a bizarre coincidence when from the other side of the locked door my grandmother approaches, reinforcing the guidelines I grew up ignoring: "Calmness and modesty make up the heart of all that is good in a woman. It must now become your mission and duty to make sure you adopt these noble and pleasing qualities."

She's berating the girl in the picture, this me of so long ago, who is charged with pluck and daring. Ice cracks in my head, and my response is a cutting rejoinder: "Silence and acceptance, you mean!"

"Hold your tongue!"

"I've held it long enough."

"No shame in your bony frame, no shame," she mumbles, her voice brimming with shock and disapproval. "He's right, after all—you have gone completely mad!"

"Yes, mad," I shout back. As she trudges away I watch the rain, a steady stream that sounds like thousands of tiny clapping hands. For a long time I stay that way, emotions surging through me. What have I become? What pathetic creature have I allowed myself to turn into? These questions bring me back to the photos, which I realize have been sandwiched between my palms for quite some time. When I loosen my grip, I am careful, as if the photos were delicate flowers that might lose their petals. My sweaty hand has left a smudge on the little girl's face. I wipe it off gently. And then I am up, changing into a pair of jeans and a thick sweatshirt.

I have to get away. I have to get as far from here as I can. That's the extent of the plan I muddle through as I fill a small duffel bag with essentials. Through the window, the tamarind tree quivers and shakes. It lacks the strong branches needed to support my weight. No matter! I drop the bag to the ground and slip one foot out, then the other, until I'm sitting squarely on the windowsill. I squint at the darkness, calculating the distance, judging the best way down.

I don't hear the door unlocking, but I do hear a gasp, emitted right as I plunge. I'd aimed at what looked like the most favorable part of the tree, a thickening of branches just above the solid trunk. Now stuck to that tree and holding tight, I blink the rain out of my eyes, stunned at having made it. I have a few scratches, and some sharp bits of bark poke me in the calves, but nothing is broken.

I'm about to negotiate my way down when I see Ammiti Aisha at my window, chewing the edge of her shayla as she looks down at me with terror. "Come back! This isn't the way to do it." She leans out the window and extends a hand. I shake my head. "Wait!" she cries out as I start sliding down the tree. My grip loosens, fingers like springs coming undone.

It's a bumpy descent; the bark is rough and pitted, and it scrapes off layers of skin even through my thick clothes. When I think it's safe, I jump to the ground. It's a miscalculation. I land flat on my feet but tumble forward with the force of the fall, knocking my head on the ground. Along with the rain, blood streams down my face. I could have taken a moment to nurse the gash, but the urgency of getting away runs deeper than mere blood.

The duffel is under a hedge; I have to crawl to reach it. When it is tucked safely under my arm, I shift back and rise on shock-struck legs, my knees wobbling so hard I have trouble taking the first few steps. That's when Ammiti Aisha grabs me by the arms. I fight back. She holds tight as I slap and kick blindly. "Leave me alone!"

I pull away but she still won't let go, her fingers like iron tongs boring right through to the bone. She insists that I listen to her, because she's arranged everything. "You won't be able to get away from him without my help! You have nowhere to go, to hide." Having just lost her dearest son, she ought to have been filled with a quiet grief. Instead, she's brimming with a wildness that won't allow her eyes to stay still. "He'll find you and send you away. Do you know where?" She doesn't wait for me to guess. "He's arranged to send you to Bombay."

We stare at each other, the rain still falling in sheets. I'm stunned, caught between believing her and not believing her. I think of my mother and father in that photograph, standing in front of the Gateway of India. "Why would he do that?"

"He's decided you need help, professional help. So he's sending you to a clinic there." I cock my head and blink, still unable to grasp what Ammiti Aisha is telling me. She must think I'm an utter idiot. "A mental institution," she adds in the gentlest of tones, loosening her grip to pat the cut on my head with her sodden shayla. "So please, come with me."

47

DALAL

ꕥ

It's midnight, and I slide into the car waiting outside my apartment in upscale and trendy Zamalek. We head to the venue at Cairo's Semiramis Hotel for the last of 1998's big summer concerts. Each was planned and scheduled to coincide with the Khaleeji traveling circuit. I debuted in London at the Royal Lancaster Hotel, then performed at the InterContinental in Geneva, then at the Concorde La Fayette in Paris—a full house every time.

It's quiet in the car. Normally I would relish a moment of peace when I could empty my mind before stepping out into the lights, but not this time. I'm wound up as tight as the coiffed strands of hair that curve and twist like a hundred snakes on my head.

Mama Al-Ouda died yesterday in her sleep. But that's not the reason I'm tense. It was the first thing Mariam told me when I called her earlier in the afternoon in a panic, insisting that she come over to my apartment before the group arrived to get me ready. But she was packing, getting ready to travel to Dubai in the evening for the mourning period. It will be the first time she's been back since her daring escape nearly three years ago.

I fell silent when she gave me the news and waited for something to happen—a lump in the throat, an ebbing spirit, some small piece of sympathy—just as I had felt two months earlier when I got that other news, about my father. I waited, a granddaughter who never knew her grandmother, and when nothing happened I tried to stir up some sad thoughts, hoping to draw tears. They came with a might that rattled me, but it wasn't because of Mama Al-Ouda's death.

"Did he hurt you?" That's what Mariam asked as soon as I bridled my hysteria long enough to tell her about last night's row.

How to tell her that he did? "No, no, that's not what happened," I said, with too much ardor. How to explain that he doesn't think I'm good enough (worse, he called me trash!) without giving away the real nature of our relationship, the intimacy, the way I've let him possess me? I've sketched only a vague picture for Mariam: a scribble of a respectable suitor with honorable intentions. He can be crude and hurtful, but I can't tell her any of that, because I know what she'll say: "Leave him, Dalal. You deserve better." And that's the one thing I can't bear to do.

"I'm not yet twenty-one. Why is this happening to me?" I said.

She asked, "So, what did he do?" And all I could manage was a hacking sigh that sounded as if it were my very last breath (or close to it) while I searched for the best way to describe my distress. I could tell that Mariam was losing patience as she waited for me to say something. I could hear her opening a closet and pulling out a suitcase.

I never thought it would be possible for me to be smitten to the point that my mind is always occupied with a man. He's hard to ignore, impossible to resist, an addiction, and I've racked my brains trying to figure out why.

I was introduced to him last summer at a restaurant in Geneva and immediately registered his age and status: thirty-three years old and single, a successful Saudi businessman. In the middle of that big group, drunk on lighthearted humor and champagne, he had a way of seeing me without actually looking at me. He'd rub his chin, the sharp line of his close-trimmed beard, and seem to be focused on something in another world. But then he'd slide into the conversation, aiming his interest at me only, as if I were the only person burning my tongue on fondue in that restaurant.

The next few weeks were exhausting: I built up my worth by resisting him, a delicate game that involved keeping him interested at the same time. In addition to a few of my own tricks, I used all the ones I'd watched Mother perform with those lowly people in Imbaba (even though they'd brought her more trouble than good).

It was pointless—all of it. I might as well have been made of glass, because he saw right through me. Finally I stopped trying and just gave myself to him.

Not for the first time, Mariam said, "Well, at least tell me his real name," and I had to tighten my lips against the temptation to reveal his real identity because of everything else that might just spill out: the nights—so numerous—spent with him at his penthouse in Garden City, the vacations on his yacht in Hurghada, and the trips to Europe.

In Cairo we never venture out together. In Europe he relaxes his guard somewhat. I know what is expected of me, and, wearing dark glasses that cover most of my face, I always make sure I'm a few steps behind him whenever we are out in public, just in case he bumps into someone he knows. We might be walking down the Champs-Élysées when suddenly that someone appears. And I'll quickly stop at a café or pause in front of a shopwindow or make an abrupt swerve to the back of the line at a cinema's ticket booth—whichever is nearest. Sometimes, once whoever it is moves away, he'll come back to find me surrounded by a cluster of passing admirers. With a forced smile, he'll watch the inevitable photos-with-the-star being snapped. I know he gets a thrill out of being in a secret relationship with the Arab world's number-one singer. But there is jealousy, too, a mean-spirited silence and resentment that can go on for days.

Mariam will never understand that that's how it is with someone like him—so educated and worldly. He often says to me, "Dalal, habibti, do you realize how many enemies I have who would like nothing better than to take all that is beautiful in our relationship and rip it apart?" (Why do the men closest to me—first my father and now this man—insist on keeping me a secret?) I always nod, convinced that I must stay quiet just a little bit longer—until we get married. Then, last night, I finally asked him when that might be. He looked at me as if I'd committed a crime, and then belittled me with all those insults.

We cross 26 July Bridge and veer right, decelerating into a thickening sea of taillights on Corniche Al-Nil Street. My manager, Gino Ghazal, sits next to me in the backseat of the BMW, which heads our convoy of three cars. He dials the concert organizer, and as he informs him of our delay, I pull out a compact mirror to dredge up some enthusiasm over how glamorous I look. I've been prepared by the best; both the top hairstylist and the finest makeup artist were flown in from Beirut. I turn my head this way and that, catching bits of my face: the sleepy eye that has woken up for good, the smooth bridge of my nose—both improvements that my man pushed me to get—and my skin, a velvety sheen under layers of expertly blended makeup.

Outside, an old man, outfitted in traditional baggy trousers with a broad satin waistband, sways from side to side, singing praise for the cold licorice juice sloshing in a large copper container strapped to his chest. The night is alive. Cars honk; boat owners call out offers for late-night trips on the Nile to the stream of strolling couples and families who are either in the middle of lively conversation or busy chewing on libb. There's laughter all around. Music blares from a small radio somewhere. The noise of the street seeps through the windows of the BMW . . . and so does the smell, as we inch past a vendor fanning corn in one of the many mobile kitchens. I scowl at the *tirmis* seller farther down, who keeps spraying his lupin beans to keep them moist. "It's past midnight," I grumble. "Why can't all these people stay home and watch television?"

"End of the week," says the driver. "No one stays home on a Thursday."

I lash out at him. "It's good and proper for a star to arrive late: it shows she's in demand. But I want that delay to be of my making. I'm the one who has to be in control. You hear me?"

The driver and the bodyguard sitting next to him reply together, "Yes, Sitt Dalal."

"Fools!" I mutter, and hold the compact mirror at arm's length to inspect my canary-yellow dress. It's an extravagant one-shoulder Zuhair Murad creation. The fitted top is studded with rhinestones and hugs me in all the right places. The bottom part is a gush of chiffon, fresh, alive with strips of yellow and lime green. Gino Ghazal squints at me with tiny green eyes that look like dried-up peas. My dazzle blinds him. For the third time this evening he says, "Spectacular!"

I indicate my agreement with a grunt and, wisely, he says no more—unlike Madame Nivine, who never knew when to shut her mouth. It's been a year since I replaced her—just as she'd predicted—with the Lebanese manager. The greedy, turbaned glutton uttered her final *habibchi* when I found out she'd been skimming money, cheating me out of my profits.

How is it possible that I actually looked up to her? I considered Madame Nivine a mentor, a protector, and even a replacement mother at one point. That other one is still trying her best to win me back. After my career took off, Mother waited to make sure that my fame was not a passing thing. Once she felt assured that her daughter was a star who would not fizzle out, she went ahead and divorced Sherif bey. (Why keep him?) I support her financially because that's what is expected of a good daughter, but there it ends. I have a new family now.

A new family: it's an attractive thought. I scrutinize my manager, who has one long leg crossed over the other and is dabbing his clean-shaven face. He wears a gray suit and a pale-pink shirt without a tie. His thinning hair is gelled back in distinct rows of chestnut-colored strips that gather at the back of his business-minded head—no space in it for anything other than success and profit. Gino Ghazal is not someone I can embrace as family, I decide, and neither are all those other people—never less than seven or eight, all of them mirrors of Azza and Hannah—who surround me for no other reason than their own selfish desires. I take a fatigued breath and blow it out through lips colored a screaming fuchsia.

Gino Ghazal cocks his head to indicate his concern. Even though he has seen me distressed before, it's never been before a concert. Like all the others, my entourage and attendants, he knows something is seriously wrong. From the moment they filed into my apartment a few hours ago to get me ready, I've been in a sour mood. I accused the hairdresser of grazing my scalp with his pins and complained about the selection of colors the makeup artist had chosen, insisting they did nothing to brighten my features—anything to vent steam. They were apologetic, obviously used to the whims of a star. They were so accommodating it made me feel frivolous. So I turned my attention to Azza and Hannah. That good-for-nothing duo received the brunt of my cranky mood, and that still didn't satisfy me.

Mariam had kept pushing to find out his real identity. She said, "How did you come up with it, anyway—Ustad, this name you've contrived?"

To me, that's what he has been—an *ustad*, a professor, who has taught me so much: to dress well and eat well, to pose and speak like a lady. He cares that I look my best, and even arranged the appointments for the surgical improvement of my nose and sleepy eye. He's done so much for me. When a nasty reporter wrote in a review that my voice sounded strained and went so far as to call me "tone-deaf" (the ultimate insult!), Ustad arranged for the most famous music teacher in

Egypt, an old, retired Greek-Egyptian woman with blue-gray hair and a mustache, to give me voice lessons.

Mariam persisted. "Well?"

I almost told her that it came from my ignorance. There is heat in Ustad's eyes and strength in his face—and a nose that, early in our relationship, he described as Roman. He was amused when I told him that I'd never met any Romans, and he vowed right then to educate me, beginning with a series of lectures on that ancient empire that went on for way too long. The lessons on Rome were thorough; he even cited dates. The information floated into my head and stayed there for seconds before turning to vapor. But he couldn't tell. He didn't know me well enough to understand that I've mastered the art of looking interested when I'm not. At the end of it all I decided to call him *Ustad*, a code name he approved of. Yes, I was ready to tell her this little story. But Mariam scoffed at the name, and that made me feel protective of him. I snapped, "It suits him, and he likes it."

"So," Mariam said, after a short pause. "Will you cancel the concert?"

"Of course not," I said. "Think how unprofessional it would be to let a fight with him affect my work. People have flown in to see me from all over the world. They've bought tickets!"

"No, I mean in light of our grandmother's passing away."

"Hmm." I'd forgotten about that. "*Allah yarhamha*, may God bestow his mercy upon her."

"Right."

For Mariam's sake, I closed my eyes tightly and tried to shape some thought of Mama Al-Ouda that might help me mourn her. The only image that popped into my head glowed in colors so bright I felt the onset of a headache: Mama Al-Ouda on the bridal stage, telling me to get off and sing. The old woman couldn't tell I was her granddaughter. "Anyway," I said, "you know as well as I do that no one wants us there."

She grew silent and I told her not to be like that, to understand that I had made a commitment to perform, signed a contract. She smiled then, or I like to think she did, because Mariam always could see the good in me.

I'm smiling. Gino Ghazal notices and tells me that it suits me. The driver and the bodyguard turn around briefly to nod their approval. I touch my mouth, a little shy, somewhat bewildered to find that I am indeed smiling. As the car halts at the back entrance of the hotel, I realize that something else has snuck up on me: a quickening of the pulse, vitality—yes, the familiar enthusiasm that always precedes a performance.

The doors of all three cars open at once and we shuffle through the back entrance, where the concert organizer, a short, round man with no neck, greets us as if we are long-lost family members. He looks set to cry, so great is his relief at our arrival.

He leads the way, raining compliments on me while half walking, half hopping to the service elevator. The elevator bell dings, and we step out on the top floor. As we walk down the corridor toward the suite, the concert organizer tells me that I have barely ten minutes for last-minute touch-ups, that he'd like to keep the evening going smoothly, with everything running on time. "When has that ever happened in Cairo?" I joke, and the whole group laughs heartily.

A C star would have commenced the evening's entertainment at 10:30 p.m., and a B star would have followed an hour later. Then a break, during which dinner would have been served for the two thousand guests before my dazzling performance, the A star, at 1:30 a.m. I'll sing for a couple of hours, plus another half hour for the encore.

Once we reach the suite, Gino Ghazal asks him, "Do you have the balance payment for Sitt Dalal?"

"Of course, of course," says the concert organizer, nodding too eagerly. "Right after the show."

"No, now," Gino Ghazal says, and this starts an argument, which I act as though I don't hear. Sitting at the vanity table, I steal glances at their reflections while the hairdresser puts a spring into some of the ringlets on my head and the makeup artist sharpens her black pencil, having been given permission to see whether a beauty mark might add to my glamour. She makes a mark in the center of my right cheek.

"I told you to make sure that money was with you when we came: the full balance, cash, in crisp dollars. Didn't you hear me?" says Gino Ghazal.

"I thought you were joking."

"I said it a thousand times. Would I make the same joke that many times?"

The concert organizer is flustered. He looks at his watch. "Listen, we're late already. I have a ballroom filled with distinguished people who have bought tickets, mostly Khaleejis who have traveled all the way here to see her." He stomps his foot. "They want her now! What am I supposed to tell them?" When my manager remains unimpressed by the performance, the concert organizer closes his eyes and cracks his neck—once, twice—and utters his next words calmly. "Look, I understand what you're saying. But for now let's get her on the stage, and, wallahi, I promise you I'll have your money before she finishes her first song."

"No."

"No?"

"What guarantee do I have? You could keep stalling and then disappear after she finishes singing."

"You insult me!"

"That's not my intention. But I have to put my client's interests first."

"We have a contract!"

"Yes, we do. But I still say she won't go on until she is paid fully."

"Please." The word hangs in the air, and when Gino Ghazal hardens his demeanor the concert organizer scurries toward me and begs. "Sitt Dalal, please talk sense into him. The audience is impatient for you: Dalal, the Gazelle of the Desert!"

He stands behind me, the suffering of a hungry beggar in his eyes, while I take my time trying to decide about the beauty spot, which has already been tested and failed in two different locations on my face. In this third trial it sits just below my lips, on the left side. Should I keep it or not?

"A thirty-member band is waiting for you onstage. They're playing Umm Kulthum to pass the time. How long can they keep doing that? The audience is already fed up."

Having decided that the beauty spot stays, I turn around and shrug. "What can I do? I know nothing about such matters." I smile at him sweetly. "I'm the artist here."

He opens his mouth, but before he is able to utter a word Gino Ghazal squeezes his arm and leads him away, scolding him for causing undue stress to the star. The concert organizer starts yelling and threatens to call his lawyer and the police, too, to make sure we get thrown in jail for breaking the contract. Coolly, my manager tells him, "We haven't gone anywhere. We're here, waiting."

The situation seems to be getting out of control. I'm gripped by fear when I realize I might not step on that stage after all. Azza mouths the time: ten minutes late. I turn around. I'm about to tell my manager to back down when I see him reaching into his jacket and pulling out what he calls his "cigar of success." He will light it once I get onstage and will follow a ritual of finishing it only with the concert's end, nearly three hours later. He sniffs it, rolling it under his nose. He's ready to celebrate another success. And there's the concert organizer, snapping his fingers and whispering something to an assistant who has suddenly materialized and who then flies out the door.

Ten minutes later the assistant is back, breathless and clutching a fat envelope, which the concert manager snatches and hands over to Gino Ghazal.

There is light chatter while my manager counts the money; every person in the room feigns uninterest. How to sit still? Everything dims as the excitement rushes through me like a crazy river. I can see them, all those adoring eyes focused on me. Under the lights, I'll be a golden glow. I won't just stay on the stage, like so many other performers. Once or twice I will step down and weave my way between the men and women, all those distinguished Khaleejis, seated around the tables. I shall sing from my heart because that's the only way I can, and at the end the stage will turn into a garden of single red roses flung at my feet by the adoring audience.

I'll start with my first hit song: "Only Me, Lonely Me." The musicians will play an extended introduction to key up the audience before I come into view, mike in one hand, the other posed in a floating salute. It will not sound the same. There's a twist in the melody, with layer upon layer of newly added harmony. It's enriched, not so simple anymore, just like the girl who first sang it three years ago. She's not the same, either.

It's 1:55 a.m., and Gino Ghazal's cigar is wedged at the edge of his mouth. He pulls it out and calls, "Everybody."

We're looking up already.

"Five minutes."

48

MAJED

❧

She takes me straight from my doctor's appointment to the palm grove in Al-Khawaneej. I'm in a foul mood. Strapped in the front passenger seat of my Mercedes, I glare fiercely at the blur of dunes running along the road. Once we get there, I watch out the side mirror as Ophelia jumps out from the back seat of the car. She delivers the wheelchair, and I have a ridiculous notion that I'll be able to get into it on my own. I heave and twist around, succeeding in getting my legs to dangle out of the car. But as I try to shift onto my feet I run into trouble; the car's seat is too low.

Aisha surveys my reddening face with the most awful expression of indulgence and worn-out pity, as if to say, "Let the old man have his moment." It makes my blood boil and I shove Ophelia, who is standing in her assisting mode—arms stretched out, hands swimming like a pair of fidgeting fish at the sides of my ribcage—at the ready to scoop me up.

I swear at her: "Daughter of a whore!" From my warped mouth it sounds like a crow's caw. She beams at me, humoring me as if I were a baby practicing his first word. I pause, the pressure building in my head as I use every shred of concentration to shape the next insult: "*Ya bgara!* You cow!" It comes out as a stutter, sounding like "ha ha ha"—slurred, too. Ophelia claps her hands good-humoredly before latching them under my armpits.

Nothing comes out the way it should. Thoughts clamber over one another in my head, like those tiny red ants that scurry around, looking to build something out of chaos. Only I never succeed. My mind is in perpetual tumult. Sometimes I have trouble remembering things: names, places, people. Other times the memories are as clear as the winter sky over my head. My brain busies itself by sending signals, futile commands I have trouble following. It looms like an overblown balloon, a dubious far-reaching world pressing against my skull. That's how it is, how it has become, now that this stroke has rendered my whole being senseless.

I am up. Ophelia hands me the cane. I had rejected the medical crutch—an embarrassment!—raising such a fuss that they had no choice but to get me a wooden cane with a rubber cap at the bottom, which I'm tempted to use on her immediately. But I wait until I've taken the two steps to the wheelchair and settled into it safely. As she positions my feet onto the footplates I jab her back with rough pokes, pushing her away. When she secures the worry beads, weaving them between my fingers so the string doesn't slip out of my contorted right hand, I strike at her ankles.

"Leave her alone," Aisha says. "Let her do her job." But I am trembling, working up a fit that has me lashing out as best I can. Horrible noises are coming out of me. My limbs jerk in every direction and I'm deaf to Aisha's pleas to "look at your palm trees, how lush they are!" as the women wheel me over to the end of the patio. It has yet to be completed; they park me in front of a sharp dip of dug-up earth, near a stack of bricks, and walk right past me, roaming off toward the palm trees to give me a chance to calm down. Time to punish the wild old man!

I object aloud, "How can you leave me like this in my state?" Of course no one understands a thing, but Aisha assures me that she'll be right back. She mocks me! How dare she treat me this way? Even though her constant presence irritates me more often than not, I'm outraged that she would walk away like that—my own wife!

It was a bad stroke that affected the left side of my brain. The doctor kept saying I was lucky it didn't finish me off. After the surgery to remove the hematoma, I remained in the hospital for more than a month before being sent home. But the recovery, the grueling physical-therapy sessions to retrieve my lost strength and mobility, was so quick that I was sure I'd soon be as I once was. The doctor was impressed with my progress, and this drove me to continue—until my visit to his office this morning.

I can't see Aisha, who, although close by, is concealed behind the layers of palm fronds. She says something to Ophelia in a voice too soft to hear. I hate her. I hate them both. I hate myself. I contemplate what would happen if I just got up and plunged over the edge and into that dirt hole. I'd probably break my neck. And that would be that. But at least I'd succeed in making them feel sorry for having neglected me—my whole family, the despicable lot of them.

My eyes moisten and I close them against the humiliating threat of spilling. God knows, it's hard to control! There doesn't have to be any particular reason or emotion to set it off. It just happens, leakage from a warped garden pipe. And then I'll start bawling for what feels like an eternity, unable to control that braying noise and the sticky dribbling of spit. Eventually I'll sink into a heavy dispirited sulk.

I try to make as little noise as possible as I weep. They don't know anything. They don't know what the doctor said to me, the cruel truth that this, this me, is as good as I'll get. Eight months on and this is the full recovery: the nerves damaged beyond repair, my face melted on one side, my life flushed to nothing.

I look for a diversion, something that might steady my whimpering, my sniveling, which will only get worse. There's the string of worry beads Hareb gave me all those years back, which I've taken to carrying with me all the time, wrapped around my benumbed fingers. I snatch it out of the useless hand and start twirling it to recover some sense of control, of dignity. I focus on one bead at a time, rubbing it between thumb and index finger before flicking it down along the string.

It works. It plugs up the torment, and I make my calculations. How many steps to the edge? I'll just have to get up and walk—if one can call it that—to find out. The longer I stare at the drop, the fiercer grows my determination to take action, to make a statement. I can't punch or kick or rage effectively, but I can alarm them. I want to give them all a piece of my mind: the so-called friends—Saeed, Mattar, and even Mustafa—who don't visit anymore because they got sick of my tantrums; my sons and daughters who all this time were looking forward to the day when I'd be suffering like this, just so they could get their hands on my money; and Mariam and Dalal and Aisha, too. I want them all to know that the force that kept them in order is still . . . still . . . I don't waste any more time probing for the word, the exact meaning, because I've slid to the edge of the wheelchair.

Planting my right foot to the ground, I push up on my left foot using the stick. I stand unassisted for the first time since the stroke. I don't move. I wait for a signal to go ahead, quivering slightly with apprehension in case it does not come. But then it does: I'm able to shift on my good leg and sling the other forward in a wide arc. I can barely contain my groan. Two more steps; I know I look awkward, my body shifted to the side, my right arm twisted into my chest, the fingers crowding my tucked thumb. I don't care, because here comes the plunge.

It's a pathetic tumble. Instead of crashing into the earth headfirst, I stagger to my knees and then proceed to half slide, half swim down on my belly: no more trauma than a mouthful of mud. I would jump back up and climb into my wheelchair quietly if only I could. Instead I stay motionless, waiting to be rescued.

What happens next I have to imagine, because I keep my eyes closed. There's the wheelchair being shifted down to my side. There's the grip under my armpits. There are my feet dredging clumsy lines in the earth without the sandals, which have slipped off. I tighten my eyelids against Aisha's rebukes, high-pitched with distress, against her swatting palms as she brushes the clinging soil off my face and kandora. I don't dare open my eyes. I am too ashamed.

49

MARIAM

❧

"Ah, you should have seen him, all shaky, all muddy."

She fusses over him to chase away the anxiety of being somewhere she shouldn't be. "There's no one here in the middle of the week," she says, and pats his head as if she suspects a fever. She covers his shoulders with a shawl, then joins me on the wicker chairs. They are newly unpacked, their tags still on, as is the matching low table in front of us. "You should have seen him," she says again, still quite baffled at the way he fell off the wheelchair just before I arrived. "I don't know what he was trying to do, but he must have tripped."

It's January, and a mild sun shines. The trees swish and break its rays, casting splotchy patterns on my uncle's face. I catch him in profile, his jowls saggy under a head that hangs heavy in sleep over his chest. His arm is twisted and pressed to his ribs, the fingers frozen into claws. A string of amber worry beads winds tightly around his hand; he clutches them as if they were valuable gemstones.

The maid arrives with a tray, and Ammiti Aisha lifts the flask, pours the tea into a couple of tulip glasses, and adds a teaspoonful of sugar to each. "I bring him here because it usually relaxes him, but not today," she says, frowning. Her fingers quiver slightly when she hands me my tea. "They won't like it if they find out I'm here. So I don't tell anyone, and I don't stay too long."

We are in the shade of a palm-frond awning held up on wooden beams. A cool breeze blows and we lean back and inhale deeply at the same time. We sip the tea quietly. She doesn't need to explain anything. I already know that whatever worth she had in her household disappeared the moment she smuggled me out of the house.

I often wonder whether she considered what she was giving up, and every time I come to the conclusion that Khaled's death must have snapped something in her. Her children were sickened by her action. They considered it a betrayal. More than three years later, she still has not been forgiven.

I remember that stormy night as if it were yesterday. How strange that she launched her plan just as I'd jumped out of the room! She'd acted quickly after discovering my daredevil escape, dragging me under the pelting rain toward a waiting car.

The doorman caught sight of us through the window of his little room by the gate. The flickering blue light of his television set highlighted the alarm and confusion on his face. He scampered out of his hut, getting drenched within seconds, and waved his arms in panic, trying to block our escape. Ammiti Aisha shoved him aside and pushed me into the backseat of her sister's car. Slamming the door shut, she waved us off—her figure a watery blur as I looked back through the car's window—and stayed behind to face the consequences. Ten days later she walked out and joined me at Shamma's house, and soon after, she asked for a divorce, which she never got.

My uncle is a little distance away, still turned toward the spread of palm trees but wheeled a safe distance from the edge of the broad patio. The patio has been newly built just in front of the small rest house at his farm in Al-Khawaneej. Saif and Ahmad had decided to make it a play area for their children. They run the company now, and from what I understand, this has caused a catastrophic rift between them and the rest of the siblings. The girls accuse the two older brothers of being greedy tyrants.

Ammiti Aisha reads my thoughts, it seems. "They argue all the time," she says. "The girls want to see the money, and Saif and Ahmad won't allow it. 'It's not ours,' they tell their sisters, even though they spend it as if it were." She fixes her sight on the six bicycles. New and gleaming, they stand in a neat row, arranged according to size, at one side of the house. "Saif says that it's a responsibility entrusted to them. Ahmad always makes sure to add the word *temporarily*, meaning until their father is capable again." She scoffs. "Of course, the girls don't believe that. And who can blame them? I mean, all these months and he's worked so hard just so that he can . . ." She shakes her head and waves her hand at him. "Just look at him."

My uncle is still asleep. A trickle of drool slides down one side of his lips. The maid, who sits on her heels in front of him, massaging his right foot and looking as bored as can be, reaches out for a tissue and dabs at it.

"I asked them to employ a nurse, but they said he doesn't need one, that the maid is strong enough to deal with him and clever enough to administer his medication. Isn't that right, Ophelia? Clever, nah?"

Ophelia snickers and beams a sunny grin at us before moving on to rub his left foot. I hadn't recognized her with the weight gain; she now has a wrestler's body. "The girls are preparing a case against their brothers," Ammiti Aisha continues. "Mona and Amal are the engines, insisting it's the only way. Nouf, of course, is always spoiling for a fight, without a thought spared for the damage that will certainly follow. As for Badr, well, he was hesitant, but in the end they bullied him into joining."

"And Nadia?"

"Ah, that one. As you know, she's slightly softer, doesn't like making too many waves." Ammiti Aisha lets out a heavy sigh. "But she's left in want of money since that husband of hers finally made good on his threats to divorce her. He left her and their five children after he decided that it was a scandal to be married to one of the Naseemys. He said it tainted his name in the eyes of society and opened him to ridicule, because everyone knows that no respectable family can stay that way with a singer in it. What excuses he came up with! We all knew he'd taken another wife long before Dalal appeared on the scene." Her shayla doesn't need adjusting, but she fiddles with it anyway. She pulls it down to just above her eyebrows and then slides it back up to her hairline. "The fights, the bickering, the ugliness all around me. And you know what, I don't even bother trying to repair the situation. I watched the way they fought over Mama Al-Ouda's gold when she died and thought, *What's the point?* Which of them pays attention to what I have to say, anyway?"

Sunlight falls in strips across her face. I listen and keep very still. It's the first time Ammiti Aisha has opened up to me like this. But then again, there hasn't been an opportunity before. I've stayed away these past three years, carving a life that I can call my own. Every so often I call her, but they're typical phone conversations, filled with nothing more than pleasantries.

After Mama Al-Ouda died last August, I'd packed and was heading to the airport to be with my family for the mourning period when Ammiti Aisha telephoned me. She told me not to come, to stay in Cairo and mourn privately, because she knew her children would not have allowed me into the house.

She is shaking her head. She continues where she left off. "The married ones hardly come to visit now that their father is in this condition and their fortunes don't depend on him anymore, and the twins, still living at home, hardly have a word to say to me. My grandchildren are no better." She leans forward and starts rocking. "All the plots, all the nastiness," she mutters, her face frozen in a heavyhearted expression of pain. "No sooner did the doctors get your uncle stable and send him home than they appeared like vultures, ready to peck and rip. Then, during one of his emotional bouts, Saif and Ahmad were there to take full charge of the business and make sure the transfer of power was legal."

They are their father's seeds. It's a morbid thought, and I look away. The sky is a vivid blue with scratches of cloud. Glossy-feathered mynahs call to one another and white-cheeked bulbuls chirp and chatter. Wishing for some of their lighthearted cheer, I follow them with my eyes as they flit about from tree to tree. I watch them and count my blessings.

After the escape, Shamma used all her resources to retrieve my government scholarship, and within a month I was on a plane back to Cairo. I have started afresh with my studies, this time following my passion in botany. I share an apartment in the Emirati girls' sakan with none other than Buthaina (now studying for her doctorate), who has proven to be the guiding sister I'd longed for. And there's Dalal, elevated into a world so different from mine—one day up, one day down—rushing about, always busy, so that it's hard to catch up with her news. On the outside she looks different, more refined and self-assured. On the inside I don't know, because she only tells me what she imagines I want to hear. I don't scold anymore. I don't push. I stand back and wait—for a time when she might really need me.

And love—I think I might be finding that, too, in a fellow Emirati student who has shown an interest in me. It's not there in the sense of that overwhelming longing I used to feel for Adel, which made me forget everything just as long as I was near him. (I heard he dropped out of college and went back home soon after my return.) No, this is taking its time: a sprouting of little moments, a dawdling smile, a slow gathering of feelings that leaves behind a sense of serenity and security.

"They did to their father what their father did to yours." There's a tremor at the back of Ammiti Aisha's throat. "You were cheated, Mariam. We all knew it, and we kept quiet about it." Her lips quiver; she looks ready to cry. I shake my head to indicate that she mustn't.

"It's fine," I say, giving her hand a gentle squeeze. "I'm fine."

I think about that and realize that it's true—I am fine. I find myself rising and walking toward Ammi Majed. With every step I anticipate that familiar wringing resentment, the cramping fretfulness, that I used to stifle whenever he was close. It doesn't come, and I wonder if that's because of what he has become—old, powerless, friendless, and dependent, a picture of wretchedness and defeat.

Standing to the side of the wheelchair, my hand moves as if following a will of its own. It floats up and hovers just above his shoulder. Ophelia keeps ahold of his foot, but her fingers have stopped moving. I stand there for a moment with a mind gone blank, and then I ask, "Why did you go back to him?"

Ammiti Aisha is unfaltering in her response. "Because it's my duty."

My hand drops to my side and I nod. My gaze drifts over the grove, its lush palm fronds rustling with a hasty breeze, and settles on the late-afternoon sun, a grand ball, bright as a tangerine, poised and ready to descend into the distant dunes. My breathing is even. There is peace.

ACKNOWLEDGMENTS

First and foremost, I am deeply indebted to my family for their boundless love and support: my father and mother, my three brothers, Samir, Anwar, and Shehab, and their wives, Souad, Cyma, and Lamees, who are the sisters I never had.

Special thanks to my good friend Ali Khalifa Al-Rumaithi, for his nuggets of insight of all things Emirati, for his limitless imagination when it comes to plot twists and narrative possibilities.

Tons of gratitude goes to Mimi Raad and Lina Matta for their energy as they pored over the various chapters of the book as they were being written, for their enthusiasm at each of our regular meetings to discuss what they'd read. Every writer needs such a dynamic pair.

A salute goes to my vivacious editor, Jillian Verrillo, for her acute observations and grasp of the big picture, both of which have made this a stronger novel. And not forgetting my copyeditor, Julie Hersh, for her exacting expertise.

My sincere gratitude goes to my agent, Emile Khoury, who always delivers when it counts, and the HarperCollins' team for embracing the novel wholeheartedly.

A big applause to the spirited Dr. Hala Sarhan, Arabic talk-show host extraordinaire, for the valuable information she provided and a bow to all the film, music, and media celebrities of the Arab world whom I met for getting excited about the book to the point that they felt they had to divulge a behind-the-scenes secret or two. Much appreciation goes to Mahra Al-Shamsi and Badriya Al-Marri for the vivid accounts of their days living in the sakan as Emirati students in Cairo, and to physiotherapist Semir Bakija for information on recuperating stroke victims.

Thanks to my team of first-draft readers: Cyma, Pia, Samer, and my cousin Sana', who also created the lyrics to "Only Me, Lonely Me."

And finally, now and always, hats off to everyone I meet who says, "I can't wait for the next book."

ABOUT THE AUTHOR

❧

MAHA GARGASH has a degree in radio and television from George Washington University in Washington, D.C., and a master's from Goldsmiths College, University of London. In 1985 she joined Dubai Television to pursue her interest in documentaries. Through directing television programs that deal with traditional Arab societies, she became involved in research and scriptwriting. Her first novel, *The Sand Fish*, was an international bestseller. She lives in Dubai.

ALSO BY
MAHA GARGASH

THE SAND FISH
A Novel from Dubai

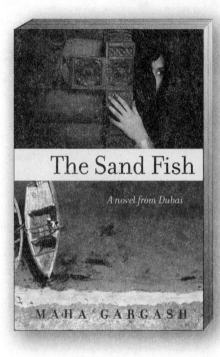

Coming of age in the 1950s, seventeen-year-old Noora is unlike other women of the sun-battered mountains at the tip of the Arabian Peninsula. Though she shares their poverty and, like them, bears life's hardships without complaint, she is also fiery and independent. Following the death of her mother and her father's descent into dazed madness, Noora flees the threat of an arranged marriage, only to be driven back to her unwanted fate by disappointment and heartbreak. As the third wife to a rich, much older man, Noora struggles to adjust to her new home by the sea, thinking of herself as a sand fish—the desert lizard she observed in the mountains, which, when stuck in the wrong place and desperate to escape, smashed itself again and again into unyielding rocks. But then a light is shone into her miserable darkness, resulting in an unexpected passion, a shocking indiscretion, and a secret that could jeopardize Noora's life.

"Gargash weaves an enticing tale of a fiery, independent woman. . . . Intimate, well-paced prose. . . . An exciting, passion-filled read that illuminates an intriguing culture through the eyes and experience of a fiesty heroine."   —*Publishers Weekly*

"Unadorned, poetic language, filled with well-integrated cultural detail. . . . [A] terrific choice for bookclub discussions. . . . This may find appeal with fans of *The Kite Runner*."   —*Booklist*